BOWL
OF
CHERRIES

—A NOVEL—

by

MILLARD KAUFMAN

McSWEENEY'S BOOKS

SAN FRANCISCO

www.mcsweeneys.net

McSweeney's and colophon are registered trademarks
of McSweeney's, a privately held company with
wildly fluctuating resources.

ISBN-10: 1-932416-83-8
ISBN-13: 978-1-932416-83-1

To Lorraine Paley Kaufman with love and gratitude,
for her warmth and wisdom shared day and night, in every season

TABLE OF CONTENTS

BOWL

OF

CHERRIES

ONE

THE LAST MILE

If you look closely at a detailed map of Iraq, you'll find somewhere to the south, between the western shelf and the equally monotonous eastern plain, the province of Assama, a flat depression in the shape of a chicken.

The more ironic of Middle East scholars have for years hypothecated that the name comes from some sour old joke, lost in antiquity, because *Assama* is Arabic for "Paradise," and this place isn't even close to the minimal consolations we might expect on earth, much less heaven. There are in Assama geographical nooks that are yet to be charted, chronicled, demarked, but unless they turn out to be a decided improvement from what we've seen so far, you might conclude from Assama that the earth is a very grotesque and tacky planet.

Even remotely, Assama has never reflected the exotic Araby of the Europeans who romanced about it more or less convincingly in the nineteenth century, managing to assure their armchair readers that they, the talespinners, were living in the middle of a travel poster chock-full of exotic flora and fauna. Lions and panthers (much bigger than presently existing species) did at one time, according to no less an authority than H. G. Wells, roam the wasteland, which is to say the entire province. These days there's nothing to kill around here but humans and gerbils, the sand rats of the desert, and a few other wee beasties that manage to survive the desolation of the Rub al-Khali, the Empty Quarter of Mesopotamia, as the region between the lower Tigris and Euphrates was called for millennia.

A rumor persists among a minority of the locals—the majority are skeptical and secular—that Qurna, where the rivers converge, was the biblical Garden of Eden (perhaps the source, however dubious, of Assama's name). Down through the centuries, the province has never achieved anything to match its mythic eminence. Triumphs are rare; history has behaved disruptively with the place. With the oldest cities on earth, Mesopotamia is often called the cradle of civilization. It might with equal certainty be called the birthplace of sustained barbarism. There were clashes from 4500 BC on, hot spots, flare-ups, skirmishes, even pitched battles among Arabs, Persians, Mesopots, Assyrians, Babylonians, Berbers, but manhood didn't show signs of deep, irreversible impairment until warfare on a grand, gangrenous scale was introduced around 2076 BC, when the first big parade of bullies and kleptocrats stormed into Assama.

Assama was the jumping-off place for invasion because an east-west road spills irregularly across the Rub al-Khali, from the beak of the chicken to its tail. But the legionaries from Europe or Asia spent little time in the Empty Zone. Didn't take them long to determine that the southerly wasteland, scalding by day, freezing by night, had little to offer. There were no beads or bangles to snatch, no fields of bright minerals to pluck. Nothing to fossick for or fight over. Consequently, Assama achieved neither fame nor notoriety as a battlefield; rather it supplied a warpath to an access road running north, along the chicken's midsection. It led to the flush and fabled cities of antiquity—Baghdad, Babylon, Ur, Urik, Nineveh, Samara. The intruders plundered one or another of them or as many as they could.

King Rim-sin of Larsa (Ellasar in the Old Testament) defeated Babylonia in 2076 BC. His successors were decimated by Hammurabi around 1770 BC. Tiglath-pileser I, ruler of the Elamites, took Babylon in 1110 BC, calling himself "King of the World." Shortly thereafter he lost the world title, along with the city-state, to the Assyrians. Doggedly the Elamites tried to retake it, finally succeeding under Tiglath III in 728 BC. Then came Sennacherib, King of Assyria, who spent most of his reign (705–681) warring against Babylonia.

In 586 BC, King Nebuchadnezzar of the Chaldeans took Babylon; Cyrus the Great took it from the Chaldeans in 539 and founded the Persian empire. King Xerxes of Persia took the road west, leading an expedition against the Greeks. He was slaughtered at Salamis in 480.

Alexander of Macedon took Babylon in 381 BC, defeating Darius III of Persia. The Persians took another dreadful beating by a Roman army invading Mesopotamia in 242 AD. A raggedy-assed swarm of Arabs conquered southern Mesopotamia (at the site of present-day Iraq) in 640 AD. The Saracens crossed the road and got as far as Tours before the Franks, led by Charles Martel, Charlemagne's grandfather, crushed them in 732 AD.

Saladin defeated Saif ud-Din to take Mosul in 1176 AD. Hulagu Khan, grandson of Jenghiz, sacked and burned Baghdad in 1258. The mongul Tamerlane, who hated jokes and was said to have been born with bloody clenched fists, took Baghdad in 1400.

The British arrived in 1915 and took over the territory six years later when they invented Iraq by gerrymandering a large, irregular cut—as much as they could grab—of Mesopotamia, which is why Assama looks like a chicken. Cartography was determined by oil; it was known that just about all the rest of Iraq gushed with the stuff, but somehow it had given Assama the slip. Damn place was indeed a desert eccentrically surrounded by a vast oasis of oil.

Nobody knows what tomorrow will bring. Assama's boundaries may zig or zag once more, to the degree that it no longer resembles a chicken but perhaps a kangaroo or a porcupine, or it might be gobbled up by a neighbor, even by a neighbor on the other side of the world, and disappear, as it once nonexisted, like a guppy ingested by a piranha.

It's in the air—the air once redolent of myrrh, spiceberries, and frankincense, the kind of balm associated with Omar Khayyám. There were palm plantations and marshlands festooned with moss until 1991, when Saddam destroyed them to clear his fields of fire.

Now the air is troubled by an infinitude of invisible mites combining gunpowder, cordite, and corpse-rot, and churned up by Humvees and tanks and the decay of young people torn limbless by land mines. The devastation is eerily illuminated by the combustible blight of burn-off from the oil fields. Dysfunction and instability as far as your red eyes can see.

Midway across the chicken road at about the fowl's navel (designated for geographic, not anatomical orientation) it is bisected by an offshoot to the north. Where the two arteries converge is the provincial capital, a dilapidated town called Coproliabad, christened by the Romans when they passed this way to consolidate the eastern reaches of the empire in 242 BC. At the center of Coproliabad is the jail. I am in the jail, which proves that despite the more heralded hazards of war and mountaineering, deep-sea diving, and space probes, man's ancient and honorable pursuit of tight corners can still be satisfied in the most disreputable places.

I've never had a tendency to feel sorry for myself but this time I think I might justifiably yield to it. Incarceration even in polite societies is, I'm beginning to suspect, a galling experience. *Languishing* is not the word for it. There's no chance of busting out, and I'm tired. My stomach is deranged from Assamic cooking. Worms and wavy arrows, pinwheels and hieroglyphs dart and wheel and collide across my peripheral vision. I suffer from the clanks, which I suppose is not unusual for a man charged with murder and condemned to die by a provincial mandate. I've tried suicide by the only means available, which is by eating the food they serve me. That accounts for the diarrhea, a fate certainly not worse than death, but it'll serve till the real thing comes along.

The jail is a shithouse, and that's not a metaphor. It is fashioned, like all the public buildings and private dwellings in the capital, of human excrement, well salted with sand, an additive of shale, and, most important, an agglutinate, marvelous but unidentifiable, to solidify it in a state as costive as concrete.

The Mesopots have a tradition of urban ingenuity that goes back 6,000 years to Ur and Kish. They built fantastical structures—towers and ziggu-rats, buildings seven stories tall of sun-broiled bricks painted in unexpected combos: pastels of green, blue, pink, and yellow.

But the buildings of Assama are unique. Nobody else in our planet's freaky past has ever constructed works of art and architecture whose chief ingredient was excrement. It is not only feces that the Assamans make practi-cal use of; they are a relentlessly retentive people who hate to part with any-thing of themselves. They preserve toenails (ground) for curatives, hairballs (plaited) for amulets, and urine for use as a skin conditioner.

Pondering such eccentricities as well as my own predicament, small wonder I can't sleep. I pace my cell in the hot, dead-aired dawn, which holds the fierce stench not of my surroundings—in Coproliabad one grows used to that in about two weeks—but of death.

4

My death, of course. It's in the blue-black air, a raw, acrid chemical stink. It's in the dirgy music strummed on a two-stringed gourd of a guitar and plunked with a jagged shard of coconut to the beat of two coconut shells bouncing off each other like cymbals, while a discord of rackety voices sings my disaster, in the process rattling my fillings and scaring off the bustards poking through the garbage.

I glance at my watch, a gift of our Assamic sovereign, in fond commemoration of our eternal friendship (ha ha), sealed when he and I were young, just two years ago; it is 4:18. In precisely twenty-three seconds the dawn's first flash of lightning will send me reeling, and I steel myself for the thunderclap to follow, and then the blessed rain that washes away if only for a short while the smell of death, the plink of gourds, the eldritch keening.

Now don't get the idea that I'm taking literary license, invoking the pathetic fallacy so dear to John Ruskin and the lesser Romantics, to distort all nature into harmony with my plight. It is a fact that every day this time of year, at twenty-three seconds after 4:18, the entire Parthenon of animistic godlings and demons, trolls and sprites and the spirits of dead chiefs that predated Muhammad, flex their bronzy thews and proceed to gang-piss on Assama. The earliest invaders clocked their movements by it; the lightning, the thunder, and the rain are the sole consistencies of this drowsy, turbulent land, ceaselessly full of surprises, none of them pleasant, all of them keeping you from ever feeling at home.

A great bolt of fire tears a white tunnel through the sky and turns the square outside my window a sullen violet-red. The thunder explodes and the square reappears, like the afterimage on a defective retina, flat, blank, and grayish. The shit-buildings across the street take shape, impossible buildings beyond the madness of Maurits Escher, separated from my jail by a wide brown dappled river.

The rain falls, the wind shrills, rising, fading, and, in fifteen minutes, dies. The brown river subsides, and the painted statues in the square are fresh and gaudy after their bath. They are carved, of course, of mud and shit, but, I must say, skillfully. Slim, elongated figures with a hint of caricature, the illustrated index of Who's Who in Assama.

Just as some books are best read, I've been told, by candlelight, so Coproliabad's gallery of the great is best viewed at dawn, after the rain. In less than an hour its paint will be cracked and cobwebbed by the sun, and our newly minted sheikh and the woman we both loved, his ministers and his General, all will be afflicted by a new day's scruffy assortment of botanical growths, more distorting than leprosy. But now they are astonishing as they stand uncertainly, that is, lifelike, with an abstracted air, solitary ghosts and strangers to each other, rich in irony as if they were not statues at all but flesh and blood transfixed into stillness by some capricious spell.

The young sheikh, Abdul al Sadr, is something of a jumped-up tribal chief who inherited the hefty title from his father, Saeed, a shrewd but otherwise ungifted warlord. When the Americans arrived in 2003, they paid little attention to him or to his wasteland people in the south. They concentrated their forces in the north, on the opposition and the oil.

Being ignored was an asset the old man made the most of. He lived quite well on a sandy flat above the muddy Shatt El Arab, at the confluence of the Tigris and the Euphrates. Switching a few channel lights and buoys, he lured boats to the sandbars on the banks of both rivers. Then, in America's disregard, Saeed sniffed a prodigious opportunity. He declared Assama a kind of independency within Iraq and installed himself as boss.

Nobody, least of all the intruders, saw any point in contradicting him. The U.S. Army was groveling to get the cooperation of the region's assorted bandetti and to press swag on anybody who didn't shoot at them and whose fealty they could buy. It took Saeed about ten minutes to realize that by declaring his rebelliousness he could benefit from American perks and pork-barrel diplomacy. He became an eager recipient of anything they offered—handouts now, electricity later. He died before the grid's installation, leaving his statue to stare sightlessly from the square with a mien of silent, cunning, stationary greed. There is a hint of wiliness on the face of his son, who stands next to him, but Abdul's is a magnetic face, holding the symmetry and the luster of an iron door-knocker, the handsome features attesting to his Arab-Persian roots. His sculpted body seems to have less poise and assurance, perhaps, than he actually possesses. (Or had the sculptor fathomed something I didn't?) The indecipherable eyes (seeing what new reform, what next outrageous improvement?) stare into my cell window with imperial aloofness and no understanding whatever.

Not like the eyes of General Kalid Qazwini at the right of the young overlord. Qazwini's ashy eyes are cold, the eyes of an interstellar hit-beast. He stands like an army with banners...

But wait a minute. Why should I be wasting whatever time I have drawing word-pictures of the notables in Assama's Parthenon? Hell with them, with all of them—the General and the Reverend Doctor Lipgloss and Shakir bin Zaki, the asshole intellectual, and squashy, pear-shaped Hashim Pachachi, captain of nonexistent industry. Maybe I'll get around to them—frankly, I doubt it. In the meantime...

Look out! Here comes the sun! It does not rise or simply appear in Coproliabad. White-hot and unruly, it slams down like a sledge on an anvil and bounces off your skull with such force that dust devils whirl around the streets and the very air goes tremulous, and things you'd swear were immobile begin to dance behind a curtain of Vaseline—the schizoid buildings, the spavined tower on the right, the statues in the square. Mesmerized by the glinty eye of the sun, they undulate like a company of cobras standing on their tails.

My stomach rumbles, not in sympathy with the now distant thunder, but in protest of last night's dinner: fish rot and scorpion salad, the jail's blue-plate special. I hardly have the strength to wave at a buzzing fly. Soon, I console myself, it will be over. My eyes stray to that tower on my right.

It has a sort of sinister gaiety, rising like a vast untidy beehive, and surrounded at its base by bamboo stakes, repetitive as files on parade, their butts driven into the earth, their razor-sharp spikes pointing to the belvedere five stories above.

What we have here is the topography for ganching. Perhaps a few words on the subject are in order; fortunately, not too many nice people are familiar with the process. Unhappily, I know more about it than I care to.

It was practiced, according to the best authorities on grisly behavior, by both the Ottomans and the Mongols of Hulagu Khan. Who introduced the procedure in Mesopotamia is a point of some disagreement, but the experts concur that the Mesopots, particularly the Assamans, were quick to appropriate certain foreign ideas and instruments that appealed to them. They took to the ganch, it appears, with enthusiasm, executing some poor bastard by flinging him off the rooftop onto the stakes below.

In this case, I'm the poor bastard. I'm having trouble avoiding another wallow in self-pity and a burst of bromides like "I'm too young to die" and so forth. What I need is distraction, not constant meditation on my predicament. I grab at straws. It takes all the resolve I can muster to concentrate on a yellow mongrel skulking out of the jungle. He shifts uneasily through the caked mud, delicately raising and lowering his paws as if with each step he expects the earth to cave in under him. He sneaks past three or four statues—obviously they hold no interest for him—until he arrives, with some sense of achievement, at the foot of Hashim Pachachi, Assama's leading and remarkably inept industrialist. He raises a leg and, with a sly grin of ecstasy, pees. Is the beast aware that the man is an infidel and a glutton who eats a puppy for lunch whenever he can trap one?

Assamans are aware of it; Hashim isn't the only dog-eater in town. Nobody gives much of a damn about the contents of a fricassee; Assamans are essentially secular, with few if any dietary prohibitions, and Islam's habits and customs are rich and varied. Cultures thrive within cultures, with subcultures bubbling beneath every sect and deviation.

I wondered how long the dog with the sly grin, happily pissing away, would press his luck. Long enough to get laid: another yellow dog walks prowlingly down the mucky pike, and, ignoring all the best manuals about foreplay, my friend with the sly grin mounts her.

I watch.

Now what, you might ask, am I doing, an intricately calibrated man like me, watching a pair of decrepit beasts fuck in broad daylight? And what, I counter, what else is there to do? Coproliabad lacks even the homely slob diversions afforded by the most destitute of towns, like watching the streetlights go on (there are no streetlights) or listening to the plumbing (there is no plumbing) or peering at a sitcom (no TV).

And so I watch, a little enviously, the dogs with their eyes of molten wax, the yellow arch of lust, the throbbing, thrusting, connecting rod, redflaked and marbled white and veiny blue. The colors of the mammal race. I yearn, I yearn for one more day, one more hour of love and lazy exertion in that slow, unstately dance, ancient, eternal, that primal nepenthe beyond drink and drugs.

That's what pleasured me in Coproliabad, why I had come here in the first place, why I remained, and, ironic joke, why I would die. I look out at her now, eyes damp, throat dry. She stands there, pedestalized in the square, more of an idealization than a woman, extravagantly remote, faintly smiling. Oh, the prodigies we performed, in essence nothing more or less than what those yellow dogs were doing, dancing beast to beast, but with certain nuances, certain eerie refinements, breathtaking explorations.

There is about her a curious quality: no matter what she wears she appears to be undressed. It is the kind of nakedness from which the beholder cannot unglue his eyes. Her face in a ring of shining hair, the freckled button of a nose, the upswept breasts with the chiseled nipples pointing at you, tracking you like the eyes of a Rembrandt. The legs so long they look skinny, the perfect scut. There! Now maybe you have some idea of what Valerie is to me.

And she is somehow greater than the sum of her parts. Indeed, each part has its own summation, and this I find disturbing. The oval eyes are blue-green and deep as a sunless sea, but the total effect is of an oceanic vacancy. The brows so smooth and pale are unwary; what seems to emerge is a kind of unobtrusive numb inertia, as though she were beyond all worldly contest, or ran a subnormal temperature, or didn't give a damn about anything.

She didn't give a damn about much. Early in our relationship (shallow, aseptic term), indeed before we had one, her slackness led me to believe that she was kind of dumb.

I was mistaken, having somehow overlooked what was spectacularly obvious: that her air of dopiness derived from her beauty. She didn't do anything; she didn't have to. Beauty's coign of vantage and its perks she accepted without question or analysis or the least expenditure of effort.

I on the other hand have always been striving. That's what got me into this mess that can only get messier. I've always tripped and floundered—is it any wonder I trip and flounder across these pages?

And romanticize. But lest you confuse me with some love-swacked swain in an Elizabethan madrigal mooning after a buxom shepherdess, let me scrawl a compensatory note. If I were lured to Coproliabad by Valerie, it is equally true that I was driven here by greed or its euphemism, enlightened self-interest. Dr. Joseph Grady, that cunning gray eminence of UGH, had fanned the flames of my insolvency with tales of untold wealth. It was he who had discovered that riches were waiting to be snared in this unpromising, scorched chicken of a place, and from the most unlikely source. It was the secret formula of the shit bricks he was after, to isolate that mysterious elixir which would transmute dross into gold for the two of us by supplying an eager, overpopulated world with an endless, inexpensive supply of the most workable building material ever stumbled upon by man. The multinational consortium, Ultra Global Husbandry, would, through its subsidiary, Resource Analysis and Technology, finance the launch of our magic upon a receptive world. And launched we were.

For a brief and splendid moment we soared across the financial heavens, Grady a comet and I his tail, his instrument and ambassador.

Only to come to this. I hardly need a reminder of my plight but there it is: the caretakers of the tower are reporting for work, like groundskeepers of the college green tidying up for class-day japes. They manicure, pluck, and sharpen the pickets to receive my ventilated body. What a vulgar way to die.

When my jailers graciously complied with my strange—to them— request for a ballpoint pen and a clutch of legal pads brought from home, it was, I told them, to keep me from going mad. This may be true, if I could only limit my meanderings to the soothing fellowship of the past, thereby obliterating the perilous present. But how can I write of the past without evoking my father's disappearance, which defeats my very reason for writing? It tends naggingly to remind me of my own impending departure.

I find nothing soothing in thoughts of death, particularly my own. But to die in compliance with the penal code of Assama—what a way to go. What they do—what they intend to do to *me*—I'm going to be prodded at spearpoint off a tower of shit and mud onto those impaling stakes a hundred feet below, and soon. But exactly when I haven't an idea. When the British, the last of the Europeans, departed in '48, leaving only the legacy of their language behind, the Assamans reverted to precolonial customs and institutions, which they found infinitely more appealing than those imposed by their Western rulers. They revived the stone-tipped whip for all manner of misdemeanors—that is, behavior that the sheikh did not condone. For serious offenses they preferred ganching to the British noose, possibly because a stout rope was difficult to come by, and in that climate prone to swift decay. The sentence carried with it a fiendishly cruel corollary: for a capital crime, an unspecific time of execution.

I am due to appear at the top of the tower sometime in the month of May. Today is the twelfth or maybe the fourteenth. Under these suspenseful circumstances, precise dates grow furtive. I can be fed to the stakes any time now; it is this lack of specificity—I wouldn't wish it on a steer in a slaughterhouse—that scrambles the circuitry, sunders my peace of mind, and plays hob with my nervous system.

And now I hear the flat resonance of calloused feet padding down the corridor, each footstep falling like cowflop in a pasture. I listen in a trance of anxiety, straining to hear above the pounding of my heart. I have already been served my scummy breakfast bowl. It is too early for my scummy lunch. A sharp searing pain ricochets off my chest and tears like a raging Skilsaw through my shoulder and settles high in my left arm. Are those footsteps coming to get me? Is this the end of my muddle of a life, as short and unpredictable and insignificant as a sneeze?

The cowflop footsteps come closer. I cradle the agony in my arm close to my body. I turn my eyes, the pain prowling behind them, back to the window, to the statue of Valerie. I drink in her slow, assured beauty, those gently flaring hips—I can feel, I swear, the heat of her thighs.

She is, I suppose, all I ever wanted. All else is trumpery.

TWO

DIXIELAND

The year after I was born, in Charlottesville, Virginia, the only child of two teachers, the family moved south, where my father accepted a post on the English faculty of a state-endowed university, otherwise undistinguished. It was on the outskirts of an unpleasant place which qualified in population and industry as a city, but in every other way it was a farm. Here I was toilet-trained, went to school, read from *A–AND* through *MUN–ODD* in the *Britannica* (Scholar's Edition), and was hit by a tractor. I twist the ignominious facts. Actually the tractor was stationary. I hit it, absentmindedly. God knows what I was thinking about (something in *MUN–ODD?*). So much for the bewilderment of boyhood.

The university had not too long ago emerged from the cocoon of an agricultural college; it still suffered the pangs of afterbirth. It was like some sprawling mutant, misshapen and without fingerprints, the tail wagging the mongrel, and its proud traditions were for thoughtful men embarrassing—a long devotion to the cult of the plow and the Confederacy. The undergraduate body, peasants in saddle shoes, were full of sweaty and ill-conceived pranks, like dressing up as Ku Kluxers on Halloween or energetically waving the Stars and Bars at football games.

The football games were what I hated most, marching down the field in the band, caparisoned like a hussar with a shako of imitation fur slouching over my eyes and frogs of imitation gold braid curling across my chest. But I had to do it; performing on the tuba was a contractual obligation that went with my scholarship.

There was constant conflict between the farmers and the philosophers. I can't remember all the petty maneuvering my father reported to us at dinner, but I'll never forget the Honorable Orville Wiley, who rose in the state legislature to lead the impassioned fight against an expenditure to enlarge the French faculty.

"The English language," he declared, ape eyes burning, "was good enough for Jesus Christ, so it ought to be good enough for yew-all." And that was that.

My father had a certain sardonic sense of humor in those days, before life in its incessant pursuit of perversity turned him sour and obsessive. He relished those bitter inside jokes of the humanities people. Unfortunately he was himself an inside joke to his colleagues. I think he annoyed them with his fastidious precision, which made him unable to resist such infelicities of speech, however apposite, as "the *rice* of American civilization," and "the Don *Joo*anism of Byron."

True, his tweeds were as rumpled as theirs, his ties were knit and his shirts were buttoned down. But there was something else, most vulgarly expressed, I suppose, in a dialogue between two of his confreres I happened to overhear one day when I was an undergraduate. I had stopped off briefly in the men's room of the humanities wing and was minding my own business inside a cubicle when the outside door opened and two Professorial Voices proceeded to the urinals.

"Ah don' know where he gits 'em from," the First Voice boomed and echoed in the tiled chamber. It was the voice of the head of the English Department, who had an untidy penchant for ending sentences with prepositions. "Don *Joo*-an, indeed."

"Ah fear," resounded the Second Voice (it belonged to an instructor of freshman English), "Dr. Breslau's *Joo*-an is a *Jew*-ism." They shared a roupy chuckle.

That, essentially, was the problem, but there were complications. My father could have accepted anti-Semitism with the sort of superior forbearance that made him say "rice" for "rise." He would not have felt like a failure in the ugly face of discrimination alone, but he harbored the suspicion that there were other elements that undermined his success. He was a lousy teacher and a dubious scholar, and he knew it. He was no worse than the rest of that dismal congregation, but those his age were full professors and he was an associate; they had tenure and he did not.

Had Morton Breslau's discipline been other than English Literature, in those days a WASP monopoly, or had he lived in a country with a long history of hard-core anti-Semitism—Poland, for example—there possibly would not have been a problem. Jews in Poland knew where they stood—on thin ice to be sure—but their position was defined and unambivalent. A Jewish teacher had simply to embrace Catholicism, no more than superficially, and his academic permanence was assured. But here in democratic America, religious relationships were more subtle, and seldom discussed by gentlemen outside toilets, so to speak, and to endorse the reigning faith in America would not have helped. In America we pretend to take pride in the melting pot which only simmers, coming to a boil now and then; the juices seldom assimilate. We like Jews to be Jews, to attend their exotic synagogues and pursue their alien customs and traditions, and let the rest of us the hell alone. I think my father's associates would have accepted him with a faint, bemused tolerance if his accent were Yiddish. It was his goddammed superior phonetic dandyism that so sorely afflicted them.

My father never faced his chortling, democratic oppressors; they were contemptible, unworthy of his steel. He refused to pursue the gratification he might gain and the reward he would harvest in a public confrontation. I could not have resisted such a dustup, if only to relieve my frustrations by snapping off a few of their teeth, hitting the bastards with the nearest chair, pissing on their flag, burning down their sheep-dip library—all those books about animal husbandry and the cross-fertilization of squash—but that was not my father's way. When things got too sticky, as sooner or later they did, he'd saddle up and shove off. Thus he had come south from Virginia, and before that, in inverse chronology, from Pennsylvania, Connecticut, Massachusetts.

It was hardly a solution. Frustration that is unrequited in one corner finds, like a confused and famished rat in a maze, sustenance in another. Dr. Breslau among his colleagues (neither he nor they considered the other peers) maintained his rigid politesse. His most virulent public expletive remained a quiet "son of a biscuit" without even the mild explosive of an exclamation point at the end. For major irritant and inconvenience, ranging from a cut finger to a dented fender, he would say "sugar." Still, they got to him, vultures pecking away at his entrails. In private, in the secret shell of our small house, it wouldn't even take a cut finger to elicit sheer red-eyed choler, the veins beating at his temples like the wings of a blind bat, the wales of his cheeks pulsating. In our house all was rampage—the price of a can of soup jumping a nickel, a trace of starch on a shirt collar, a broken shoelace and he'd be off, apoplexed, calling my mother a fat cunt, striding across the length of a room to push me out of his way, invariably followed by regrets, remorse, pronouncements of self-hatred. Then he would put an arm over my shoulder and ask with grave deference what I wanted to be when I grew up. I would mumble, shifting my weight from one leg to another, kicking imaginary shit like Jimmy Stewart in a stable, "I don't know."

Once, I'll never forget, this oblique, irrelevant armistice led to an even nastier war. I was perhaps ten at the time; he asked me that persistent question I had until then successfully evaded. But now, "I want to be a teacher," I said sturdily, eager for his approval. His eyes went red again, his face twisted as if his stomach had suddenly gone sour, and something obscure, monstrous, and terribly uncomfortable flashed between us. I didn't realize until years later that the conflict was oedipal, that I was giving him notice of competition, but I knew enough to be frightened. "You miserable little coward," he screamed at me, and pushed me away as if I were unclean.

My mother had given up teaching when she married and moved for the first time, that trek from Massachusetts to Connecticut. She paid surprisingly little attention to her husband's outbursts, even when he called her names, not because she was inured to them but because she paid little attention to anything outside her "work." You had to ask her questions twice and still she'd look at you with the glazed fixity of a sleepwalker. She wrote poetry constantly; that was her "work." She was a slow bleeder and she slaved over it for long, exhausting hours, and many a middle of a night I could hear her creaking around the dead house with a pen in one hand, a clipboard and flashlight in the other, refining her poems, jotting down the lines of a conceit. Writing never came easy for her; it gave her calluses. She never courted the muses, she wrestled them, mauled them all over the house and came up, after weeks of peripatetic labor, with a slim Spencerian sonnet, fourteen lines of imagistic jabberwocky. Or she'd shape her stanzas to form a geometrical design on the page. Her favorites were wings, stars, and shields.

She was a handsome woman, my mother. If you like largeness, you'd call her statuesque. She looked like Amy Lowell, but there the comparison ended; unlike Lowell my mother was silent (although she sighed loudly and often), she never swore, she did not smoke cigars, and she could not write her way out of a net brassiere. But she did pack a lot of brisket.

My mother's output, starred and pseudonymous, appeared regularly in one of those little, irregular periodicals so limited in readership that they might be called incestuous. Subscription was by invitation only, and contributors would go into a rage over a misplaced comma and brood for days if their poems were understood. All this called for constant and voluminous correspondence between my mother and the editor, about what I never knew, because the whole system was built along the lines of a secret society whose secrets were kept from everybody, including the membership.

There was one time of the year, however, when my mother could not ignore the rages of my father. It was when his name came up for tenure, and for weeks the poet and I would scarcely breathe, would speak in whispers, and only if spoken to. She continued to write, of course; to her the production of poetry was like a ravaging disease, but she didn't put her usual body English into it. She'd walk the house day and night, but carefully, not bumping into chairs, and with her head bowed as if she were balancing something, a bottle or a cane, on the back of her skull. For my part, I shunned all contact with my tuba as if it were the carrier of some dreadful virus.

He had a disconcerting way of fantasizing about tenure, advancing arguments to us (as if we weren't on his side) to prove his appointment was inevitable. This year he couldn't miss, he'd tell us, not that he was a whit less Jewish but because never in his fifteen years of teaching had his competition been so entirely composed of cretins. We'd nod in total approbation at the invincibility of his logic, knowing that logic had nothing to do with it.

That year, the great day came, and went. My mother walked the floor with something on her mind besides her latest carmen figuratum. I called his office on campus, that shit-faced head of his department, the hospital, the police. He had disappeared totally.

Years later, when I told the story to Valerie, she had shaken her head slowly and said, "Unbelievable." It was, of course, but not to me until the pronouncement tripped off her tongue. Nothing that happens to you is unbelievable. Or maybe everything is.

We had to get out of that town, but how, and where to go, and what to do? We had no money, and not the wildest chance that Old Mom could turn a buck with her dilapidated rhymes. I still had at least another year of graduate work before I got my doctorate; with or without it there was no way I could land a job to support us, not even bagging burritos for take-out in a mini mall. Did I mention that I was fourteen years old at the time? And also I was for some reason resisting the move; at least I was ambivalent about it. I hated that school and all the people in it, those I knew and those I didn't, and their fathers and their cousins and their state fucking legislature, with more passion than I had ever vented on anything in my life. I wouldn't even miss my girl in town, a precocious junior-high-school student who was getting to be a large pain in the ass anyhow. But something absurd and totally irrational, something I couldn't quite get a handle on, prompted my sticking around for a few more days, another couple of weeks, a month maybe. I knew he wouldn't turn up, but maybe, just maybe he would, with the same unaccountable abruptness that had characterized his leaving. He'd explain everything perfectly and then we'd leave, together, and he'd get tenure some goddam place and... and...

Each day my mother waited for the mail. And then, about a month after the day he left, she came into the room where I was working. She held a letter.

I turned so fast I spilled coffee all over my father's desk.

"Pop?" That's what I meant to say. One syllable, but I managed to mangle it. What I said sounded more like "Pulp," but she understood.

"No," she said, "but it's all set."

"What's all set?" I asked nastily. I had of late been taking out my confusions on her. "What the hell could be all set?"

"We're leaving," she said. "First we are going to New Haven."

"What for? I've got to finish this..."

"You've been accepted at Yale." She waved the letter at me. "It's all arranged—just dash off a few forms and an essay."

"Do I have to march in the band?"

"No. You'll have a job, with enough money to get by."

"How come? Who arranged it?"

"Mr. Quillet," she said placidly.

"Who?"

"Dilmore Quillet of *Callipaedia*." She was beginning to sound like one of her poems.

"Where's Callipaedia?"

"*Callipaedia*," she said once more, running her tongue all over the word as if it were a delicacy, "the magazine that publishes me."

"What about Pop?" I said, as if there were no such thing as a forwarding address. "When he... if he comes back, we ought to be here..."

She said nothing.

"What do you mean," I finally filled the silence, "*first* we go to New Haven...?"

"We'll go up and I'll help you get settled." She looked down at the letter in her hands fondly, I thought, as if it were a rare parchment, unlocking some riddle of vast significance. "Then," she went on, "I'm going to Ravenna."

I shook my head. The cobwebs persisted. "Ravenna, Italy?"

"Ravenna, Colorado. I have a staff job with *Callipaedia*. That's where it's published, Ravenna."

And so we went, each our separate ways. She was understandably eager to start work, and I was, frankly, glad to be off alone. In the bus, all the way to the county airport, I kept staring out the windows for—that's right—my father. I kept thinking it was my fault he had left. I had been a disappointment to him. Certainly he had not wanted me to go into English. If I had shown some inclination for medicine, law, architecture, plumbing, maybe things would have been different. And now it was too late.

Maybe it wasn't; I could change to whatever the hell he wanted, if he ever came back. If. Shit. Sugar.

THREE

THE INSPECTOR GENERAL

The door of my cell creaks open. Monstrous, malignant, the figure of General Kalid Qazwini fills it jamb to jamb. Behind him range half a dozen grunts from his ragtag militia.

It is fitting that he and his rowdies should escort me into oblivion. He is my host; among his military duties is the operation of this sorry lockup.

He wears a dish-dash, the traditional men's robe, and over it a gaudy assortment of gifts from various Europeans who had shown up to prowl for riches—a khaki topee, an infantry jacket with four pips on each shoulder and a triple row of gongs on his chest. With such peacock adornments above the waist, what he wears below can only be disappointing: between Sam Browne belt and combat boots there is nothing but the gruelly skirt of the dish-dash.

He leans forward tautly, as if he's ready to spring, a man of unsuppressed mayhem who thought napalm, once he learned about it, was an instrument of social change. In one hand he grips a knife, in the other a large pistol, and he seems, suspended in time, undecided which to use—shoot and be sure, or stab for the fun of it? General Qazwini has a sturdy drive toward tumult; if, implausibly, he were ever to find himself without his steel companions, he might throw a rock at you, or a jar, just to test his marksmanship, and see which way you'd fall.

I know he wants to make my valediction as difficult as possible, but I'm not going to give him the chance. Shakily but not without a certain clumsy dignity I wobble toward the door. He stands there blocking me, eager to play smashmouth.

"Where," he asks, "do you think you're going?" The heel of his hand slams into my chest and I fall. My dignity, fragile at best, collapses with me; I have no real desire to reassert it.

"Get up," he says.

"What the hell for? If I'm not going anywhere...?"

"On your feet. We'll start with some deep knee-bends."

I can't believe it. I lie there in my prison-putrid pants. "I'm not moving," I say.

He draws one of his pistols and fires. The round kicks up dust a few inches from my ear. The son of a bitch is insisting I die healthy, but here is an opportunity to turn his spleen in a useful direction, a swift, relatively immaculate end to all the pain and the bullshit, certainly preferable to death by multiple perforation. But Lord God Jesus, how we cling to the earth when we're faced with the possibility of never seeing it again. Let the void swallow me up, but not yet.

I do deep knee-bends until my legs are spasmed and my brain goes numb. "Pick it up another notch," Qazwini says. "*Stretch!*"

I duckwalk in circles, covering a country mile, staggering with uncertain nausea. Push-ups follow, he sounding off in the pitiless cadenzas of a Marine D.I. He seems to find excitement in my torment. I might have drowned in my own sweat, but fortunately he had a short attention span. After about ten minutes, or maybe it was two hours, he grows bored with the regimen. "Enough for the day," he barks abruptly.

At the door he pauses. "Maybe I'll be around again," he promises. "Or maybe not. It depends on how much time you got to get in shape."

I lie in my own vomit. A wavering supplication reels through the fog of my consciousness: Please, Val, don't come around today, I don't want you to see me like this. The thought is superceded by another, more intense and totally preposterous. Someday before I die, I tell myself, I don't know how or when, but I'm going to kill Kalid Qazwini.

FOUR

A GIRL IN THE HEART OF MARYLAND

A year sped by, calendar leaves exfoliating. I continued to lead a relatively sheltered life at Yale, until the day I met Valerie. After which nothing was the same.

Like most days that alter our lives, this one gave no indication of radical changes to come. It all began a week earlier, and blandly enough, with a note to:

> Phillips Chatterton, Esq.
> 13520 Dumbarton Oaks
> Baltimore
> Maryland

> Dear Sir:
> Dr. Guthrie Armbruster, my faculty advisor, suggested that I write you about my being a graduate student in the English Department at Yale. My research has determined that you are a direct descendant of Thomas Chatterton, the subject of my doctoral dissertation. It would be of great value to me if I might talk with you about him. Perhaps there are family letters, notes, addenda, memorabilia that you might grant me the privilege of examining.

I intend to be in Baltimore next week, working for few days in the stacks at Johns Hopkins. May I phone you at the time, and come to see you at your convenience?

Sincerely,

Judd Breslau

The Chatterton house, a great Georgian brick pile with a gallery and a hipped roof crowned by a balustraded widow's walk, dominated a gentle rise in the Green Spring Valley. Delicate gates of wrought iron opened on a quarter-mile of driveway lined with oaks.

Before you get carried away in a magnolia trance of antebellum splendor, let me inject a few apt modifiers. The gallery wanted painting. A few planks of the widow's walk, essential to any sentinel who wasn't an acrobat or a mountain goat, were missing. The iron gates were rusty and asquint on their hinges. The approach was rutted with great potholes hosting a cancerous proliferation of damp toadstools and beasties with opaque wings that droned in the stillness of the hot, shimmering afternoon. The oaks, ridden by something like scurvy and badly in need of a surgeon, formed a blighted tunnel smelling dankly of decay. The whole place looked as if the ghost of General Sherman had bivouacked there; it needed extensive repairs before it could be condemned.

The doorbell did not work; it hung from two wires on a tarnished metal plate. No one answered my knock; I had hitchhiked from Hopkins, walking the last mile or so to the rusty gates. I was hot and tired, and irritated by all this soundlessness. Could Chatterton have forgotten the appointment? We had talked only that morning.

An emptiness hung in the air, nothing sinister or ominous or oppressive. I had no premonition of entanglements as I stood at that bleak and crumbling portal. My joints were rubbery and my movements slubbered and ponderous, and inside my mouth, between my thick brown cottony tongue and my rubber lips, there hung an invisible bridle that made swallowing difficult. Perhaps it was the mile-long walk; I was in terrible shape. The only parts of my body I regularly exercised were two sedulous fingers on the computer. But the dominant feeling, of depression, was connected with my work.

I was weary of groveling after varnished truths, petty dissections, specious interpretations, the same old source material, the stale sad smell of school libraries. Who cared? Certainly not I. Out of the dusty womb of my scholarship, Thomas Chatterton was taking shape not as the "marvelous boy" eulogized by Wordsworth but as a deranged and pitiable fraud, less the victim of society than of his own self-inflicted wounds, which destroyed what embryonic talent he had years before he swallowed the poison which ended his life. And all that a long, long time ago.

I felt I had somehow allowed myself to be cheated by myself. A sudden dull current of apprehension filled me with doubt about my own sanity. My life was short-circuited somewhere; it needed rewiring. Was it too late? Standing there at that dilapidated doorway, I thought of my father. Like him I felt a vague longing for some homeland I'd never had but where I belonged. I didn't even know where to go for a visa.

And then from behind the house came a girl's voice crying "Love..." And another word, I thought, which in its disembodied flight from her to me, drifting through the trees, bouncing off the dark red bricks, had become hopelessly, irrevocably lost. I stood there another moment, in thrall to that sirenic voice.

I followed the red facade of the house through a path of pale, scruffy grass, a gap in the tangled underbrush leading round to the back. I turned the corner and pulled up short.

A man with a swirl of gray Medusa hair sat with his back to me in one of those tacky chrome chairs with plastic webbing, the kind of prize cut-rate gas stations in the South bestow with a full tank of regular. He wore a filthy bathrobe, much too large, as shapeless and unreal as a papier-mâché rock in a stage setting.

Now he hunched over while a flock of sparrows wheeled and flapped and screeched around his shaggy mane and landed trustingly at his feet. He leaned back in his chair, a grungy Saint Francis, and I approached, deferentially clearing my throat. I hawked two or three times before he favored me with a disgruntled glance.

"Mr. Chatterton...?"

He nodded abstractedly, his eye still on the sparrows. He reached into the pocket of his robe and came up with a handful of peanuts. Carefully, bending forward once more, he planted the peanuts between the toes of his mother-bare feet and, with superb self-satisfaction, watched his flock dig them out and hoard them away.

"Yes...?" he said finally. It was a moment before I realized he wasn't talking to the birds.

"I'm Judd Breslau. I..."

"Who?" Again he reached into a pocket.

"I talked with you this morning about Thomas Chatterton..."

"Oh," he grunted, perception dawning. He held out a hand, cupping a dozen peanuts. They were oily, with bits of grayish fluff sticking to them. Altogether they looked like rat shit.

"Peanuts?" he asked.

"No thanks."

He popped them into his mouth. The birds screeched with deprivation.

"Beat it," he snarled at them, throwing a bedroom slipper. "Kitchen's closed." He turned back to me. "Goddam gluttons," he said. He got to his feet, chewing, wiping his palms on the buttocks of his bathrobe. "I got some of his papers," he said. "I'll get 'em from the attic." He shuffled into a side door and I stood there, my heart pounding, thinking, Good Christ! *Papers.* What a break, what a windfall, there was something new and undiscovered under a scholar's sun, socked away in that unpropitious old house. Maybe I hadn't wasted my life after all.

A voice roused me from my delirium—that girl again.

"Balls!" it bellowed, mellifluously.

I was snared on that voice like a hooked catfish. At the back of the house was a bosky dell, another unrefreshing eyesore. A wooden table, black and pitted with age. A couple of benches ready to collapse if a field mouse danced across them. An abandoned refrigerator with stains like rusty tears running down the chipped enamel. A hibachi under a coat of grease held a few disintegrating lumps of charcoal, like thousand-year-old eggs in a sooty nest. Everything considered, a nice place for a picnic.

Beyond this garden spot was a windbreak of dusty trees draped with a green canvas. It was torn and faded; I squinted through the shreds at a tennis game. The ball bounced off a racquet with the hard hollow beat of a tight drum and shot across the sagging net. It bounded from a crack in the court and squirted over the head of the young man poised to return it. He had moved with muscular grace to meet the ball; its crazy bounce tied him into a congested knot. He unraveled, waved wildly at it—he looked as if he were falling out of a tree—and missed. The girl on the other side of the net laughed deliciously.

"That's a takeover," he said. His voice had a sinewy, theatrical ring. "Bad bounce." He was tall and flat-bellied in his spotless white shorts and fashionable T-shirt. I didn't like him.

"The hell it is," the girl said. "You know the ground rules, Derek."

Turning, the girl walked to the baseline. She had an effortless way of walking, as if a substance more volatile than blood—helium perhaps—were coursing through her adorable veins. Her legs seemed to flow while her hips remained motionless, her breasts bobbing and weaving as if the sap and the fire of life were racing through them. Then all was quiet again, no movement of neck or slim shoulders or ponytail. Elegant little beads of sweat glistened on her forehead.

Now she glanced off at a second young man standing at the net on the sideline. He was paying absolutely no attention to the game, and small wonder.

"Balls!" she cried at him. "You're a lousy ball boy, Abby." She shook her head and the ponytail flew this way and that and then settled down again.

"He's all the time dreaming, for Christ's sake," said the young man on the other side of the net. She laughed again. She knew damned well what the ball boy was dreaming about.

Abby roused himself. First he frowned with embarrassment, and then, as if he realized his expression was inappropriate, rearranged his long face into the grin of a slave trader. He trotted onto the court, retrieved a couple of balls, and tossed them at her as if they were orchids. Then he melted back to the side of the court, aware that his skill as a retriever had been challenged. More likely his discomfort stemmed from his fantasies, if they were anything like mine.

He was a most incongruous ball boy, dark-skinned with a shag of black hair falling over his soft dark eyes. His nose, his cheekbones, the mild thrust of his jaw—all of them were prominent, none of them dominated. His was the face of an unintrusive factotum—a good flight attendant perhaps, or an assistant sommelier. But that face was joined to a hard body that somehow conveyed, at least to me, a guarded turbulence, a suppressed defiance. Ferment seemed to seep through the filter of his skin and unsettle the very air around him. Or maybe it was my imagination.

The girl tossed a ball into the air. Her racquet circled and slammed it across the net. She darted forward, on her toes, and Abby and I were delighted, entranced as she performed her caprioles. She swerved to the center of the court, her tight little ass all but bursting the snug cutoffs, her ponytail flying, those plangent breasts in the man's shirt uncontaminated by a bra, alive alive-o like two playful puppies under a thin blanket.

I watched, Abby watched, but Derek, poor bastard, had to watch the ball, and he wasn't even good at that. He took a few stagey, self-important steps, swerving heroically, and hit a clinker. The ball thunked against the rim of his racquet and fell like a dead bird at his feet.

Derek stared at his racquet, holding it in front of his face as if it had committed some unforgivable breach and he were admonishing it silently. He tugged at his immaculate shorts the way pros do on TV. He *looked* like a tennis player, but his game had more form than content and his racquet categorically refused to do his bidding.

"Thirty-love," the girl said solemnly, and I laughed to myself. I was having a great time, after all those months in the stacks. Out there in the open, sportsmanlike reticence I suppose precluded any wild demonstration (crying for joy, foaming at the mouth, cartwheels, rape). Abby's eyes held a look of mute blind rapture like the eyes of a lap dog clotted with adoration.

Someone was breathing heavily down my neck. I turned; it was Phillips Chatterton lurching toward me in his hair shirt of a bathrobe, like a fat penitent on the road to Canossa. His burden was a thick bundle of newspapers, yellowed and foxed with age. He dumped them on the rickety table and it staggered. What a windfall, I thought, what a veritable windfall. With trembling hands I picked up the top sheet. The logo read THE COCKEYSVILLE WEEKLY CLARION, and under it the date: Thursday, May 12, 1923. To the left was the weather forecast (cloudy, with possible thundershowers) and to the right a box enclosed a rather formidable statement: "The World's Greatest Weekly," it said forthrightly.

"What is this?" I asked.

"Tom Chatterton's newspaper. I thought..."

"Who's Tom Chatterton?"

"Don't you know?" He looked at me dubiously. Our styles were not jelling at all. And my disappointment took the form of rudeness and that didn't help either.

"He was my grandfather," he went on in a subdued but edgy voice. "Editor and publisher and quite a wit. He did this column, 'The Compost Heap'—most amusing if you spark to rustic humor."

"I don't," I said. "I think you've got things twisted."

"But you said…"

"My Thomas Chatterton was the youngest major poet in the history of English literature. Chatterton—*my* Chatterton," I went on icily, "was born, as the illuminated will recall, in Bristol, 1752, and died by his own hand in 1770." My father's son, right? I sure was creeping the hell into his heart, right?

Chatterton chose to ignore my contentiousness. "He was a relative of mine?" He frowned with perplexity. "You're sure?"

"Sure I'm sure. Look—your name's Phillips—that's my Chatterton's mother's maiden name. Valerie Phillips. Moreover…"

"Valerie? That's my daughter's name…"

"You see?"

"I'll be a son of a bitch. And he did himself in? At eighteen?"

"Seventeen. 'A fate-marked babe,' he called himself in *The Storie of William Canynge*." I shook my head in frustration. "What could possibly have given you the idea I'd be interested in the Cockeysville Weekly Nosebleed?"

He flushed. "How the hell would I know?" His eyes went sullen and hard. "People nowadays write dissertations on the goddamdest subjects, or so I've been told."

Pouting, he fussed over the stack of newspapers as if he were tidying up a favorite room, aligning them gently, lovingly.

He had been told right. I remembered my father, years ago, telling my mother and me in that pursy, gleefully contemptuous way of his about a doctoral candidate at Corn Pone U. whose discipline was animal husbandry. His thesis, "Does a Bull Control the Sex of His Get?" was accepted, and later printed in some scholarly barnyard journal.

But here, in the momentary silence and the everlasting heat, what made matters worse was my unreconstructed nastiness. I had to watch myself; I should have known enough to be respectful, to be courteous toward people who were trying to help me, whether they succeeded or not. Try to remember, I told myself, it's not Chatterton's fault that my father walked out on me.

"Listen," I said, "I'm sorry…"

He sniffed the air querulously, cocking a cold eye at me, as if I were bilboed under his microscope and my true self were suddenly revealed to him—a Muslim spy with false papers, or some kind of goddam freak. I knew what was coming.

"How old are you?" he asked suspiciously.

I had long ago learned not to lie about my age, if for no other reason than that, despite my six-foot frame, I actually looked younger than my years.

"Fourteen," I said.

There were other reasons for telling the truth. I had *because* of my freakishness established early on a wary ascendancy over adults of seasoned determination, and not in spite of it. It was precisely my freakishness that made me acceptable at Corn Pone and at Yale; my oddness gave promise that one day I might add a footnote to their fame (were they ever wrong). And in situations where my background was known, I was accorded a certain esteem out of pity; my father had deserted me at a tender age.

Both areas I had exploited to the best of my ability; I discount those rare occasions when my customary success was blunted by rudeness. Even a freak can't be expected to suffer fools gladly. (Here I go again.)

Chatterton continued to stare at me, a sly expression on his pelican face. He clacked his beak loudly.

"Valerie!" he yelled. "Hey, Valerie!" in a kind of malicious triumph. "Come here!"

Beyond the canvas curtain a tennis ball plopped on the court and dribbled into silence. The girl, still holding her racquet, appeared, her lovely face solemn. Chatterton swung his rheumy eyes back to me with a kind of grudging respect.

"I want you to meet an authentic prodigy," he told her. "Two years younger than you, he's getting his goddam doctorate and you can't even sneak by algebra."

"Jesus," the girl said. "The way you yelled I thought it was some kind of big deal."

The bland young man called Derek and Abby the ball boy came trailing along. They stood in the background like a couple of dithering supers on a summer theater stage who, disinterested in the action, had signed up just to be near the star. She gave off an aura of excitement just being there, turning the blighted patch around her into something more vivid than dirt. How does she manage it? The question crossed my mind, and such is my capacity for bullshitting myself that I thought, I swear I thought, Interesting thesis material.

Another and noxiously pervasive ambiance was in the air; immediately I traced it to Derek. He exuded the sharp spiced reek of some muscular toiletry—I visualized the spray can, crown and phallus emblazoned with an inspired trade name—CROTCH, perhaps, or GONAD, or TOAD REPELLANT.

Chatterton noticed it too. Curling his big nose indelicately, he jabbed his thumb toward Derek. "My sore back," he said. I must admit I liked the old man for that.

Valerie said nothing (was it possible she agreed with him?), and Derek ignored the impeachment. He had the narcissist's blockage to everything but praise. Leaning against a tree, full of little self-enchantments, he shifted his weight to his heels. His hips were shot forward, his legs spread wide, forming two sides of a triangle that pointed up to the apex of his jock. His thumbs were hooked in the belt-line, the fingers pointing down at the same target. I wondered if among his athletic accomplishments he might be a sprinter. I pictured him, spikes flashing down the stretch, legs pounding like pistons, digging, digging in an agony of triumph, and then the last eternal split second as he hit the tape with his cock.

Chatterton made no attempt to introduce me, and I was tongue-tied; it somehow seemed inappropriate, pushy, for me to introduce myself. The silence was growing oppressive. It was as if each of us were packed in his very own hermetically sealed container, and each container isolated from the others by cotton wadding. I—my presence—had erected the barriers, I was uncomfortably certain. I was the outsider who had altered their easy chemistry, inducing general asphyxia. I was the unassimilated child among adults, the impendent PhD, the oddity. Put it all together, and that one irreducible denominator rumbled painfully around my skull—*freak*.

And then Valerie floated toward me, her chaste little hand extended. I was tempted to kiss it, bite it, lick it like a fawning dog while Derek eyed me enviously.

"I'm Valerie Chatterton," she said, and I thought, She's an undiscovered municipal treasure. Tourists, if they only knew, would flock to Baltimore to see her.

"I'm Judd Breslau."

"This is Derek Bronson…"

"How are you?"

He nodded with an extreme economy of motion, as if any warmth might raise his temperature and expose him to grave danger.

"…and Abdul al Sadr."

"How do you do?" He shook my hand rhythmically, as if he were jacking up a car.

Silence again. Everyone frozen in place, like those mock-ups in the Museum of Natural History. Then Derek sauntered over to Abdul, who retreated to the background. It occurred to me that Derek enjoyed being in the same frame with him. All that swarthiness set off his lemon-colored hair.

"Well," I said, with the air of a man who had important things to do, "I must go."

No one made the least attempt to dissuade me.

"Thanks, thanks very much," I said to Old Man Chatterton. He unleashed a joyless grunt, took his grandfather's publication in his arms, and scuttled off. Abdul sprang forward to help him, and I was alone with Valerie and Derek. He seemed to think *he* was alone with her.

"Why don't you come back to Washington with me?" he asked.

I tried to look invisible, turning away tactfully. "No," she said. "I've got school tomorrow."

"So you'll miss a day. I'll bring you back tomorrow."

"No," she repeated. "The last time it was three days."

"I promise."

"What'll I do while you're working?"

"You could see the Capitol or the zoo or something."

"I don't think so." She made an adorable little face. "I don't want to wait around all day."

"I'll get Abby to drive you back."

"He's got classes."

"He won't mind."

"No," she said with finality, and I turned and walked off.

Down the rutted driveway, along the switchback road, I swerved my neck now and then, scanning the empty countryside for a hitch. She had hesitated. She had said, "I don't think so," and then, severely, "No."

I was beginning to feel better. It started to rain. The rain felt good, fresh and soft and cool. I had her phone number. What if I called her? Would she go out with me? Impossible, she'd have to hitchhike. Would she make me over, a stranger, a child, a freak? Certainly it was a fantasy worth pursuing down a rainy road. She invites me over, her old man is out of town for the night, tracking down a new grungy bathrobe, and I...

The car approached, a rusty old bull-bitch of a Chevy sedan, the tires bellowing in the rain. I raised my thumb. The car snorted past, spraying me with a curl of water like a wave boiling over. It roared on, but not before I recognized the couple in the front, beyond the blisters on the window, and Abdul in the rear. The old bull-bitch plunged on, diminishing, swallowed by the next switchback. I dug my hands deep in my pockets and kept walking.

FIVE

CONSOLATION

He strides athletically into my dark chamber, enshrouded in a tangle of hair that covers his face and his gaunt frame. Gym shorts as brief as a bikini support little more than his modesty.

The Reverend Doctor Dewey Lipgloss—just what I need—raises a benedictory hand in a striking simulation of his statue in the square, his tapered fingers slightly splayed, ready to field a blessing or a high fly ball. His attitude of athletic piety must have been familiar to those who knew him when he first came here, before the war, righteously armed with his trusty antimasturbatory tools—tennis racquets and golf clubs and a fundamentalist Bible. But that was before he renounced baseball and Jesus in one fell swoop to embrace all the virgins of his wide-ranging parish. He's a bristly-coated little animal with a thicket of wiry hair on his face and body (a source of fascination to many Assamans), and on his pedestal in the plaza that's all he wears.

Particular care had been lavished by the artist on Dewey's scrotum. Penis, testes, and pubic hair had been carved beautifully to mold in miniature a pious replica of Dewey's face. There is about it, and him, a mischievous ambivalence, half saint, half satyr, his image forming neither but suggesting both, in that attitude of supplication. But whether he's beseeching God or a local girl is difficult to determine.

Now, in the swelter of my cell, "Abide in light," he mumbles behind the thicket of his beard. "What can I do to ease your burden?"

"What do you have in mind?"

"First of all, I want you to know that I forgive you for having been so snotty with me. So please don't let it gnaw at you. And second," he settles down for a nice juicy chat, "I hope you're not wasting what little time you have with creepy thoughts of repentance. All that can do is give you pain."

"I thought pain was purifying."

"Perhaps, if you can outlive it. But in your case…" he coughs delicately. "Anyway, only pleasure is purifying."

"Most of your colleagues would disagree with you."

He nods sadly. "Too many of my brethren seem to be of the opinion that pleasure, particularly sexual pleasure, is a perversion. It took me a long time to realize that man's only perversion is celibacy. What I'm here to discuss…" He pauses, as if to make sure his deep sermonic voice has my unwavering attention; then: "What kind of funeral would you like?"

"I haven't thought about it."

"You should," he says, "but don't worry. I'll take care of everything. You want flowers? Those wildflowers we're allowed to pluck?"

"No."

"Would you prefer I take up a collection? A gift in your name for a favorite charity?"

"I don't have one."

He shrugs, running out of patience. "It's your funeral," he reminds me. "You'd do well to give it some thought."

A fat green fly buzzes loudly, beating its iridescent wings in the shadows, swooping and soaring in swift, eccentric circles. Lipgloss swipes at it, and the thing, sensing danger, takes sanctuary in the unassailable fortress of his beard, looking for a nice place to lay a few million eggs.

Undaunted by either the bug's persistence or my resistance, Lipgloss presses on. "What about the eulogy? I'll say a few words, touching on whatever you deem appropriate. You know the problem with eulogies—the person most concerned is never consulted. What would you like said?"

"I really don't care."

"Well, frankly, *I* care. After all, I'll be conducting the service."

"I'd rather you didn't. Would that be asking too much?"

"If I don't," he looks hurt, "what's there for me to do?"

"Well, frankly, I'd like to avoid a funeral altogether."

"How do you intend to do that?"

"Maybe you can help get me out of here."

The idea, from the confused cloudiness of his eyes, clearly hadn't occurred to him. "How could I?" he asks.

"I've heard you get away from here from time to time. For rest and recreation."

"Man doth not live by bread alone."

"Wherever it is you go, there's got to be an American consul or a U.N. agency."

"I can't go anywhere anymore," he says bitterly. "Not since the war began and they sealed off the borders."

"You can still get to Baghdad. Any American general or chaplain or the Coalition Provincial Authority would…"

"Baghdad's full of thieves, assassins, and thousands of trigger-happy kids."

"All you have to do is tell anybody I've been kangaroo'd."

"I go a yard and a half out of Assama I'd be scragged by somebody I don't even know. Thing is…"

"What?"

"They got an ugly war up there. They don't want anybody disturbing the peace down here."

"Abdul al Sadr's going to kill the hell out of me."

"What I'm tryna say, nobody up north is going to reverse Abdul's verdict—it's a done deal. So why can't we just talk about your funeral?"

"No."

"How can I help you if you won't cooperate?"

"You can't, really. Good-bye, Dewey."

We share a limp handshake and the visit is over. But at the door, waiting for a guard to unlock it, "Still," he says, "if you change your mind, I'd appreciate your letting me know as soon as possible. I have to prepare, you know, if my remarks are to be creatively structured."

SIX
FAREWELL TO COLLEGE JOYS

I never did get my doctorate. I fooled around, trying to work up some outrage toward John Lambert, the lawyer Chatterton was apprenticed to. Lambert used to search the youth's desk drawer and tear up his manuscripts, but the more I studied Chatterton's poetry, the more I sympathized with his employer.

Such depravity in intellectual circles does not go undetected. It was not long after my return from Baltimore that I was summoned to the office of my committee chairman.

Dr. Guthrie Armbruster was usually designated to the off-campus community as "our metaphysical man," not because of any deep transcendental leaning but for his discipline, the metaphysical poets. He had a certain peculiarity: he sat on pillows, for he suffered from hemorrhoids, that occupational hazard of scholars. We've all known people who elicit thought with some autistic gesture, wrinkling the nose, rubbing the chin, chewing a lower lip—that sort of thing. Armbruster achieved the same effect by leaning to his left and, using his right hand as a sort of tamper, pushing back his piles. One got the impression that his most inspired ideas came out of his ass.

Between him and me was his desk, and on it was a talus slope of papers, books, pens, pipes, unguents, a coffee mug, and, somewhere toward the base, my preliminary draft. When finally he found it he frowned, fingering a few pages with one hand and his ass with the other.

I had entered his office with high hopes, although I didn't know at the time what had prompted the invitation. It was quite late on a soft September afternoon; we had come directly from a reception for a visiting academician who had regaled us with a wok of stammering anecdotes about his work in China, collecting material for a biography of P'u Sung-Ling (1622–1679?). Or as he put it, "Kneading the d-d-disparate conca-ca-catenations of P-P-Pu's vitae into a workable t-tessellation." When, mercifully, the lecture dribbled down to a flat and inconclusive finale, we all repaired with the inconspicuous speed of sleepwalkers to the revivifying buffet.

Dr. Armbruster filled his plate with a wedge of cheese, a school of anchovies, and a mound of potato salad. He pushed back his piles, poured himself about four fingers of vodka, and was interrupted, as he proceeded toward a chair, by Shelby Drake.

Shelby Drake was another graduate student under his aegis, a smarmy, prematurely balding young man with a large Phi Beta Kappa key dripping from a chain across his ample vest. His doctoral thesis, on which he had been working for five years, was entitled "Punctuation as Emotional Caesurae in Joyce's *Ulysses*."

"Dr. Armbruster," Drake called, "I've just remembered the first time I heard you praised."

"Let me tell you something, Drake," Armbruster said. "Your overtures, despite their delicacy, are valueless. Your deference is nauseating. Your presence is dispiriting." Without rancor he added, "Go away."

Nicety dictated that I move out of earshot. My attempt at self-effacement failed; as I veered away from the two of them, "Breslau!" Armbruster snapped. "Come with me."

So I dogged his footsteps (Drake the toad-eater watching me hatefully), and sat by his side, peripherally aware of his long pistonlike arms working alternately to pass food to his mouth and push back his piles, as if he were shifting the gears that made his jaws mesh.

He said nothing for a good five minutes; then: "Sorry about your little contretemps with Chatterton."

I shrugged dismissively, careful not to agitate the meatballs on my soggy platter.

"My fault, actually," he said, "putting you on to him." He chomped awhile, ruthlessly, every tooth a pulverizing weapon. He said, "We share an addiction, Chatterton and I—tennis. One should have an outdoor hobby."

I tried to contain my surprise, although I couldn't have been more astounded if he had told me his outdoor hobby was riding a barrel over Niagara Falls.

"You look stunned," he chuckled, enormously pleased by my reaction. "Odd, that just about everyone should think of a teacher as totally enveloped in the nimbus of his own discipline. Do you play?"

"Unfortunately, no. And I know little about the game, other than it seems to have derived from ancient Persia, and was popular among the Arabs before Charlemagne. Louis X died from a chill contracted after playing. I believe it was Charles VI who watched the game from the room where he was confined during an attack of insanity, and Du Guesclin amused himself with it during a lull in the Battle of Auray."

"No. It was at Dinan. The siege of Dinan."

"Of course."

He got to his feet and I too rose, his faithful shadow. "Come back to the office with me," he said. "What *were* we talking about?"

"Your friend Mr. Chatterton."

"*Doctor* Chatterton. Yes, Chatterton thinks the game originated in Egypt. He's an Egyptologist, you know."

"No, I wasn't aware…"

"But I agree with you. Persia. Anyway, we had gone to Forest Hills together and between the matches, over a couple of brews, it occurred to me that Chatterton wasn't all that common a name. So I asked him if by chance he numbered among his rather substantial antecedents the poet Thomas, and he told me about *his* Thomas. I suppose," he said lamely, "I was only half listening—should have pressed more deeply before I passed his misinformation along to you."

"That's all right. I appreciate your trying."

We lapsed into another silence, crossing the quadrangle in the cool, calm evening. A group of undergraduates was playing softball in the mustering darkness; second base was a light stanchion in the middle of the quad. Their melancholy voices hung in the air like wisps of autumn smoke, punctuated now and then by the hollow resonance of bat meeting ball.

Armbruster and I skirted the players, young colorful ghosts floating across the forlorn grass, haunting that medieval pile of stone resurrected among the encysted slums of New Haven. The Silliman dorms rose around us on three sides, a chalcedonic fortress bravely a-glisten, the vaulted windows shot row on row with fire reflected from the iron-red sun.

I had never enjoyed my rare excursions into Armbruster's office. The room was permeated with the lingering stench of old and laminated farts, the stench building up until it reached apogee at nose level. The furnishings gave me claustrophobia; it was the kind of room that always seemed to be closing in on you. I found it difficult to concentrate on whatever I was there for; my thoughts ran to defenestration.

A turmoil of books with foxed leaves, papers veined with the tributaries of age, dog-eared clippings from literary journals, monographs mussed and frayed were on every shelf, on every wall, in every cranny. A helix of books loomed up from the floor. Most of them were unmanageably thick and long and wide.

A promiscuity of mysterious and totally unexpected artifacts was partially buried under the books on the floor. I recognized the thick shaft of a Wright and Ditson racquet that might have seen action in the hands of the redoubtable Du Guesclin in the Hundred Years War, and a lamp whose light bulb protruded from the maw of a sneering, stuffed alligator.

A meandering trail led through the thicket from the door to the desk. Armbruster sat behind it, having graciously cleared the only other chair of books for my comfort. He dug into a wavering column of documents, hands burrowing like a pair of underground animals. At the very plinth, under an offensively murky jar of olives, he pulled out my preliminary draft. He stared at it. I stared at him, waiting.

"It's full of seepage," he said.

"I beg your pardon?"

"Your dissertation. I find a certain subjectivism seeping into your exegesis," he explained. "No place for that sort of thing." He flipped a few pages. "Undeniably you have *talent*..." The way he stressed the word made it sound dangerous, as if he were diagnosing a rare disease. "...But," he shrugged his goat shoulders, shaggy in the ill-fitting Shetland jacket, "why do you suppose the seepage so stubbornly persists?"

It was my turn to shrug. "What do you think, sir?"

"Breslau, I'm not one to beat around bushes, so I'll give it to you with the bark off. I think you should pursue some endeavor where your imagination would be better appreciated and your flair for theatrics and adjectives handicap you less."

Pursue, he said, but pursue what? All I could think of was Shakespeare's line, "Exit, pursued by a bear." All I wanted was to get out of that evil-smelling chamber. But Armbruster was still trying to be helpful.

"Have you ever thought of writing, maybe for television? Or a gossip column for a tabloid? I know a man at the copy desk of the *Courant...*"

"I don't think I could write fiction. Or semi-fiction."

"Thing is..." he tugged at his piles for emphasis, "you're not pushy enough. I attack your preliminary draft and you don't even defend it."

"I was pushy with Dr. Chatterton and..." my voice trailed off. My thoughts at times ran to pushiness, but, outside of Chatterton, I couldn't think of anyone I'd been pushy with.

"Passivity," he plunged on loftily, "is never an asset."

For a moment it was so quiet in the room I thought I could hear the worms feasting on the spines of the books that confined us in this noisome cell. My problem was deeper than the passivity Armbruster observed. I was a total washout, once more having blundered, just as I must somehow have gaffed up with my father (why else would he have abandoned me?). Outside and from far away came the sad consolation of bells tolling. Someone, probably one of those music majors, had again gained access to the keyboard hammers of the carillon in Harkness Tower and was banging out a baroque rendition of "Melancholy Baby," and a sudden wave of peace and contentment washed over me. At last, I thought, an end to abstruse striving, to dogmatic bluster, Talmudic dissection, to the fractured assignment of Meaning and Levels to a phrase, a clause, a guiltless comma which the author, pinned like a butterfly on a board, probably never intended when he wrote it (who can fathom the mind of a writer?). An end to the inkhorn vocabulary of literary scholarship that was like a throat disease. A host of favorite terms bounced around my mind, derived from half a dozen legitimate languages, melded into a kind of lobotomized Esperanto so piss-elegant they self-destructed on the tongue into parody: *logaoedic, sestina, litotes, stasimon, meiosis, burletta, diverbium...*

Hooray and hallelujah, I told myself, an end to the absolutes of the pundit at the podium, that mild, murderous voice of orthodoxy which brooked no contradiction. An end to puny, pedantic jokes, to jabberwocky that was meant to clarify...

Hermeneutics, pleonasm, vorticism, catecresis, prosopopoeia, peripeteia... I rattled them off with the ease of a combat veteran reciting his rifle number: *dibrach, prolegomenon, choriamb, chiasmus...*

Was I going mad, or was it the euphoria of reprieve? The gibberish charged around my skull like a squirrel on a treadmill. The seizure continued, I couldn't stop it. The panic grew, the idiot internal voice persisted *anacoluthon tmesis rodomontade virelay...*

The spillage was ineradicable, but the mind is a palimpsest, and if its images can't be painted out they can be painted over. The trick is to concentrate on something else, on... on... A jingle of childhood burst into my head, that holy couplet of release we used to shout on the last day of school when the long unending summer beckoned and flashed like the Grail, all sun and silver:

> *No more lessons, no more books,*
> *No more teachers' dirty looks.*

School was out for me, forever, and sumer icumen in. The balm of relief spread over me like the cool, sweet sweat that follows a consuming illness. I felt kindly toward Armbruster, amorous toward life, and joyful toward the world *erziehungsroman ubi sunt enjambent Freytag's Pyramid...*

"You all right, son?" Armbruster's concern cut through the bombardment.

"I'm sorry. What were you...?"

"I was saying, well, what are you going to do?"

I hadn't thought about that. My euphoria evaporated. I resented his bluntness. His doubts about my ability could have at least been mollified; he had made no effort to conceal them.

"I don't know," I said. "Maybe I'll be a rock star or join the circus. Play tuba in a band."

He ignored the pallid attempt at insouciance. "I do feel a certain responsibility, and you're much too young to assume the emeritus." He smiled supportively. "You're just a colt."

"An aging colt. I'm pushing fifteen."

"Just a colt," he repeated, cherishing the phrase, "with talent, and an unlimited potential for... for..."

His voice broke off, a contrail of uncertainty. Now he was trying to be kind, and it was more concussive than his bluntness. He didn't know what

I had a talent for, and neither did I. I remembered my mother, proud of my dash through high school in a year, indulging me (and herself) with the same sort of vague encomium. "I do not think you will die," she had said on that occasion, "without making a Real Contribution."

"...Or perhaps let it lie dormant for a couple of years, until it asserts itself."

"It'll have to assert itself in about a month, or I'll starve to death."

"Come now, boy. Can't you live with your mother?"

What could I do in Ravenna, Colorado? I thought of life with the remote fortress that was Old Moms, in her flowering black robes and heavy gold-plated chains, going sadly, oppressively bump in the night as she walked the house shaping her odd-shaped poems. I could hear her sigh like a leaky bellows, feel her inflexible eyes on the back of my neck, perplexed, perhaps embarrassed by the presence of this foundered son of a defeated father.

"I'd rather not," I said.

He frowned. Deep in thought, he swung his torso to the left, slipping a hand under his elevated right ham, and pushed back his piles.

"What about research?" he asked. "If you care to give it a go, Chatterton might take you on."

"Phillips Chatterton? Researching what?"

"He would of course brief you."

"But he's an Egyptologist. Didn't you say...?"

"He is indeed. With solid credentials. There was his paper on the mastabas of the Old Kingdom..."

"That's hardly my field."

"He is a man of many disciplines. Protean. One of those clever people," he added mysteriously, "clever enough to conceal his cleverness."

"Would he have me? We didn't hit it off too well..."

"I'll speak to him."

"Where would I work? Baltimore? Washington? College Park?"

"He is no longer affiliated with a university, choosing to devote all his time to his, ah, project. His home is his laboratory, shared with a few others of the same ah persuasion. You'd work at his home."

Would I indeed? Interesting...

"Any other questions?"

Just one, but not for Armbruster's elongated ears. The question was, of course, was I clever enough to suppress my own cleverness? Because, of course, the only reason for taking the job was to bask in the glorious proximity of Chatterton's daughter.

SEVEN
CHATTERTON

I should have known there was something weird and tilted about Chatterton and anything he was involved with. But Valerie beckoned.

And so it was that on a dank, dark autumn day, before the hermetic snows of winter gripped the world and everything went bare and shriveled and icy, I sloshed through the melancholy leaves down the tree-lined corridor of Chatterton's ancestral seat. This time there were no sweet muffled cries of "Love" and "Balls" to greet me, only the burned-out silence of the invisible sun as it dipped below the equator far away.

I hammered on the water-warped door. I'd be damned if I'd touch the bell hanging from the two frayed wires, not in this kind of wolf-weather.

From within came the irregular pad of galumphing footsteps, rather like those of a gorilla with corns.

The door groaned open, as if in pain, and Chatterton stood in the portal. His shag of linty hair hung round his face. The considerable nose protruded in my direction, as if he were sniffing me. He seemed ill-defined and slightly out of focus in that offensive bathrobe (his usual at-home vesture, I was to learn) that contained his nakedness. He managed a sour nod of welcome and stomped off, down the hallway, past a shadowy staircase. From somewhere high above in the house the thin, sharp notes of a fipple flute spilled down the steps. Was it my darling practicing demisemiquavers?

I followed Chatterton into a high-ceilinged room, darker than the entry and furnished with a lumpy couch, a straight-backed chair, and a scarred chess table. He closed the door behind us, snuffing out the sound of the flute as he would a candle.

An old-fashioned safe with a stolid hard look squatted in a corner. Thick and aggressively ominous, like a mugger in a black trench coat, it probably weighed more than a wrecking ball. By every law of Archimedes, the state of Maryland should have collapsed under its weight.

Built-in bookcases lined three walls from the peeled varnish of the parquet floor to the faded polychrome ceiling bloated with stucco relief—rosettes, garlands, foliage, fruit—all mildewed and decayed. The shelves were empty of books and unclotted by those sentimental little fragilities the acquisitive bourgeoisie sometimes substitute for them—Dresden shepherdesses, Steuben swans, stoneware urchins, polyester pussycats. Nothing destroyed the austere symmetry of those naked shelves except one battered tin container, about shoulder high, labeled

HEINZ'S PEARLS

KEYSTONE PICKLING & PRESERVING WORKS

PITTSBURGH, U.S.A.

Despite the frivolous ceiling, the room, all things considered, was as barren as a Trappist's cell.

The old man flopped into the chair and with an imperious gesture assigned the couch to me. He planted his elbows on the chess table, forearms slanting upward, making a steeple with his hands. He favored me with a meager smile.

"Armbruster," he began, "has told me quite a bit about you. Recommended you highly."

I tried not to register surprise.

"I can understand why—your being so removed from the usual run of doctoral candidates."

True. But why would he consider my ineptitude an asset? What had Armbruster told him? I figured I'd find out soon enough, any minute now, if I just let him rave on.

"I refer of course to your maturity…"

Me? Mature? I rearranged my face into a saint's mask of huckdummy humility, a violet by a mossy stone, in Wordsworth's lapidary phrase, half-hidden from the eye. A conspiratorial hush descended on the fuggy, frost-bitten room, profaned by the disintegrating smell of meals. Indeed, we were conspirators; of all the world's burgeoning population of six billion souls, only we two shared an awareness of my maturity.

"…your zeal to face life's rough and tumble, your ardor to accept the responsibilities of adulthood is hardly congruent with the aspirations of most graduate students…" He shook his head of disagreeable hair. "I need not tell you," he deplored, sinking to paralipsis, "that there resides in almost every one of 'em the unconscious desire not to grow up. For once the academic goal is attained and the doctorate irradicably abbreviated after the name, the problem of facing the world is confronted. The subtlest, most unremitting drive of the student is his unconscious proclivity to postpone the acceptance of responsibility as long as possible."

I said nothing; my lack of response seemed to bother him.

"I don't seem to have your rapt attention," he said crustily. "Aren't you listening?"

I was listening intently, not to him but for some little manifestation of *her* presence. I strained to the trill of the fipple flute, no more than a memory, lost beyond the portal that confined me in this black hole with her father. Somewhere she was in that misshapen house, in a quiet room made luminous by her magic, her long, gracile fingers curved around the stem of the flute. I saw before me the mirage of happiness. Reverie soared on gossamer wings.

"Well," Chatterton was saying, "that's not my way." He stared at me belligerently, like a big old bison staking out his claim to a patch of prairie. Perhaps he thought I was toying with the notion of refuting him—saying something nice about the fellowship of graduate students.

"What is your way? What do you do here?"

"You might say we practice good citizenship."

"'We'?"

"I and my brave little band of brothers. We work, we live in harmony, with mutual respect and understanding. We pursue a common, or perhaps I should say," he smiled a smile that had no gladness in it, and his gleedy eyes narrowed mysteriously, "…an *un*common goal, in this calm and pleasant manse."

"What?"

"Manse." He sniffed querulously. "Dwelling, abode, if you prefer."

"I mean, what do you do?"

"Research, of course."

"Research on what? What am I supposed to do?"

He squinted at me as if the answer to my forthright question was too obvious to merit a response. Finally: "Why, to play the tuba," he said. "You do have it handy?"

"Handy enough." I had left it along with my minimal wardrobe in the checkroom at Union Station. "You've got some kind of orchestra around here? A military band?"

"Goodness, no," he chuckled, deep in his throat. For a moment I thought he was choking. "You play solo," he said, "observing as you play the response of, well, we'll start with this." From his bathrobe pocket he plucked a small stone rectangular block about the size of a domino. "This," he said, "is your audience. But we can't expect you to spend ten to twelve hours a day blowing your horn without a break, can we? So," he added with the sanctimonious air of a vigilant shop steward concerned over the exploitation of the workers in a salt mine, "so I want you to take time out every now and then."

"To do what?" I asked warily.

"Think." He tilted his head to one side, lolling his tongue out of the corner of his mouth, winked a watery eye, and tapped a finger against his temple. "I mean, that's your job, along with the tuba. What you do here is think."

"About what? Anything in particular?"

"Suicide," he said, favoring me once more with his murky, fraudulent smile. He rose from his chair and lumbered across the room like a famished wolf. He plucked the solitary tin can from the bookshelf, lifted the lid, and peered inside.

"My own?" What the hell kind of job was this?

It was as if he hadn't heard me. His face went livid, as if it were lit by an internal torch. The ropey veins in his neck seemed about to burst through the skin. Combusting, he lunged to the door and threw it open. "Gorelik!" he roared, head thrown back, like a statue trumpeting on a pedestal, and the muted strains of the fipple flute were silenced. "You running sore!" Chatterton shouted. "You've been at my peanuts again!"

A guttural voice from high in the house stumbled down the stairs. "Tzadderdon," it advised wearily, "go fug yourself." The flautist resumed playing, and Chatterton continued to shout, accompanying the recitative with a set of emotionally charged stanzas characterizing Gorelik as a crapulous lout, a relic of barbarism, a Levantine prick, and a musicologist with an ear of pure tin.

The tantrum subsided. Breathing heavily, Chatterton slammed the door against the invading flute. "The gods forgive my foolish rage," he said huskily. Then: "Where were we?"

"This suicide business."

"Oh, yes. I want your ideas on... on why some people in deep trouble, in despair about whatever—it may be something personal, or the state of the world, or the lack of money—why certain people do something positive about it, sail on, accepting or overcoming any manner of obstacles, while others self-destruct."

"Different people do different things, that's about all you can say."

"What about that poet fellow who did himself in? One of my ancestors, you said."

"He just gave the hell up. He didn't fit in anywhere. He didn't get enough to eat. He had no friends. So he swallowed a little arsenic."

"Give it some thought. Try to come up with something seminal."

"Well, Freud said..."

"No, no," he cut me short. "*I* know what Freud said—a cul-de-sac! And Durkheim and Jung and Schopenhauer and Menninger and the Hopkins studies—culs-de-sac, all of 'em. What I want is your original thinking on the subject—what the physicists call a *gedanken* experiment. That's what we do here, I and my crisis cabinet, so to speak. We are a phalanx of thinkers with unmortgaged minds, who have never been inclined to accept the rules and values and interpretations which have been imposed upon us." He popped a few peanuts into his mouth. "Thinkers," he repeated thickly as he chewed, "not readers. Look at this library," he directed me, gesturing at the shelf. "Note that there's not a book in it."

What was he driving at? Chatterton's approach to scholarship was a new departure from research as I knew it. But to what purpose?

Perhaps I was assigning to him some ulterior motive, deep and baleful, that the situation didn't warrant. Perhaps, like a clown in an outrageous cloak, he wasn't to be taken seriously. Perhaps he was just another harmlessly eccentric pedagogue chasing his intellectual tail in a maze of reverie which passes for thought. Or some kind of nut with the tilted intelligence that is a variety of *Dummheit*.

And yet—he had introduced the subject of suicide; I found that worrisome. Did he want to gaslight an enemy? Create a sociological order conducive to *felo de se*, a self-inflicted murder? Did he intend to use me to supply the means?

And as for his brave little band of brothers, what was Gorelik's role in the opus? And the crisis cabinet he mentioned—what was the crisis?

"Yes...?" His croupy voice penetrated my gloom, showered my thoughts. "What is it?" he asked, not unkindly.

"I'm thinking..."

"Splendid. Your brain is a castle of fertility."

"...about this *gedanken* thing..."

"Take your time. Explore those silent areas of the mind. Open 'em up, break through those inky thickets that are contaminated by cant and bibliolatry. Free your instrument and your vision becomes limitless."

"Yeah, sure, but why am I to do this?"

"For reasons," he said mildly, "which seem sufficient to me. The only issue is, do you want the job? It's light, indoor work," he said, "with no heavy lifting. You can do it sitting down."

"What about salary?"

"I assume your needs are modest?"

"Well..."

"Good. You'll be doing significant work. Breaking new ground."

"You mind spelling that out for me?"

"You'll have the opportunity to do battle against the world in order to save the world. Don't you find that an enticement?"

The job was only an enticement because of you-know-who. After seeing her that first (and last and only) time, I had returned empty, depressed, inflamed, to New Haven, bewildered by the sense of loss of something I never had. It took months before a sort of partial amnesia set in, until at last I could work on Thomas Chatterton for days on end—well, make it hours—without thinking of her.

There was also the conscious desire *not* to see her. In the isolation of the stacks I cringed with self-loathing whenever the blistering shame of my oaf-ishness that day in Maryland returned to assail me. Forget her, I told myself, and I tried. You'll never see her again, that stern, internal voice persisted, and I believed it.

Then, miraculously, things had given way to a future full of hope and bright promise. How could I give it up, even if it meant short wages and slow starvation? Accepting Chatterton's indecent proposal was small tollage for the privilege of her proximity, of sipping beer from her tennis shoe, of stroking the back of her dimpled knee. Still, the enterprise begged for nego-tiations; that knee was no less tantalizing with a bit of silver in my kick. In case of an impasse, I could always capitulate.

"It's difficult to *gedanken,*" I began, "without resources."

"By which you mean money," he said haughtily, drawing his bathrobe about him, as if I were a cold wind. He looked like a giant hairball. "What's money compared to serving the cause of humanity?"

"Do I get paid at all? I mean, it sounds like I'm to pay you for the oppor-tunity..."

"Of course you get paid."

"How much?"

"That depends."

"On how well I do?"

"On how well *we* do. We are funded, you see. Our finances vary from time to time."

"What kind of funding is that?"

"Voluntary. We have certain associates, culled from academic ranks, who believe in our cause, who think of us as a... a lighthouse on a stormy night. Still, it's all very irregular," he added wistfully. "Sometimes they forget their pledges altogether. And now we're really up to our hilt. The house is mort-gaged, the bank has threatened to foreclose..."

So he embroidered his poverty-stricken project, while I tilted with more practical issues like where would I live? I had a sneaking suspicion that I wouldn't be able to afford a room in a skid row scratch house. How would I get to work? There was no bus line within miles of Chatterton's labora-tory. I couldn't even cough up a down payment on a bicycle. Hell, if he gave me the use of a car, which was highly unlikely, I couldn't drive it. At fifteen I couldn't qualify for a license. As for Valerie, how often could I expect to see her? And on the rare occasions when I did, what was I to expect, other than a fresh chapter in my bitter book of wounds?

"I'm sorry," I said, "but I don't know how I'd manage..."

"The same way we do," he said. I'd wondered about that—Chatterton and Valerie and Gorelik and God knows who else, garrisoned in that Moorish keep with the defective electrical wiring and the crumbling widow's walk— how did they live? On the old man's harvest of peanuts?

"Somehow we get by," he intoned. "You'll break bread with us and live under our roof. I think you'll find it stimulating."

Under a roof with Valerie—stimulating indeed.

"Okay," I said. "I'll give it a whirl."

"Splendid." The hairball levitated, balanced precariously on two shabby house slippers. "Come on—away to shed some light."

He led me down the ill-defined corridor, floorboards creaking under us like a wooden ship in a storm. "Remember," he said, "the trick is, open all your valves."

We climbed the stairs. My foot caught twice in the frayed runner. He threw open a door and we were in a small room, no cozier than Chatterton's, but darker and louder with the wail of the wind. A gauzy sheet of rain pushed against the only window, and beyond it the wintry trees bowed in a slow demonic dance. Out there somewhere was my father. Where had he gone, what was he doing, did he ever think of me?

"Here we are," Chatterton said. "Settle down and air the corridors of your mind." And he was gone.

The wind fell to a murmur and before it rose again the strains of Gorelik's fipple flute sloshed over the room. I groped for a blunt shadow, hoping it might be a chair. It was, and it was upholstered. I flopped, twisting my body, throwing a leg over an armrest. Not bad; there's something about wind and rain, when you're sheltered from it, that makes for contentment. I counted my blessings—a loaf of bread, a leaky roof, and Val, beside me in the wilderness. I hoped our friendship would not be long in deepening.

EIGHT

THE MARVELOUS BOY

The figure appears like a small, curdled cloud floating on the hot wind across my prison cell. Slowly it takes substance: a rickety stool dangling in the middle of the air and on it, cross-legged, sits Thomas Chatterton, boy poet and faded star of my mangled doctoral thesis. A coarse scarf ripples at his throat; a threadbare linsey vest of a mottled hue goes well with his yellow teeth. A wen pokes through his spiky hair. On his pen finger is a callus.

"You blew it," begins whey-faced Thomas, sneezing into his scarf, then dabbing his eyes with it. "You blew it when you dumped me."

"I had no choice," I say. "I was bounced out of Yale..."

"Yale's not the only school in the world—in my day it was considered a slough of godlessness way the hell and gone out in the colonies—so you could have taken me elsewhere. But you thought I was, don't deny it, a no-talent, dismissable asswipe. Well," he favors me with a powerful sneer, "the experts, among whom you hardly qualify, thought otherwise. If you'd really read through *MUN–ODD* of the *Britannica* as you've claimed, you'd know that my work had (and I quote) 'sustained power, originality, rare merit, lyrical beauty.' My poems were 'wonderful for their harmony and spirit, by far the most remarkable example of intellectual precocity in the history of letters.'

Moreover," he went on, "I was the first writer in the entire canon of English literature to live in a garret. Of all the major poets who died young," he says proudly, "I was the youngest, while you…" His eyes burn contemptuously. "So," he trumpets, gulping air, "so who's the asswipe now?"

I want no quarrel with this squalid apparition, certainly not at a time when my spark is about to go out. But he would not let up.

"When you abandoned me, you abandoned yourself. You gave up the tranquillity of scholarship to make a noise in the world and now you have doubts about your decision—small wonder when you see where it's gotten you. So you summoned me…"

"I never summoned you. I…"

"How else can you explain my being here? Certainly I'd never return of my own accord." He shudders. "And the words you put in my mouth—*asswipe* and, and—I gag on them, I, in whom the spirit of piety, veneration, and rectitude was so deep." He settles back on his stool, taking solace in his own virtue.

"Why would I put words in your mouth that allow you to praise yourself?"

"To prove that I was indeed the inflated fraud you took me for, to justify the rightness of your course, *or* because you thought there might be some truth in what I'd have to say, thereby confirming your secret suspicion that you were wrong about me when you threw in the towel." He grins unpleasantly. "Think it over," he says, "but take your time about it. No one else is haunting me at the moment, and I rather like the equatorial heat. I was always cold in England, you know, seldom had a fire to poke. And anyway," he adds slyly, "I'd like to stick around for the show. For which you have nobody to blame but yourself."

He was a vindictive boor, defeated in life, defiant in death, the epitome of all the young geniuses who failed. But there was indeed something remarkable about him…

"Maybe that's why I called you back," I say.

"For the show?"

"For your… I don't know, your indomitability."

He long-faces me, fraught with mistrust.

"I think I admired you for that. Envied you in a way, because you knew what you wanted to do with your life and you accepted no compromise. You honored it in the face of defeat, you pursued it until you died. "

"While you, on the contrary, sold out."

"Not exactly. I just stumble from one damned thing to another, never knowing what I want."

"I never had the luxury of stumbling," he says. "There was no other road I could take and survive, even to my seventeenth year. Wherever else I turned I was repelled by the ceaseless, senseless bustle." He loosens his fusty scarf and turns his face to the sun streaming through the window. "Do you know now?" he asks. "What you want?"

"No. But it makes no difference now. Although I won't waste more time with visitors. Except Val, if she comes. They're all ghouls, the rest of 'em."

"You might reconsider—seeing them, that is. Never can tell who might provide a clue to survival."

Suddenly I'm tired of talking. He seems to be just warming up.

"I think I'll have to ask you to tear yourself away from me," I say.

"It's your decision," he says. "You're calling the shots."

He touches his forelock in a small salute and fades slowly away, beginning with the bottom rung of his stool and ending with the wen on his head, until he has disappeared altogether.

NINE

BAND OF BROTHERS

My workday. Up at seven, summoned by the extravagant outburst of an alarm clock, compliments of the house. Half-drugged with inflamed sleep, I'd drag myself from my onanistic bed, wash, dress, and stumble downstairs.

Breakfast was whatever remained from last night's dinner, usually hard-boiled eggs or Spam or canned spaghetti, a diet that might have caused rebellion in a holding tank for felons. Then back to the frozen solitude of my room, to slump into the chair and get to work.

Still I did it, if not industriously, because it was preferable to doing nothing, which was even more irksome and somehow induced melancoly.

And I didn't make much progress gedankening about suicide; it was a subject easily resisted, more so by my confusing awareness of the clangor and clatter of Gorelik and the others scattered around the house. Were they too in their time-outs mulling over suicide?

It was a puzzlement, and I for the most part was uneasy, cinched in the serpentine coils of the sousaphone, um-pah-ing for hours on end for the edification of that damned stone block (Chatterton maintained a discouraging silence whenever I asked him why I was so engaged) or thinking about self-immolation, an exercise in unfulfillment unless, I suppose, you have a personal interest in the subject. I needed stimulation, source material, reference works, and like a wretch in a famine intoxicated by the remembrance of a full pot simmering on the stove, so my nostrils inhaled the imaginary smell of books, that delicate and overpowering perfume nothing on earth could match, not fresh-mown hay, not automobile leather, not vulval musk.

I was a prisoner of my own resources, which I found were surprisingly limited, and of a silence that was daunting. I came to welcome the sneaky and infrequent infiltration of Gorelik's fipple flute, but I cringed when, suddenly and violently, those shadowed corridors were rattled by Chatterton's voice booming some displeasure, the cause of which was never made clear. "Gorelik!" he would yell. "You double-humped Bactrian...!" or "Pierson! You yellow-bellied sapsucker...!" It was unnerving, and to regain some modicum of reason I would have to remind myself why I was there.

From the time I had crossed the threshold of my frowsty cell, a postulant closing the door on the outside world to worship my goddess, what equilibrium I had previously possessed gave way to confusion, an aphrodisiacal compound of great expectations and sheer panic. Poised like a cunning little animal in a wilderness of predators, I listened for her footsteps, her voice, some small sign of her presence.

Thinking of her had its compensations—there was a kind of perverse enjoyment in it. Her incorporeality neither discouraged my vigilance nor restrained my speculations. Somewhere she was, but where I hadn't a clue. Where she was not became increasingly obvious as the days shambled by: she was not in her father's house. Had I committed myself to this underendowed asylum for nothing?

The morning after my arrival I was the first at that septic breakfast board and the last to leave, for it was there in the company of my colleagues that I sought (beneath a mien of indifference) information regarding Valerie's whereabouts.

Shortly after the grandfather clock in the downstairs hall groaned, wheezed, and, with extraordinary mechanical effort, struck eight, Chatterton's brave band of brothers struggled through the French doors of the dining room. They were a loutish crew, with dull eyes, sloped shoulders, and heads hanging like heretics about to be burned at the stake.

All of them were old and most of them were irascible. No one took the customary initiative of introducing himself. They might have been members of some seedy club in which they took no pride; each, however, seemed to view his colleagues as so lacking in respectability or accomplishment as to merit expulsion.

No salutations passed among them as they jockeyed, with the glazed, greedy self-absorption of children, for position around the stove, then lunged across the uneven floor to gain a coveted spot by the clanking radiator.

Once they had eaten and thawed out, they grew expansive, garrulous. I listened closely, eager for some clue as to their calling.

"…the angle fish. Fastest gun in the sea. Strikes in four one-thousandths of a second."

It was (I learned later) Gorelik speaking. He was short, with pale, hooded eyes which gave him a look of sham inscrutability. A Russian *rubashka,* the kind Tolstoy wore, but dirtier, encased his slab-chested torso and the hump on his back; altogether he was built like a doorknob. But what had angle fish to do with his assault on the fipple flute?

The man he addressed smiled knowingly. "The sargassum fish will eat its own kind," Norman Baker said. "That, too, takes a sort of gruesome energy."

Gorelik drew on a brown cigarette. "And what about the saber-toothed blenny?" he asked, exhaling. He held the butt between the tips of finger and thumb, palm upraised as if to catch raindrops from a leaky roof.

Norman Baker, the authority on sargassa, smiled again, a corpse-smile this time. "And the hummingbird," he said, "beating its wings seventy times a second?"

So their discourse leaped and glanced from fish to birds and then to deceptively fragile butterflies, particularly the monarchs, whose energetic excesses were exemplified by their migrations between Canada and Mexico, laying their eggs under milkweed along the way.

Who were these people? Ichthyologists? Ornithologists? Lepidopter-ologists mured in a convalescent home for declining academics? They droned on, sipping their vile coffee, Gorelik chain-smoking his long, mud-colored cigarettes, holding them like a mittened ape, and Baker smil-ing, smiling, smiling. He had a smile for every occasion, an unending vari-ety of smiles. His round, defenseless eyes, presumably the mirror of his soul, relayed nothing, but that smile ran the gamut of passion. He could beam a smile of excessive intimacy, a rictus of ferocious ill humor, a melting sim-per of benevolence or rumpled self-effacement, a smirk of wry mockery, an insinuation of mysterious complicity. Yet each smile was incongruent with whatever he said, so that his words always sounded banal or frivolous.

I tried picking up on other conversations in the huddle around the ingle-nook, but they seemed to be nothing more than trivia, however exotic. There was about the group a kind of conspiratorial affinity, as if they were all ful-filling a need, but what it was I didn't know. Nor would any of Chatterton's accomplices tell me. My presence among them as time went on was acknowl-edged from meal to meal, certainly not with relish but with a timid waif of a nod from George Desmond, a fubsy piglet of a man (he seemed afraid of offending anyone), or the gimlet eye of Ridgeway Mainwaring (who seemed to enjoy offending everyone). Mainwaring's brief survey would spear me for only a second or two before it passed on to a vista more alluring.

One positive corollary of being ignored: nobody asked me my age or evinced the slightest interest in my past. If indeed they had questions about it, they thought it best for whatever reason (the foremost being total uninter-est) not to pursue them.

That first morning their talk drifted on, hushed and aimless and in a miscellany of accents I'll not attempt to reproduce. I nodded off, exhausted from my Homeric debauchery with the girl of my dreams.

I willed myself to think of Valerie—oily, priapic fancies—but some dark undeniable compulsion wrenched her from my grasp and death took over. I saw myself slightly out of focus, in that kind of iridescent light we associate (thanks to motion pictures, I suspect) with the supernatural. Whatever the hell, there I was in shiny black leather, a hangman hanging myself, with an ugly knife in one hand and a darkly gleaming gun in the other. A shot rang out with the blast of a sonic boom, and a voice from an echo chamber said, "Murder. It's sheer murder," and I woke, instantly alert and cringing.

Karl Gruenfeldt sneezed again; it had been his first sneeze, I realized as the clutch of the nightmare subsided, that I had mistaken for the gunshot or sonic boom.

"It's the cold," said the sneezer, running a red knuckle under his hairy nostrils. "He'll kill us all." Karl sniffed and probed deep into his nose with a finger.

"Stop that!" commanded Zygmunt Wolenciewicz. His elongated, aristo-cratic countenance took on the aspect of a man who had detected the reek of month-old crabmeat.

"Why should I?" Gruenfeldt asked. His face bore a waxy jailhouse pallor.

"It's unaesthetic," Wolenciewicz said.

"Some people make an art of it," the sneezer insisted, "like the Italians of the Piedmont."

"The Piedmontese are barbaric," Wolenciewicz said with insufferable hauteur. "Their amusements are limited—what else have they got to do?"

"The nail of the little finger of a Piedmontese is grown long and spade-like to facilitate the procedure..."

"You exhaust me with your erudition," a tall, gaunt man said contemptuously, his eyes splashing with distemper.

"Stay out of this, Treblant." Gruenfeldt turned back to Wolenciewicz. "And it is not only the Italians. Everybody picks."

"Not everybody." They turned to me. I should have kept my big gob shut.

For a moment the heavy silence was relieved only by the clanking radiator. Then Gruenfeldt sounded me with his watery eyes. "And who is this person to whom you refer—this paragon who does not pick?"

"What I mean—some very remarkable people didn't have a nose to pick," I said lamely.

"Boy," said Henri-Jacques Treblant, "you are ridiculous." He had the mien of a warrior, fierce, straight-spined, unfrivolous. Without a doubt the prickliest pear of the common room.

"Tycho Brahe lost his nose in a student duel over who was the better mathematician."

"He must have been a pretty sight," Baker said with a heartwarming smile.

"He was," I went on. "He had the original replaced by a gold one."

"Now that's the kind of nose I would pick," Wolenciewicz said. "Imagine the satisfaction of mining gold from your very own nose."

"You may think it's funny," Karl sniffed, "but I think we should draft a petition..."

"Splendid idea," said Zygmunt. "Gold noses for everybody."

"...If everybody signs it maybe Chatterton will turn up the heat."

"Gruenfeldt," George Desmond said, "you've got to realize that one man's cold is another man's comfort. When I was at Harvard..."

"There he goes again," Gorelik said in a loud aside. "Hey, Desmond, you think you can say your little piece without boring us with your triumphs?"

"...at Harvard," Desmond went on, "we had as efficient a heating system as any in an American institution, and I for one am happier here than I ever was there."

"Why," asked Treblant, "do you Americans place such emphasis on happiness?" His voice was solemn and emphatic, like thunder bounding across the Juras. "Nothing of value was ever accomplished by a happy man. Happiness is for children, if they're lucky."

Ridgeway Mainwaring nodded sharply. "People work best when they're uncomfortable," he said authoritatively. "For best results, the human brain should be refrigerated, like a good cut of pork."

"I cannot be happy when I am freezing," Gruenfeldt insisted.

"Seneca!" cried George Desmond.

They all looked at him.

"Seneca," Desmond repeated. "He led a plummy life. He was productive, functioning well on many levels—philosopher, playwright, politician, cocksman—one of his mistresses was the daughter of Germanicus. And he was rich, the possessor of more than five hundred ivory tables. Seneca," he glared at Treblant, "was a happy man."

"Some happy," Treblant sniffed. "So why did he suicide himself?"

"He was forced to, accused of political conspiracy. For all intents and purposes he was murdered."

The grousing lapsed for a long moment. They sat there, presumably contemplating the end of Seneca, hunched over their coffee cups and brooding within their jackets with patches at the elbows. They were all over the hill and they knew it, put out to pasture. Each was undoubtedly a specialist, confined to his own narrow arena of expertise, a discipline indecipherable to his colleagues. They didn't talk shop as fellow workers are wont to do. Rather they simply ventilated the esoterica of academics, holding anxiety at bay with their hostile rhetoric and their rudeness.

Karl Gruenfeldt had not yet exhausted his disgruntlement. He zeroed in on the one subject all workers have in common: the enemy in their midst, the Boss.

"I consider myself the victim of Chatterton," Karl insisted, "no less than Seneca was the victim of imperial Rome. What difference if one is forced to open his veins or to freeze them solid?"

"You make our helmsman sound like one of those bonker scientists in the movies," Desmond said.

"He does get his ideas in the dark of the moon," Gorelik declared.

"Ideas are one thing," Treblant said. "Solutions are harder to come by."

"If he can cut the mustard," Wolenciewicz said doggedly, "he should be able to spread it. If he can't, he shouldn't be holding the knife."

"One thing," Desmond said. "He does keep rooting. If a blind pig roots long enough he's going to get an acorn."

"He doesn't root," Mainwaring said, "he uproots—not allowing a book in the house. You don't pull anything up by the roots till you're bloody well certain it's dead."

So they sat there, gassing away like cavemen around a fire, relieving their fossil fears, and I sat alone among them, surrounded by their lost whispers. Why were they fearful? What were those ideas of Chatterton's, begat in the dark of the moon?

At last they grew bored with each other and filed off, each to his respective room, a clutch of solitudes in search of solutions for God knows what.

I found myself alone at the table with Joseph Grady, by far the youngest of Chatterton's soldiers. No more than sixty-five, he had contributed not a trifle to the morning's rough symposium; he had simply been there. A sort of cautious curiosity glimmered in his eye, the mark of a man who takes all things into earnest consideration but adds nothing to their explication.

For a while neither of us spoke. Then, "Hemlock?" he said.

Hemlock? All this talk about murder, being shot at, Seneca's suicide, death by freezing, and now hemlock. The morbidity rate in Chatterton's house had to be among the highest in the nation.

"I beg your pardon?"

"More coffee?"

I shook my head. He got to his feet slowly—he must have been six feet four—and poured from the blackened pot on the stove.

Quickly I assessed the situation. Here I was, sharing a heartburn with a man of scrupulous courtesy, somewhat outgoing, an excellent target of opportunity. Yet there was that sort of curiosity in his eye that I couldn't decide whether I liked or not. And the tone of the place was such that certainly it would have been presumptuous if not gauche of me, the cub of the company, to ask him what he did, even if I could manage the question nimbly. Perhaps I could ask about Valerie? By the way, I might say, whatever happened to

Chatterton's daughter, the young lady with the fabulous tits?—something like that but more dignified, less personal.

My misgivings were unwarranted. Out of nowhere he turned his unruffled gaze on me and said, "It must be difficult for you around here—no one your own age..."

A man of vital perception; the seal that shut me off from Valerie was broken.

"Where is she?" I asked, bewildered by my own daring.

"In Fort Lauderdale, I'm afraid, with that handsome barrel of noxiousness, her great friend Derek What's-his-name."

"When will they be back?"

"Soon, I suppose—after the Christmas break. She'll sashay in here, exhausted from... doing nothing, freighted down with sunburn, beer, and a supply of porno comic books."

I managed to utter not a word.

"You too?" he asked with a solicitous grin.

"Me too, what?"

"Smitten."

"I'm too busy," I said. "I'm working on..."

"Don't tell me!" he fairly shouted. "Chatterton doesn't like team sports. We all work individually—keeping him posted, of course. He feels strongly that good work can never come out of collaboration."

He returned his empty mug to the stopped-up sink, where a culture of velvet gray mold and some green slime bubbled gassily. "See you around," he said, "and by the way—I manage to smuggle a newspaper into the house every now and then. You're welcome to them, if you like." And he was gone.

TEN

YEARNING JUST FOR YOU

It was the first week in January before the pale, sickly sun reappeared. The soggy earth settled under it and the house settled into the earth and I settled into the house.

I huffed and puffed on my tuba. I gedankened, more or less. My days seemed pointless and overcharged at the same time, posing twin, unsettling questions. What was Chatterton up to? And what was I doing, chugging blindly along with him? A yoke of crepuscular companions shared my snuggery: Tedium crouched in a corner, while Horniness occupied my bed.

To escape my roommates I prowled that wreck of a house, its fathomless shadows and its funky air. Furtively avoiding my confederates, searching mostly for books but willing to settle for anything, I found nothing. Not even a map. But the expenditure of energy did me no harm.

I might add that my colleagues afforded no relief. They were at best fugitively visible, other than at meals. I heard Gorelik's fipple flute now and then, and other sounds which in their convoluted passage through the house were less easy to identify. A muted metal clangor, as if a pair of steel dice were being clapped together like castanets. The sostenuto of what might have been the vibrations of a tuning fork. The reedy shrill of a pitch pipe, or was it a boatswain's whistle? The tinkle of arrhythmical bells and the sudden, unnerving anguish of a siren. And always the confrontational blast of Chatterton's a cappella mood music bullhorning across the stage, flogging his tonsils over some balls-up which was never made clear. He roared like thunder but he struck like lightning and, so far as I was able to determine, with the same whimsicality. No one except Gorelik ever talked back, and their dialogue was unnerving. "You toad! You fart-infested camel!" Chatterton would yell, and, deep-voiced, as if from a rocky cavern, Gorelik's borscht accent would bellow, "Tzadderdon, vy don't you take a flying fug to the moon?"

Stressful, yes, but those brief and warlike exchanges did relieve the heavy consistency of my lassitude, and in their wake I would re-rouse myself and re-slink around the house looking for something, anything, readable, besides labels on bottles. I'd rattle along one dreary, unpopulated hallway to another, lurch up and down the stairs, wondering if she'd ever come back. I stood entranced before the door of Val's room, trying to find some runic significance in the notice pushpinned on the door:

PRIVATE KEEP OUT

THIS MEANS YOU

(The majuscular print was slanted, slubbered.)

CURSED BE YE WHO EVEN

THINK OF ENTERING HERE

V.C.

Of course the door was locked. I put my nose to the keyhole and sniffed for perfume, but all I inhaled was the frowst of dry rot. There was, so far as I could determine, not one square inch of that infirm house which wouldn't give you a cauliflower nose.

So I'd speed to the countryside, striding over the wintry moor with a gait that was purposeful and a mind that was not. The dull, tingling, perpetual twilight of January hung over the chestnuts, painful to the eye, drained of all color. That semisolid grayness, the texture of dust, played hob with depth perception—perhaps I needed windshield wipers—for the trees seemed to be gliding blindly toward me. At times the earth and the sky became one and I'd lose all sense of direction, lose sight of the widow's walk, the entire house. A feeling of loneliness and isolation cut me off from the world as it reeled on its own axis, and the image of my father would thud across my mind like the memory of some weighty transgression (not his but mine).

Some world. Something was wrong with it, a world in which I walked alone, while Val frolicked like a fawn on a tropical beach with Derek the self-enchanted satyr. I'd break out in a cold sweat thinking about her, them, until Take it easy, I'd tell myself. Be patient and one of these days she'll return.

But hold on.

It occurred to me that my obsessive frenzy over Valerie might tumble into a bottomless fixation—and then what? What if I never saw her again?

It was possible. People go to south Florida and other such lotus-eating communities in the horse latitudes and never come back. They letch around with beach bums (like Derek). They catch wheezy-engined planes to Mazatlán or Zanzibar. They... you get the idea. So I knew I'd better be ready for any importunate contingency, of which there are legion. But I wasn't folding my tent like Longfellow's Arab and quietly stealing away. If she was dumb enough to curl up with Derek, I'd get by, no matter how I felt at the moment.

Yeah, yeah, yeah.

ELEVEN

THE CANDY BOX

Surfeited in riches, I sat within a fortress of impacted books, magazines, monographs, journals of the International Association of Egyptologists, anthologies, chrestomathies—enough cud to chew and swallow for a long time. I flipped through the leaves of an old *New Yorker,* feeling warm and happy about all the consumables in the ads I had not the least desire to own. I practically caressed a copy of *Light in August.* Nestled among its cozy, big-shouldered siblings was my old friend *MUN–ODD* of the *Britannica.*

Discovery of the treasure trove was purely *gedanken.* On my somewhat demonic tours of Chatterton's ancestral acres, I was at times inattentively aware of the widow's walk, but I had never found access to it on the rare occasion when I roamed the top floor—the third; nothing there but empty rooms. The brave brethren were foxholed on the deck below, while up here only one cubicle showed signs of habitation, presumably a workshop of sorts, with a carpenter's bench, a scattering of tools, and a ladder on its side, angled against the wainscot.

Was the platform purely cosmetic? Or was it sandwiched like an end of cheese between the third-floor ceiling and the slab roof?

And then it hit me: the *attic.* Chatterton had said, the day we met, "I'll get 'em from the attic," referring to the oeuvre of his grandfather, that sterling editor-publisher and belletristic wag of the *Cockeysville Clarion*. That brown and brittle clump of newsprint resided there, with god knows what else?

Peering up through the gloam of the third-floor corridor I made out a trapdoor. It gave when I pushed against it, while beneath me the ladder protested, creaking.

The first thing I saw among the graveyard of junk was a sewing machine table and, on it, a framed photograph of a woman of about forty with wide, piercing eyes and a Gioconda smile. Beside it was a bud vase holding a dusky red rose too perfect for this world; it was made of plastic.

I gave it no more than a glance, eager as I was to get at the books, and now I was devouring them in great swinish gulps. For how long? I don't know. I was only conscious, and vaguely, of a shaft of cathedral light that slanted through the bull's-eye and pearled a patch of the attic and then moved on. The distance between my nose and the page narrowed as darkness fell; my sanctum had no electricity. I closed the book and stared at a dark spot at my feet; it became a beetle. I tracked its stiff, erratic trek. Rather than walk, it seemed to push and pull its black shell through the dust. Its joints creaked loudly, like some tiny primitive tank. Which couldn't be; it must have been the floorboards, which also couldn't be, not under the weight of an insect, and oh shit, I suddenly realized, it was the ladder in the hallway below. Chatterton was coming to catch me red-handed among the forbidden fruit.

A head appeared above the trapdoor, a halo of hair shining darkly as if it were the focus of a full moon, and beneath it the face of a suntanned divinity. She anchored a long, slim leg on the floorboards and her skirt slithered upward, revealing a flash of silky brown thigh that slammed into my ventricles like a shot of digitalis. She favored me with a smile, polite and listless, as if we had last met an hour ago at the supermarket.

"Hi," I said eloquently, my voice a husk of its former self, my mouth tasting thickly of glue. Did I speak loudly enough? Too loudly? Both?

"Hi," she answered in perfect pitch.

"Nice to see you."

"Yeah," she said remotely, going to a bookcase.

"Perhaps you don't remember me. I'm..."

"I know," she said, and I was elated. She *remembered* me.

"When'd you get back?"

"An hour ago. I don't know. Two or three."

"Have a good time?"

"Yeah. It was a ball."

A ball, was it? I hate that word. Visions of my love throbbing in Derek's embrace was like a rain of blows from a bludgeon.

"Not really," she went on, and I was delighted. Maybe, I thought with the desperation born of hope, everything went wrong—holidays are like that. Derek was a bore, he ran after other women, he was stoned, pissed, reeling from the day they left, impotent upon arrival.

"Derek had this bad cold," she explained. Great. Colds can lead to influenza, gallop to pneumonia, scar a man for life. Or better yet, his brave young heart gives out, finds peace at last in an unmarked grave in an unplowed field along the road to Disney World.

"But he's okay now?" I asked, hoping for the worst.

"Yeah," she said, squinting through the darkness at the books. "For sure."

For some reason her words jarred me back into reality, more or less. To ignore her relationship with Derek was unproductive.

I would simply have to take her away from him. How I didn't know, but he was despite his seniority such a redundant asswipe, six feet of a fool, I felt I might have a shot at it.

Across the dark attic, she stood balanced on the bale of *Cockeysville Clarions,* playing a small flashlight along the volumes on an upper shelf, rising on the toes of one leg like a light-loined ornament, waving the other in the increasingly warm air.

"Hmmmmmm…" She frowned as she scanned the titles. She pulled a wide book from the shelf. "You think this thing's worth anything?"

"What is it?"

"*Who's Who in America.*"

"What do you mean? Worth reading?"

"Worth money. My father never gives me a fucking dime. All he ever gave me was a collection of whatchucallem, you know, that read the same backward or forward…?"

"Palindromes?"

"Yeah. Once for my birthday. Like 'Able was I ere I saw Elba.' In a kid's notebook. It's around here someplace."

She climbed off the newspapers, bouncing the flashlight along the book spines in search of her only birthday present. She gave up and turned to me. "So what I do, I take an armful of books to the Salvation Army in Pikesville." She slid a random book off a shelf and dropped it at her feet. "They're good for a few bucks," she said.

"Next time I'll help you, if you like." The enormity of my overture struck me immediately. But of course I'd steal for her. Hell, I'd kill for her.

"We do it in the car. Carry the books, I mean. Abby's car."

"The Chevy? I thought it was Derek's."

"No," she said. "I wanted to ask you something."

I waited breathlessly.

"Now what was it…" Her sun-kissed brow creased a little as if thinking caused her pain… "Oh yeah." Her eyes reflected the light and a starburst of violet diamonds fell on me.

"Who," she asked, "was Elba?"

"It's an island in the Tyrrhenian Sea. The palindrome refers to Napoleon's exile."

She sat on the throne of newspapers, facing me. "You ever hear of Stanislavski, some ginzo in show business, Russian or Polish maybe?"

"Konstantin Stanislavski?"

"That's the one. Yeah."

"Russian. Born in the 1860s, died in the 1930s, I think. A director, teacher, and actor. He created the so-called Method technique. But perhaps," I was just getting warmed up, "his greatest achievement was an ability to flourish under both the Czars and the Soviets. His real name was…"

"Derek's all the time talking about him."

"Derek's an actor?"

"Kind of. He wants to be, you know?"

It was sheer witchery, the way she talked, the constructs that rolled off her tongue. Stanislavski, "some ginzo in show business…"

Outside the wind howled over the frozen earth, but here by her side (well, across the width of the attic) all was aglow with the radiance she generated. I felt splendid for the first time since I had entered Chatterton's turvy world. After all, I was batting a cool 1.000 in our game of Twenty Questions, and she was impressed, I think. It was hard to tell. On the one hand she upheld her end of our fragmented duet; on the other she relayed a distinct impression of indomitable torpor. There was about her the aura of a mild trance. I thought of opiates—perhaps she was still in recovery from an overdose of beer, sunshine, and porno comics consumed in Lauderdale, as Grady had augured. Or was it an habitual disenchantment with everything, the rooted sluggishness of a cow? Another thought struck me; I was quick to dismiss it, but... could it be possible that my pedantry was boring the bejesus out of her?

She was stacking a dozen or so books in two neat columns on the floor. She paused and again her tranquil brow creased. "What are you doing here?" she asked.

"Scrounging around for something to read. I thought maybe..."

"I mean *here*. In this house."

"I..." I clamped my mouth shut, succumbing to a mute sense of panic. According to no less an authority than Joseph Grady, what one did under Chatterton's quirky roof was not to be bandied about; indeed, he had made it emphatically clear that silence was requisite.

"I'm working for your father."

"Doing what?" She continued to rummage among the books, stretching, bending, twisting her torso shamelessly; all her parts engaged with elegant grace. Then she turned and tilted her head to one side and gave me an absent, reassuring smile that obliterated my defenses before they were properly constructed. "You can tell me," she said. "I don't talk."

"I play the tuba," I told her.

"In his rinky-dink band of brothers?"

She was not impressed. Perhaps I needed to intensify my contribution to her daddy's enterprise, whatever it was. "I'm also doing a study on suicide."

She stiffened. Two books exploded out of her hands and landed thuddingly at her feet.

"You know why?" she asked in a flat voice.

I shrugged. "Because he wants me to. He didn't confide..."

"He didn't tell you about my mother?"

My eyes went to the picture on the sewing machine table.

"Is that your mother?"

"Yeah. She killed herself."

That kind of jolted me.

Valerie stared down at the fallen books. "Why'd he hire *you*?" she asked.

"Well, maybe because I did a study about a suicide. A young man, seventeen."

With infinite care she restacked the books, aligning the spines with the tips of her fingers. "This kid," she said, "who did himself in... why'd he do it?"

"I think he was just overwhelmed. The world was too much for him."

"I think that was the trouble with my mother."

"When did she...?"

"I was thirteen. Three years ago. September 2001." She hesitated, then, "I think my father still feels guilty about it."

"Why?"

"Because she gave him certain signs. He never picked up on them. Like the first time she tried. The sixth of August, 1995." She picked up a book, put it down. "So maybe he wants to prove it wasn't his fault—that there was nothing he could have done to prevent it. Or maybe he just doesn't understand."

"There was no hint why? No suicide note?"

"There were lots." She stood quite still, as if she were weighing a decision of vast import; then she weaved past a console radio removed from its housing, the metallic tubes and coils and tuners like the towers and domes of some miniature, futuristic city. She bent over the sewing table and slid a glitzy red box from a top drawer. Under the beam of the flashlight she handed it over.

In the candy box was a thick cluster of three-by-five index cards. The sickly sweet fragrance of chocolate was still on the first I pulled out.

We make war (I read) *on all creation and in the process we kill ourselves.*

The words were penned in an urgent, erratic hand. I plucked another random card from the pile.

The world will end soon with a bang. All of us, everywhere, are prisoners of our own destructiveness.

And:

There's no way out for the human race. We're running in reverse, back beyond Methuselah, back to the nothingness of the void.

It seemed to me, after a sampling of only three cards, that any moderately dispassionate observer would conclude that Mrs. Chatterton was paranoid, possibly to the point of madness. Which obviously didn't disburden Chatterton; he couldn't or wouldn't let go.

I read on:

Phil dear, your gray suit is at the cleaner's. Also two of my dresses. I've been wearing the same thing for a week. Maybe you noticed.

And:

I feel limp, hollow. I know I shouldn't succumb to these thoughts.

And:

I don't know what else to do. All I know, I won't spend the rest of my life weeping.

So it ran on. Chaotic, repetitive, interlaced with domestic banalities, fearful admonitions.

I [a few words scratched out] *and we need coffee, sugar. It is the end of the world. Tonight for me, anytime now for the rest of humanity. Goodness no longer exists in the world. Ingenious brutality, ceaseless bloodlust on one side, and corruption, greed, and arrogance on the other.*

"She took more than a hundred Seconals," Valerie said.

Why is it that nobody cares?

"The notes were pinned to her nightgown," Valerie said. "More than a hundred. You could hardly see the nightgown for the notes."

Phil, this is important. Get me out of the house before Valerie sees me.

I had read enough. "Who found her?" I asked.

"I did. Wouldn't you know?" She tried to smile. The attempt was a shambles but she made no effort to wipe it off her face. "That's how I met Derek," she went on. "He was the son of the undertaker. He used to help out around the shop."

"But you were thirteen, you said. That's pretty young…"

"He called me a year later. Out of the blue."

"It must have been tough for you. I mean without your mother."

"Most of the time everything's okay, but once in a while I have this feeling…" Delicately she peeled a flake of skin from her forearm and examined it minutely. "And my father—he's kind of weird. It's hard to explain."

"You don't have to. My father was kind of weird too."

"Yeah," she agreed, not listening. "I don't know. All I know, every time I do something he just like stares at me. So I do nothing."

"Don't you think it's obvious why she…?"

"Yeah. I suppose."

"Isn't it obvious to your father?"

She shrugged, tracing a finger through the dust on a book jacket.

"I mean like when she chose to do it. The fiftieth anniversary of the bomb drop on Hiroshima. And then just after the Twin Towers fell…"

"I don't want to talk about it anymore." She snapped the flashlight off and on again, off and on. Little orange-red flares tailed across my retina. She went a bit out of focus, as without another word she stepped over the books she had so assiduously collected and disappeared down the ladder.

TWELVE

THE PRINCE

I hung in there, lurking you might say around Valerie, Abby, and Derek, trying to penetrate that magic triangle. I hung in there, lonely and slack and dim-witted, like a moth on a window attracted by the warmth within.

Not that there was much warmth among them. The tone was set by Val, who seemed as little interested in them as she was in me. Three isolates they were, inseparable but strangers to each other.

Let me not distort. In truth, Val and Derek got along well enough; they seemed to have so little in common that there were no grounds for conflict or resentment.

I tried to be fair about Derek. Certainly he must have been a vessel of incandescent sorcery—why else was she so taken by him? Was it his pretty face? Like so many scumbags he had the features of a mass-produced android, one of those shallow-eyed washouts who populate TV commercials flogging a cure for dandruff. His wit? Derek's eloquence was that of a rather backward monk immured in silence. On those rare occasions when words were indispensable, his speech was limited to the laconics of a telegram ("Val. No toilet paper in bathroom").

His sartorial virtuosity? Perhaps. When he wasn't sporting his spotless tennis whites, his style of dress was Early American Saddle Tramp—tight-crotched jeans, scrolled boots, Western shirt with smile pockets (and rivets yet), and a half ton of burnished buckle on a wide leather belt billboarding his name, each letter hyphenated by stars. A coxcomb cowboy, old D*E*R*E*K, whose linkage with the range was not easy to determine.

Was the attraction the sensuality he was forever flaunting? Did he have a cock as big as King Kong's? I didn't know, and I never would, unless we managed to share a urinal sometime, and that was unlikely.

I also didn't know why Abby was always in evidence. Certainly he was smitten; did he insist (however indirectly) that in exchange for the use of his heap, he be allowed some little patch of her sunlight, to bow in benediction as she passed his way? Maybe he cherished the hope of winning her favors (was I projecting?); maybe he had already done so. It was not totally unimaginable that they shared some kind of *débauche à trois*. But no, his attitude toward her—the furtive half-smile of appeal, the soft, uncertain gaze of worshipful submission—was hardly proprietary. No; he was a walk-on waiting in the wings, and she wore him on her bracelet, accepting him simply because he was dangling there. Truth was, she accepted everyone, but distantly, and therefore no one. My Last Duchess in reverse, as it were:unconcerned, uninvolved, unresponsive. Never relating to anyone, never resenting anything, she rolled (so I thought) with every punch. I was soon to learn differently.

Derek's excursions to our cozy little nest were constant. On those days when the eccentricity of the Maryland climate banished winter for a few shining hours, he and Abby and their hostess would repair to the court, where the splashy son of a bitch would prance about like a spastic peacock. I'd hover on the periphery, melting out of the background and into their awareness only when a ball bounced my way before Abby could retrieve it. My overtures, few and puny as they were, did not meet with Derek's approval; we showed toward each other that grim reserve evidenced in so many cases of undesired proximity.

Sometimes I'd see them lounging in the Chevy, passing around a joint, and sometimes they'd see me (I made sure of it, parading down the avenue of oaks, feigning unawareness, deep in meditation ha ha). But they never offered me so much as a toke. I would have tried it, of course, just to play in their magic garden, although getting stoned was a skill I'd never mastered. Like that snatch-happy president of way back when, I didn't even know how to inhale.

Most of the time, the cold and the damp and the darkness forced us indoors. We took refuge across the hall from Chatterton's study, in a room of dusty, haphazard charm. All of its mismatched furniture—Victorian, Federal, a Louis Quinze escritoire—was worn out, beat up, stove in, but polished to a high gloss by the brush of time. The self-contained trio had commandeered it as their own, although of course I managed to hang in during their occupation.

I was not the only alien infiltrating the sanctum. While Chatterton and his brave band steered clear of the young people, Joseph Grady did not. He encamped in a corner, behind the widespread pages of his newspaper, and they ignored him. He offered nothing; neither did Derek, who seemed to be of the persuasion that we were amply rewarded by his very presence among us. Abby, on the other hand, acknowledged the pleasure of Valerie's company by bringing her things: a silver miniature of a llama, a string of amber worry beads. Once it was an ivory netsuke of a mouse whose charm, not unlike her own, induced breathlessness.

Tonight they sit on the grungy rug, the two visitors like steadfast planetoids around the star that holds them in place. Derek sprawls against a cushion. Beside him is Valerie, her bare legs airborne, hinged at the knees and crossed at the ankles, perpendicular to her prone body. Facing her is Abby, kneeling in an attitude close to supplication. Between them is a chessboard. They're playing checkers, more or less. She studies the pieces, nibbling the petals of a bright chrysanthemum, another gift from Abby. Trying not to be obvious, he tilts his torso to run his feverish eyes inside her open-throated blouse, just as I am doing. Derek, of course, has all the best of it. While Abby's contortions and mine compete for a less impeded vista, Derek is running his hand up and down her leg, rounded knee to slim ankle, again and again, slowly, maddeningly.

I can't stand it; I try to concentrate on the game, not easy because I've never found much stimulation in checkers, although no less an authority than Edgar Allen Poe had written something like "the higher powers of the reflective intellect are more decidedly and more usefully tasked by the unostentatious game of draughts than by all the elaborate frivolity of chess." But I doubt if Poe's concentration was ever contested by a spectator's reaching out to cop a cheap feel off one of the players.

Valerie's leg shot out reflexively. "Cut it out, quit it," she said.

"Cut out what?" Derek asked with a kind of sly innocence. His grin was close to a hyena's.

"You know what." A film covered her eyes, as if they had been daubed with a damp cloth, and her mouth trembled ever so slightly. She rolled over and sat up, cradled a leg in her lap and examined it. On the brown calf were two scarlet little half moons like parentheses where his nails had bitten into her flesh.

Abby leaned forward, attentively silent and with a hound's devotion. A dog-smirk of embarrassment for his friend's savagery shadowed his lips.

The light twist of my mouth must have telegraphed my censure to Derek.

"What?" he asked.

"You," I said, "you make me sick."

"Stay out of this."

"You're a louse. Your whole head is sick."

"Fuck you," he said, and with that brief exchange, something ugly and evil passed between us. His mark on her was the brand of possession; by challenging it I had made for the first time in my rather uneventful life an unallayed enemy. I wanted to kill him, to scalp the lemon-colored hair from his skull, to flatten his perfect nose until it split at the seams and bloodied his face, but most of all I wanted to cornute that sadistic bastard, whose meanness was in double figures.

He said, "Look, kid, you're not wanted. Why don't you go to bed like a good little boy?" It was to my knowledge the most elaborate outpouring of words he had ever managed to string together.

Valerie said, "He's got as much right here as anybody."

He looked at her with grim censure.

"Fuck him," he said again, and thickly, "fuck you too."

"That's enough!" Grady lowered his newspaper. And then gravely, almost courteously, he added, "You two have renewed my faith in juvenile churlishness."

Derek chose not to meet his gaze. He scrambled to his feet, upsetting the checkerboard, and stormed out of the room. Hopelessly, Val looked after him. Grady said, "Don't worry. He'll be back." Altogether I considered the episode a promising, an enriching, experience.

But not for long, for back he was, within a week, he and Valerie going off together, disappearing in the woods, in the back of the car, wherever, while Abby and I, like two abandoned lepers, were left to our own resources.

Our conversations at first were merely courteous, the static of politeness. Never more than muted, they would at times drift off and fade altogether, like a bad telephone connection. He'd look out the window, waiting for Val to turn up even while we were talking, his voice with me while his thoughts hovered over the woods or the car or wherever he thought she might be. So we sloughed through the swampy, extended silences until once again we'd pick up the wayward dialogue. We seemed to agree on any number of subjects I didn't care much about, and I had the feeling that Abby didn't either. We had become entangled in each other, a couple of alien twigs grafted to Valerie's disregard.

When the fruits of our rhetoric withered and died altogether we played tennis, badly, which in that foul climate had the salutary effect of a cold shower, that classic cure for satyriasis. Until the day I slammed a ball over the raggedy green canvas that enclosed the court and in retrieving it found Chatterton slouched on his chrome and plastic throne like some noxious growth out of nature's own garden.

He was bundled in his bathrobe and an overcoat that would have left Richard Evelyn Byrd sweating in Antarctica. We exchanged a cautious greeting, but that in itself provided a strong disincentive for my returning to the game, for I was pricked by a small but nagging guilt that I should be applying myself to the tuba instead of freezing, self-indulgently, to death on his cracked playground. After that I stayed in my grotty room. Abby would bop in on me for our desolate chats.

"What are you taking at Georgetown?" I asked one day.

"I already told you, I think. Sociology, diplomacy." He stood at the window, his back to me, staring out. "I would like to make her my queen," he added. "It's very awkward." He bowed his head, chagrined.

"I suppose it is, you and Derek being so tight."

"I suppose we are. *Ur haft yik gorill.*"

That's what it sounded like. "What's *Ur haft*... what you said?"

"A gorilla, in my language. Dialect really, spoken where I come from."

"Which is?"

"Iraq. A province called Assama. Never heard of it, right?"

"Exchange student?"

"No. I have a full ride, courtesy of the U.S. government."

"Who's a gorilla?"

He didn't answer.

"Derek?"

"I shouldn't have said that."

To my mind Derek wasn't an ape. He was an insult to apes. Still, coming from Abby, it was an epiphany of sorts. "Why is Derek an ape?"

"Well… literally it means, 'one who is like people but cannot talk with us.'"

I grinned at him and slowly he rearranged his sad face and grinned back. It was the beginning of friendship.

"What else about Derek?"

"There's nothing that you don't already know. He's like a celebrity."

"In what sense?"

"Have you not seen those people on TV?"

"Has he been on TV?"

"No. But he *acts* like he has—as though millions of people are *aware* of him. Isn't that what a celebrity is?"

"I suppose."

"Yes," he said, "he is like King Kong in the cinema. A celebrity gorilla."

He grinned again and then the fingers of his right hand played a few silent notes on his left wrist and he held out a watch on a fine leather strap.

"Here," he pushed his Patek Philippe toward me.

"I can't accept this."

"I got another one. I want you to have it."

"Why?"

"Because you are a sympathetic listener."

I hefted the watch in a palm. "You must be a wealthy man," I said, tempted by the overture.

"There are gradations of wealth. I am moderately rich, not princely rich."

"Only princes are."

"But I am."

"Rich?" The conversation had gyred toward a confusing circularity.

"No. A prince. Well, sort of a prince. Heir to the throne of Assama." His face was set in a somber, quizzical half-smile, as though I were feigning unawareness to the obvious. "No one told you?"

"No one tells me anything."

"Well, actually my father is not a king. More of a tribal chief. But he prefers the title 'King.'"

"Isn't there kind of a big difference?"

"From the time the Europeans first arrived bearing gifts, hoping for any kind of concession that would give them a foothold to hunt for treasure, they called him 'king,' and he liked it. He also liked the stuff they gave him. The French gave him a wad of Patek Philippes. I got a couple of them."

"But still I can't..."

"Will you just take it?"

I hesitated, said, "Thanks," and strapped it on.

"Want to play checkers?"

"I'm supposed to be working."

"The old man knows you're not working. He knows I'm here. I think," he added, "he has Grady spying on me."

Another revelation. Just as he defined Derek as an ape and a celebrity, so he exposed himself as a faux prince and a genuine paranoid. Such was the taint of this vile house that everyone who crossed its tilted threshold was certifiably bonkers.

THIRTEEN

FAT CHANCE

Through the slit of my window I look out on the feculent buildings around the square. Many of them are multistoried like the jail. At first glance they seem to be made of sun-dried bricks splashed blue or green or red or yellow. The bricks are made not of mud but of shit, plus that unidentified substance that solidifies them.

For six thousand years Mesopotamia has adorned its urban centers like Jarmo and Tel Halaf with brilliant, unexpected structures. Elaborate. Fantastical. The walls of city gates, mosques, and towers throb with bolting, slab-chested bulls prodigiously hung and scaly, fire-breathing dragons prodigiously hung.

Little remains, but in full bloom are the excremental ingenuities of Coproliabad.

Walking toward the jailhouse is the provincial secretary of commerce, fatso Hashim Pachachi, whose life from an early age has been dedicated to finance. He had served an eager but unremarkable apprenticeship to a Baghdad branch (long abandoned) of a bin Laden family consortium.

Hashim never got over it. He drifted from one unfulfilling enterprise to another, emerging as Assama's secretary of commerce, a job that lacked substance in the real world. But he went on trying mulishly to rack up a big score.

With Hashim is Shakir bin Zaki, resident intellectual and poet laureate. He is steeped in the works of William McGonagall and Edgar Guest—he loves them both and is known to quote them on solemn state occasions, although nobody seems to know why.

The guard outside my cell door stops snoring long enough to let them in. I offer them a range of salutations, in accordance with custom. No response, which is unusual. Most of the time we signify in a kind of Choctaw, a simplistic and infelicitous mix of English and the regional misspeak of Persian, although Hashim has been known on occasion to drop a precise zinger of a construct into the otherwise loopy dialogue.

Finally bin Zaki says, "We thought we might give you one last opportunity to help us before you..."

"I can't help anybody. I can't even help myself."

More silence. Then Hashim says, "Just one question. It might even take your mind off..."

"What?"

"Before you go climb a tree..." Shakir says.

"Who," I ask, "is climbing a tree?"

"You know," Hashim says, "what we do in a tree when somebody dies."

"I mean, what's the question?"

"Well, here in Assama we have not kept up with the world." Pachachi heaves a leaden sigh. "Now we got to make up for lost time."

"We need to get something going," Shakir says. "We got to bust out of our rut."

"We need foreign investment," the Secretary of Commerce says. "Tourist trade. Some kind of international attraction. Something big."

"Big as a rock," bin Zaki adds.

"Spectacular but refined," Hashim says. "Transformational."

"In the arts," Shakir says. "A poetry festival with two prizes. In Arabic and English."

Pachachi frowns. Bin Zaki has thrown him a curve, momentarily impeding his plunge toward tycoonism. "What I had in mind was more like a World's Fair," Pachachi says. "Or the Olympics. Maybe a heavyweight championship fight. The Miss Universe Contest. World Cup soccer—we could put an all-Coproliabad team together. So," he turns to me, "what do you think?"

"Do you know," I ask, "what *fat chance* means?"

"Don't you want to help us?" bin Zaki asks back.

"I don't know how."

"Yes, you do," Hashim insists. "You're a Yank."

"There's nothing I can do in jail. Maybe, if you could get me out..."

"You want me to go against the will of the Sheikh?" Hashim is shocked. "That wouldn't get you out. It would get me in."

We seem to be hitting an impasse. For a long moment I hear the rats jigging in a dark corner.

"Take care of yourself," Shakir says.

They shuffle toward the door. Before they get there I ask, "You happen to know where Valerie is?"

They exchange a guarded glance, their eyes avoiding mine. Finally, "She spends a lot of time with King Abdul," Shakir says.

"Probably trying to talk him into letting you out of here," Hashim says.

"Probably," Shakir adds unconvincingly.

"Probably? Why else would she spend time with him?"

Now they are staring at a dirt-lodged crack in the floor.

"I don't know," Shakir says. "I'm sure she has her reasons."

Abruptly, Pachachi says, "We got to go."

And they went, leaving me uncomfortably alone with my thoughts.

FOURTEEN

THE SECRET OF THE PYRAMIDS

Darkness fell long before the day succumbed to evening. I walked the hall outside my room, flapping my arms to keep warm, trying to think, finding little but worms in the gedanken apple. Chatterton's voice tore up the stairs.

"Bud," he shouted. "Come down here!"

He was paging me. I had told him about twenty times that my name was Judd. When I gave up, I'd even thought of changing my name to Bud. But I had a bothersome notion that if I did, he'd call me something else.

He sat at the chess table in his cell, wrapped in his bathrobe. All that protruded above the upturned collar was his sworl of sauerkraut hair, while below the hem his legs like asparagus stalks took root in the frayed vegetation of the carpet. Trousers were invented by the Scythians of Carpathia back in the Bronze Age, but Chatterton apparently had never heard of them.

"How are you?" he asked with unexpected civility.

"Cold."

Civility vanished. His face—what was visible of it—twitched, like gruel coming to a boil. "Don't be cheeky with me," he cautioned. "If you're so cold, why are you sweating?"

What could I tell him? That from the time I scrambled down the steps in

91

answer to his call I was taken in a fit of free-floating, corrosive anxiety? That I found no joy in being confined with him and his hair and his bathrobe in that bleak black hole of a study? That I wasn't prepared for the inevitable inquisition on the progress my sousaphone had made on the little steel domino?

Thomas Henry Huxley, up there with the brainiest, once noted that there was "the greatest practical benefit in making a few failures early in life." Something like that.

Not for me. The domino's refusal to dance to my tuba I found of no benefit whatsoever. Although once, just once, I thought I saw the damn thing shudder. More likely it was my imagination, exhaustively impatient for progress.

"Perhaps you're working too hard?" he asked with a smirky, derisive smile. "Perhaps the work is too stimulating? But never mind," he said magnanimously. "How well do you know Abdul Whatsisname?"

"Not very."

"You are of course aware of his background?"

"Somewhat."

"Thing is, our revenues have become increasingly idiosyncratic, and now the cupboard is just about bare. You think he might be interested in funding us for a while?"

"Possibly," I said. I didn't think Abdul could be pitchforked into funding Chatterton and his project, whatever it turned out to be. Moreover, I knew he was on a Georgetown scholarship with the U.S. government picking up the tab, which did nothing to allocate him among the philanthropic rich. But then it occurred to me that the old man had handed me a wedge. If I played along with him for another five minutes I might learn the significance of Gorelik's assault on the fipple flute, and find some meaning for the assorted disharmonies that rampaged through the house.

"Possibly," I repeated, "but he'd want to know what you'd be using the money for."

"Yes. I suppose he would." He tugged thoughtfully at his pursy lip.

"You'll have to guide me," I purred.

For a while he said nothing. From somewhere in the house came the sharp emphatic resonance of what might have been two steel rods slammed together.

When his reply came it was hardly fathomable. "We live in Hamlet times," he said, "a new ice age of self-doubt and indecision."

The sound of the rods expired; now in its stead came the percussive click of metal on metal, or perhaps a pair of hardwood blocks bouncing off each other.

"The world," Chatterton went on, "has always had its systemic crises—peripheral brawls, bushfire squabbles, wars of every size and shape. Still, there has always been a glimmer of hope in history—the sign of the phoenix—the capacity of the crucified to rise again. The Jews, the Armenians, the Ch'ins who had the lousy luck to live in the swordlands of Genghis Khan, the peoples of the Roman Empire who fell before Attila."

He paused again, warping his mouth as if to dislodge a peanut particle. "Yes," he lamented, "the human race has always lived intimately with pain, but now, since that August day in 1945 when that terrible act of destruction was put to use in Hiroshima, the dread has intensified. And this time," the jeremiad swept on, "this time every tree in the forest will fall, every living thing will die, give or take a few weeds and insects. Certainly the globe's human population will peg out, flash fried on a nuclear griddle. However," he glanced up at the fruitcake ceiling, the color of faded tattoos, "unless you recognize life's dangers, you'll never try to fathom its mysteries. It's fear and peril that make one think. Don't you agree?"

"Totally," I said. "But what shall I tell Abdul?"

"Don't rush me," he answered. "To arrive at that point, we must first plow through a few more unpleasant clichés. Would you please," he added in a voice treacly with sarcasm, "stop toying with your watch?"

"Sorry. I didn't realize…"

"Today, just about every civilized, explosives-loving country on earth has a thermonuclear arsenal. And so the unthinkable is very much on our minds and the minds of our leaders, whose limited vision is set in a vise of prejudices. We are beset on all sides. Presidents and premiers may vary in size, shape, and luminosity of eye twinkle, but they are collectively clueless and arrogant, masters of the big stick, scoundrels flexing their muscles.

"As for the U.S., in just the past century we've picked a fight with Spain and Cuba…"

"That was 1898," I said, to show him I was paying attention.

"We fought two world wars, we've invaded Korea and Vietnam. The Soviet Union was our reliable enemy for seventy years—"

"Seventy-three," I said.

"—and since then we've stormed Iraq twice. Twice," he repeated.

His words were an excitant; the more he expounded, the more indignant he got. The eyes bulged, the lips quivered, a little vein on the side of his forehead throbbed like an inexact metronome. He was a disturbing ambassador for all the eccentric teachers I had ever known.

Now he reset his face into an empty half-smile of superiority. "You do follow me, young man?"

"I do."

"What do you think? Your input is breathlessly awaited."

"I think you should take it easy."

He snorted. My input, rather than mollifying him, had increased his agitation.

"Let me tell you something." He twitched and churned within his bathrobe. "Practically everything of value to the human race that has been said or done since the beginning of time had its genesis in indignation." He settled back in his chair, breathing heavily. "Where were we?"

"You were talking about presidents..."

"As for the ordinary citizen, he is engulfed, reduced to the compliance and corruptibility of a listless victim, as devoid of honor as his gauleiters. He has stumbled and bumbled about the thin crust of our fragile old planet, enduring the wrath and the indignities of fools and megalomaniacs for ten thousand years, but a new scourge has caught up with him. The fools are about to turn his home into a crematorium. They would reduce the world to a pellet of muck where not even a hair will grow, and he is asked to admire the excellence of the plans and policies by which he is deceived."

He stared at me while I tried to maintain the impassivity of a mandarin, which wasn't enough for Chatterton. He wanted a visceral reaction.

"Doesn't it strike you as preposterous that a few men of questionable sanity have the power to destroy what nature has preserved for a hundred million years?"

"I guess so," I said tentatively.

"You guess so," he boomed mockingly. "That's your considered opinion? That's all you can say?" Scornfully he shook his shaggy head. "Well, young snot, we're coming to the crunch. The world is marching off a cliff and," he said, "you 'guess so.'"

"What are you doing about it?"

"Ah-hah!" he said. "Then you do agree that it calls for something other than resignation?"

"Sure. But..."

"Wouldn't you further agree that steps must be taken to unseat the barbarians?"

"How?"

"I'm so glad you asked," he said with glacial indulgence. "We have gathered here, my brave little company and I, to wage war on the warriors—to end war forever." He rose theatrically from the chair and paced up and down. "We, perhaps more than most, are prepared to challenge cant and the cult of conventional values, for we have never in our academic lives been inclined to accept the dictatorship of science. And now we are on the verge of a revolutionary breakthrough." He paused in the middle of the carpet.

"You seem to be going against the vast majority of world opinion."

There was in his lightning-shot eyes the look of a vulture with its remorseless ill will against all creation. "If a hundred million people embrace a stupid concept," he said, "it's still a stupid concept. Look at our American electorate."

"Are you allied with any of the anti-nuke organizations? The grassroots movements?"

He sniffed contentiously. "They're all on the wrong tack. We need stronger initiatives to keep the peace. We need instant alternatives."

He was becoming unbearable again, with his indignant and grandiose generalities, his handful of dottering communards trying to impose a sense of order on a resistant and chaotic world.

"What are they, precisely, these initiatives of yours?"

"Let me remind you that all wars, essentially, are economic. We spout ideology, but we pillage the earth for real estate, for fossil fuels, for markets. We fight for power, I tell you, although we call it principle. We kill to hold on to what we've got, or to gain what we haven't. To the lesser nations we give money to assure their support, but we don't share the technical know-how that would make them self-sufficient. Our benevolence is predatory; to paraphrase the poet what's-his-name—Housman—we give megabucks and rubles, but not our hearts away."

"But what do I tell Abdul?"

"Now, suppose there was a way of dispensing to everybody in the world an equal share of the planet's wealth, and the means of developing it at no cost, absolutely free? To produce all the good things in abundance? Free access to energy for agriculture, transportation, industry, communications, for leisure. An end to starvation, the beginning of physical well-being, mental health, even happiness. Under those circumstances, war would become obsolete—what purpose could it serve?—and wouldn't that be a hell of a thing?"

"Sure it would," I agreed, "but how would you accomplish it?"

His eyes held a dry, soft shine. "I know how," he said. His somber face seemed to glow with evangelical rapture, as if he were the anointed herald of some glorious annunciation.

I know how. What the hell was he? A savior or just another charlatan, panting for immortality? A sage consumed by the splendor of a Cause, or your average neighborhood wacko with a mind full of scrimshaw?

He flapped his flat feet to the far corner of his cave, where the black safe crouched like some sullen, overgrown toad. He twirled the knob clockwise and counter, then back again. He gripped the nickel-plated bar and managed, miraculously, to swing the thick door open. Within its cavernous iron belly there was nothing (I half expected a cache of peanuts) but a few pages of white foolscap. Chatterton gathered them up.

There was something about the way he handled those papers—with grave respect, and a kind of adroit and casual grace—the way a batter knocks dirt from his spikes, a surgeon scrubs up, a priest offers a wafer in the Eucharist. It was solemn and beautiful, the way his fingers slithered down the page.

"Read this," he said, handing them over. "It'll give you some idea..."

Across the top of the first sheet were two urgently admonitory words in ragged block print. TOP SECRET, they enjoined, and beneath them, without further preamble, was an intricate scramble of hieroglyphs, row on crowded row to the last page.

"I can't."

"Thought as much." He snatched the papers from me, returned them to their prison, and locked them in. He fell, silently, into his chair. He had no idea of the effort I expended, just sitting there, waiting for him to get on with it. And he looking around furtively, as if he half expected his office was bugged. He opened his mouth, closed it again, sucking air like a fish in a dirty bowl.

"What," he asked finally, "do you know about the ancient Egyptians?"

"Not much. Only what I've read in Herodotus."

"They were unique," he said unequivocally. "A people of genius, with the longest record of first-rate art in the history of mankind. Four thousand years—an outburst of undiminished productivity—quite a period when you consider that western Europe has been occupied by our ancestors for less than half that time, and it's only been five centuries since Columbus set foot on America. What," he asked, "do you consider their crowning achievement?"

"Well," I said, "they invented oars, I believe, and folding chairs, safety pins and boxing and apple orchards and... I guess it was the pyramids?"

"The pyramids." He nodded weightily. "There are those who wouldn't agree with you—Mister H.G. Wells for instance. 'Vast, graceless bulks,' he called them." Chatterton smiled disarmingly. "But I think you're absolutely right."

I was hardly prepared for the enormity of that accolade. Beware, I told myself, beware...

"The Great Pyramid at Gizeh is the most astounding, the most intense and mind-boggling single achievement by any people in recorded history. It covers thirteen acres, seven hundred fifty feet square at the base, and rises to a height of four hundred eighty-two feet. A solid mass of masonry containing two million, three hundred thousand blocks of limestone, each of which weighs between two and seventy tons, nearly ninety million cubic feet of masonry, enough to build thirty Empire State Buildings. They were hewn to slope with an extraordinary exactitude of angle and surface, and with such subtle craftsmanship—artistry, if you will—that the stones are cut and joined within a thousandth of an inch." He paused and slowly pressed his hair down on his skull. Immediately it rose again, like the thrums of a stiff mop. "Shall we play a little game of contrast and comparison? The Gizeh Pyramid is taller than a forty-eight-story skyscraper. The Houses of Parliament and St. Paul's Cathedral could be lodged within its base. According to the estimates of E. Baldwin Smith, there was room inside the area for St. Peter's, the cathedrals of Florence and Milan, Westminster Abbey, and again St. Paul's tossed in to complete the package. It is longer than the Colosseum. And it is solid, while the Colosseum is no more than a shell built around a hollow enclosure. Question is, how did they build it?"

"Sheer muscle power, I guess. According to Herodotus, it was built by a hundred thousand men. They must have died like flies—Herodotus says the workforce was renewed every three months, over a period of twenty years."

"Doesn't that strike you as odd? That's four hundred thousand workers a year. Eight million in twenty years?"

"Why odd? I don't follow..."

"They were recruited from the Nile Delta, a tiny patch of arable earth, around 2600 BC, when, according to modern demographic experts, the entire population of the world totaled twenty million people, including women and children."

"But it's no illusion—they built them stone on stone."

"But how?"

"The blocks were hewn in quarries beyond the Nile, brought over the river, and dragged across a plain to the site."

"How?" he repeated.

"On wooden rollers, or sledges..."

"Where did the wood come from? There were and are very few trees in the area, and they were date palms needed for food. Moreover, the wood of palm trees is soft and spongy, unable to withstand the weight."

"Perhaps they imported timber."

"They lacked a sizable fleet. And their ships were infinitesimal by modern standards."

"How do you know?"

"From the remnants of an inscription that describes the shipment of two granite monoliths—'trees were gathered in all the land and a very great boat was built to load two obelisks...' Ships, rafts probably, to transport two slim daggers of stone, each a hundred feet long, and it took all the trees in the land. For the pyramid, each of the limestone blocks was about thirty feet long. Mathematicians have determined that if the blocks were subdivided into cubes measuring one foot square, they would span two-thirds of the earth's belly at the equator."

"They could have used horses and carts."

"Horses and carts were not introduced in Egypt until a thousand years later, in the Seventeenth Dynasty."

"They had to use rollers," I repeated.

"What makes you so adamant about rollers?"

"Because Herodotus writes of a great causeway five furlongs in length—five-eighths of a mile—to convey the stones to the site."

"Why five-eighths of a mile, and only on one side of the Nile? If the road had been built to transport limestone, wouldn't it have covered the entire distance between the quarry and the site? A distance of ten miles, according to some authorities, and as much as six hundred, according to others."

"Then what was the road built for?"

"Let's first consider what it was built *of.*"

"According to Herodotus, polished stone, covered with carvings of animals. But what has that to do with...?"

"Does that sound like a roadbed for heavy rolling stock?" Old Mop Head favored me with the smile of a raptor. He said, "Cheops liked to watch the men at work. He came out every day from the summer palace he had built—five-eighths of a mile away." He smiled again, this time impishly. "What Herodotus described, although he didn't realize it, was the royal road, the King's road, and not an expressway for grunt labor. However," he added, "we mustn't be too harsh on Mister Herodotus. He visited Gizeh two thousand years after the pyramid was built, and he believed what his guide told him. Although anybody who accepts the word of an Egyptian dragoman..." He shook his unlikely head in disbelief, adding brightly, "But for the moment, let's accept everything he tells us, and approach the riddle—this superlative release of energy—by another route. Do you think that one block of limestone, weighing somewhere between two and fifty tons, could be quarried, cut, dressed, ferried over water, lugged overland to the site, sloped upward at a fifty-degree angle of ramp—more than half-perpendicular—locked into place to meet perfectly at the apex almost five hundred feet above—do you think the work on one such block could be completed in an hour?"

"It seems unlikely, not to say impossible."

"For the sake of argument, try to accept it, like a good little reader of Herodotus. And to further suspend disbelief, let's say our workforce labored in shifts, twenty-four hours a day including Sundays and holidays. That's a daily assemblage of twenty-four blocks, which in a year would yield...?" He frowned heavily. "I don't seem to have a pencil..."

"Eighty-seven hundred and sixty," I told him.

"Then how long would it take to complete our pyramid of two million, three hundred thousand blocks?"

I winced.

"Well?" he scolded triumphantly. "Cat got your tongue?"

"Two hundred and sixty-four years."

"So there you have it. Unlikely," he mimicked my voice with uncanny fidelity, "not to say impossible."

"But the pyramid was built—it's no illusion. How did they manage...?"

Again he said, "I know how," and the hair on my neck woke up. His voice continued, the intonations of a pedant before a captive seminar. "Egypt in so many ways has provided the furniture of our minds..." Now the voice came as if from deep in a vault, a sepulchre. "But they also knew something we don't know—how to harness the most incredible source of energy the world has ever witnessed. They did it," he said, as I looked at him bleakly, "with sound and music. The sharp, clean notes of a horn, the timpani of a taut goatskin drum, the crash of cymbals, the peal of bells, the rattle of bones, the percussion of copper rods that fanned the air and set off great vibrations—and those blocks of limestone rose from the quarry like birds, like perfect arrows from perfect bows, and sped through the sky and settled, stone on stone, at Gizeh. Can't you just see them?" he asked.

And incongruously I could, the pliant limestone shaking loose the fetters of gravity, rising with the dream-slow grace of a blimp, trotting nonchalantly over the desert, galloping above the papyrus sedge, gathering speed, soaring... I shook my head hard. Reverie crashed.

"...flow of forces through the universe," Chatterton was saying, "sonic energy, pulsations of power, and music the propellant."

"I don't see how," I said.

He flushed. "You are a willful and obstructive boy," he roared. "Your attitude fails to captivate. You're fired!"

"That's okay with me," I told him. "You can talk to Abdul yourself."

"I'll—no." He tugged at his robe. Surprisingly, he added, "I apologize. Let's not be hasty."

I had no intention of being hasty. What I didn't need was to get canned, now that Valerie was back.

"All I meant to suggest," he said soothingly, "was that your criticism lies within a limited concept of logic. Certainly you realize that our orderly universe is disorderly, and riddled with incongruities."

There was more than a pustule of truth in what he said. Even legitimate science has at times become discomfited by the forays of irrationality and made to recant its earlier, inflexible certitude. The theory of relativity by

Einstein (another mop-head) violated all proper laws of logic. Was Chatterton's seemingly absurd premise—that harmonics have a physical effect on a solid body, with no apparent exchange of force or energy between them—any more bizarre than Einstein's?

Yes, it was—the product of crude, thalamic thinking, sloppy, quasi-scientific experiments with gongs, clappers, fipple flutes. Unless...

"How far have you gotten in your research?"

"We're on the verge of victory. The key's in the lock. With a little money from Abdul, we can turn it. The door will swing open, like the gates of heaven, to reveal..."

"Have Gorelik or Grady or any of you succeeded in moving physical objects by the manipulation of sound waves?"

"You first," he said. "What have you come up with?"

I could have told him in one word: nothing. Or I could have recounted that strange isolate, that perceptible stutter-step I thought I saw when my domino moved maybe a wink before the onslaught of my solo. More likely not, so I shook my head and said nothing.

"What would you say, young man," and he eyed me gravely, "if I told you that I have observed a metal jackstone tremble when the air around it was charged with the notes of Gorelik's flute? That I have seen a cube of beech-wood, not large I admit but large enough to swear by, startle like a fawn to the ring of two thin cymbals?"

"But under what conditions? I mean, when the wind blows around here, not only a block of wood but the whole house shakes. I can't see..."

"Then you are the victim of your own selective blindness." He put on the face of one who detects a skunk. "It's as if you wear defective glasses that make all that is relevant invisible. Well," sadly he shook his fungoid head, "I cannot change that. I cannot give you vision, any more than I can give you brains. And I cannot give you a lobotomy."

"Let's just say I lack the faith of St. Paul—I can't believe in the evidence of things not seen. I can't believe in witchcraft, or comic-strip magic."

"The study of any science begins with a comic-strip vision of the universe. I don't suppose you know anything about acoustics?" he said.

"I know that sound, like heat, is a vibrational phenomenon. It can strip the rust off lead pipes."

He nodded. "It can break up the blockage of fatty tissue in arteries."

"The boom of a cannon, bouncing off a mountain, can cause an avalanche."

"A human voice can shatter crystal."

"It's a question of control, I suppose." And even as I said it, up croaked another, inner voice, monitory and more rational, "Don't be a schmuck. Don't get *engrenagé*,"—as the French say, "caught in the gears."

"Precisely," intoned old Mop Head, eyes burning like banked-down coals. "A matter of intensity, frequency, pitch..."

"The size, shape, and composition of the instrument to produce..."

"The required effect. Yes," he said, "yes. What shall it be? Copper rods, silver tuning forks, the golden trill of harmonics?"

"Separately?"

"Or combined? The way Joshua used voices and trumpets to tumble the walls of Jericho?"

"I wouldn't go that far..."

"I tell you, son, he knew something we've forgotten, and we must find it again. God!" he whispered hoarsely. "Just think of it...! It's like the second discovery of fire!" He slumped back in his chair, exhausted by the gymnastics of his mind, waiting for my reply.

"I don't know," I said feebly. "I just wish I knew, you know?"

"That's the chance I'm giving you. Wouldn't you like to be a part of our effort? Incubating a revolution to redesign human society? Save the earth while it's still salvageable?"

"Yes, sure, but..."

"Well then...?"

"Frankly, it seems impossible."

He stared at me. "Young man..." The embers in his eyes took fire, "We're facing a global meltdown. People all over the world despise and envy us—an explosive combination—and we don't seem to be the least bit aware that our arrogance and insensibility toward them might have something to do with it. Right now they're all of 'em in hot pursuit of the bomb, and once they get it, the very chain of life will be..." He didn't complete the thought. It wasn't necessary.

"But it's implausible, the idea of building a pyramid by tooting a flute."

"Implausible, you say? More implausible than what's being done right now? A preemptive strike against Iraq? Carving up space? The space cadets up there dividing the moon with the Russians? And what'll they find?"

"I don't know."

"They'll find a pretext to fight, if only to get the side with the best view. Boy," he said, "I don't claim inerrancy, but something must be done."

Well, it would have to be done without me. It was all too goofy—contributing to the second coming of fire, indeed; reclaiming a lost stitch in the fabric of time, unraveling a riddle unsolved for five thousand years.

And yet... I was tempted. I thought of my father—I was always thinking of my father—he would have jumped at the chance; for him the pursuit of the unattainable, the unresponsiveness to reality, put him in a bracket with Don Quixote. I thought of my mother's prophetic fancy: *I do not think you will die,* she had said, *without making a Real Contribution.* But even she on her most unworldly wavelength would have rejected old Mop Head's sales pitch. Still...

There was Armbruster. "Talent," he said I had, as he probed his ass with his fingers, "and an unlimited potential for... for..." He didn't know what, but it certainly wasn't as a facilitator in Chatterton's cabal.

"You don't trust me," he said flatly. "Not that I give a damn. I don't want your approval, I want Abdul Whatsisname's money."

Another long silence. "I suppose," he went on, "he would want to see what we've accomplished before he puts up a dime. So, tell you what—I'll give you *and* Whatsisname a demonstration as soon as he shows interest in the project." He smiled bountifully. "Isn't that a good idea?"

And only then did it occur to me: What was I so exercised about? I was no more than a courier delivering the pouch to Abdul. Let him get incensed, let him expose the old man as a buffoon, let him get banished from the violet eyes of our darling. But definitely not me.

FIFTEEN
THE INCENDIARY

"No," Abdul said, clipping the syllable rather emphatically. "I don't think so."

"It's difficult to visualize," I told him, "it's like, well, like a butter-fly—you can see the wings but not the engine. Wouldn't you care to see Chatterton's engine?"

"No," he repeated. "First, it could be a trick, an illusion. Second, I don't have the money, so it's all kind of academic. And third," he added forth-rightly, "he's crazy."

"A little eccentric, perhaps, but crazy...?"

"They're all crazy. All you've got to do is look in their eyes and there's nobody home."

"Not all of them. Grady's sane."

"I don't like Grady. He's always sniffing around. He spies on me."

Jesus, here he goes again. Abdul al Sadr, prince of paranoids. "Well..."
Yet I knew what he was trying to say. I had the feeling, when his nose was in his newspaper, that Grady was *listening,* his nobody-home eyes tracking us.

"Why do you think he'd do that?" I asked.

"I don't know why," he said impatiently. "But whenever I'm alone around here, when Val and Derek are off together or something, he pops up out of

105

nowhere. Once he popped up in Washington on Connecticut Avenue—suddenly appeared as if by accident, and asked me to have a drink."

"Did you?"

"No. Not that I'm that much of a Muslim. It's just I don't drink with people I don't like."

"You might have found out what he wanted. If anything."

"I don't want to know what he wanted. I want him to let me the hell alone."

"Maybe he's just friendly. He tried to be friendly with me, when I first got here. I didn't know anyone, and..."

"Maybe he wants something from you."

"What could he want from me? Will you think it over—Chatterton's proposal?"

"What for?" A shadow of annoyance crept across his narrowed eyes.

"There are certain precedents, you know. Joshua at the battle of Jericho—"

"He also made the sun stand still," he said. "If you believe that you'd believe anything."

"But what about... what about...?"

"There are no precedents in defiance of gravity."

"If sufficient thrust were generated..."

"Sure," he mocked, "with a fipple flute."

I decided, for the moment, to press him no further. Why, you might be wondering, did I press him at all? Here's why:

Valerie had returned, to be sure, but for all I saw of her lately she might still have been in Florida. Not precisely true: I glimpsed her once, floating like a wraith down the hall, chewing abstractedly on a pencil. I called to her but my vocal chords fogged up; what emerged was a kind of fluttery bleat. She disappeared inside her room with a great, resounding slam of the door before I caught up with her. It occurred to me that because of my dustup with Derek, perhaps he was determined to keep her away from me. If so, he had gained her total cooperation.

She never appeared for meals in the commons refectory. I didn't know when she ate (or what; roses, perhaps). Presumably she dined with Daddy Mop Head, and I could imagine, if that were the case, the bleak atmosphere they shared. I never saw him either.

Patience, I told myself, have patience. But patience is a lonely virtue; a depressive emptiness consumed me after the sweet fire of seeing her so briefly.

And then the unkind, uncaring, and ceaselessly vigilant stars that wrote my destiny veered off course. Suddenly I looked up, Grady looked up from his newspaper, and there she was. She walked into that room of mismatched furniture and everything went aglow. She clutched a notebook against her breasts; it didn't know how lucky it was. She came right to the point.

"Something's wrong," she said to Grady. Reluctantly, he put down his paper. "I'm writing the story of my life," she went on, "for school. What you call an autobiography." She opened the notebook and frowned at it. "I'm up to 'once I went to camp when I was a little kid' and I dunno, something's wrong."

"Valerie," Grady said, "if I understand the academic process, your teacher meant for you, not me, to figure it out. That," he went on, uncharitably and unmoved, "is the way to learn." And he stuck his nose back into the kettle of print.

She turned abruptly toward the door. "Maybe I can help…?" I heard my voice saying.

She hesitated and, with a lovely, what-have-I-got-to-lose shrug, settled beside me on the floor. I shot a fleeting glance at Grady. Immersed in his paper, he didn't give a damn that our respective philosophies of education were at variance.

Valerie pointed a slim finger to the smudged and questionable page. I leaned toward it, her, my God our shoulders were touching. Still I managed to get my eyes back in focus.

> *That's when I met two new girlfriends* [I read]. *One of them was Cindy. She was weird and Nancy. We climbed a mountain. Some of the girls climbed down. I was one of the some.*

I showed her how to fix it. "Thanks," she said. She pulled up a leg of her jeans and licked an adorable scab on her knee.

"Could I do that for you?"

"What? Usually I'm pretty good with words," she confided. "When I look up a word in the dictionary the same day I never have to look it up again. But," she went on, "I'm not as good as you are." It wasn't a compliment, the way she said it, but a realistic evaluation of the evidence at hand. "What do you want to be when you grow up?"

I let it pass—the intimation that despite my syntactic skills I was still a child. "I don't know," I said airily. "Maybe I'll star in a porno flick. What do you want to be?"

"Me? Nothing."

I furrowed my brow critically. The response was not totally lost on her.

"Hell," she said, "there's a lot of nice people who don't work." Her wayward loyalty to the pariahs of the Hebraic-Protestant ethic was, I thought, admirable. "What I like," she went on, "is to just let things happen. Just let 'em fall into place, you know? Instead of trying to like direct them."

It had been my experience that things, given half a chance, fell chaotically out of place. However, "I agree with you totally," I said. From behind the wall of his paper, Grady tried, unsuccessfully, to suppress something between a snort and a snicker, and sank deeper into his chair.

Valerie stared gravely at the curtain shielding Grady from us a few feet away. Calmly, leisurely, she took from a pocket a book of matches. She stretched full out on the floor, struck the match, touched the flare to the spine of the paper. I watched the cremation in a catatonic frenzy, gawking at the burst of orange flame, at Grady flying upward among the sparks, then stomping the conflagration to embers. The whole room reeked; by the time the dead flakes curled blackly across the floor, he was gasping and she was gone.

Jesus. I spent the rest of the evening, of course, thinking about my little incendiary. About her fractured, inspired syntax. *She was weird and Nancy...* Her slither across the rug to firebomb Grady. I wondered what next, how I'd manage to see her again. And when, the following afternoon, I ventured to the window of my cell—Glory be to God there she was, swinging through the woods with long coltish strides, wrapped in a low-lying mist, wading through blood-red leaves, kicking at pinecones. She picked up a rock and threw it: a flutter, a flash, and a rabbit, swift as a wind-up toy, bolted through the bosk and disappeared like an illusion. With the speed of the rabbit I plunged down the stairs.

"Hello!" I yelled above the wind.

No answer, not from her, but she paused. I sped to her side. We walked in silence, which was trumped by a torrent of sound, a cascade entangling the rude orchestration of winter. The clinging cold wind wailed around us like the disembodied voice from the moors that cried Heathcliff. The disorderly leaves cackled as we plowed through them. Beneath us the earth smelled of sour apples and the antique rot of vegetation, while over us hung a cloud as large as a continent.

The thorn bushes whistled at her and that wind like a wild river pressed her jeans to her thighs. The peppergrass and the gnarled old chestnuts bowed like devoted retainers along her path. I too was enchanted, managing to brush against her as we walked, feigning awkwardness.

And then she said softly, speaking as much to the trees as to me, "I don't like to be laughed at."

"Grady?" I asked. "I think he was laughing at me."

"Then why didn't you do something about it?"

"Because, because, because I, I..." My tongue went bankrupt.

Her lips curled. "Men!" she said scornfully, kicking at a moldering acorn. It shattered explosively. "That fucking Derek," she muttered.

"Derek? You say Derek?"

"He's gone."

"Gone?" It was as though I had been slammed on the back of the head with a mallet. "You don't know where?" I asked hopefully.

"Of course I know where. New," she kicked a rusty can about twenty feet, "York."

"What for?"

"To be a *nactor*. What else do you go to New York for?"

"When's he coming back?"

"Who the hell knows?"

So old Derek had split, to tilt with skyscrapers. Ho ho. Ha ha. I hoped fervently that he'd fall on his histrionic ass, the gaudy fucking vagabond, and be reduced to working in a deli, where he'd cut off his thumb in the pastrami slicer and bleed to death. Even without that vivid eventuality, he was still two hundred miles away; here was my opportunity ho ho (would she ever be more vulnerable?) to make her wish he'd never come back, or not give a diddly damn if ever he did. We'll begin, shall we, with the disarming bond of friendship, the epicene sedative which would give way imperceptibly to stronger medicine, a steamy philter to enflame her with a passion as ardent as mine.

"I appreciate your entrusting me with your confidence..."

"I'm not *entrusting*," she said querulously, "I'm just pissed off."

"What are you doing tonight?"

"How do I know? That's *hours* away."

"Want to go to the Captain's Ball on B Deck?"

She didn't appreciate my drollery. If I could scrape together a load of books from the attic, hitchhike to the Pikesville Sally, and pick up enough tease for a movie... Or hock my tuba, or borrow a few bills from Grady. He'd comply; all I had to do was hint that I'd sic my little flame-thrower on him.

"I'm tired," she said. "Too tired to go anywhere."

"I'm sorry. Maybe some other..."

"What are you sorry about? I *like* being tired. Next to absolute, pure boredom, it's the most satisfying feeling."

"Well, if you mean *satiety*..."

"I meant like exhaustion, what I said. Christ," she added, "this conversation is getting just too damned strenuous. I'm warning you," her eyes narrowed, "this kind of heavy talk is a threat to our relationship."

"What relationship? I wish we had one—just a waif of a relationship for starters."

"Jesus, you talk a lot. You know," she added like a placid sage, "what I think it is, why don't you find somebody to go to bed with?"

What is more maddening than the girl you adore trying to interest you in someone, anyone, else? I wanted to kick her insolent ass, belt her across that scarlet mouth, I wanted to...

I kissed her. She saw it coming and ducked. My lips sought the moving target, flayed air, brushed the cunning lobe of an ear. Bungled though it was, still it made for a certain intimacy.

What to do now? Once at long last having taken the initiative, retreat was unthinkable. I asked myself that desperate question of last resort: What did I have to lose? And the destitute answer was Nothing.

"Confidentially," she was saying in a mild and reasonable voice, "you really are an asshole."

Again I lunged.

"Stop it!" she ordered.

"What's the matter?" I said with an inspired smirk. "You afraid of *not* being bored for a change?"

"Come off it," she said dismissively.

"*You* come off it," I said, sinking to her blather. "You find your school-work about as exciting as stacking pants. You live, the only girl, in a dilapidated monastery where you... nonexist."

"They've got other things to think about. And I have my weekends and tennis and, and…"

"Derek. That benighted son of a bitch"—I was appalled, perversely elated by my own rashness—"he could put an upper to sleep."

"You bore me more than… anyone."

"Isn't boredom what you like?"

"I don't like all this talk. It's dull and tedious and pointless. Like… like…"

"Like what? Life?"

"That's right."

"Only for dopes."

"That's enough!" she snarled. "I'm not a dope, I'm dangerous. I'm ready to pounce. Anyway, fuck you," she said, but her wide, unblinking eyes shone damply, and I felt a scalding shame for the ferocity of my attack. I fumbled toward a pocket to offer my handkerchief, just like in the movies, but I hesitated because it was filthy.

"Don't think I'm crying," she said. "I got these windy tear ducts which when it's leaky…" She was aware of the spoonerism even as it trickled off her tongue. "Jesus," she said despairingly, "I get everything backward."

"That's not true," I said stoutly.

"I get things wrong," she persisted.

"Me too. Maybe we could help each other."

"Nobody ever helps anybody."

"I'd like to try."

"What would you do?"

I hesitated. Moments ago I had botched my first foray into crisis management. I was afraid I'd do it again.

"Well…?" she said impatiently.

"I'd talk to you."

"You mean you'd tell me about Stanislavski," she said, unimpressed, "and palindromes and stuff like that?"

"And I'd listen to you, *feel* you…"

"What?"

"Feel your *presence*," I was so oozing with sincerity I spoke in italics, "always be conscious of it. I'd *touch* you."

"Let's not get carried away."

"What I mean, like scratch your back if you wanted me to—say you got an itch in an unreachable place."

"That sounds like a thrill and a half."

"I want to know you..." I might have added "in the biblical sense," but instead I played my trump card: "I'd help you with your homework."

"Tonight? I got to write a poem..."

"It's a deal."

"...about nature? You can make it rhyme?"

"We'll do a springtime number—lambs gamboling in a vernal grove where the woodbine twineth, a purling brook and tender buds unfurled..."

"You're crazy," she said quite matter-of-factly. "Would you like to kiss me now?"

I nodded dumbly. Unblinking, she waited, as if to prove her immunity to my caresses. And it was more than that: a tacit acceptance of our contract, and with it an insistence on not taking greedily without giving a little something in return.

And so I planted a whisper of a kiss on her sculpture-still mouth and held it there for an eternity. She raised her hands and placed them lightly on my shoulders and my arms encircled her, drew her to me, and Oh Lord God Jesus the sweet excitement of holding her. It flowed from my arms through my body and I was secretly exultant, as if I had found a treasure. In the dark and glacial wood she seemed by some astonishing chemistry to throw off light. Her hair, tumulting in the wind, whipped the corners of my eyes. She smelled like some exotic sundae of peaches, strawberries, cream, and hot chocolate. The point of her tongue slipped into my mouth. Immediately it was gone, and gently she drew away. I stood there, glass-eyed and shaky, breathing like a bellows.

"Now," she said huskily, "just don't get any ideas..."

What could I do to top that? I threw myself backward on the forest floor spread-eagled and spent, staring up blindly at the leafless trees.

"What's the matter?" she asked, only mildly concerned. "You okay?"

"Ecstasy robs me of consciousness."

"You're crazy," she repeated, and dashed off over the frozen field.

I lay there on that soggy turf, slowly regaining my feeble strength, happy at last, full of the ideas she had forbade me from entertaining.

And so, you see, I had the best of incentives to keep Chatterton's shop in business, and the most propelling of reasons to stay on there.

SIXTEEN

HEAVEN

Soft rain, whippoorwills and flowers,
Dreaming kings in lonely bowers,
I've got fever, can't get going.
Sit and watch the sky, enjoying
Fleecy wisps of clouds that sheen,
While far below all gold and green

She looked up. "Jesus," she said, "that's *good*." And, frowning, "You think it's *too* good?"

I didn't know how to make it any worse.

"What does it mean, 'I got fever'?"

"Spring fever."

"Wow," she said. "It's a real pisser, it's really something."

Something? It was the portend of a week that was the best I had ever known. Slowly it began, our heads together, bending over a book, the soft fire of her breath on my cheek, the days unfurling like a banner and soaring beyond expectancy. I was wired to the wonder of the world, a garden of delight, and cut off, at long last, from all the lost, snakebite days, the sleepless, storm-tossed nights of what seemed to be an earlier incarnation.

Monday night was the night of the poem.

Tuesday: $m \sin (A + B) = m \sin A \cos B + m \sin B \cos A$. "Jesus," she said in a whisper of disbelief as we tiptoed through the prickly thickets of trigonometry, "I think I got it."

Wednesday we walked in the woods. It was a mild and delicate evening. An oriole sang, unconcerned that he had missed the last thermal to Dixie. We held hands. I told her about my father.

Thursday night was Latin. *Amo amas amat. Venite adoramus* and all that.

Friday, "I want to show you something," she said, leading me through the dark house, up the stairs to the workshop. Stealthily we raised the ladder and climbed through the trap. Moonlight silvered the attic, dusting the accumulated junk with a luminous wand. I stumbled over a mattress on the floorboards as she steered me to the bull's-eye and, as if from a height far greater than an eagle's nest, we looked out over the shrouded countryside. A solitary star poked a little white hole in the sky, then another. They doubled, trebled, multiplied mysteriously—a tumult of stars—until the night was no more than a frame for their cold fire, and the moon a pale medallion. Beneath them stretched a flat and tarry canvas without dimension, but even as we watched it took shape, its stencils sharpened, until a perfect toy landscape emerged, as still and immaculate as a village under a Christmas tree—gently sloping meadows and rock-ribbed hills, forests and farmhouses with one light quietly burning, gray smoke flecked with the spindrift of orange embers flaring from the chimney tops. The headlights of a car sliced through the trees and from far away a train whistled a wild, lost chord, ghostly, timeless, unbearably sad.

"Isn't it great?" she whispered. "I come here all the time."

"What's that over there? The lights?"

"Pikesville—where I go to school."

She was so achingly beautiful, standing there in the darkness, her lips full and rounded in a half-smile. At the sewing machine table she took a matchbox from a drawer and lit the candle stubs. They flared up and her trembling shadow fused sinuously with mine on the wall of books. She turned to me, direct and grave, while in the portrait on the table her mother's eyes in the long-dead face stalked me in the candlelight. Far from dead she was, terribly alive in that attic with that still, enshrined Madonna look of hers, watching over her child.

I was stunned by that ghost on the table, and all the while Val waited, expecting something more from me than paralysis. But how is it possible to ravish a daughter before her mother's eyes? Where was the electric spark to ignite my engine? Was Val already aware of my panic? Had she anticipated it? Was that the meaning of her knowing half-smile?

"What's funny?" I asked.

"Once—did I tell you?—I went to Sam's Peerless Fresh Fish in Pikesville and bought a live lobster and took it to school on a leash."

I faked an appreciative cackle. All this chatter, amusing as it might be, was preliminary, a prelude to the big embrace. After all my plotting and scheming and imaginary forays into lust, I had no conscious intention of aborting the mission now. Yet my apprehensiveness increased. All the signs of disaster were chaotically evident—the cold sweat, the dry throat, hyperventilation, the diastolic hammer in my chest, the dead soldier in my pants.

She rambled on, rooting among her memorabilia. How she sniffed glue when she was a little kid, but now her candy of choice, when she could get it, was grass. How she loved to drive Abby's car backward. That she was allergic to underwear. And all the while her mother watched and heard everything and waited with me in the flickering light of the candles for the next revelation. But there was silence. The moment of truth had arrived, a cosmic event, and I greeted it without zeal or spontaneity. I kissed her, yes, but kind of woodenly, a mannequin's kiss, praying for rejection, for reprieve, I don't know what's the matter with me, something I ate at your father's repellent table, how about a rain check?

She walked away. "What's the matter?" I asked hopefully. "You're not feeling well?"

"Of course not." She smiled. "It's just—this is not a good time…"

"Yeah," I said, grateful for deliverance.

"…to be standing up." She reached back, recaptured my sweaty hand, and led me like some docile zombie to that lump of a mattress. Oh God! went the weird machinery of my mind, Let me function like a proper man, don't let her know that I'm dead in the water, that the root of my manhood has shriveled to a worm. And all the while Valerie lay there like a calm sea awaiting my assault.

I kissed her again, gropingly. We sprawled into each other but my body was like an alien interfering presence in a plaster cast—grotesque, unmanageable, an object of hate and outrage, shame, humiliation. I began to bang my head against the floorboards.

Valerie put a cool hand on my shoulder. "It's all right," she said, eyes glassy.

"That's good news."

"It's easy," she said soothingly, "easier than trigonometry. So take it easy." Her words, her trembling voice, then her hand on my limp sprout of spaghetti—that did it. Miraculously the cast flew off and my whole body became one blazing tumescent cock. With a deep anguished breath, I tumbled on her again and this time, bumblingly and with her help, I succeeded.

We lay there cozily. She smiled. I kissed her once more, inwardly exultant, like a young general who has brilliantly concluded a world-shaking campaign. We gazed at each other. On a sudden impulse I bent over and licked her nose.

"I'd better be getting to bed," she said reluctantly.

"I'll walk you to your room. Can I walk you to the school bus tomorrow?"

"Tomorrow's Saturday," she said, "we've got all day."

Lord, I thought, as the predictive delights of the weekend impacted on me, my cup runneth over. I went to bed aglow with lost innocence, having gained heaven by abandoning virtue.

How, I wondered, had evil endured in the world, persisted, once copulation was discovered?

SEVENTEEN

KNOCKOUT

I awoke to a pounding on the door, disoriented, vaguely aware that I had been interrupted in some irretrievable dream of deep, surreal merriment.

"Yeah?" My voice was a knot of frogs. The door opened and Abdul stood in the threshold.

"Sorry," he said solemnly, "but I wanted to say good-bye."

I pulled on a pair of shorts, pants—where the hell had I dropped last night's shirt? My watch said 11:40. "Where're you going?" I asked.

"We're going to New York, with Derek."

"Well," I held out my hand. And then the pronoun struck me. "You say 'we'?"

"Valerie and I."

"She can't go," I said unequivocally. "She's got to finish school."

He looked at me as if I were talking nonsense, which I was. I threw on a sweater and he followed me out the door.

They were in that squalid garden behind the house, Derek leaning slackly against the abandoned refrigerator, she seated stiffly on the bench beside the rickety table.

"What's going on?" I asked coldly.

She pulled her terry-cloth robe tight around her and looked away. At least she had the goodness to not meet my gaze, and the dignity not to say a mumbled word.

Derek tilted his ten-gallon hat far back on his head, revealing a face that was all smirk. "What's going on," he said, "is none of your beeswax."

Beeswax. His was the loose vocabulary of a child; like a child he was to be ignored in the serious business at hand. I took a step toward Valerie. He lurched between us with the rolling gait of a bronc-buster and stood taut.

"I'm gonna crawl yore frame," he said, which was positively logorrheic for Derek the Silent, and with a Montana twang yet. We stood there, glowering at each other. "Messin' with me," he added, "is like tryna jerk off a wildcat." He curled his hands into fists.

She said, "Derek. Don't."

"Don't, my butt," he drawled.

Pause for thought. I realize now, putting pen to paper about what happened not too long ago, that I'm trying to reconstruct the episode with a wry sense of Galgenhumor—a denial of fear in the sickening face of violence—but truth impels me to report that I was scared shitless. He was as large as I, and six years older. In only one respect was he more mature, and that was physically, but unhappily in this confrontation nothing else counted. I tried to bolster my waning courage (or banish my cowardice) by dwelling on the prize at stake. I had to be heroic in her eyes or suffer everlasting pain, eternal damnation by caving in before this ersatz actor, this cowboy manqué, this scuzzbucket weaving his fists before me, leaking brio from every pore.

He had a hard grin on his face, the Plexiglas fixity of a TV hero about to kick calamitous ass. He shriveled me; yet I had mangled that blustering son of a bitch so brutally, so meticulously, so often in the bloody butcher shop of my dreams that I was for a crippled instant exhilarated by the event—at last it had arrived.

But only for an instant. He rocks, feints, and deals. I move backward and to one side, slipping his awkward lunge. He stalks me, coming on with all the tortured grace of a one-hinged gate. Derek is not a bruiser, but then again neither am I; you couldn't get me in a ring with thirty-two-ounce gloves and football pads. Two things I know: I can't elude him forever, and the tumult can only end disastrously if I remain the passive target of his punches. Then I remember that a really good shot to the liver (or was it the kidneys?) can maim a man for life. But then I figure, no, if I've got to fight, at least I'll try to bust this bastard's beautiful nose, whack out a few of his perfect teeth.

As fights go, it was not a cowtown brawl on TV; it was, by comparison, deplorably tame and gracelessly choreographed. Nevertheless, having no choice, I went after him like a dog for a bone. He popped me a few times, insignificantly, and I looped a right that bungled past his ear, following it with a left that missed again. Oh shit, I thought, if my fists refuse to cooperate with my intentions, he'll kill me. But with an intensity of purpose that merited a more uplifting cause, I continued to target his impeccable nose. My third shot glanced off his chin, my knuckles barely grazing it. Closer; I was getting the range, the hang of it, but no cigar. Try again.

But before I could, a strange thing happened: Derek pulled up short. The muscles along his handsome face were twitching. "No hitting in the face," he said, with an uncertain voice. It was a rule peculiarly his own, as if our klutzy ballet were a knightly joust and there were niceties of violence to be observed. But this was warfare to the death and I had him, I knew I had him. My next offering, a roundhouse right, caught him solidly, sickeningly, on an astonished eye, and suddenly everything became tension-clear. For me, at least; for poor old self-infatuated Derek, all became confusion. I hit him again. I think I even connected with his goddamned liver. He clawed at me, all talons, as he fell backward on legs which had suddenly sprung a leak. He slammed into the table and went down with it, flapping his arms like the useless wings of a prehistoric bird. He came up—his rage had overcome his narcissism—swinging the hibachi's poker. I snared a redwood board from the wreckage. He swung at my head. I parried the blow with the two-by-six as if it were Excalibur. The old wood splintered with a sound of an ape biting into a bamboo stalk. It broke jaggedly in half, but the concussion knocked the poker from his hand. He backpedaled, his jaw hanging slack. A glaze coated his eyes, and then that idiot clown-smile took over again. I was all over him like a second shirt, a swarmer glowing with that rarest of possibilities: a victory for the oppressed. I battered him, grunting as each punch landed, while he in duet uttered a strange strangulated rasp, the song of pain. Still my fists continued to pump. I was elated; never had scholarship afforded such rapture. I couldn't have stopped hitting him had I wanted to; wiping that awful smile from his bloody face had become an obsession.

He bounced off the fridge and into me. I pushed him away, calibrating the shortest distance to his nose. But before I could unload the cannon I became aware of Valerie's screaming among the trees. I froze, his legs collapsed, and slowly, still smiling, the boy fell dead.

Not quite. She knelt beside him, her hands fussing. A suddenly activated Abdul helped him to his feet. He wobbled there, heavy-footed, a dreamy kindle in his eyes, as if what he managed to see with his backward stare was no more than a freakish illusion, not to be believed and hardly worth his interest.

She crooned to him softly, unintelligibly, but the meaning was clear enough. He leaned on her, ever so still, his arms like waterlogged sponges hanging over her shoulders, and she clung to him.

Is it possible to feel ecstasy and agony, triumph and defeat at the same time? I stared at them, trying to be objective, she in her anguish, he with a fat lip and festooned in gore. Still, I had to admit, they made a plummy couple. Was it possible that they fueled each other, that he was indeed more to her than a sport-fucking hobby? Or was it that this simpleton, this petty, posturing, mirror-loving blowout patch had the skill to abandon her at precisely the right moment and because of it was once again her desire? Had his suspension of caresses revitalized her love?

So I stood there, sapped of strength, watching their ardor unfold. Abdul had disappeared; some innate good sense had told him they should be left alone. And I too realized that anything I might do or say was best stifled. I hated the idea of her casting me out of her life like yesterday's tabloid, forsaking me thoroughly, but my love for her wasn't going anywhere and it never would. If I had the nine lives of an alley cat I might have considered devoting two or three of them to Valerie, but no, not this way, not even when her shadow arched over the one life I had. I had to get away from her, from Chatterton, from the blight of that wretched house. Maybe time, that sweet restorative, might induce forgetfulness. Maybe I'd leave a note to be forwarded to her after I left.

> *Dear Val,*
> *Yours to command, perhaps*
> *someday.*
> *Your worshipful*
> *Judd*

I tore it up in my head, then and there.

EIGHTEEN

KEEPER OF THE FLAME

"It's an outrage," Phillips Chatterton proclaims, shuffling into my cell.

As if I didn't know.

Chatterton is followed by his adjutant Gorelik, who hands me a carton of Sherman's cigarettes. He knows I don't smoke, but he also knows that people of the most uncompromising disciplines are apt to disregard them under stress. Perhaps, his reason dictates, I might find solace in the weed.

As if to win me to its magic, he tears open the carton, lifts out a pack, breaks the seal, and sticks a butt in his mouth, lights up and inhales with deep pleasure.

"Terrible!" Chatterton rages.

"This place," Gorelik observes "iss enough to puke a pig."

Chatterton shakes his shaggy mane. "Who would have thought...?" He makes a few damnatory noises. "Why I don't understand—why did you do it?"

"Do what?"

"Behave so abominably."

Slowly perception dawns: the outrage he refers to is not my confinement but some heinous crime of my own making.

"What did I do? I'd like to know."

"Espionage," he says. "I have it on good authority."

"Abdul? Abdul's a fucking liar. Why don't you ask your daughter?"

"I have. She of course denies it. But I'm trying to maintain a certain objectivity."

"How could I be a spy?"

"It's always the one you least suspect," he says sagely.

I glance at Gorelik, the hunchback. He is totally absorbed in forging a faultless smoke ring. If he doesn't agree with Chatterton, he disagrees as silently as possible.

"If you're not guilty," Chatterton says, "what are you doing here?"

"I was kangaroo'd by a court with Abdul as judge and jury. Because he wants your daughter."

"Valerie?" He asks as if he has a dozen daughters, and she was the double-ugliest of them all. "Why Valerie? He could have any woman he wants."

"Because she's beautiful and desirable and..."

"Funny. I never saw her that way."

It was hardly the time to educate him about his own issue when another, far graver issue required his immediate attention.

"Why don't you take your objectivity and give it a real workout?"

"What do you have in mind?" he asks warily.

"Send a wire—just state the facts—to the President, to the State Department, to Amnesty International in London—it's got to be fast. Tell them that an American citizen is about to be executed on the dubious findings of a Coproliabad court. Hell, I'll write the message, all you'll have to do is hand it to one of Grady's pilots on the next flight stateside."

Chatterton hesitates. I put a steadying hand on his shoulder to pluck up his courage, to support him in his moment of decision. He slides from my grasp and studies the wall as if he might take instruction from it. His survey completed, he looks down again at his feet.

"Well?"

His eyes mirror his ambivalence.

"Can't Valerie do it?" he asks.

I still haven't heard from Val. But it's not the time to share my benightedness with her father.

"Valerie is being watched," I tell him. "They won't even let her come visit me."

"I don't want to jeopardize my program. We're on the cusp of something big. Gorelik's been producing undulations you wouldn't believe."

"A life is at stake."

He squirms, his face drained white with indecision. Again he examines the lava-like floor, looking for a patch of sand to bury his head in. For all his drive to incubate a revolution, to elevate the wretched of the earth with his fifes and drums and cymbals, here he is, shunning the chance to relieve the wretchedness of one incarcerated solitary. Perhaps he thinks that anybody comprising less than a plurality isn't worth saving.

"I'm sorry," I say, "if I've made you uncomfortable. And I hate being irksome. But I need help."

"I'm thinking about it. Just don't hammer me."

"If you don't act now, you'll be thinking about it the rest of your life. You've got to help, if you ever want another good night's sleep. Suppose a year from now, five years, you realize you should have helped and you didn't—wouldn't that be unbearable?"

"God," he says, "you're pushy. You're holding a gun to my head."

Precisely what I intended—either that or slipping off the bottom of the page. Honor, dignity, pride, and all the other trappings of grace and heroism were no longer luxuries I could afford. I'd have to live with ignobility, at least for the moment, if I were to live at all.

"It's a matter of preservation," I plunge on, citing, as most men do, both truth and falsehood. "Yours as well as mine. If you don't send those wires…"

"I told you I'll think about it," he mumbles. His chin hangs. His eyes droop. He has dried up. So far as I can see, the subject is dead.

Gorelik carefully grinds out his cigarette under a heel and says, "Excuse him. But there is nothing to be done."

NINETEEN
A DAUGHTER OF THE WILLIWAW

Chatterton wanted to see me before I left the jute mill forever. I knocked on his door; he ushered me in for our last (and first and only) supper together. On his desk were two stoups of Campbell's borscht, half a loaf of sliced white bread, and, befitting the festive occasion, a fresh tin of peanuts.

"You've been like a son to me," he said, unclearly, because his mouth was clogged with goobers, "so what I'm going to tell you will, I hope, be interpreted as it is intended—for your own good."

"Of course."

"Of course. You know by now how reluctant I am to dispraise anyone, but I must try to be helpful."

"Please tell me." And get it over with, I was tempted to add, there being no convenient escape hatch available.

Popping peanuts, he settled back in his chair, like some great old dugong munching on lily pods. "The best advice is always the least heeded," he reflected, "especially by the young."

I said nothing.

"You're just a chicken..." he plowed on.

"I'm not all that young."

"...with its head cut off. Clucking aimlessly from one barnyard to another. You must find your métier and stick to it like grim death."

Good point.

"If you were to return to university, you'd never be more than a... a limp-wristed scholiast."

"I have no intention of returning." Damned if I'd become an academic tramp like my father.

"What then?"

What then, indeed? "What are *you* going to do?" I said, switching the spotlight. "How long can your project last without funds?"

He shrugged. "I'll go on trying to keep the old wreck afloat." So he was still hell-bent on hatching his hippogriff. "The subject, however, is you," he said. "Your plans."

"I don't have any. At this point, I don't really expect things to go well for me."

"You're behaving badly." He snorted. "Pull up your socks and get on with it. You're a secondary talent of a fairly high order. You should be able to mesh tractably with *something*."

Just what I needed. Positive reinforcement from the dugong. I winced perceptibly.

"It hurts?" he asked with more feeling than I thought him capable of.

"I don't seem to mesh with anything. Or anybody."

"You could," he said, "but your carnality seems to have blocked your intelligence. I refer," he added soberly, "to Valerie."

"Valerie?" I blinked at him with wronged innocence.

"Your *adorata*," he nodded. "Certainly you remember?"

Another impeachment I should have been quick to deny. Instead I heard myself say, "I didn't think you'd noticed."

"Everybody noticed. You were absolutely sock-eyed about her." He thought for a moment. "Her problem," he went on, "she's *too* tractable. Her brain power—it's difficult for a father to admit—can be mercifully described as inadequate."

"That's not true," I said staunchly. "It's just she has an uncluttered mind."

"There's nothing in it. But there will be someday, I think. She has the earmarks of a late bloomer. Perhaps the same might be said of you. Tell me," he said, retrogressing to the old nastiness, "has she enriched your life, the little backbreaker? Your six months with her weren't exactly a priceless memory? And what about your six months on the tuba? Did you even once manage to get a wiggle out of your block? Whatever skills you possess, you flunked harmonics cold."

"I gave it my best."

"Not good enough."

"You're being unkind."

"Never to you. I took you in, gave you food and shelter, listened to your inflexibly jejune absurdities, opened your window of opportunity, and you slammed it shut on my fingers. Nonetheless," he glowered at me, "Grady, for whatever reason, has taken a liking to you. He has asked my permission to allow him to buy you a plane ticket, one way to wherever. And I have granted it."

"That's very kind of him," I said, and quickly added, "and of you."

"Yes," he agreed. "I have a nature soft and warm as swansdown, if one cares to dig for it. And you never can tell, I might call on you for repayment, with interest, when like Antaeus you rise from the earth, renewed after your fall."

Now I was falling, the sky was falling, as the plane plunged earthward. Would I be renewed like Antaeus at the bosom of his mom, or was I in for another premature midlife crisis?

No time now to dwell on my croppered career. I squared my shoulders, looking around the Denver airport: Judd, Crown Prince of Failure, reporting to the Queen Mother. For a long while I peered at a large, inelegantly formed old lady in a sort of monastic cloak, but no, it was not she.

A man approached me with a wide smile, baring a set of heroic teeth, not one of them homegrown. "Judd?" he asked, with tentative familiarity.

I nodded. Despite the teeth, he was not robust; rather he wore robustness the way he wore his clothes. The Pendleton jacket was a multicolored plaid dominated by magentas and greens; his red hunting cap was a polyester approximating rat fur.

"I'm Dil Quillet," he said, extending a hand. An impressive knife hung in a leather sheath at his belt, the holding strap unfastened, as if at any moment he expected a marauding band of Sioux to storm over the hill and infiltrate the terminal.

"Where's Mother?" I asked. "She said she'd meet me."

"Working."

"On a poem?"

"Mucking out the horse stalls. She loves it."

"She's okay?"

"Fine. But you know—once in a while, when she gets into the cooking sherry…"

I didn't know. We walked down a bleak corridor and out into an ice age, the snow piled high on the side of the tarmac.

Quillet opened the door of a Dodge pickup. Immediately the clean mountain air was poisoned by a stench that combined ammonia concentrate and overripe shrimp. It emanated from a large, villainous dog seated behind the wheel. He bared his long yellow teeth at me, then found the spoor of his master. His tail beat against the upholstery, his mustard-colored body writhed with pleasure.

"Lee Roy!" Quillet barked. "Get in the back!" Lee Roy squirmed, twisted, and obediently vaulted the seat.

For a while the three of us drove in silence, Quillet concentrating on the road, pointing the rig in the direction that the sun, a raw red blister, was taking across the sky. Old Lee Roy's cumbersome head hung between us, his slobbering muzzle close to my ear, his fetid breath on my nostrils.

We rumbled over the tracks of a railroad yard where a dirty sign, with the compelling ineloquence of a piney-woods preacher, emblazoned the Mosaic imperative: DO NOT HUMP.

We climbed on a wide turnpike—five lanes—and barreled down a steep declivity.

On each side of the highway was open country, vast under the gun-metal sky and blanketed with snow. A skulk of fox padded daintily over a stream-slashed meadow, and a herd of deer like iron ornaments stood stock still in their winter pelage. Suddenly they bolted like a burst of explosives and were gone among the pines.

I drowsed, fanned by the warmth of the heater humming beneath the dash; more likely I was etherized by the stench of that vile dog. His breath was of the stuff that withered crops.

And then, abrupt and unmistakable, a flurry of shots rang out, a flat, ominous staccato that penetrated the closed window. Lee Roy, sharing my apprehension, started to whimper.

"What's that?" I asked.

"Nothing," Quillet said with a superior smile.

"It sounded like rifle fire."

"Deer season," he explained. "They're hunters, not assassins. They shoot for the pot."

Another volley rang out, uncomfortably closer this time. Now that malodorous, flop-eared dog was wailing like a wolf. Using my shoulder as a springboard, he hurled himself into Quillet's lap. The Dodge swerved, weaving from lane to lane, dancing madly to the tortured orchestration of tires, torque, and the trumpeting Klaxons of the jehus around us who apparently were under the impression that their impulsive blasts might soothe our pickup's frenzy. For a terrible moment I was sure Jesus had tapped the three of us for sunbeams. I managed to grab Lee Roy and toss him like a sack of shaggy cement over my shoulder while Quillet skillfully brought the rig under control on the runaway vehicle ramp. "Fucking dog," Quillet said, and the fucking dog belched again and again until Quillet had to turn on the wipers to clear the windshield.

"You made Lee Roy nervous," Quillet told me. "He's got a nervous stomach."

"So have I."

"I told you—there's nothing to worry about."

Easy for him to talk, dressed as he was to make sure deer hunters saw him, but I thought it would be prudent not to remark on it.

"You've got to realize," he said, "that out here hunting is a way of life. Out here we go back to basics. Where you come from," he added accusingly, "the cities crumble, standards deteriorate, morality declines. But here," he glanced out the window across a field where a dead cow oozed stiffly into a snowy quagmire, "out here there are constant and salutary reminders that we are of the earth—a legitimate concern not only of ecology but of our very ethical fiber as a people."

"Do you hunt?"

"Wish I had the time." He smiled wistfully. "But I'm too busy with the Morgans."

"Who are the Morgans?"

"Morgan horses. You'll love them."

"I will?"

"Your mother does. They're the first American breed of horse, developed by Justin Morgan, a Vermont music teacher, at the beginning of the nineteenth century. They're proud and swift, although," he added reflectively, "our Morgans seem to run without vanity or ambition. Actually," he went on, "they're not as smart as old Lee Roy here."

God forbid. Lee Roy, that pus-hound, barked a couple of times, as if to asseverate the master.

The house sat on the crown of a snowy hill, gleaming in the twilight. A big-shouldered stone fireplace dominated the living room, and next to it stood my mother. She wore the white robes of a vestal, cinctured with the silver and turquoise of the Navajo. From her neck depended a silver chain, and her earrings were like quoits. I had never seen her so gussied up, but the style was matchlessly Mother's.

She acknowledged my presence, but not directly. "Look at the size of him," she told Quillet. Raising her kohled eyes heavenward, "Where's the little boy," she asked, "who used to melt in my arms?" Finally she focused on me, floating in my direction like one of M. Montgolfier's gassy balloons. "I feel almost sentimental," she admitted.

Working on a ranch is like sailing a windjammer around Cape Horn; there's always something to be done and you're always uncomfortable doing it.

Stables had to be swamped, the tack room tidied, gear repaired, firewood cut in the forest—a dangerous exercise, for an ax or a chainsaw can bounce off a frozen branch and bite a chunk out of a leg. Lugging the harvest a half mile home through ass-high snow was like wading through a wind tunnel. I fed tons of evil-smelling stew to Lee Roy, who inhaled it faster than I could prepare it. He was big enough to eat hay, the only provender he didn't relish. His thick tongue polished the bottom of the bucket and like a hockey stick whanged it across the kitchen floor until the last granule was gone. I learned to drive the pickup, tooling over the rutted roads, in and out of ditches, ignoring the piteous whines of protest whenever I shifted gears. I foddered the Morgans and led them to a high meadow potholed under the endless snow. Wherever I went, Lee Roy trailed after me. He seemed delighted with my company, particularly when a pothole got me. I'd go down and he'd pounce, joyously, kicking up a blizzard, blindsiding me, sniffing and slobbering in a cloud of frosty air. I knew that his was a cupboard love, but I yearned for companionship. Once he licked my hand and I was moved by the endearment until I realized it had nothing to do with affection; he was trying to eat the bandage that covered a nasty cut I had picked up rebuilding a lodgepole fence.

I was always numb with the cold and the wet, but there were days of compensation. When the huddle of horses pawed at the earth and shook their splendid manes and the dog raced in wild circles and the sun was a white shadow of itself— then I would feel the wonder of nature's own cathedral, Quillet's phrase, and without succumbing to Quillet's convulsions of piety, yield nonetheless to the beauty of field and forest, mountain and sky.

The long periods of work were relieved by brief flurries of idleness which were worse than the labor. They gave me time to think, and remembrance brought with it an aching loneliness. Then Valerie would dance uninvited but provocative across the mirror of my mind, and I'd try anything to shatter the image.

Even Quillet's company was preferable. "I've got to go to Paxton's," he'd say. "Care to come along?"

We'd park beside the lumber-loading platform under a sign that proclaimed Paxton's slightly veiled contempt for the summer people:

SHOES

NO SHIRTS

SERVICE

as if anyone in his right mind would venture into the redundant cold without armors of insulation. I'd heft the plywood or the siding or whatever onto the truck bed, adding to my already substantial collection of splinters, scars, and calluses, while Quillet stood well to the side, observing, supervising, knocking the dottle from his pipe. "Interesting place," he would say as I busted a nut struggling with a four-by-twelve. Interesting place indeed, but only if you happened to be a woodpecker.

In the evening I'd sit perishingly close to the fireplace, staring at the red embers in a rapture of exhaustion. The varnished room was full of reflections from the flames that threw a soft luminosity on the books on the shelves, books I was too tranced out to read. Mother sat embracing a legal pad, cultivating not her poesies but a long list of horse and hound groceries that I was to fetch in the morning. Quillet in a thronelike chair exercised his sovereignty, editing copy for his magazine, pausing now and again to discourse learnedly on our ecosystem with a tutorial, ironed-out smile on his face. Lee Roy lay at his feet, snuffling and farting in an excess of contentment, competing with the gale that roared down the high valley.

It was Quillet's passion to embrace all the diverse manifestations of nature that characterized his realm. He knew the names of all the local animals, vegetables, and minerals in three languages—English, Latin, and Arapaho—and he shared his knowledge with us. It didn't take much to get him going.

Inspired by the blasts that rattled the house (or perhaps it was the borborygmus that rattled Lee Roy), Quillet treated us to a sermon on the williwaw, the sudden, violent wind that roared down from Alaska. As it cracked branches and toppled trees he lectured us on the ponderosas, growing on the sunny slopes, and the blue spruce, which flourished only in the bottoms where water collected, and the hardy juniper, which grew everywhere. He preached while it wailed across the meadow like a scourge, like God's own bulldozer, peeling the blanket of snow from the bed of the earth, scraping it clean, exposing troves of what the Arapaho called *knic-knic,* delicate pale green tendrils with pale pink blossoms. Then the pronghorns would gather, loping over snow fences eight feet high. They seemed to be forever in flight, even when standing still, feasting among the *knic-knic.* And the coyotes would join the party, prancing high in the arctic air to land stiff-legged on the scurrying mice and gophers that their intimidating diet comprised. And finally the crows and the magpies would sweep down like chars to nice up the earth, pecking away at dead animals disinterred by the wind until nothing was left but bone.

So Quillet would favor us with the lore of his wilderness years, listening to himself with the keenest enjoyment while my mother, his partner in pleasure, would gaze on him fondly. "He knows so much," she would say in an awed whisper, as if he were asleep, "and he never forgets anything." She heaved a heavy-breasted sigh. "There's so much I wish I could remember, but my mind abdicates."

Every couple of weeks Quillet shared his erudition with Harry Swift, his lawyer and the only guest I ever saw in that house. Harry tried now and then to squeeze in a word or two—he knew something about *knic-knic* and the

Arapahos and such, possibly more than Dil, for he was a past president of the Colorado Conservation and Historical Society, but he never had a chance. Quillet wouldn't have shared his podium with John Muir.

Dil's monologues seemed to take a lot of out of Harry; still, he kept coming back to listen politely and fidget incessantly. He must have been lonely, a short-assed, thick-bellied, solitary man on a mile-high, big-shouldered mountain.

Now our host was crowing about his Morgans, how strong they were, how docile, the lovely arch of their necks "so unlike the giraffe neck of the Arabian." He stressed the need for breaking them gently, his preference for snaffles to the brutality of bar bits or rowels. Some ranchers, he hinted darkly, twisted, even bit the ear of an animal to instill obedience, but once you bite or twist, a horse becomes head-shy.

"Not Dawnette," said Mother with a delicate shudder. "Dawnette would never…"

"Certainly not Dawnette," Quillet concurred.

"Which one's Dawnette?" I asked. All the Morgans looked alike to me.

"Dawnette? Dawnette's the trainer," Mother explained.

"Dawnette," Quillet said, "understands that horse-breaking is an art."

Mother allowed her gaze to rest on him for another long, rewarding moment. "Dil's life," she told Harry Swift and me, "is a work of art. He resonates to the pull of the earth. He has a higher focus."

Jesus, it was unsettling. Harry Swift burrowed deeper into his armchair, somewhat removed from the rest of us, avoiding Dil's eyes, pressing over and over again the button on the bezel of his massive wristwatch and staring at the digital readout which recorded the time in twelve of the world's major cities. He never smiled—a lawyer's prerogative. Sheer willpower dictated his unforensic silence.

I too felt embarrassed for Quillet, but strangely he seemed prepared to be admired, to enjoy the eulogy. Still she raved on, to the metronomic accompaniment of Lee Roy's farts. "He seeks perfection, that is his Grail."

"One seeks," Quillet bowed his head with becoming modesty, "but one does not find."

"Of course you do!" she cried.

"Not always." He pointed out that all was not perfect in his little corner of Arcadia. The Morgans, despite all his efforts, got the botfly warbles; his war against the toxic locoweed was unending; pine bark beetle and spruce budworm laid waste his woodland.

"He works so hard!" she said.

This was confusing; I had never seen him lift more than a cup of coffee since I arrived. He was our strategist who read a little copy and assigned the calluses to Mother and me.

"You should learn to ride," he said. I knew what was coming.

"Do I have to?"

"Then you might ride out and take over the locoweed war. Your mother will show you how to do it."

"It's very simple," she said. "All you do is cut the roots about two inches below the ground and spray them with Dr. Dummit's Deadshot Insecticide Number Four."

"Have you ever tried Killoco?" Harry asked. "It's..."

Dil ignored the suggestion. "Dawnette will teach you to ride," he told me.

"You'll like Dawnette," Mother said. "She's a remarkable young woman."

"How so?"

"Shy and woodsy. Almost elfin, with a rare blend of sweetness and courage. And for one so young..."

"How old is she?"

"...she's had more than her share of tragedy. Seventeen."

"What happened to her?"

"It's her grandmother. But Dawnette copes, never complaining, doing the work of a dozen men, running the old lady's ranch."

"What's the matter with her? The old lady?"

"Booze." Her kohled eyes made fleeting contact with the lawyer's, enough encouragement for him to speak up again.

"And litigation," he said. "Dell White spends most of her time suing people."

"It's a source of grief for the poor child," Mother said.

"Enough!" Quillet got to his feet, crossing the room to a cabinet. "Enough of Dawnette's grief. Shall we fill the night with music?" He opened a long slim leather case and took out an oboe. "I don't believe," he said to me, "you've heard your mother sing for quite a while."

I had never heard my mother sing, but sing she did, and I listened, astonished at the range, not of her small, breathless voice, but of her adaptability.

With my father she had played the slave, tiptoeing through the night, maintaining an elective muteness. Like a backward schoolgirl, she spoke only when spoken to, as if her very presence were an excuse for a caning. But here on this storm-lashed mountain Quillet said sing and she sang to his obbligato. Good God—if she had taken up with Clyde Barrow she would have robbed banks.

And yet I wondered. Was this another of her disguises, put on like a mask in her overeagerness to please—the only feasible basis, however fraudulent, in her secret mind, for a relationship with a man? What was she, mouse or canary? Would I ever know? Would the essential Jenny Bernstein Breslau cum Quillet please stand up?

"*Plaisir d'amour ne dure qu'un moment*," she was singing. "*Chagrin d'amour dure toute la vie…*"

I eased my mother from my mind and in her place was Valerie, by the song remembered. A flood of sadness and longing and tenderness tinctured with pain washed over me. "*Chagrin d'amour dure toute la vie…*" How true, I thought, how true.

The freeze broke, the mist lifted, and one morning in May the sun like a frail, feverish stranger reappeared. It burned the rime off the muddy road and melted the snow in the meadow. A thousand streams crested and little waterfalls carved their way though the dingle.

Down the road came the fused figure of a horse and rider. From the deck of the house I stared down at Dawnette White, sitting tall and easy in the saddle. I was expecting her, but I had anticipated nothing like this.

She rode like a jeweled mirage, a princess in Levi's and boots, a pilgrim from a perfect place. She fairly glinted, from the shine of her yellow hair beneath the bull rider's hat to the gun belted at the narrow waist. A red-tailed hawk wheeled slowly over her head, an auger of nothing but good.

Old retarded Lee Roy bounded from my side and down the stairs, racing toward the horse, circling the burnished hooves, barking with sharp pleasure, the way he would at less auspicious enchantments, like the rising moon. The godlike horse ignored him, throwing back his elegant neck, snorting, mane flying, and the dog's tail spanked like a pennant.

That horse. Lightning eyed, muscle plated, high stepping. A horse bred in heaven. And the girl riding him wrapped in a sort of golden halo. Chaste, chiseled, a divinity on a celestial steed, a creature blending earth and sky, on loan from the Kingdom of the Centaurs.

I strode casually to meet her. She smiled down at me, teeth glistening. She said, "Howdy."

I swear she said "Howdy," and I said "Howdy," just like a couple of cowpokes in one of those schlocky paperbacks about the purple sage. For the first time since my arrival in Ravenna I was aware of being up to my ass in the goddamned golden West.

She was one of those rare people who look even better upon close inspection, a clean-limbed, leggy paragon, a 4-H poster with the wide, wise eyes of a virgin. She moved in an aura of immaculateness, her glossy shirt illuminated with birds and flowers like a medieval manuscript. Good God, had I at long last found someone more innocent than I?

She showed me how to saddle Eohippus, the Morgan Quillet had assigned to me. We worked shoulder to shoulder, her apple cheeks glowing with vigor. She smelled of mountain pines and clear freshets. She gave me instructions, her little white teeth clamped on a straw aromatic with horse shit. She told me about the art and etiquette of horsemanship and I listened, although it was hard to concentrate on the lesson: "...so the horse reacts to cues—words, clucking, or the roll of the tongue, pressure of your legs, shift of your body, and always with a loose rein..."

All this would have been rewarding (at least to Quillet) were I able to report that I thereupon mounted the Morgan, that we forthwith galloped off through the buckbrush, but it was never meant to be. Matter of fact, we never got out of the stable.

"...and never, never jerk on the horse's mouth. A good horse has a soft mouth..."

She paused, but her voice still lingered in my ear. It was sweet and low, gentled with grace and gravity, a warm wind, a whispered spell. Calmly she said, "What are you staring at?"

"Me? Nothing."

"Yes," she said. "You were staring."

"At the gun," I said. "What's it for?"

"Rattlesnakes."

"This time of year?"

"You never can tell. You were staring," she said gravely, "at my breasts."

"I'm sorry," I said.

Her lower lip quivered. "It's embarrassing," she said. "Just because one of my boobs is bigger than the other..."

Boobs, she said. I wouldn't have guessed that she was aware of the vulgarism. "I couldn't tell," I said. "I swear."

"I guess I'm self-conscious about it. If you look real hard..."

I looked. With a mustering of courage I asked, "Can I feel?"

"Sure. I guess so."

Gently I cupped one of her flawless jugs as if the procedure were entirely academic. I transferred my hand to its sib, probing scientifically, frowning with concentration. She too frowned, and then a set, cryptic smile replaced the quiver on her lips. She pulled me to her, unleashing a kiss that liked to rend my shorts.

"Now," she said, suddenly businesslike, "what are we going to do about that little yucky in your pants?" With a quick, sure motion she unzipped my fly. "Interested in a little beef jerky?" she asked.

I was too concussed to come up with even a nod. Suddenly Miss Goody Two-Shoes had before my eyes transmogrified into Mistress Dolly Drop-Drawers. All efficiency, she snared a horse blanket from a rack, whipped it open in a cloud of chaff, and climbed the ladder to the loft. We spread it on the hay, sowing havoc among the mice as they squealed and bolted for cover. We tumbled on it. Below us the horses stomped and whiffled. Lee Roy wailed and pawed the bottom rung of the ladder, affronted and excluded from the fun.

Fun. We came together, love-locked, a ruttish and inelegant entanglement. She went about it with a kind of grim, irruptive persistence, an approach I never expected from a creature who somehow combined the angel essence of Rima the Bird Girl with the tramp proclivity of Sadie Thompson.

And then, as quickly as it began, the revelry was over. She lit a cigarette, puffed on it ravenously, went to a corner, and squatted. "Got to wee-wee," she explained, flipping the butt into the puddle. She had the mannerisms of the backwoods and the vocabulary of the suburbs.

"Get your dee-lights?" she asked, rummaging through the pockets of her discarded jeans.

"It was wonderful," I said untruthfully. She nodded in agreement—one lie begets another.

"Now—" she sat down beside me, holding a little blue notebook and the nub of a pencil. "Will you kindly answer a couple questions? It's May...?"

"Eighth."

She wrote it down. "How do you spell your name?"

I told her. "What's all this...?"

"Kind of a diary," she said. "Your age?"

"Sixteen."

Passionately she said, "Shit!"

"What's the matter?"

"What's the matter?" she repeated. "It won't count, that's what's the matter."

"I don't know what you're talking about."

"You wouldn't," she said disdainfully. "You probably never even heard of the Daughters of the Williwaw, right?"

"I'm always willing to learn..."

"It's like a sorority, sort of."

"At school? You go to school?"

"It would be easier if I did. At the university or Colorado State, or even at Denver Secretarial, I'd have a chance to meet some people. But out here there's horses and cows, that's about it, and like you they don't count."

"Why don't I count? Count for what?"

"Membership. I'm a pledge. I've been a pledge for six months, almost seven."

"What have I to do with your qualifying for membership?"

"According to the bylaws, you have to screw a hundred guys. Jesus," she went on hopelessly, "I'm only about halfway there."

"A hundred *different* guys?"

"Of course." She shook her head with the enormity of the burden. "And it don't count if a guy's under eighteen."

Half a hundred guys. Her experience diminished me a little. But only a little. "Can I see you again?"

"For sure," she said. "I'm to teach you how to ride."

"I don't mean..."

"What good would it do? I just told you..." She sighed.

"Maybe you ought to impact a few changes in the bylaws."

"Yeah," she said. "Some of the other girls have trouble too."

"Is there any way I can help? I mean, if you introduced me to some of those pledges? Maybe if I lied a little about my age…"

"That's not fair," she said, a victim of her own integrity.

"There must be some way…"

"I don't know. Believe me, I've given it a lot of thought."

"Why don't we talk more about it…?"

"What's to talk about? Not that I don't appreciate…"

"…Tonight?"

"It would have to be in the barn. My grandmother doesn't like me bringing boys to the house."

"Barn is fine. We could talk while you're, I don't know, cleaning your gun."

"Well…" she said noncommittally, getting to her feet.

I reached out, clutching her slim ankle.

"What are you doing?" she said. "We got to get back to the horses."

"Not yet."

"What do you want?" Was it possible she didn't know?

"I want you," I said emphatically, "even if it doesn't count."

"You're sweet, the way you tried to help…"

"You madden my blood."

"Yeah. Your poor little old lollipop is stretched all out of shape."

"Isn't that the sincerest form of flattery?"

She considered the calculation. "Yeah," she said, "I suppose," and sank to the blanket beside me.

And then a voice rang out, carrying across the grange and into the barn. "Judd," came the howl of doom, the resonant whine of my mother. "Judd… are you in there?"

"Goddammit!" I whispered fiercely.

"You ought to answer her."

"Maybe she'll go away."

But she didn't. She said, "Telephone." I threw on my clothes, buttoning, zipping, all thumbs.

"I'd better go," Dawnette said.

"See you tonight," I called over my shoulder. "Eight o'clock."

* * *

Two hours later I braked the pickup before the Brown Palace in Denver. "It's a little late for lunch," Joseph Grady said. "Can I offer you a drink? And tell you that I'm most pointedly delighted to see you?"

I was impatient to hear what had motivated his calling me, and equally eager not to show it. On the phone he had said he was passing through Denver on business. He had something to tell me—"something pivotal that you might find interesting"—that was the way he put it. There was in his tone a hint of mystery, of promise; it could only have had something to do with Val.

Now we sat facing each other across an aspirin-size table, next to a window, raising our second martinis. "Usually," he said, impressed by my performance, "you have to acquire a taste for them."

"I like 'em already," I told him. "Particularly the olives."

"Waiter!" he called. "A plate of olives." Grady sipped from the long-stemmed glass. "Now," his great bald dome reflected the pallid burnish of the underlit room, "I hope we can agree on what I have in mind."

I leaned forward slightly. There was about him a certain discomforting steeliness, the solemn intractability of a man willing to break faces to achieve a consensus. "You took off," he said accusingly, "faster than a rumor."

"I would have said good-bye, but…"

"Doesn't matter," he said, "but remind me—what were you in civilian life, before you signed on with Chatterton?"

"A graduate student in English."

"And what are you seeking out here…" he looked pained, "in God's own graveyard?"

What could I tell him? A shelter for my fears, a comfort for my disappointment, an antidote to sorrow? "My mother lives here," I said.

"That's it?"

I shrugged.

"That's a terrible reason. That's a reason to be anywhere else." He raised an authoritative arm and ordered a couple more knocks, wearing all the while an expression of deep interest. "You don't look particularly happy," he observed. "Maybe you're not programmed for it."

"Happiness?"

"Your life in the forest primeval." Almost casually he asked, "How'd you like to work for me?"

"Back at Chatterton's?"

"God, no. Until I retired, I was a roving vice president—a trouble-shooter, with Resource Analysis and Technology. RAT is an offshoot of Ultra Global Husbandry, for which I serve as a sort of flack-master and talent scout, recruiting young people of promise." He took an embossed card from a leather case and flipped it to me.

"To do what?"

"The field is unlimited, depending on what interests the recruit. UGH is the parent corporation of a number of American firms—a packing plant in Des Moines, sports equipment in Newark, the Calvary Construction Company in Oklahoma City, coal mines in West Virginia, a printing press in Chicago (specializing in the publication of church periodicals), as well as plantations—rubber in Southeast Asia, coconuts in Melanesia—latifundia in Hungary (a consortium with the Russians), ranches in Argentina, to name a few."

"Nothing for an English major."

"Let's not jump to negative conclusions."

"What did you have in mind?"

"You could start anywhere; obituaries, for example." He drained his third martini. "I believe you were doing research on death for Chatterton—some sort of exploration into the valley of the shades. You write them in advance, the obits, keeping them up to date, for all our executives all over the world. So when the inevitable time comes, as to all men it must, the media will not lack appropriate copy."

"What does it pay?"

"Exceedingly well." He settled back in his chair, poised to send me a sparkling flash of congratulations as soon as I said yes. I hesitated. Something was ass-backwards. I should have been begging for such a plum, yet I felt that he was pleading for my complicity in accepting it. "A career in public relations is as demanding as scholarship," he went on, "and possibly a great deal more significant." He shared a solemn smile with me. "If Jesus Christ had got good press, he probably wouldn't have lost the big one."

"When do you want an answer?"

"Now," he said. "I'll have to arrange for your using a company flat in New York, until you can find a place of your own."

"You say New York?"

"UGH headquarters."

Well. So there it was. The meeting did indeed have something to do with Val, if only indirectly. The idea of finding her in the phone book had its appeal. But when I did, I knew, she'd wear another hole in me.

I glanced out the window at the signs of spring. The sky was almost blue, the trees were almost budding, the sun was almost bright. Springtime in the Rockies. Somewhere over the almost green mountain was my newfound female friend, galloping through the *knic-knic*. No complications there, just a favorable shift in my life situation; I'd be wearing a hole in *her,* so to speak. Thoughts of Valerie receded and lost their talent to intoxicate. I wasn't even curious to explore what might develop, one way or another, if I were to see her again. Hell with her.

"No," I said, "I don't think I want to live in a place where all the trees are cut down."

"There's always Central Park," he said. And he added, just in case I hadn't made the connection, "What about Miss Chatterton? Not interested in renewing a beautiful relationship?"

"No, but thanks for the offer."

I thought for a moment that he might debate the issue, but he shrugged it off, smiling that solemn smile. "You're a promising young man. I'm convinced you have talent."

Here we go again, another unspecific allusion to my endowments. But this time I said bluntly, "For what?"

"That's something only your destiny will determine. A destiny we might share if you were to change your mind."

"I'll know where to reach you." I pocketed his card, got to my feet, a bit unsteadily after all those olives. "But I don't think so," I said.

TWENTY

GOOD-BYE AGAIN

She lived in a small crooked house of mud-chinked timbers, set in a sea of melted snow.

She introduced me to her grandmother, whose faded eyes and uncompromisingly tight lips were breached by a piddling mustache that seemed to grow out of her nose. The old lady shifted her raddled raw bones under the prim Mother Hubbard and looked at me as if seeking grounds for a lawsuit; she didn't even say howdy. Nor did she offer the usual amenities of parting as her granddaughter and I (with uncivil celerity, I must admit) hied out of that stunted house.

The yellow eye of a flashlight led me through the sentinel trees, across the stubbled fields to a hulking barn. Together we shouldered open the wide door and she with a chatelaine gesture bade me enter.

Horses pranced and snorted in a row of stalls that smelled bittersweetly of hay and horseshit. On the far end, beyond the skittish beasts, was the tack room, only one corner of which housed stable gear. The rest held the genteel imprimatur of Dawnette's other self.

Along one wall was a spavined divan and a lamp with a beaded shade connected by a snaky wire to the only electrical outlet, across the room and far away, above the tack bench.

"Cozy," I said.

"Yeah," she agreed. "Now, you interested in a little uppin' and downin'...?"

"What?" If I understood her correctly, the invitation called for some small, oblique preamble. Which was not Dawnette's way.

"...innin' and outin'?" she went on. "What do you say?"

There was nothing to say. Without further elaboration, I jumped her. Of course we were not lovers, nor would we ever be in any sense of the word that transcended an almost jarring physicality; lovers make love in countless ways, seeking contact as well as connection. They hang on to each other, linking arms, touching, intoxicated by the perfume of proximity. They are constantly in each other's pockets, especially hip pockets. They whisper fatuities and assign vast significance to them. They weave small conspiracies that set them apart from all the world; they go underground. They nuzzle and nibble and chew on each other. They cosset and quarrel and eat from the same spoon. They sigh or scream hilariously, redefining wit for the outsider, who sees nothing funny there. They beam into each other's eyes, seeking and finding the mirrored fusion that isolates everybody else. Or together they focus on the moon or the page of a book or—with what tender mercy—on the inflammation of a bug bite. They tingle with the stupefactive awareness that no duad in the long history of the earth has been so privileged or so blessed. They say things at the same time, as if other people don't, astonished by the miracle of simultaneity. They invent pet names, sometimes cute, often playful, invariably infantile. Dawnette had a pet name for me—I guess you could call it that— she called me a little ole scum-sucking buzzard fucker—not totally, I like to think, without affection. And of course we touched and grabbed and bit and bruised, but for connection only. And with a kind of sluggish, glassy-eyed, unendearing deliberateness. Our lovemaking was like a preemptive strike, aggressive and immediate. Only once upon entering our passion pit did she postpone (for maybe five minutes) my nailing her to the springs. I had brought us a couple of hamburgers from Mother's table, not having eaten in my haste to join Dawnette. She sat down and scoffed the cold meat in the soggy bun. "Can't fuck on mush," she said between bites, in her soft, musical voice.

I got to know every nook and cranny of her. Most of our moves she herself initiated. "Wanna try like this?" she would ask, and gladly I'd acquiesce to her every delinquency, however daunting or inventive, and soon the place would erupt with the brays and means of our flexions. Then I'd fall back, clamp my eyes shut, and breathe like a tortured bellows while she, the sweet-purring, fine-tuned engine of my burnout, would grin slyly at me.

"Needle on empty?" she'd ask.

"I am Judd whose sword never sleeps."

But of course it wasn't true. For at least fifteen minutes I'd lie there ragged and lifeless while cross-legged and bare-assed on the couch beside me sat my inexhaustible symbiont. Gravely and patiently she sat, like a good wife awaiting my recrudescence, dry-firing her gun, sipping a Diet Coke. Then we'd collide again, a couple of acrobats coupling on the couch, the earthen floor, the tack table. Nothing could keep me from her, from pawing and pouncing and plugging her gaps, not even when she wore jumbo pinks in her hair.

I knew she would respond to any man so long as he was ithyphallic; still (such was my selective blindness), she was a bundle of charm. A darling, dirty-minded, filthy-tongued scamp, a gem carver bent on sculpting the perfect fuck. The more explosive bodily functions were always on her mind. "How are you?" I greeted her one evening, in bland conformity to custom. "Had a pretty good day," she replied, "didn't get fucked but sneezed twice." I came to expect that sort of touching, uncalculated revelation; it was only when she resorted to the patois of suburbia that she surprised me. "How can you drink that stuff?" I once asked as she drained yet another Diet Coke and sucked the bottom of the can. "It's conducive to my own personal lifestyle," she said.

What could be said about my own lifestyle, except that it was random and unruly? The nights with Dawnette, expanding the frontiers of human endurance. The days riding the range, rooting out locoweed, sprawling, sometimes sleeping in the saddle. Dawnette, between the more pressing exercises that brought us together, had insisted on carrying out her contract with Quillet, and so I had learned, squeamishly, the rudiments of horsemanship. But nature never intended me to become a cowboy. There dawned a shuddersome day when destiny, bored or perhaps shamed with what had become of me, intruded.

Quillet stood in the center of the stable and eyed Fritillary, the alpha mare of his herd. He puffed on his pipe, a monument of profundity. "She's in estrus," he said. "I think she's ready."

"How can you tell?" I asked warily. Already I knew that no good could come of this.

"See how she urinates? And switches her tail and holds it to one side?" Puff, puff. "I'll phone old Mrs. White and have Dawnette bring over the stud in the morning. You and your mother can oversee the operation."

"I don't think I can do it," Mother said limply.

"I know I can't," I said emphatically.

"It could be dangerous," Mother said.

"Don't be absurd," Quillet said between puffs. "I'd do it myself, but copy's piling up, there's a deadline to meet, I got those back spasms again..." A facial nerve twitched, as if to certify his infirmity. "All you've got to do," he went on bravely...

"*No,*" said Mother.

That night Quillet sat on his living-room throne surrounded by reams of copy, ensconced in so vast a remoteness that he didn't even lecture.

"More tea, dear?" Mother asked miserably, her head slightly inclined, her voice flat and dry.

He would not acknowledge her existence with so much as a shake of his stormy head. He had a babyish aptitude for pouting when he felt only fleetingly neglected, but this was an irritant of another dimension: betrayal, a denial of the loyalty he thought due him, and he responded with the aggressive resignation of a martyr. My mother simply sat there, fixed and frozen, the primary target of his silent accusations, until she could stand it no longer.

"I suppose I could do it," she said. "It's no more difficult than a thousand other chores I've managed..."

"You'll need some help," he said bluntly.

What could I do? Suggest that he snap out of his exploitative shit? Tell him to go shit in his Stetson? That I didn't intend to be in the same county with two horse-beasts innin' and outin', ramming each other like jousting battleships? And let my mother, armed with good intentions and ineptitude, go it alone in her eagerness to please the absentee mastermind of the revels?

I looked at her, at her wide, leaky eyes pleading for me not to make trouble, to help her in her travail, wasn't that what a son was for?

The grassy floor of the pasture was swathed in layers of silent light, and dappled by long, still shadows.

We hovered outside the stable, Mother and I, looking down at the horse van that moved toward us over the mustard-colored road. From the house a hundred yards away drifted the dismal howls and yowls of Lee Roy. Quillet had taken the sensible precaution of locking himself and the dog inside.

"Morning!" Dawnette shouted to Mother, still some distance away, and, as I helped her down from the cab, "How's your ass?" she asked me. "This here is Sailor," she added, as if she were introducing the guest of honor. She unloaded the chestnut steed, leading him into a stall. He clopped behind her, docile enough. Mother clopped after them.

"He's a sweet little guy," Dawnette said. "Up-headed."

He didn't look any such thing to me; Sailor was an iron-hoofed, wind-sucking behemoth. "He's hammer-headed," I said, "dish-faced." Sailor glared at me, aggrieved by my bluntness.

"He's got good genes," Dawnette said, and Sailor's ire subsided somewhat, his family honor upheld by an advocate who knew a hell of a lot more about him than I did. "Your first mare ready?"

"I guess so," Mother said dubiously.

Dawnette strode over to Fritillary, chomping at a bale of hay. "Now Miz Jenny," she said reprovingly, "you haven't dressed her?"

"I haven't?" Mother asked.

"You got to wash her down with soap and water."

"You mean like a car?" I asked. To wash down Fritillary would be like washing down a galleon. I wanted no part of it. "Won't she catch cold? Shouldn't she finish eating?" She could eat all day, I figured, which would give me time to invent another, possibly more valid excuse to avoid stress.

"You just wash around what you call her vulva," Dawnette explained, "and wrap her tail to prevent germs and injury to old Sailor boy here. I mean," she shook her head sternly, "you wouldn't want old Sailor to get his penis all slashed up with a wild hair, now would you?"

Frankly, I didn't care what happened to old Sailor boy's penis; I wasn't going to wash out some goddam horse's snatch just to make him safe from wild hairs. "Not me," I said firmly, and Mother looked as if she were about to faint. Her fortifications, built on cooking sherry, were crumbling.

"It's easy." A note of impatience crept into Dawnette's voice. "For Christ's sakes…"

"You do it," I said.

"Can't," she said. "I ain't nothin' but a little ole shirttail girl delivering a stud. It says in the contract between Mr. Q. and my grandmama that's what I am to do and then get him to home and that's all."

"What about the helpfulness, the traditional code of the West? I always thought being neighborly was like a sacred trust out here."

"What are you talking about?"

"Like when all the good folks get together to help a neighbor raise a barn."

"This definitely is not a barn-raising and anyway I never heard of such a thing."

Shit. I led old Fritillary to the breeding stocks; with every step she shied from her own sun-trapped shadow. I loose-wrapped her lead line around a post, rolled up my sleeves, and sloshed out her snatch with a bucket of soap and water. Her tail I swathed in an old but clean leg-wrap Dawnette found in the tack room. It was a sloppy job, made more so by Fritillary's pissing all over me.

"Good," said Dawnette, the indisputable maven in such matters. "Now get her down to the exercise run."

"What's that?"

She sighed loudly, pointing a finger of command toward an elongated enclosure, about twelve feet wide and eighty feet long, fenced in by horizontal logs with mesh wire spiked to the posts between them. Dutifully I maneuvered the mare out of the stocks and into the run. Now what?

"I think we ought to tease her a little," the maven said. "You bring old Sailor into the paddock."

"Why can't we take them down to the pasture and let 'em the hell alone?"

"No way," Dawnette said. "My grandmama says he's got to be bred in hand."

"Screw that," I told her.

"What's the matter now?"

"If 'in hand' means what I think it means," I whispered fiercely to Dawnette, "old Sailor can jerk himself off."

"It means," she said haughtily, "you got to control old Sailor with this here breeding halter and this here lead shank."

"You can't be serious," I said.

But she was. Gingerly I took the lead line, about six feet long, which was linked to fourteen inches of chain attached to the halter, and led Sailor toward the mare on the inboard side of the fence.

He sauntered across the paddock, as benign and gentle as a teddy bear. Everything was going well, and with much more restraint than my extravagant fears had predicted. It was a piece of cake, and I was inwardly exalted. I could, it seemed, control this towering monadnock with the flick of a wrist. An immaculate triumph, all the sweeter for having been spared the odium of priming his pump.

Then he saw Fritillary. He stood for a second or two drinking her in, transported by her presence, his big head cocked stupidly. And then, as if she were the executrix of some crowning accomplishment, Fritillary spread her gaskins in an indelicate approximation of a squat and peed again. Buckets, and Sailor went apeshit. He neighed shrilly, a high piercing shriek, like a hysterical, sex-starved locomotive, but there was in it a primordial echo of Eocene quagmires and flinty mesas and that untamed tenacity which in the higher species has been known to confound desire with mayhem as a means of satisfying it.

Fritillary hung her tail to the right, a flag of welcome. Sailor trumpeted, white-eyed, pawing the earth in archetypal conformance to the cliché. The muscles in his neck writhed like a nest of snakes under the twitching skin. His sculptured frame, engulfing as a wave, rose up and blocked out the sun. It was a long way to Fritillary; he shifted into overdrive. Flailing the savage air, wild mane flying, he plunged toward her. The lead line went taut. Anchored to the end of it, I went with him. Sweat caked his plated shoulders as he and I were swamped by an invisible tornado thick with the heat and dust and the rot smell of the stable. He flashed past me toward his tail-twitching seductress. With an awful effort I held on. The lead bound my hands as he jerked his head. I jerked back, hard as I could, which was a mistake. His terrible hoofs like twin pile drivers exploded into me just about equidistant from my belly and my balls. I went oozing into the corral, clutching my insides together. Everything went dark, diminished, and then in that crucible of pain the dark image intensified, etched forever on the retina of my mind. I saw Dawnette lean forward, framed in golden dust, her pretty head tilted in an angle of disbelief. I saw my mother breathlessly still, observing my punishment with unreasonable composure. I saw the neck of a small bottle protruding from the embroidered pocket of her lavender gown. I saw a deep grave, looking down at it from a great height, the grave my own. And I saw old Sailor pour over that fence, taking off as if launched by a red-hot missile up his ass. I exaggerate: he *half* poured. His forelegs got over the highest rail but the rest of him didn't and he hung there, equipoised, like some rude and ungainly scales badly in need of adjustment. Served the bastard right—after all my pains with him, he had succeeded in mounting not Fritillary but the fence. I heard Dawnette say, "Jesus, Mary, and Joseph Smith—he's rump-sprung. And his eyes are yellow, the whites of 'em!" Her words were a chant, or maybe they just seemed so, with Sailor bellowing an accompaniment like a rusty bugle. "You got any two-bys?" she shouted. "And a sheet of plywood? Before he gets his dick lopped off?"

Mother blinked uncomprehendingly, once more the languid slave of the cooking sherry.

"Come *on,*" Dawnette wailed, "before he castrates hisself!"

"Behind," I mumbled hoarsely, "the barn." She took off on her mission of mercy.

Sailor's bellows were weaker now as he swayed on the fulcrum of the fence, unable to spring forward or fall back. Dawnette barreled out of the barn lugging eight two-by-fours. She made a dozen trips before Sailor got enough traction under his ass to hop over the fence and into the run with Fritillary, still waving her tail at him. Sailor didn't even look at her.

I didn't start plugging in to the world again until I got home from the emergency clinic. I was walking gently for another week, my legs in parentheses like old Sailor's when I last saw him. Mother nursed my wounds and made me relatively comfortable on an armchair in the sunlight.

Quillet wouldn't talk to me. If communication became necessary, I was addressed in the third person, with Mother the intermediary. "Did you show him the letter?" he asked one night. Mother shook her bowed head, as if pleading guilty to a charge of dereliction. "Show it to him," he ordered, and left the room.

> Dear Quillet, [it began]
> I don't know what you done
> to my horse but his whole pennis
> is busted. He will never service
> another mare you ruint him. He

will be lucky if he can ever piss
right again.
Sincerely,
(Mrs.) Della White
P.S. I am suing you.

I handed the letter back to Mother.

"Perhaps you'd better leave," she said gently. "Dil thinks it would be best."

Dil was right. It was indeed time for a tactical withdrawal from this ragged mountainside, if I wanted to continue breathing. The air was getting thinner and in a few short weeks I'd be freezing again, under a cemetery sky.

"Would you like to come with me?" I asked.

She thought for a moment, then said "No. What are your plans?"

I shrugged. It seemed to me that I had been asked that question, or some equally discomforting facsimile of it, too many times in my life.

"You'll let me hear from you?"

I nodded. "You'll be okay?"

"Of course." Her eyes were fixed on mine with a sad, vulnerable focus. "He's a good man, Dil, basically. I guess I've always been attracted to men who are difficult. Proves they're not hypocrites—they don't conform easily."

I said nothing.

"He casts a certain spell…" she went on.

…That is irresistible, I might have added, but only to the victim. Still, I said nothing, which was tactless, because she started to cry without any particular agitation. She dabbed at her eyes, quickly composing herself, and got to her feet. "I'd better do the dishes," she said, and went into the kitchen. I heard a cabinet door open, and then one flat note—the rim of a glass meeting the neck of a bottle. I could have used a little sherry myself.

TWENTY-ONE

UNDER THE BRIDGE

The city floated, half-submerged in a dark sea of mist. Far below, the lustrous skyscrapers hung a corona around the clouds. Saint Elmo's fire flickered and danced along the wingtips of the endlessly circling plane. And then, with a deafening death rattle, the craft staggered, lost altitude, crashed blindly into the clouds, emerged in a gastric-lurching dive, and dropped its tires and passengers sighing with relief on the rain-slick runway. Immediately the passengers went into a self-important dance con brio, standing in the aisles (ignoring the directives of the stewardess), pulling on jackets and children, pulling down carry-ons, as if they hadn't been scared witless within their seat belts not more than a minute ago.

The rain had stopped. Steam rose from the still-wet tarmac like ectoplasm. People with the gait of androids scurried along an unpleasantly moist tunnel. At the end of the ramp were a cluster of men, each with a hand-painted sign hanging from a necklace of string like a blind man's pectoral. The man with my name on his chest touched a knuckle to his soiled chauffeur's cap and ran interference for me, blindsiding everybody in his inflexible impulsion through the terminal. A stretch limo awaited us, a long gray coffin.

Grady had arranged everything, including an advance on my salary toward the purchase of New York summer regimentals—a seersucker suit, a few button-down shirts, a couple of ties—and the loan of a posh company flat usually reserved for visiting VIPs, not that I qualified, and only until I could find a place of my own.

Our relationship, of protégé to patron, was a bit unusual. He never tried to teach me anything; if anything he was indifferent to my progress. My days were undercrowded because his demands were minimal. I churned up obits for the living or lavished hosannas on the Calvary Construction Co., a spin-off of RAT, whose uplift had become my province, and shoveled my harvest of hype to Grady, but the totality of his unconcern led me to suspect that he never read it. And yet, contradictorily, in our few encounters, I felt he had great plans for me. Or maybe the feeling was no more than wishful on my part; I *wanted* his attention. Christ, I needed the attention of *somebody.*

So I'd zero in on my Old Man. Once, when I was about five, when he took me to the circus. And once, on a crowded city street somewhere, when he took my hand.

Perhaps it was the need for attention, for contact (I was eager to give as well as receive), that prompted my prowling the streets of the city. I milled in crowds, drank in bars, downing bushels of olives. I plunged into the thick goulash of New York, moving with the fierce tide of its abrasive, unmanageable, shock-infested aborigines. I loitered on corners in the heat or the rain and I learned a lot. But I was always the outsider, a fish in a merciless net, living out the golden days of my youth in a kind of melancholy confusion—until the day Grady assigned me, much to my annoyance, to the task of an errand boy.

He was reading some chemistry tract and munching on Maalox when I entered his office toward the end of that day. I dropped my copy on a corner of his desk; he didn't look up. As I turned to leave, "Got a job for you," he said, unfolding his long, wedge-shaped body from the chair. He pushed his glasses up on his forehead, as if the twin ridges above his eyes had been made for them. "One of our people is tossing a little bash tomorrow night. He has an amusing hobby—collecting film."

"Classics?"

"All kinds. He's rather eclectic. There's a picture he wants to run at his party. I'd like you to pick it up for him." He handed me a slip of paper with an address on it. "And this..." he held out several crisp bills, "should cover it."

Grady's directions, unlike his office guidance, were explicit and precise. Subway to City Hall. Avenue of the Finest, where five or six of whose eponymous heroes, unpressed and blue-jowled, were tenaciously oblivious to the sidewalk hordes, the Manhattan wallahs, the moldy old drunks, the over-medicated adolescents, the rubberheads, the mumbling, fumbling derelicts scratching and talking to themselves, the tourists, all agog but pretending not to be, lugging cameras and heading for ground zero. New York, New York, God shed His grace on thee.

Beneath the ramp, between the arches of the Brooklyn Bridge in its rise toward the river, was a series of vaults made available by the city to the private sector. Climax Productions was nestled among them, a dark concrete crypt with the barest amenities of an office and few of the refinements of a keep—a low table, a couple of unmatched kitchen chairs, a butt-sprung couch, and three closed doors marked, respectively, PRIVATE, STAGE, and HIS/HERS/ITS.

A young woman in a not quite immaculate evening gown leaned over the table, her back to me, cranking a pencil sharpener. Her body swayed, pulsated, as if in a self-induced trance. Power flowing from the engine of her hand pumped the piston of her arm, then cascaded through the drive shaft of her naked shoulder, generating torque to the torso and onward, to the axis of rotation: a turning, twisting, dreamlike perfection of an ass, fluid, mind-boggling. It was the most vivid ass I had almost ever seen, an ass designed for undulation.

She gathered up her pencils and turned, and lightning struck. For an epochal instant we stood like prisoners in the gloom of that concrete cage, stunned by some smirking humorless force that ordained our personal histories. *I* was stunned, at least, and she was—well, she was more Val than ever.

"What are you doing here?" she asked mildly. "In New York, I mean."

"Working," I stammered. "I'm a young urban professional."

"You *work?*" she seemed dubious.

"I'm with Resource Analysis and Technology," I assured her.

"You into kinky flicks?"

"I'm into upward mobility. Somebody in my office wants a picture for a party." I gave her one of Grady's slips.

"I'll have to find it," she said, squinting at the immaculate type as though it were written in Urdu. "It might take some time."

"I'll wait."

"Or you want to come back in like an hour? We wrap at six."

"You're free at six? Would you like to have a drink?"

She hesitated. A voice boomed from behind the door marked PRIVATE. "Valerie!" it summoned. Val's face went grim. "Got to go," she said. "It's Mister B, and he's the whole shirt, Captain Zero Cool." She stepped toward Captain Zero Cool's sanctum. "See you at six," she threw over her bare shoulder.

I walked out of the office, hanging a right at Frankfort, cut back to Park Row, circling. Val Valerie Val Val Val. Had I detected, along with the soupçon of easy elegance in her red velvet gown, an additional spark of assurance and animation that had ignited the old languorous witchery? It wasn't yet five; I had an hour to think about it, among the clotted crowd. Somehow, I felt, I had been favored by God, who in His infinite wisdom had seen fit to renew this fateful conjugation. A last chance? Could I snatch the dream out of the satchel and polish it up again, put a burnish of reality on a lost but insistently lingering fantasy? My mouth was dry.

A speeding car lurched into the no-parking zone before Police Headquarters. The driver, in a cop's uniform, scurried to the curb and threw open the rear door for a tall, stooped man of fifty, and I reeled from another and equally devastating shock: the tall man, in nappy tweeds, was my father. It wasn't the first time I had seen him since his disappearance, yet each time on close inspection he had proved to be a phantom, a shape-changer, a pretender. Now I dashed across the street, eager to throw myself into his arms— a reunion of blood and genes, as touching and tumultuous as my encounter with Valerie, and all in the space of half an hour. He hardly glanced at me as I ran to intercept him, and for good reason: he was yet another imposter.

When I got back to Climax Productions Valerie was nowhere in sight. I stood there for a moment, feeling like an intruder in the emptiness of that concrete dustbin, when the STAGE door opened. A woman walked in, I guess about thirty, wearing a murky rayon dressing gown. Above it she had on a pair of glasses with lenses so thick they might have been borrowed from a couple of flashlights. Beneath it she wore nothing but fishnet stockings, house slippers with bunnies on them, and a dancing glint of sequins over her pubic floss. She smiled at me like any good receptionist and made no attempt to cover her nakedness.

"Hi!" she said brightly, plopping on the couch. Her jugs bounced, not quite in unison, stirring the air. She smelled slightly of sweat and strongly of a perfume derived from the glans of a Himalayan wild goat. She took off her gigs and wiped them on the hem of the murky schmatte. "You're Judd, right? Valerie said she'd be with you in a minute. Jesus," she readjusted her glasses, "I'm dead, I've been off my feet all day." She squinted, blinking affably. "That's a joke," she confided, "you dig?"

My expression must have indicated that I didn't. "You're in the movie they're shooting?"

"Me? Nooo."

"Tell me about *your* work."

"Well," she said, "I used to be a star, now I'm queen of the warm-up pit."

Again I drew a blank and showed it.

"*You* know," she said encouragingly, as if I were two steps below average intelligence, "the bull pen. That's where you warm up the male lead, so's he's ready for action when the camera rolls. You'd be surprised," she lowered her voice confidentially, "what some of 'em want. You may not believe it but you get some real flakes in this business."

"Such as?"

"Well…"

Valerie came in, wearing blue jeans and a man's cotton shirt, her hair in a ponytail… and I thought I would fall down, flattened by her beauty, her presence, totally agogged with the miracle of my finding her here under the Brooklyn Bridge. Who knew what might happen next? What happened next, the girl with the sequined snatch got tiredly to her feet and exited. I found my voice. "Who's that?" I asked, jerking my head toward the door through which she had disappeared.

"Daphne? Daphne Titsworth? She works here."

"She always sashay around in fishnets and glitter?"

"What do you expect?" Val said. "This is New York." She grinned slyly. "If you're interested, you'd better act fast. Today's her last day here."

"Not me."

Val waved a slim forefinger toward the door marked PRIVATE. "Barf wants to see you."

"Who?"

"Mr. Barfield. The big Gorgonzola."

"Me? Why?"

"How the hell do I know?"

Barfield's office was a triumph of dinginess over the forces of fluorescent light. A raw meatball of a face hovered and slowly took shape, hanging like the harvest moon above the cluttered landscape of a desk. The face floated toward me. "Sit down, sit down, young man," it said. "I understand you're with RAT?"

I nodded and Barfield nodded, apparently glad to have his postulate confirmed. He settled down behind his desk and leaned toward me, scarcely breathing, trying to convey an illusion of unimpaired interest, total attention. I could see him clearly now, kneading that hamburger face in an earnest manifestation of mediocrity.

"I have a proposition," he said, "that RAT might find interesting." He paused, anticipating an eager response. I sighed inwardly, searching for some avenue of escape. Barfield was definitely not the kind of person who grows on you. In the outer office, not forty feet away, Val was waiting and here I was closeted with an enterprising bore. Perhaps the quickest release from my captor was hearing him out.

"What do you have in mind?" I asked.

"I've been thinking of expanding my operation," he said. "Going into recreational equipment for the physically inclined, people with indoor hobbies. I need financing."

"You mean like barbells, exercise bikes, jump ropes?"

"I mean like dildos, vibrators, and a broad spectrum of beneficial accessories, including a bakery."

I nodded sagely as if I saw the connection; he knew that I didn't, and he was intent on making his pitch crystal clear.

"I'm talking X-rated cakes. Erotica and novelties for special occasions."

"Cakes. You say cakes?"

"Cakes in the shape of dicks and butts and tits and clits."

"Hmmmmmm." My expression of solemnity rivaled his.

"What do you think?"

"I'll have to think it over."

"Don't take too long. I got some other people lined up."

"Maybe you ought to investigate..."

"That's what I'm doing."

"...investigate the people you got lined up."

"They're in the porn business. You can't trust them any more than you can bankers. What I mean is, there's been a deplorable falling of standards in the trade." He wore an expression of solemn confidentiality. "These days, you got to fight tooth and nail, hand to mouth to turn out something meaningful. Everybody wants to cock up the detail with his own input. Actors, directors, they none of 'em dig the symbolism. Like in my last picture—about what you call necrophilia. People are in love with death, get it? And then this son of a bitch cutter cuts it with a helicopter. If," he added wistfully, "I could just get my hands on one hot property." He eyed me. "Val tells me you're a college man. How'd you like to write one of my pictures?"

"I don't think I'm qualified."

Pause. Then: "What you got to tell your people at RAT, tell them I think big, okay?"

He got to his feet, extending a hand. I shook it, although I didn't want to touch any part of him. "I've delayed you long enough," he said, "but I needed Val for some rush orders, and we're trying to get product out for the Christmas market." He held on to my hand. I pulled it gently. He held on. "She's something, that kid," he said. "She's got that piece of divine flame, that elusive quality that makes for immortality among performers. I could make a star out of her, bring her along slowly, start her in the bull pen..."

I jerked my hand from his and walked fast to the door.

"Remember," he called after me, "tell 'em I think big."

TWENTY-TWO

INCOMING MAIL

Footsteps in the corridor, the footsteps of my Assaman keepers who walk softly and carry weapons, my ushers to spear-sharp stakes when the time comes, and it could be now. Weakness drips from my every pore, I am a vessel of weakness, already posthumous.

It happens every day and persists like a sickness long after they deliver my lunch bucket of slop or show in a visitor. And once again, in the ominous here-and-now, a guard is at the door. It swings open and he hands me a letter. It had come in the way all our mail arrives, forwarded from the UGH flagship in New York. The envelope has of course been opened, either by Abdul or by Grady, so the contents have to be less than earth-shaking or I wouldn't be permitted to see them.

The format is unmistakable and exactingly crafted.

"My most darling son," Mother writes in an outpouring of tenderness,

How

are

you? The

most aston-

ishing series of

events has come

to pass. Della White,

Dawnette's grand-

mother, sued us just as

she promised, for aggravated

damages sustained by her dis-

gusting horse. $5,000,000. Dil was furious and put in an immediate call to Harry

Swift. That's how it started. Do you remember Harry the lawyer? A man

with gray hair? Full of fidgets? With that big watch? Hardly ever

opened his mouth, although Dil said he was a killer in the

courtroom. Harry comes flying over. Literally. At

his age he flies his own plane. Did you

know that? Well, Harry didn't seem

like a killer to me. He tells Dil he'd like

to avoid litigation and settle out of court.

"What I try to be," he tells Dil, "is an antidote

for strife, a tool for avoiding disorder." "That's a

hell of a thing for a lawyer to say," Dil says, shocked.

"I don't want to settle   with the old bitch, I want

to break her face   on the rack. I want

to countersue."   Finally Harry says,

"If that's what   you want," and

then to me,   "Can you

drop in my
office at two to-
morrow? I'll need
your deposition." "She'll
be there," Dil says. And that's
how it started. He took my deposition.
At six p.m. he says, "I'm not finished and I
suspect Dil'll be wanting you home to wrestle a
bull or something. Can you come back tomorrow?
About ten?" Well next day we worked until one and
broke for lunch. We were enjoying a little sherry when he
lurched across the table so urgently, so blindly, that he spilled
his glass of water. "What is it?" I ask. "Forget it," he says, mopping
up with his napkin. "Tell me," I say. "How can you live with him?" he
asks. "He's always seething with indignation. Or pouting. Or spouting
about nature. Or feeling nobody appreciates, everybody takes advantage.
Oppositional bastard," he says. I didn't answer. "I had a daughter like
that," he says. "From the time she was five years old, oppositional."
"She never changed?" I ask. "I don't know," he says. "Last time I
heard from her, and that was five years ago, she was whipping
around the country in a Ford pickup with a defrocked priest."
He told me about his wife, who died years ago. About how
after the Korean War he went to work for the Justice
Department. They sent him to the Denver
office, where he never intended staying
because what he really wanted, he
wanted to see the world. "I've
always had a hankering to
find out what was on
the other side of
these damned
mountains"—
that
was the
way he
put it.

"Well, there's not too much time left, but what time there is I'd like to
share with you." I almost fell into my sherry. "Why don't you leave Dil
and live with me? Or we can get married," he says, "whatever you
like." Harry filed a countersuit, I must say reluctantly. He felt
even worse and so did I when we got the news that Della took
one look at it and dropped dead. Dil refused to let me go to
the funeral but I went anyway. It was good I did because
I saw Dawnette there looking so sweet in a leather miniskirt
and she told me she was dropping the action. Dil still
insisted on pressing counter-charges against the estate,
a subject about which the two men failed to achieve
consensus, so Dil fired Harry right in the middle
of dinner. Harry walked out and I felt weak all
over when I got up and followed him. Whereupon
Dil fired me. From what I wasn't sure. A few
days later Harry took off to argue a case in
San Diego. Alone in his condo, I spent the
time pleasantly enough, getting a passport,
buying a travel wardrobe, jotting notes
from the tour books Harry had collected
over the years. It was almost the end of
the week when he phoned. He had
been thinking—"Sit down," he
said—"this may come as something
of a shock." He didn't quite
know how to say it.

He with his lawyer's gift of tongue. "Are you
sitting down?" he asked. I said, "Yes," and he said,
"I've fallen in love," and a terrible emptiness filled
my heart, my hand holding the phone shook, all in
a swift, everlasting second. "I've fallen in love" (did
he have to repeat it?) "with San Diego," he said.
"It's beautiful, the beaches and Mexico so close, no
snow. And through Jack, he's my client, I can get a
good buy, an acre on a hill facing China." So I'm off

tomorrow to take a look at the property. I'll send
our new address as soon as we're settled in. As for
Dil, he had a garage sale of my clothes and Navajo
jewelry but I learned about it too late to buy them
back. Did I mention that Dawnette sends you her
best regards? Since the funeral she seems to have
dropped out of sight. Her grandmother's ranch,
which she inherited, is up for sale. I hope this finds
you well and happy.

—Your loving Mother

TWENTY-THREE

SAY NOT THE STRUGGLE NAUGHT AVAILETH

After leaving the studio, we had wandered the streets within a cone of silence, through an evening of hot stale air, shadowed by skyscrapers. Walking beside her gave me a feeling of accomplishment, a curious tincture of excitation and tranquillity. I could have walked with her, arm in arm, forever.

It was she who spoke first. As the moon rose high and lopsided over Wall Street, "What's Queen Anne?" she asked.

"Don't you mean 'who'?"

"I mean El Supremo's got a Queen Anne swimming pool in Jersey. He told me. Barfield," she said. "On second thought, forget it. Screw him and his swimming pool."

"Where're we going?" I asked.

"The harbor?"

"Sure. Would you like a drink?"

"I don't drink."

"Something to eat?"

"I'm not hungry."

Again a mountainous sound-void settled between us; I had the feeling I was somebody else, a deaf-mute, a dumb animal incapable even had I willed it of breaking this speechless conspiracy. And I was sweating, mostly from the exertion of lugging that awkward can of film.

"Speaking of El Supremo," I transferred the can from one bloodless fist to the other, "are you going to take that job?"

"What job?"

"The bull pen."

She shrugged. "Derek wants me to."

"Why?"

"To make more money."

"Hasn't changed much, has he?"

"Derek? He's changed a lot, since he's been taking acting lessons. Always quoting this pusbag of a teacher. A regular motormouth."

"Derek?" I couldn't believe it.

"The pusbag. And Derek too." Her eyes strayed to a clutch of young men in Wall Street suits and ties, drinking beer around a keg in front of Roebling's. "I think I'll quit. Tell Barf what he can do with his job and his Queen Anne pool and his sleazy evening gown."

"He wears an evening gown?"

"You saw the damned thing—he makes me wear it. Says it gives the joint class."

"If you quit, what'll you do? You got another job?"

"We'll be leaving soon, any day now, for the Coast."

"You want to live out there? Between the San Andreas Fault and the Pacific Ring of Fire?"

"Derek wants to try Hollywood."

Of course he would. What slob actor could resist what Hollywood had and Broadway hadn't—the chance, no matter how slight, of seeing himself in living color on a giant wraparound screen? And Derek, I thought grudgingly, had just the kind of crude peacockiness to make it out there. Had I found her, ironically, only to lose her again, and so quickly? The thought was depressing: the issue with Derek had to be resolved. The time had come to surmount caution. I had, moreover, a new and lofty confidence in myself, with a well-paying job and a semiluxurious pad. No longer a daft, untested boy, I was a man of carnal knowledge, of deft experience, of Homeric debaucheries (with only one woman, but who's counting?) in bogs, in haylofts, on the dungy turf of barns.

"What do you see in him?" I began. "I'd really like to know."

"Derek?"

"Who the hell else?"

"He's extremely good-looking," she said slyly.

"He's not much good looking after you."

"I can look after myself. Why don't you just lay off?"

"But why Derek, for Christ's sake?"

"I don't know. Maybe it's like being in a groove."

"A rut."

"I hate changes, you know?"

"You change constantly. It was only like yesterday you made it clear you wanted me to make love to you."

"I did? Well, a woman can want to make love to a man without wanting to spend the rest of her life with him."

"So change again. Dump Derek." It sounded as hollow as a slogan. Buy American. Eat Wheaties. Fight Cholesterol. "You're going to shipwreck your life," I warned her.

"Sure," she said sarcastically. "The girl stands on the burning deck with a noose around her neck."

"There's a touch of the poet in you. Only it's not funny."

"I think it's hilarious, the way you think you know everything."

"What I think—everything could have been so different. If you hadn't dumped me, we would have been spared the shock of seeing each other again."

"Don't be a douche bag," she said. "Who's shocked?"

A flight of pigeons darted and wheeled, totally indifferent to my troubles. Concentrating hard, I saw my father twice, first jogging down the street, then plucking a lobster out of a fish-market tank.

"Shit," I muttered.

She yawned. "Maybe," she added, "you'd better take me home."

On we trudged in silence, our last walk together. Outside a warehouse on Twelfth Street she took two keys from her purse and twice unlocked the steel-ribbed concrete door, as thick as a sluice gate.

"This," she said redundantly, "is home."

I peered into the filthy, foreboding maw of the building. "Home looks far from salubrious," I said unkindly.

"Where's Salubrious?" And without waiting for an answer, "Listen," she went on, impervious to everything but the crosscurrent of her own thoughts, "you want to come up?"

"I don't think so."

"Don't you want to see Abdul?"

"The only thing I'd like more than seeing Abdul is not seeing Derek."

"He talks about you all the time. Abdul. I swear."

Why? I thought. He misses our little tête-à-têtes? He's lonely in an alien land? He enjoys bugging Derek? Hell, I'd enjoy bugging Derek myself... and why not? It was another chance I'd never get again; it would provide a satisfactorily malevolent closure to an evening which, now that I realized romance was thoroughly dead, would afford no other gratification.

We stepped into the cumulative decay of a century's storage to an elevator that lurched upward through the depressingly yellow light, propelled by the worn teeth of a capricious ratchet. When it clanged to a halt I followed her down a dark corridor where hairy chunks of plaster hung precariously from the ceiling.

"I don't think this is a good idea," I insisted.

"Don't make such a big do out of it," Val said. "He won't bite you." She pressed a button; a bell rang shrilly. The door opened and I stood face to face with Derek. He stared at me with a glazed and warily belligerent look in his eyes. I thought he might bite me.

Home, as she called it, was a converted bin on the eleventh floor. Amend that—it hardly deserved the adjective—it was not converted to anything. The size of a walk-in closet, it was diminished by its emptiness. The furniture was no more than a smattering of flyspecks on the floor. Patches of damp distemper festered the walls, unrelieved by windows, unadorned by art. Something pale that resembled graveyard ivy drooped from a coffee tin, sharing the top of an orange crate with an electric fan that whirled despondently and wafted strange odors.

I knew, as soon as I crossed the threshold, that I was still on Derek's demolition list. He had nodded suspiciously, his eyes asquint, unsure but somehow unsurprised by my sudden materialization in the city, and sat stiffly on a war-surplus mattress in the farthest corner, putting as much distance between us as possible. Despite the void of space and the dim lighting, despite the upturned collar of the vast expanse of trenchcoat thrown over his shoulders, I could see that he had changed. There were lines in his face, crisscrosses of dry, chalky furrows that could have used three days of rain. The skin lacked resilience. He was still a plastic effigy of a young man, but a curious one in that at times, while that old surliness remained, the mouth quivered, and while he postured, that splendid torso, once so sculptured in spotless tennis shorts, took on the boneless slump of an exhausted workhorse.

Abdul, on the other hand, looked in fine fettle. He had bounced to his feet when I came in, greeting me warmly, bowing like a Chinatown merchant. And certainly I was glad to see his calm, handsome face.

"It is so good to see you," he had shouted, because a stereo shooting steel splinters of punk rock made the decibel level of a normal voice inaudible. He took my hand in both of his, like a sandwich, and led me to the only couch in that futile living room. "What have you been up to?" he asked, and I told him about my work and my newfound affluence. We talked, he, Valerie, and I, but it was Derek's sullenness that dominated. We were unpleasantly conscious of the aura he gave off, casting his usual blight, as sharp and lacerating as a predator's spoor. It demanded attention. Val killed the stereo and turned to him.

"Did you get the job?" she asked.

"No," Derek said. "I had a thick day of it."

She lowered the corners of her pretty mouth and clucked her tongue in sympathy. "You would have been so good as Jonathan."

"Yeah," he agreed. "I would have been great. I like those biblical things—Ten Commandments, Samson and Delilah, Prince Valiant..."

"Know who got the job?" Abdul asked.

"That asshole Bernie."

"Nepotism," Abdul said, and turning to me, "Bernie's Ernie the producer's twin brother."

"I thought I could trust Ernie," Derek said bitterly. "I thought he was a nice guy, not like some of those assholes always quoting the classics and all that shit."

"I thought he said you had the job," Valerie said. "I mean..."

"He did," Derek said. "He said, 'You got the job unless you do something terrible like set my brother's ass on fire.' Those were his exact words." His face was ashen, a somatic response to outrage. "I'd like to set *his* ass on fire," he added.

Val got to her feet and ever so quietly crossed the long room and sat down beside him, as if her nearness might heal the narcissistic wound. She brushed back an errant strand of his hair, a soft corrugation which refused to stay in place. "You'll get something soon," she crooned to him, and Abdul said, "Sure you will," and Val glowered at me, commanding my support, just to make it unanimous.

"Give yourself a little time," I found myself counseling. "You're in a business with a difficult entry level."

Derek's eyes were fixed steadfastly on blankness. "I've been acting for six months," he said.

Which should have given him ample time to regret it. Suddenly my counterfeit sympathy for him turned genuine, the poor lox, six months down the drain and nothing to look forward to but many an unsung season.

"He's doing just fine," Val cried stoutly. She patted his limp hand as though it were a dog. "He's already been up for a lot of stuff. He's had some parts."

"Walk-ons," he amended, enjoying our sympathy, for once on center stage. "But I'm going to make it," he promised us passionately.

It was an adolescent promise, about as probable as a landing on Pluto, and all the more pathetic because it was lodged in the body of a man whose dedication to his craft was so much greater than his ability to master it. America, I thought, America is the only country in the world where people are allowed more than one adolescence.

"The only question is," Derek was feeling better, "how am I going to hold out? Where's the money coming from?"

"You've got a job," Val reminded him.

"It interferes with my *real* work. It destroys my concentration."

"Soon you'll be going to Hollywood, you said."

"How, without money?"

"What do you do?" I asked, caught up in the drama.

"He's got this job," Val said, "screwing light bulbs onto the marquee of a theater."

Derek scowled. Evidently, twisting bulbs into sockets was not his métier. "It doesn't pay anything," he said. He looked at me hard, evaluating perhaps the depth of my compassion. I could guess what was coming: this mouse-brained mummer, this bulb-twister was about to hit me up for a contribution in the holy name of Art. I figured I'd better change the subject fast.

"How's it feel to be up there?" I asked.

"What do you mean," he asked, "up on a ladder?"

Val too stared at me, testing for guile.

"I mean as an actor. How do you control it?"

"You serious? You really want to know?"

I nodded somberly. "I think it's fascinating."

"Well," he said, "first of all, you got to maintain the intensity level..." It was as if my question had pumped adrenaline into an otherwise sluggish metabolism. At once he shifted into overdrive, and like an excitable kid suddenly aware that all the wonders of the world were open before him, he went on and on, talking in wrinkles about elective energy, postinternalization, subtextual environments, private moments, the arc of character, pivotal pressures, submerged configurations, the identity of opposites, the parabola of change, the negation of the negation, the contribution of the deconstructionists at Yale, and the importance of getting down on all fours and looking at it from the audience's point of view. He was wired on words, a diarrhea of words, evacuated, incredibly, by a man whose mode of expression had never been speech. His cosmic insights about acting were neither plausible nor convincing, yet Val and Abdul listened like figures on a frieze, slaves to his shallow enchantment. Perhaps it was the way he did it: Derek took his glitter very seriously, pausing at times to rivet his eyes on some blazing but spectral manifestation of quintessential truth, carving the air with ill-defined, semaphoric gestures, punctuating his sentences with a cigarette before inhaling it (as if he were indeed onstage, up to his ass in Noel Coward), and then going still all over, as if to the beckoning call of a distant trumpet, as he posed for Mount Rushmore.

His monologue made a few things incontrovertible: Derek obviously derived a kind of spiritual uplift from his "real" work; he was deeply stimulated by the self-evident, so long as it was couched in a specialist vocabulary—he seemed to think that his blather clarified some elegant and abstruse scientific law; he could throughout his cumbersome recital scarcely disguise his pity for anyone so unfortunate as not to be a performer.

"And what you got to realize," he rattled on, "is that the basic symbol, what you call the prototype, of our culture, is the actor. We tell you people how to conduct yourselves, how to respond to the phases and stages of life and death, how to express courage and fear, how to care, how to make love and make jokes and make good. We are 'the engineers of the human soul'—

Joseph Stalin said that." It was good to know he was quoting a man who had never been wrong in his whole life.

The insolence of this pygmy. His very insignificance blinded him to the comprehension of his drive toward acting—the chance to lead many lives, with each incarnation infinitely richer, more exciting, more fulfilling than his own.

"And another thing," he was saying, his voice shrill with messianic fervor, "we have the responsibility of bringing culture to the people. To bring something of value to their drab lives."

I felt my face go hot with embarrassment and repugnance just listening to this shit, but mercifully the show was over. Derek sat there in a spotlight of silence, his head bowed with false modesty, like a superstar taking his eighteenth curtain call.

"That was wonderful," Val said.

"Thank you." His lips formed the words, no more than a whisper. It was in its way another form of insolence, the gratuitous insolence of an actor who has never learned that condescension, arrogance, and generally bad manners are not enough, coupled somehow with the necessary insolence of the benevolent king to the canaille, of the Enlightened to the dumb civilian-serf. It was the way you treat autograph hounds in Hollywood.

"That's why," he went on with a courageous little smile, "it's important that I keep going with my career."

"Absolutely," she said. "Someday you'll look back on these times and laugh."

"I want to laugh now," he said. "How am I ever going to reach that point, unless..." he raised his head, confronting her. "You decide about that contest?" he asked.

"No," she said, "not yet."

"If it's too much to ask..."

"No," she said, "I'll probably do it."

"When?" he persisted. "The entry blank's been around here for two weeks. It's turning brown."

"What contest?" I asked.

"The Wet T-shirt Tournament," Derek said, "at the Arm Pit Bar and Grill. Three hundred clams to the winner." He turned to Valerie. "You'd be a shoo-in," he said.

She shrugged her shoulders inconclusively.

"What about the bull pen?" he pressed on. "Where you work?"

"No," she said, "that's out."

"Then," he threatened, "I'll get the money myself." He blew a long-suffering sigh in her face. "Christ," he went on, "I can't depend on you for anything."

With remarkable composure she left his side and crossed the room.

"Don't walk away when I'm talking to you."

"You make me feel awkward." Her mouth quickened at the corners. She seemed to cringe, menaced by his flash point.

It was painful, listening to the rasp of his bullying voice, the vulnerability of hers. I knew what would happen: he'd press her, she'd resist, he'd tighten the thumbscrews, she'd comply, until once more he'd become the navel of her world. I had seen it all before, and I didn't want to see it again. I got to my feet. Perhaps they'd have the civility to effect a brief armistice until I was out the door.

But no. "All I want is a little cooperation and," he asked, "what do I get?"

"You get every damned cent I make."

"What you make is laughable. *You're* laughable."

"Don't say that," she warned, "don't laugh at me."

"Ha ha," he countered, defiantly.

"You think I don't know why you're pissed off?"

"I'm pissed off because I can't even ask a simple favor."

"That's it. What you call a simple favor. You're pissed off because of Ernie."

"That too. Son of a bitch promised..."

"Because of what *you* promised Ernie. You think I'm so stupid I don't know Ernie wanted to fuck me?"

"That's something to be proud of? Ernie'd fuck a snake if you held its head."

"You think I don't know you tried to pimp for me? To get that lousy job."

"I don't need you to get me jobs. Or for anything else. There's enough accommodating cunt here and in Hollywood just waiting to be plowed."

"Maybe if you had a decent job you'd have something more to think about than telling me what to do."

Shock waves were looping and gyring all over the warehouse. His anger burgeoned, I think, from frustration about work and insolvency, but he also seemed imperiled by my unannunciated appearance. In my upward mobility threads, I seemed to have imposed some imprecise threat on him. He'd glance at me furtively, then look quickly away, as if, once I was out of his purview, I no longer existed. Much of the time he wore a troubled frown of perplexity or discomfiture—why in the name of Sweet Jesus had Valerie reeled me home with her? Furious with blocked impulse and unanswered questions, Derek made a lame attempt to regain the offensive: "Shut the hell up," he snarled.

"Not yet," she snarled back. "Not till I tell you about your whining, your bullying, your self-pity, your flexing your abs in front of a mirror."

"Can't you for Christ's sakes just listen?"

"To you? Never!" She was a volcano on erupt, a tigress sniffing blood. "Never," she repeated, "never, never, never. And I'm not finished with you. With you brushing your hair for hours, like it's some kind of goddam show dog. Scratching your nuts in ecstasy like King Kong with fleas. Hell with you!"

"Hell with you!" he yelled, running out of source material. "That's enough of your shit."

"Not half enough," she said with a reckless quiver of pleasure. Seething with fed-up-edness, she flounced to the far end of the rookery, where her wardrobe on three or four metal hangers was suspended from a nail in the wall. She snapped back the lid of a cardboard carton (with the sound of the tether she seemed to have reached the end of), the repository of her shoes, a clutch of handbags. She stuffed a dress, a pair of slacks, two blouses, and a trenchcoat into the box, disappeared behind a door, came back, and dropped comb and brush, toothpaste and toothbrush on top of them.

She said, "You want to carry this?" It was seconds before I realized she was talking to me, and still I wasn't sure.

"What?" I said.

"You coming with me or not?" she asked angrily.

Sermon for today: Pivotal opportunities arise when you least expect them. Be Prepared.

TWENTY-FOUR

APPOINTMENT IN COPROLIABAD

Happiness, it has been observed, is best achieved by those who have been most unhappy heretofore. So it was with me. The murkiness of my life gave way to felicity; I couldn't get enough of her. Like a passionate pilgrim eager to explore every mysterious inch of Mecca, I journeyed to that holy of holies morning, noon, and night, and with a constancy that defied the clock. We'd go to bed early, to wake at dawn, and still I'd be late for work. I'd dash home at eventide, and to bed again. Most days of the week I'd bop in for a long lunch, so to speak. We gave that bed blisters, and through some startling convolutions of our bodies, nothing we ever did didn't work. As the good times escalated, I learned among other sexual arcana that coitus could be a nonadversarial sport.

We did get on together. I gave her my total and flawless attention, showing possibly an excess of chivalry. She treated me with a kind of grave solicitude that far exceeded the niggardly esteem she had granted long, long ago to the grammarian-mathematician-linguist-poet who did her homework. Thus, and quite unconsciously, a pattern of intimacy was set, something mysterious, intricate, and wonderful beyond the Dionysian frenzy of the bed. Fucking can lead to fondling.

Valerie had quit her job. She never even went back to collect the few days' pay owed her. She kept herself busy, puttering around the flat when I wasn't there, watching TV, painting her toenails, reading *Screw* magazine. We put in a supply of her favorite porno comics from which, through delicate stages, I weaned her. First to a thick little gem of a book called *Great Erotic Moments in World Literature,* then *Lady Chatterley* and *Ada,* until one watershed day, bursting through the door for my noontide pick-me-up, I found her chortling over *Pride and Prejudice.* A late bloomer, her father had called her, and now in budding she showed the same propensity for literature that had earlier propelled her to the secret recesses of effortless sensuality.

And there was, as she curled up bonelessly around a book, an extra, added attraction, possibly because it came as such a surprise: she read faster than the blink of an eye.

It is not my intention to hyperbolize her catalog of endowments, but she also set a fine table—gourmet pastrami on rye, garnished with plenty of olives, from the Stage Door Deli. Pepperoni pizza from La Stitichezza. Dim sum from the Yellow Peril. I'd come home at night, in from the gridlocked streets with their cacophony of horns, sirens, klaxons, and all was serene with her presence. "I'm home," I'd call, broadcasting the obvious. If in my haste to get to her I'd bang into furniture, knock over a vase or two, I'd hear not the discord of breakage but the vibrato of violins.

Happiness when sustained too long in print can rightly be construed as sappiness, and so I'll close the Book of Val. Anyway, my precarious lease on rapture, despite all my bleating about it, was short lived.

Joseph Grady in his prescriptive threads of power—black suit, white shirt, maroon silk tie—sat behind the desk in his office nursing a double martini. The curtains were drawn, and in the tinted pallor of evening he had the secretive air of living inwardly. The hooded eyes had the questing look of a hawk, the prominent hooked nose seemed to sniff suspiciously at shadows in the still, stifling aridity of the room. Although a staunch advocate of Progress in human affairs, Joseph Grady had little faith in air conditioning.

"Have a sundowner," he said, pouring for me from a silver and crystal carafe. "It's time to talk."

He got up, adjusting the drapes behind him where a needle of light seeped through. "What do you know about Assama, Iraq?" he asked.

"Nothing much."

"That's where Abdul al Sadr was from."

I shrugged. "I know about Abdul. What about Assama?"

He nodded. "There's nothing much to know. It's an abysmally backward blob of a desert," he declared glumly, "in abysmally backward Iraq." He snared the martini from his desk and carted it safely to a coffee table. He eased himself into a burnished leather chair beside it.

"The Assamans need tutelage," he went on. "It's our duty, our moral obligation, to lend a hand. They need..." He paused, seeking the apposite phrase. "They need some kind of charismatic enterprise to revive their dead economy. They have it, but they don't know they have it, because they're so damned *un*enterprising."

He poured himself another jolt and refilled my glass. He gulped his, vexed, as though it were medicine. "That damned sheik warlord, whatever he is, won't allow investment capital onto his turf, not even an exploratory trade delegation."

"Well," I said, "there's a war going on."

"For a while he did, but his minister of finance—that's a hoot—fellow named Pachachi, is a fool. And your friend Abdul's father, the stumblebum who calls himself king, is happy with handouts from the so-called coalition forces."

"What is this charismatic enterprise they have and don't know it? Something from the days before the war?"

"The Western entrepreneurs before the war were looking for oil and minerals," he said, "and were unaware of the riches all around them."

"You got any olives?"

"Olives? No."

"That's okay. But how do you know?"

"That I don't have any olives?"

"That these riches exist? Abdul tell you?"

"Abdul," he said, annoyed. "If Abdul had a chronometer, he wouldn't tell me the time. It was *because* I knew that I tried to be his friend. To help him help his country—when the time comes."

"Is he aware of these riches?"

"He is as oblivious to them as were the oilmen and the mineralogists."

"You pointed it out to him?"

"I never got that far. I never got anywhere."

"How did you learn about it?"

"I believe I told you RAT owns and publishes an international, interdenominational church quarterly. When I was young, and climbing the corporate ladder, I was for a time its editor. One day, across my desk came a piece submitted by a young clergyman in the Moravian Church, so fraught with possibilities that I bought it. And killed it."

"Killed it?"

"Killed it. Deep-sixed it. In the pious eyes of the Moravians it was no more than an amusing exercise in exotic trivia. But I found it to be a clear and unmistakable statement of great significance to UGH, our parent organization."

"What was the piece about?"

"Assama."

"And its riches?"

"And its riches." He fell silent, long enough for me to sip my martini until it was gone. Immediately he refilled the long-stemmed glass, but in that measureless passage of time, that lifeless, dry, unconditioned air, a curious psychological impasse seemed to have clotted the scenario and dampened its dialogue. I had been summoned to be told… something. Now Grady was concealing it, and the closer he came to the subject the more he seemed under some self-imposed prescription to avoid it.

I asked, "Aren't you going to tell me what it is?"

No answer. His sleek hawk eyes were bright but empty, as though they were buttons and he were stuffed and mounted, a miracle of taxidermy.

"I like a good mystery," I went on placidly, "but only if I'm in on it. If you'd care to clarify, fine; if not," I got to my feet, "I'll just leave."

"No," he said, galvanized at last, waving me back to my chair. "I… I must swear you to secrecy. There's a fortune at stake."

"I swear."

"On your father's grave."

"On my father's grave. If I ever find it."

His eyes went sharp and found mine in the dusk. Across the room he looked like a figure etched in frosted glass.

"The missionaries of the Moravian Church," he began, "established a foothold in Greece in 1737. It wasn't long afterward, as evangelical history goes, that they pushed east into Turkey, then southeast into what is now Syria and Iraq.

"Among the more intrepid of them was Johann Durchfall, who, after much hardship and stormy weather, stumbled, on Whitsuntide 1762, onto a land the ancient Romans had abandoned sixteen hundred years earlier after a decade of unsuccessful colonization. They had called it Putoria; territorially it's what we know today as Assama.

"Durchfall was a man of heroic design, with a spirit for daring as well as righteousness—something of an adventurer. He was other things as well—he had to be to survive. An accomplished carpenter, with a rudimentary knowledge of eighteenth-century medicine, which didn't help him much—or perhaps it did—for not unlike Martin Luther he suffered from some gastrointestinal malady. Perhaps it was his interest in carpentry that provided his basic enthusiasm for Putoria, for what he found there was for him infinitely more fascinating than what he'd gone to do. In his journals he speaks of his 'divine calling,' of the joy of 'spreading the Word of the Kingdom' by one as 'humble and obscure' as himself, of his fervent hope that the rude and barbarous Putorians 'would fall like ripe fruit before the gentle winds of the Gospel.' He also delighted in being what evangelists had to be—farmer, brickmaker, a builder of houses and churches for his converts as well as himself.

"But he soon discovered that none of these attributes was of any use in Putoria. His parishioners, if such they could be called, repelled every aspect of the culture he tried to introduce by the simplest and most effective countermeasure: they ignored him. Soon he turned, not too reluctantly one would guess, to that element of Putorian life which interested him most: it is to the architecture that he devotes most of his writings. And of course it was the architecture that appealed to me, on that day when as a curiosity his journals appeared on my desk in Chicago.

"The text was astonishing, with vivid descriptions, originally in a terse, clear German, and clean three-dimensional drawings of structures as high as ten stories (and this in 1763) in a domed and gracefully rounded style as neat and balanced as a beehive."

He paused again, knocking back his fourth martini. "And all of them," he said in a peculiarly hushed voice, "fashioned not of brick and mortar, not of wood and stone but of mud and straw and human feces and…"

"I'm not quite clear. You're talking excrement?"

"I'm talking human feces," he repeated, "and one other ingredient."

"Why excrement?"

"Why? Maybe a psychological anthropologist could tell you. All I know, hell, in early childhood kids seem to find pleasure in anal smearing, messing with their own excrement. It's a precious part of themselves, they hate to let go of it."

He bit another chunk out of his martini. "Some people carry this retentiveness into manhood. Sculptors, some say, sublimate it into art. The Assamans sublimated it into architecture—their beehive buildings look like neat piles of shit. You know what they call them? *Nagamat garas.* Which more or less means, according to Durchfall, 'It-comes-out-of-you, you-go-inside-it.'"

"How much excrement goes into the compound?"

"How much? Only the Assamans know—probably a lot. But there's one other ingredient, the most important in the mix. The magical agglutinate that binds it together."

"What's that?"

"That's what we've got to find out."

"*We...?*"

"Look," he said, "costs of materials have skyrocketed, but here we have a product that has withstood the ravages of time and the elements, an innovative substance that costs practically nothing to produce, and the supply is unlimited—God knows the world is full of mud, straw, and shit. The yield can be fireproofed, insulated, deodorized, drilled, painted, glued, sawed into bricks. All we have to do is find that one elusive ingredient that makes it work. Then we set up processing plants from here to Timbuktu and watch the money roll in."

"You keep saying 'we'..."

"I'm offering you the chance of a lifetime. If you're the red-blooded, hell-for-leather, idealistic American I think you are, here's your chance to combine benevolence and the accumulation of wealth beyond a sultan's dreams, along with a niche in the highest echelons of RAT while you're still young enough to enjoy it. Shall I go on?"

"Please do."

"Now. Abdul, of course, is the key to the acquisition of BRIT..."

"Of what?"

"BRIT. Appellation I coined, compounding BRICKS and—"

"What do you want me to do?"

"I want you to renew your contact with him, so we—you and I—can gain access to Assama."

"What about the war?"

"That's not a problem. All kinds of specialists have access to Iraq."

"What about Abdul's old man who won't let anybody in?"

"We could get around him, I'm sure, if Abdul were on our side."

"How do we get around Abdul?"

"That, son, is entirely up to you. Woo him with soft rhetoric..."

"That didn't get you anywhere."

"Promise him anything..."

"I need guidelines."

"I'd prefer not to indulge in premature specificity. However, you might tell him we're offering a feasibility study of his country's economic potential, absolutely free. Or tell him RAT is prepared to draft him a loan at minimal interest, to be diverted toward any endeavor he might endorse."

He bent over and raised a pant leg, exposing a marbleized calf, zinc white and varicose veined. He tugged on a sock. He wore, of all things, scarlet elastic garters.

"On a more personal level," he said, "we'll donate whatever it takes to his favorite charity, or perhaps he'd find solace in a retainer from the company, or a network of roads to unify his tribally sundered country, or a fleet of Ferraris.

"Sound him out, son," he rattled on, "confect your own list of initiatives, indulgences, enticements, so long as one of them is irresistible."

"Why the camouflage?" I asked. "I mean—is all this Byzantine maneuvering necessary? Why not tell him what you want, how he could benefit from it, draw up a contract..."

"Because," he said, "business has its own realities. Financial acquisitions require safeguards and imperatives which lesser minds might construe as devious. And when trust is lacking..."

"You don't trust Abdul?"

"No. And I've already told you he doesn't trust me. Moreover, we at UGH have had considerable experience with third-world nations. We've invested money, we've worked our brains to the bone, and as soon as our investment shows signs of paying off, the sons of bitches expropriate it. If you think my approach is unethical, remember all ethics are situational."

"Not any ethical system I'm aware of."

He watched me with studied forbearance. "I gather you don't approve," he said.

He gathered right; my disapproval must have been written all over my face. With mockery in his voice he said, "Dear, dear. How mighty is our moral wrath."

He shrugged and adjusted the lapels of his jacket. "Or is it because you find dealing in evacuative biodegradables," he smiled impishly, "or, if you prefer, human shit—repellant?" He shook his head, disappointed in me. "I thought you'd be above that sort of daintiness. As for myself," he went on, "*humani nihil a me alienum puto.*"

Alien to me was the discomforting awareness that my education was being expanded by a teacher whose twin disciplines were plunder and larceny. And he was asking me to become his coconspirator.

I said nothing, sitting there, blinking stupidly in the half-light, muddled by his martinis, staggered by the breadth of the man's interests—BRIT in Assama, gong-bashing in Maryland—intrigued by his chameleonlike ability to switch commitments from one all-consuming cause to another, but most of all marveling at the power of coincidence which shapes all our lives, those odd little accidents only fate is shameless enough to concoct. If the snapping whip of chance and an errant father had not driven me to Yale and to Armbruster and to Chatterton and to Grady and to Valerie in that porn shop under the Brooklyn Bridge...

And suddenly it hit me: accident played little part in the deliberate progression of events since the day I met Grady. I was his pawn, an instrument played by the virtuoso in his compulsion to outflank and manipulate Abdul.

"...thought there was between us a deep sense of cohesion..."

It was to cultivate Abdul that Grady had come to Chatterton's place.

"...relied on you to serve as my intervention with the young heir to Assama..."

To reach Abdul, Grady had brought me to New York, then steered me to Valerie and thence back to Abdul.

"...hoping you'd recognize a kindred spirit, an altruism we share..."

The dedication of the man was awesome, equaled only by the range of his espionage.

"…to work with me, shoulder to shoulder, pressing for the eventual good to spring from our agenda…"

It was a chilling discovery. I felt the resentment of the awakened dupe.

"…great responsibility, I know, going the extra mile to help Assama emerge from her cocoon and become a model of modernity, and to supply affordable housing for the world's ill-housed masses…"

I won't go along with this, I promised myself. I was always making promises to myself that I didn't keep, but not this time.

"…a time for aggressive commitment. You can't steal second with a foot on first…"

Certainly the operative if unconsciously motivated word of his sporty little apothegm was *steal.*

"…so, indeed, if I'm to be remembered at all, I'd like it to be as a humanitarian, a champion of the poor. Are you a Maoist?"

"Me? What made you think…?"

"It crossed my mind—perhaps your resistance derives from an ideological allegiance to the side of the Chinese imperialists. If you'd prefer their infiltration of Assama to ours…"

"That's not the case."

"Something of a more personal nature, then? A deep, eccentric antagonism to the accumulation of wealth? There are people like that, you know. Something born of a peculiar need to identify with an impecunious father, perhaps."

The acquisition of money, which arguably festers and fouls all our dreams, I had already learned to appreciate. I've found that its disadvantages were invariably exaggerated. What wonders a monumental bank account could accomplish! I could buy my mother a magazine to publish nobody's poems but hers. I could hire a troop of detectives to find my father. I could buy him tenure somewhere—hell, I could buy him a small but distinguished university. As for Valerie—the thought brought me up short. There are women whose desires run toward silks and jewels and the feathers and furs and hides of any number of birds and beasts, mostly the endangered ones. But Valerie… I hadn't the least idea what she might want. She never asked for anything, never fancied anything more than clean sheets and a club sandwich.

The moment of fantasy was over. "I'm afraid," I said, "you'll have to go that extra mile without me."

"Why?" he asked. "Why are you shying away?"

I was shying away from him and his duplicity. Grady's kind of money would cost too much. It was hardly the time for a true confession, but I did have a highly legitimate reason for my reluctance.

"You mess around Iraq these days," I said, "you're flirting with a Purple Heart."

"What are you talking about?"

"About a large percentage of two hundred twenty-five million people who think we are the Great Satan."

"Not in Assama, where ninety-five percent believe in some kind of off-beat animism. Or nothing at all."

"That leaves about five percent eager to blowtorch their American bene-factors, among whom I don't wish to be included. So you want me to turn in the key to the men's room?"

"Not quite yet," he said. "Think it over for a day or two."

He just wouldn't roll over. Neither would I. Subject closed.

She lay on her belly, stripped down to a pair of unbuttoned blue jeans, as I massaged the inspired slim valley of her spine. Palpation stimulates, all the more so when the masseur pauses momentarily to nip from a tapering green bottle of gewürztraminer.

Over her shoulder she asked, "No? You said 'No'?" It wasn't a question, it was a criticism. "Did you cave in," she added, "or did you bug out?"

"Neither," I said. "I simply lost my job. It was a question of ethics, per-sonal accountability."

"I guess it's good to be ethical," she admitted, sitting up, "it's just an awful lot of trouble."

"Yeah," I said, "I got this kind of internal monitor..."

"Still small voice?"

"I don't enjoy it..."

"Neither do I." She squirmed into her T-shirt. "Jesus," she said, "I hate this place. I hated it when I got here, and nothing has happened since to make me change my mind."

"Prefer your old man's funhouse?"

"That wasn't exactly heaven either—don't be such a smart-ass. I've never lived in one goddam place I've ever liked. Wouldn't you like to haul out of here?"

The answer emphatically was yes. Wherever I'd lived, it was always too much suburb or too much farm, and New York was still another, nastier ecosystem, unique with its crackling energy, its garbage, and its snarling, bursting discord. It was indeed time for a dignified withdrawal, for further exploration.

"We'll find a place," I told her. "I'll get another job."

"Where?" she demanded. "Doing what? You talk about ethics," she went on, "don't you understand? Wherever you work they sock it to you. That's what drives me around the hill."

"You're opting for Iraq?"

"I'd like to give it a shot. Get out of the whole fucking country in one fell swoop."

"You think Assama's the end of the rainbow?"

"There's *no* end of the rainbow. But maybe we could pick up a bundle, fast, and retire early from the goddam human race. Maybe we could buy an island or something."

"You talk like Grady—ends justifying means."

"That's because we're both more realistic than you…"

"But Assama, for God's sake? It's risky."

"Any more risky than eating a clam in New York? Just what do you know about the place?"

"I did a little research in the *Britannica,* back in the fun house attic, when I found out it was where Abdul came from. There's no running water, hot or cold. No electricity. Not one indoor toilet."

"There must be something…"

"Sure. Malnutrition, scurvy, dengue, jaundice—Christ, the diseases read like a textbook on pathology."

"Isn't that a challenge? You could be a big help to those people by introducing modern medicine. All you got to do—get off your ethical ass and insist that Grady take along a medical team."

It took all of a minute before I nodded in approbation at the invincibility of her logic. But not without a certain queasy disturbance attending the acknowledgment that she had so easily skewered the meat of my argument. Not that logic had much to do with it. I had grave doubts about the road I was taking. But if she wanted Assama, I'd just have to get us there. Hell, if she had wanted the moon, I'd have sat in my old tuba and flown into space.

Subject reopened.

* * *

"So he wants to steal into my country." Abdul al Sadr grinned unpleasantly. "What he really wants is to *steal* my country."

"He's offering…"

"You told me. He's offering toys."

"…and medical aid."

"I'm not interested in a few doctors and a carton of antibiotics. For Assama that's like charging hell with a bucket of water. What ails us is poverty. Cure that and we'll buy our own pills."

"Don't you have to begin somewhere?"

"Where we have to begin is with electrification, which your country's been promising us since the war began. We have to develop our own industry, and I don't mean beads and bangles and imitation weapons for the walls of American rumpus rooms. What I want," he crossed the room to lean over Val and empty her ashtray, "and you can tell Grady to write it down with a grease pencil on his refrigerator door—what I want is nuclear power. And I'll settle for nothing less." He smiled at her. "How about a game of checkers?" he asked.

Subject closed.

Joseph Grady browed his glasses, narrowed his eyes, pursed his lips. "Nuclear energy for Assama…" He snorted scornfully.

I said, "I know it's absurd, but…"

"Nothing's impossible," Grady said. "It would require a whole gamut of procedures." He got to his feet, pacing. "It would take some doing," he said, "but I happen to have a good friend who just might be able to bring it off."

Subject reopened.

The Marine in dress blues snapped to attention. We were ushered down a succession of corridors by a series of escorts to a final door. Behind it a familiar voice answered our knock with a booming "Come in."

At a suspiciously neat desk sat a large, heavy-shouldered man, baring his perfect teeth in greeting to Grady. "Bum diddily bum diddily bum bum bum," vocalized the big-shouldered man, beating out a tattoo of jungle drums with the palms of his hands on the top of his desk. He got up and reached out.

"Hey, Joe," he said, shaking Grady's hand, "how they hanging?"

"Fine, Mr. President," Grady said. "You're looking fit."

"Yeah," said the President, "I feel fine as a little ole frog with his hair parted four ways."

Grady introduced me as his executive assistant, as if that were sufficient reason for my presence. Which it was not. I had been deputized by Abdul, who trusted neither Grady nor the President. "I am suspicious of great men," Abdul had told me, "and these two are no exception."

"So you're off to Africa," the President said, grinning with robust good humor, "on the trail of jungle bunnies. You want to bring 'em back alive? Corner the market on black slavery? What can I do to help?"

"May I speak frankly, Mr. President?"

"Haven't you always? Go ahead, Joe."

"Well, sir, for a long time now I've been disturbed about Washington's diminished credibility in Assama."

"First things first," the President said. "Where the hell is Assama?"

Geography, evidently, was not his strong suit. Perhaps it was just another deplorable example of the failure of our schools to teach the subject; nevertheless, Grady was prepared for the eventuality. He took from the pocket of his dark suit a map of Iraq, spread it, pointed.

"That the place?" the President said. "It's just a lousy province and it looks like a goddam chicken."

"Assama," Grady said, "is a glittering geopolitical prize. In the difficult days ahead, I know you don't want to find it's fallen into the terrorist orbit."

The President frowned. "The Iraqis," he said with slow emphasis, "are our good friends. The only thing I'd like to find in their orbit are those damned undetectable weapons of mass destruction. I know they're still buried in some hole somewhere."

Frowning or grinning, he spoke in that bourbon-and-branch baritone, renowned for his State of the Union speeches, his justly famous jokes with journalists, his congratulatory messages to winners of the World Series, the Super Bowl and the Westminster dog show. I felt the weight of the man's magic.

"I'm speaking," Grady insisted, "of any thug element that might view with antagonism the expansion of our freedom and our markets, our attempt to build a democratic world for the private sector."

For a moment the President did not reply. He brushed back his splendid mass of dyed hair; he was *thinking*. He touched one of a battery of buttons on a console beside the desk. A subdued grinding of little gears spawned a chain reaction: the Great Seal of the USA sank like the setting sun from its perch on a wall to reveal a backboard from which slowly descended a metal-rimmed basket and an attached net. The President reached down into the leg-well of his desk and came up with a basketball. He dribbled around the desk and fired a seventeen-foot fallaway jumper. The movement was graceless, inelegant—the lurch of a cow tripping over a rock. But the ball swished through the net. I couldn't help but admire him. He recovered the ball, dribbled to the far corner, shot again. But this time it crashed off the back of the rim, bounced in a high arc, and landed on the keyboard of a computer. The screen was shot with lights and glitches. On the video display appeared a message: *This is the Duty Officer. Are you requesting emergency access to Turkmenistan? Over.*

The President pecked out his reply: *Get lost.* He slammed a switch and the instrument went to gray. Turning to Grady, "About Assara," he said, "what are you trying to say? Just remember," he cautioned, "it has to be cost effective."

Grady's face went grave with the solemn resolve usually associated with those granitic posters flogging patriotism.

"I think, sir," he said selflessly, "we must stand by our friends."

"Friends? In fucking Assoko?"

"We must create labor-intensive jobs for these people, just as we've done for our accomplished friends in South Korea, Taiwan..."

"What can these people do?" The President's voice was etched with acid. "I've never heard of 'em doing anything, so their accomplishments must be a well-kept secret."

"We can help them mobilize what resources they have, and they're a resourceful people. What they need is encouragement."

"What kind of encouragement?" The President was wary.

"We must build an infrastructure for the province. In order to produce, they need electrification."

"They'll get it in good time. For Christ sakes, we still haven't got enough wattage or voltage or whatever the hell in Baghdad. So why have we got to kick Assoria to the head of the line?"

"Because, sir, we need them more than they need us. Strategically."

"Run that by me again?"

"We could use a nuclear component."

"Now, J for just-a-minute, Joe. You say nuclear?"

"Yes sir. For the generation of electrical power," Grady repeated. "It's what's needed to stabilize the region."

"It's madness," the President said, "to spread that nuclear stuff around. Add a trigger to it and we'll all be fissioned and fusioned, vaporized."

"Only," Grady reminded him, "if you add the trigger. Nobody's adding the trigger."

The President's handsome, craggy face canted to one side, an attitude familiar to the readers of the world's illustrated gazettes; evidence, it was claimed, of cerebration. He blinked a few times before he said, "Nuclear is out. It's impossible."

"Is it?" Grady asked reasonably. "That's what you said when I told you we were raising fifty million dollars to get you elected."

"Christ sakes, we simply can't do it."

"That's what our Board said when I came to them for the fifty big ones."

The President rearranged his face to say something. He stared off into space, looking for a teleprompter.

"We intend to at least match it," Grady purred, "when you're up for reelection."

"That's a whole different kettle of fish," the President said. "Things like that—contributions to your Party and its presidential nominee—that's what makes America great." For emphasis he opened a desk drawer and snared a baseball. As he massaged the horsehide, "But you're talking dual-use dooms-day material which an international body of Boy Scouts will scrutinize and, I guarantee, condemn. There are certain procedures set down for the peaceful use of atomic energy. Any transfer of technology has to be approved by the whatchamacallit. You know..."

"The Nuclear Regulatory Commission and the Department of Energy."

"Right," the President said. For emphasis he whipped the baseball at the backboard, missed by ten feet, hit a portrait of Millard Fillmore in the teeth. He reached down into the desk well and came up with a bowling ball. Christ, I thought, if he throws *that*...

"And," the President went on, "we'd have to get the approval of the Limeys and the Frogs and the Krauts and the Russkies and the good Lord knows who else, particularly now that they're all back in Iraq, although they all of 'em owe me a favor. As for the International Atomic Energy Agency, I know a thing or two about the director general to make him my slave."

"Then, what, sir, is the problem?"

For a long moment the President was silent. He dropped the bowling ball back in the well with a major thonk and then a few minor ones. He said, "What is it, Joe?"

"What's what, sir?"

"What's in it for you?"

Grady's jaw squared like General MacArthur's and his eyes locked with the President's. He said, "I don't quite know how to say this, sir, but in this age of cynicism and uncertainty, I have a deep commitment to my country."

I fell off my chair. Grady helped me to my feet.

"I don't see the patriotism in supplying thermonuclear power to a swarm of scroungers in bedsheets," the President said, "so let's just forget..."

Then a curious thing happened. The President's eyes took on a fierce glow, as if he were suddenly stricken by awe. He whispered, "By God, that's brilliant."

Grady said, "Yes," modestly but vaguely, because he didn't know what the President was talking about.

"That's pretty damned smart," the President said. "Smart *and* patriotic—lemme see if I read you completely." He paused, gathering his thoughts, and then, "People are still saying we went into Iraq for WMDs, which was a wild goose because we didn't even find a hill of beans. But if we ship those Assamies some kind of a nuke power plant, and things get stickier, we can always say that they're in the WMD business—proof at last to win American hearts and minds..."

"...and the reelection," Grady added.

I flopped off the chair again, like an exhausted old dog. Still on the floor I heard myself saying, "I don't think that's what Mr. Grady had in mind."

"That's precisely what I had in mind," Grady said, staring me down with a basilisk's fiery eye.

"Still," the President said, "if the word gets out, I'd be thrown to the wolves by every hyena on the Hill, by every nitpicking blabbermouth in the press. So we have to give them a head-and-shoulder fake before we run with the ball. We've got to make it crystal clear, if any of those bastards start goosing me with a cattle prod, that our thrust is humanitarian as it is in the rest of Iraq—reaching out to help our brown brothers. So the question is, how are we going to get you to Asexual?"

"Mr. President," Grady said, "why not create a back channel? I could go to Assama with a few atomic specialists, to study the area's potential for economic growth, then..."

"Back channels are out," the President cut him short. "Like I said, all you need is some shlub to blow the whistle and my nuts are in the wringer. What we need, just in case, is some manifestation of goodwill." For a moment he whistled aimlessly, discordantly, deep in thought. Then, "These Assos big, tall guys?"

"Not particularly. Why, sir?"

"I just had a wild hair. Like maybe we could say you were coaching a basketball team or something."

A moment of silence; he and Grady seemed equally at a loss to come up with a solution.

"Well," said the President, taking a football from his cornucopia, "I've got to get back to work."

I snapped to my feet, glad to be dismissed. Grady hesitated, drifting slowly, reluctantly to the door. There he halted, turned, and said, "What about..."

The President eyed him impatiently.

"What about," Grady went on, "a scientific expedition?"

"Such as?"

"I know a man—it would be perfect—a man, formerly a distinguished university professor..."

"I don't trust professors. They're all of them full of shit, a bunch of garbage."

"This one is totally innocuous. He has some sort of inoffensive project studying acoustics. He could front for us, and he wouldn't even know he was doing it."

"He's stupid?"

"Naïve. Zealously naïve."

"What's in it for him?"

"He needs funding. And a place to establish his laboratory."

"How much would that cost?"

"Nothing, sir. I'll take care of it."

The President toyed with his football, tossing it high in a tight spiral, catching it with one hand. Then: "That's interesting," he said, "why don't you sound him out?"

"I'd be honored to."

"I hope it works," the President said. "Maybe I'll drop in on you down there. I always wanted to see the Taj Mahal by moonlight."

We rode down Connecticut Avenue in silence. At a red light I stared out the window of the stretch. A smattering of pickets filed past some rhetorical monument, carrying anti-nuke placards, shouting slogans strapped to sandwich boards exhorting the administration to get out of Iraq. The light changed. Grady said, "I know what you're thinking. Lofty thoughts."

"That friend of yours wants to pin WMDs on the Iraqis. And you're supplying the blueprint."

Grady fingered a chrome switch above an armrest and a soundproof window rose snugly, isolating us from the driver.

"What is it *you* want?" he asked. "How can I help *you* achieve it?" As if I were holding him up, breaking a contract, as if he were flexible, reasonable, prepared to renegotiate, a little more up front, a more favorable division of the gross, a few more points of the net. As if the subject were money.

"What I want is an end to the war. What I don't want is to rev it up."

"Don't be apocalyptic. That'll never happen."

"It's already started to happen. It's the only reason the President went along with you."

"Anything we start we can stop. The ball's in our court," Grady went on, using an idiom he might have borrowed from the President. His eyes burned like the arctic sun, flaming and chilling at the same time. "Christ." With puzzled concern he asked, "Do you think I want to blow up the world?" He shook his head, protesting, astounded by my intractable perversity, and then he grinned, "For one thing it would be bad for business."

"Then why'd you plant the seed?"

"To get where we've got to go," he said. "What's good for business is a reactor for the Assamans."

"To which could be added fortified fuels—a little uranium 235, a sprinkling of plutonium 239—and you got yourself a handy little A-bomb."

"Abdul'd never do that."

"I don't trust him." He knew what I was saying. *I don't trust you.*

TWENTY-FIVE

THE SWEETHEART OF SIGMA KI

My jailer hands me the missive.

"Hey you!"

So reads the letter's salutation on a pink page freighted with perfume, an essence sharper than the writer's pen and reeking like a call girl's pussycat.

> First of all you should know that I am not only a Member in good standing of the Williwaws but I am President of the Club and I want to thank you for your help which I sincerely appreciate along with bad news my Grandmama past altho the good news is she left me you wouldn't believe it a shitpot of Money and so I enrolled at Comanche College in Eureka not far from Denver which it is a ball. I'm majoring in French and my French Professor who is a doll says I have a real nack for it altho I have decided to go on and be a vetinarian because there's nobody in my whole class who has the Experience and the Advantages I have like slicing the balls off a bull. I got to tell you I think of you often when I have the time you see I live in Town now and am very busy what with being a Cheerleader for the Black and Blue Cliff Dwellers at Hockey games along with all the rest like Football and Basketball and being chosen Homecoming Queen and Winter

Carnival De-Icer at Steamboat Springs as well as the Sweetheart of Sigma Ki, Fi Epsilon Pie, Kappa Sig, Lamda Ki Alf and I forget the other one, everybody but those dorks at Fi Gam who don't have a Sweetheart what about you? I hope you are taking good care of your skinny little tush.

Your friend,
Dawnette.

TWENTY-SIX

GIFTS AND ENDEARMENTS

A mist shimmered in Abdul's molasses eyes as he spoke lovingly of his father. "If you really want to make the old man happy," he said, "get him a movie star."

The conference had been going from bad to worse. It hadn't even begun well, and it was a sticky, tricky enterprise even before it began, a test of faith, patience, and stamina. Getting Abdul in the same room with Grady was a trial. He refused to step across the threshold of UGH headquarters. He didn't welcome Grady at his flat. Summit meets between superpowers were more easily negotiated.

We convened for our power breakfast, finally, at a comparatively neutral site—the pad I shared with Valerie—to exchange essential information, iron out the wrinkles, and, hopefully, reach accord.

Grady opened the proceedings on a gracious note of tribute, a demonstration of esteem for Abdul's father and of gratitude for being allowed entry into Assama. What would he like? he asked Abdul. What do you think? as if the gesture were prompted by pure generosity rather than what I was certain motivated it: an attempt to narcotize the man's well-founded xenophobia, in case it flared up again.

Abdul was rather disinterested in gifts and tokens—he seemed to consider them frivolous—but he did suggest the movie star. Other stratagems, most of them introduced by Grady, were immediately ratified: toothpaste and a washing machine driven by a portable, hand-cranked, compact, state-of-the-art generator. Valerie thought tennis gear might be a good idea. She also recommended a nice, even-tempered puppy, and volunteered to research the project. And then Abdul nominated the most cumbersome piece of baggage imaginable: Derek.

Derek? Grady demurred. Valerie said, "That's fucking ridiculous," but Abdul was unbudgeable.

"He is my good friend," he insisted. "When my allowance was slow in arriving from the government, Derek kept me solvent."

Derek? Was he capable of keeping anyone solvent?

"He'd peel off instruments from his father's mortuary and hock them. And anyway, I promised."

Promised? Promised him what?

"That when I went back to Assama, I'd take him with me."

"Why?"

"To bring Western culture to my people. We often spoke about it."

"Perhaps he could join us later," Grady suggested.

"He goes with us," Abdul said. His jaw was set firmly, his body rigid, signaling no brook of compromise.

Silence ensued, loud with the resonance of pique, dictating a change of subject.

"What about the language?" I asked. "I think we ought to learn it."

Abdul's eyes strayed, to hold on mine uncomprehendingly.

"Learn *it?*" he asked.

"As an expression of respect. If we're in Iraq, we should speak Arabic."

"There's no such thing as 'it,'" Abdul said. "More than four hundred tribes in Iraq speak more than eighty languages—nobody knows the exact number." He wasn't entirely appalled by my ignorance, saddened perhaps. It was simply something he had learned to expect from people who insisted on becoming involved in Middle Eastern affairs, and who knew next to nothing about them. "All of Mesopotamia," he went on, "is a Tower of Babel, a confusion of six hundred to a thousand spoken languages."

"But isn't there one, a kind of lingua franca that…"

"English," he said. "My father, his court, and his council speak English. It was introduced years ago by the British, who schooled the ruling class—my father went to an English school—and the people had some familiarity with it. Plus its usage was expanded by Dewey Lipgloss when he came to preach."

"Who's Lipgloss?" Grady asked. Abdul's words had managed to shake his steely composure. If this Lipgloss had infiltrated the country, despite the ban on foreigners, he was there for financial gain, and what was to be gained in Assama other than the evacuative biodegradables that Grady had set his heart on? Had this Lipgloss beaten RAT to the draw?

"The Reverend Dewey Lipgloss," Abdul said, "is an American evangelist. He's still in Assama, so far as I know."

The identification did little to assuage Grady's fears. He knew that commerce followed the flag, the flag of the Church Militant.

"This Lipgloss," Grady said, "he taught English for purposes of conversion? He converted the people to Christianity?"

"You might say they converted him. Dewey's a badly lapsed Christian. As for my father, he was particularly keen on the English language because of the publications the Reverend Lipgloss brought into the province."

"You mean before the man lapsed? Like the Bible, religious tracts?"

"Oh, nothing like that. You see, when I was a little boy, Dewey would repair periodically to Beirut or Damascus, for the hell of it, so to speak, or as he put it, to restore his wasted tissues…"

Lipgloss always returned from his sojourns with periodicals unavailable at home. Stroke magazines, like *Playboy, Penthouse, Hustler,* all of them immensely appreciated by the King. His favorites were *Photoplay, Silver Screen,* those dealing with film, their pages adorned with stills of all those fetching ladies. He spent a lot of time writing to them in their own language, although the letters were actually penned by Dewey to the old man's specifications. He proposed marriage and offered an extravagant dowry of junk jewelry showered on him by European engineers and geologists in their passage through Assama. His quarry numbered many a dish; their magical, lyrical names, like velvet on the tongue, conduced palpitations and heavy breathing. Over the years they expanded, it seemed, into a cast of thousands from which only Lassie was excluded.

"Any of them bite?" I asked.

"Of course not," Abdul said, "although some studio publicity flacks sent him glossy eight-by-tens of half of them."

The King's addiction to goddesses never diminished. When the Sheikha,

Abdul's mother, died a few months after the birth of her only child, the King refused to elevate any of his ninety-seven concubines to share his throne, still hoping that some knockout, however belatedly, would claim his jewels.

"So give him a movie star," Abdul repeated.

We were properly stumped. Then Valerie said, "I think I might know somebody…"

Daphne Titsworth squinched up her moss-green eyes and pulled at a twist of yellow hair, unaccustomed as she was to public thinking.

"Let me see, give me a little time, okay?" She wound a few strands around a finger and poked them in the corner of her mouth. "I don't know," she said through the hair in her teeth, "although it's better than waitressing, and something to do till I get a new agent and make my comeback." Her eyes behind the sequin-studded glasses were chary. For more than fifteen minutes now she had been wallowing in a fog of indecision.

"There's nothing funny about this?" she asked.

"What could be funny?" Valerie said.

"I mean, I saw a piece in the *National Enquirer* about this prince, his family claimed the crown of Rumania or someplace, who wanted to marry a policeman. Nothing like that, eh?"

"Nothing like that," Valerie assured her.

She turned to me. "What did you say he was? Tell me again."

"An authentic Stone Age sovereign, with a certain rugged appeal."

"And what did you say he wanted?"

"A movie star."

"I'm a movie star?"

"Queen of the pornos, Val tells me."

"Well, I once was," Daphne said, "and, well, to tell the truth, I've always been kind of tender-minded toward royalty, and this…" She squinted at a photo Abdul had supplied. "Well, he's definitely not a ringer for that king of Spain or the Prince of Wales, but he sounds a hell of a sight better than most of those stammering, limp-wristed, pointy-headed, rabbit-toothed, chinless inbreds I read about in the papers. So," she took a deep breath, expelling hair, "what the hell—why not?"

TWENTY-SEVEN
THE JEWEL OF IRAQ

The first thing I learned, once we had rattled down the automatic walkway at Kennedy, boarded the big UGH jet, belted ourselves into our seats, and bounded into the precarious air, was that I could not sleep on an intercontinental flight. I knew that if I so much as shut my eyes, let concentration lapse—it takes no more than a moment—the pilot would plunge all of us into a watery grave.

Valerie beside me swallowed two pills and smiled warmly. "See you in Wherever-the-hell," she said, and was off in balmy dreamland. But I found I couldn't sit still. Something about the decompression system or the supersonic growl of the engines, *something* exposed a nerve. I got up, carefully, in order not to disturb her, and walked across the ocean, pausing along the aisle to stick my nose in card games and conversations, while at all times bending an alert ear and a peripheral eye to my responsibilities in keeping that big-assed bird aloft, a condition about which my fellow passengers seemed shockingly unconcerned.

Derek and Daphne were comparing professional notes. He glanced up at me guardedly, looked away, holding me in the corner of an eye, like Bambi in the piney woods treating a pit viper with circumspection. He looked great,

I had to admit (now that he was no longer a candidate for Valerie's affections), his raging blondness projecting the aura of a sun god. Cute as a bug he was, warm as an ice cube, while Daphne beside him rucked her skirt above her thighs and acted saucy.

"The camera was always good to me," she told Derek, unzipping her travel bag and showing him a deck of publicity stills. "My bod holds a lot of light."

He nodded sagely and said in that sinewy voice, "Wow," and "Right on." He was full of such feeble expressions, to which he invariably appended exclamation points. Fortunately, she wasn't listening to him any more than he was listening to her.

"In a good screw-action flick," Daphne said, "you need rape and a couple lesbian scenes. Something sweet and gentle, you know?"

"Yeah," he agreed, "as Stanislavski says—"

"Yeah, well, my twin strengths have always been energy and intuition." She tittered, larking it up, pointing to one breast. "This one is energy," she said, and caressing the other, "and this is intuition."

"Aeschylus," Derek said, "invented the tragic *kothornos,* the sandal with the platformed sole, which gave an actor an additional three inches of height on a raked stage."

"Yeah," she said, "lovely."

"When you make contact," Derek said, "you *know* by the way the audience reacts."

"Yeah," she said, "it's blissy."

Derek pulled on his cigarette, exhaling a great histrionic contrail of smoke. "This Assama thing is just a brief excursion for me; I'm doing the prince a favor."

"It'll put me," she said, "in the same league as Wally Warfield Simpson, you know the Duchess, and that Princess Di and Betsy Patterson who married Napoleon's little brother Jerry."

"When I come back, I'm going to make it big," Derek confided like destiny's own tot, "and when I do I'll never forget the little people."

I walked on. A familiar voice was saying, "...prefer truth to delusion. That is the crux of science." Then, looking up, "Ah, *wunderkind!*" Chatterton greeted me with a smile suitable for framing. Without a pause he turned back to Grady and said, "So what is at stake is neither more nor less than global habitability. If we keep it up," he warned, "we'll be a few grams of dust on the slaughtered planet."

Grady nodded abstractedly, tapping the palm of one hand with a rolled newspaper held in the other.

Chatterton was in a festive, expansive mood, as he had been since the uplifting day when Grady told him of the new home for his project.

Only one element had dampened his enthusiasm and threatened to nullify the undertaking: when he had assembled his band of brothers and told them of the move, Mainwaring had blurted, somewhat uncharacteristically, "Fuck that shit." Thus the rebellion began.

Only Gorelik had remained loyal. The others, each in his own fashion, had echoed Mainwaring, who decided to write his memoirs, but definitely not in Southern Iraq. Norman Baker retired to live quietly, he hoped, with his daughter and her brood in New Jersey. George Desmond had no immediate plans, but he did have family, money, and a modest pension from Harvard. Henri-Jacques Treblant became a cultural attaché at the French Embassy in Washington. Zygmunt Wolenciewicz took his hauteur to Hollywood, where, through the good offices of an ex-colleague at USC, he got a job as technical advisor on an epic about Hiawatha.

Now old Chatterton sprawled contentedly in his bucket seat, his dreadful bulk oozing over the aisle on one side and Grady on the other, popping peanuts by the peck. He even offered to share a few with Grady and me while gently he waved an arm to brush away an orbiting fly. It veered toward Grady, changed its mind, and landed on the back of the seat in front of him, rubbing one tentacle against another. And then Grady's newspaper slammed down on it, and the fly became a bottle-green, custard-yellow blob.

"Why'd you have to do that?" Chatterton was furious. "That fly had as much right on this earth as you have. It had its own spark of divinity."

Grady leaned forward until his nose was an inch or two from the gruelly corpse. Elaborately he said, "I humbly beg your pardon, Lord Beelzebub."

Chatterton looked up at me. He said, "It's hard to like some people, isn't it?"

But his glower subsided and quickly his distemper receded. Nothing could derail his dither of delight at the prospect of dominoes and other such lumps dancing in southern Iraq.

"It's certainly," he said, "felicitous that Assama has given us a home.

These people have much in common with fourth-dynasty Egypt, when Cheops built his great pyramid twenty centuries ago."

I thought I noticed the slightest flicker of doubt—possibly of refutation—crossing Grady's face, but his features maintained their armor of impassivity, which encouraged Chatterton to go on. "They both had a flare for spectacular architecture, each in their own way. The Nile dwellers developed their pyramids while the Tigris-Euphrates crowd was into gigantic beehives."

He was just warming up. "Both regions," he pointed out, "built cities, shared traffic and wealth..."

I might have added that they also shared pestilence and disease, but of course I didn't. Uninterrupted, Chatterton's solo continued, "They developed doctrines and idealogies..."

Along with, I might have added, wide-ranging incompetence and obstinate confusions.

"Each had great periods of conquests..."

"And chaos," I heard myself say.

Chatterton ignored my input. "Perhaps," he said thoughtfully, "they might have used harmonics in their building. We'll see," he joyfully added, "we'll see."

Abdul looked down at the darkness rising from the earth. In the empty seat next to him were Gorelik's mud-colored cigarettes, his fipple flute, and the poems of Yevtushenko in the original Russian.

Gorelik on the aisle bent over a plastic tray, pushed the last crumb of chocolate pie from his plate into his mouth; after his years at Chatterton's table, airplane fare must have tasted like ambrosia. He put down his fork, explored a molar with the tip of his tongue, and lit a cigarette.

"Is it not true," he asked Abdul, "that we must approach your father on our knees?"

"Absolutely not," Abdul said. "It is customary only to bow a little and avert one's eyes."

"Don't you find that sort of thing obsolete?"

Abdul smiled. "What I find isn't the issue. It's what my father wants. And while his wants are few, what he wants, like that girl in the old song, he gets."

Night invaded the cabin. The jets knifed through the black air, their drone at once subdued and urgent, the black ocean gliding past. I felt a kind

of stupefactive excitement, propelled by an unnatural and (to me) unfathom-
able force, a risky business. Was it possible that none of my fellow aerialists
felt it, each in his own cocoon, each secure with his own sense of mission?
Chatterton slept, Grady read. Daphne and Derek talked in undertones.
Abdul and Gorelik, glaze-eyed and self-absorbed, had stopped bickering
out of sheer exhaustion about a thousand miles back. Grady's scientists and
engineers were bored, accepting the monotony of the flight with the stunned
acquiescence of a rootless, itinerant tribe that plied its trade resourcefully,
humorlessly, in any country for any cause, men who could deliver anything
except a joke.

Carefully I lowered myself down in the seat next to Val.

Her mouth was slightly ajar, a piquant bubble of saliva at a corner. Her
soft breath wafted a buoyant tuft of hair that hung over her face. I smiled
sentimentally in the darkness, feeling warm all over. Daphne and Derek ran
by and locked themselves in the aft toilet.

The airplane bounced across the virgin runway, newly completed by an
advanced corps of Grady's engineers. It stopped with a mechanical sigh, and
was immediately attacked by a squadron of angry mosquitoes as large as bats.

We boarded the bus and took off in a fog of asphyxiation. The dashboard
radio, beamed into a coalition patch, played loudly that most oedipal of
songs, "I Want a Girl Just Like the Girl Who Married Dear Old Dad." The
bus plunged through scrub and sand with a grinding of gears, coughing
and clanking. Brown grasslands gave way to desert, silent and menacingly
still. Inside the bus the scorchy reek of oil mingled with the stench of the
passengers. We were uniformly filthy, the men in need of a shave, Valerie
sweat-stained and rumpled, Daphne's hair a tangle, her bare arms and legs
mottled by the heat.

A hot wind fanned the creepers beside the washboard road, and beyond
them, as far as the eye could see, stood that immensity of wasteland. Every
once in a while appeared a cluster of Mazari palms where ratlike animals, gerbils I think, flew from frond to frond, working without a net. "Are we there
yet?" Daphne kept asking, until finally, suddenly, Coproliabad ghosted into
an unreal substantiality. Rounded huts clustered here and there like melting
scoops of coffee ice cream. Indeed in this land where the desert encroached,

enveloped, invaded, and conquered, the fragile designs of man should have been as fleetingly ephemeral as his dreams, but the great, multistoried buildings seemed as permanent as the surrounding wilderness. We staggered off the bus, greeted by Assama's plenipos, while the plebeians stood on the sidelines and gawped. Hashim Pachachi, Secretary of Commerce, led us to the Square, proudly pointing out the statues of the provincial paragons, himself among them. Draped between two hairy trees was a hand-painted banner that smacked of a press release:

WELCOME TO ASSAMA THE JEWEL OF THE IRAQ AND TO
COPROLIABAD ITS DYNAMIC CAPITAL

We all would have preferred a bath and a bed—by this time we looked as if we had got here on a collier—but protocol had to be served. A man with a mushy paunch and short legs rounded like logs wabbled front and center.

"Permit me to introduce myself: I am Shakir bin Zaki, poet of the people. I am also Minister of Information, Communication, Planning and National Guidance, Popular Education, Pacification, Civil Service, Specialized Organs, Memorializations, Women's Advancement, and Amenities."

"He carries a thick portfolio," Gorelik said in my ear.

"Now I give you some thoughts of my people, your genial hosts. But before I speak," the fat lips smacked, "I would like to say a few words."

"Didn't he say 'Women's Advancement'?" Daphne asked. "Outside of Valerie and me, there're no women around."

"In the past, economics-wise, we have been victims, we have been at death's door, but now our guests pledge to pull us through and usher in a new era of prosperity. We welcome Lord Grady and his potentates, for they are deluxe people. I truly believe that there is not one second-rate scuffler among them, trying to pass himself off as an expert in Assama. So we can relax, we can rejoice together in the knowledge that we won't have to eat them as our brave forefathers did to protect themselves against the plunderers of the past." He smacked his lips.

I swallowed nervously. Derek's bright eyes ransacked the pitiless trees beyond the square, searching for sanctuary. But Grady's countenance in the torchlight maintained the serenity of a saint.

"And so," bin Zaki went on, "we raise voices of joy, voices of shout..."

It is so insolently easy to record the misspeak of people who mangle

English. I draft the poet's words, fully aware that he speaks my language a hell of a sight better than I'd ever speak his. But to get on: bin Zaki's was the only voice of shout. At the edge of the clearing the people were silently, cautiously malevolent. Their tan skin held a patina of grayness. "Why are they gray?" Gorelik asked.

I could answer that one: "Ashes," I told him. "They smear their bodies with ashes to keep off mosquitoes. There are fifty-eight known species of bloodsuckers in Assama."

"Fun City," Gorelik said.

"Where is the King?" Daphne asked.

"You'll meet him," Abdul said, turning to me. "My father, like your Andrew Jackson, does not understand diplomacy."

A sudden wind swept across the square. The trees tossed their branches, leaves like elephant ears swung in slow tranquillity, nature's answer to the mobile. The glow of the torches dwindled, creating dense pockets of darkness, reducing the dignitaries to silhouettes. The torches drank what light they could siphon out of the darkness, their flames darting, plunging, writhing.

A muster of warriors stormed onto the square. They screamed in a savage falsetto, and their faces shone with sweat. Their robes billowed like sails as they galumphed about, scimitars flashing. Each man was further armed with a scrawny chicken, which he twirled above his head like a terrified pinwheel. The wind died again, the torches flared. The thick silhouette slouching toward Gorelik took corporeality and became General Qazwini, rotund, dripping with medals. Responding to his presence as if to a command, the warriors tore the chickens apart and in a flurry of squawks ate them alive.

"You will review my troops?" he ordered. "I have army of two hundred and ten men and four women who would to be men, you know?"

"Not me," Gorelik said. "I don't know one end of a troop from the other."

"Follow me!" bin Zaki shouted, snaring a torch. We did, uncertainly, as if he were a crimp, and we were press-ganged into unconsenting service. From under the trees, a band struck up a creaky rendition of "The Star-Spangled Banner," then with equal dubiety, "Anchors Aweigh," Assama lacking an anthem of its own. The instrumentalists whacked away with sticks, stones, and tambourines, and snorted extravagantly into nose flutes. Chatterton was enthralled.

Beyond the square was a clearing of tramped-down grass, altogether like the coat of a dog with the mange. A path meandered through a courtyard, where a raggedy-lettered sign, barely visible in the torchlight, warned:

THERE IS A FINE OF TWO CHICKENS

FOR BOTH OFFENCES

PLEASE NOT TO SPIT

AND LITTERING!!

Beyond it was the palace.

That so insignificant a path could lead to such an imposing structure lacked congruity. But there it was, a whimsical pile looming, dominating the land as an iceberg crowns the surrounding sea. It soared up and up, surreal, audacious, like some enormous, irregularly rounded candle dripping tallow, its wick lost in the mist beyond the gleam of the torches.

We entered a long rectangular room lit by saucer lamps.

"The Hall of Great Fragrance!" bin Zaki announced. "Guaranteed to produce subduing atmosphere for your endearment." All the surfaces of the chamber—floor, walls, ceiling—seemed to be made of a blistered, lavalike stone. It was of course not stone at all, but the amazing masonry of Grady's quest.

On one side of the room a row of twelve sausage-fat pillars, about ten paces apart, was carved in the round: squat effigies of men on one side, facing on the other a parallel row of women.

Neither group was tall enough to support the ceiling. No matter, for from each male figure protruded a penis, thick as a phone pole, sinuous as a hose, that curved upward, rose to become a beam as it stretched horizontally across the hall, snaked downward to a compliant woman, to embrace her in its corkscrew grasp, and then lodge in the snuggery of her pudendum.

The group comprised an unintentional parody of licentiousness—those engorged penes in frozen transit across the oblong hall—in a display of misbehavior that was anything but erotic. The orgiasts wore uniform expressions of numbness, their round eyes grim and vacant, all their faculties resigned to satyriasis. It was perhaps the lack of enthusiasm in their revelry that confused Daphne, and then prompted her to say, "What're they doing my God."

Under a phallic arch a table held a variety of food. Some of the dishes were hot and some were cold and none of them were recognizable.

"As we always say," bin Zaki bellowed jovially, "a hungry man is an angry man. So take a lot of these sumptuous delicacies prepared in your honor and you will soon discover that our cooking is an art."

I bit into a cheesy spread that might have been bat shit.

"Why," asked Valerie, "is it called the Hall of Fragrance?"

"Because," bin Zaki answered, "it is washed every year. Cleanliness," he added, "is our main forte. Although you'll find that we have many other fortes."

The room, large as it was, swarmed with the King's ministers, plus a sending of chieftains from the outback. Their faces were stern with authority, accepting or yielding homage. The lees of a rather assertive beer clung to their lips.

The brew was brown and bubbly, and reeked of sorghum. Daphne, born to be bad, made a dive for it. Soon she was clinking glasses, I should say clunking bowls (which could only have been made from Grady's magical compound), with a short splinter of a man in a sackcloth robe held loosely together by a penitential cord. He drank with an air of smug piety, but his eyes never left Daphne's nipples, bursting like two swollen buds against the imprisonment of her tight bodice.

"Hey, Juddie," she said to me, sloshing beer on my pants, "say hello to Reverend Lopgas."

"Lipgloss," he corrected her.

Other eyes were on Daphne, hungrily, as if she were some glittering passion flower. But not all; many turned to Val, the party's matchless adornment. She stood coolly within a circle of ministers, comparing canapés. The eyes of the Sheik from the North never left her, not even when he threw back his bulgy bald skull and belted down his beer. Those eyes were cloudy and red-rimmed, like those of a nocturnal carnivore. I in turn watched him.

Gorelik had planted himself at the table, making a god of his stomach. He ran his tongue against his palate, savoring a dish he couldn't quite identify. "Delicious," he told bin Zaki. "Do I detect a touch of cilantro?"

"It is one of our specialties," Shakir answered. "Baby-rat stew, fresh from the trap." He reached out, catching the elbow of a dignitary in a Winnie the Pooh blanket. "This is Mr. Yussuf Chapouk, our rat-killer first class."

"My wifes are fine," Mr. Chapouk said, "and yours?"

A blood-curdling screech, feral and prolonged, burst from the trees beyond the courtyard. "What's that?" Daphne asked.

"Monkey," Lipgloss said.

Daphne's eyes went soft. "Once," she confided, "I did it with a monkey."

Boisterous, full of imbecile rancor, General Qazwini thonked about, his pitiless eyes darting from one white face to another, wondering who next to confront with the honor of inspecting his troops. A big hand rested on the grip of the heavy weapon at his belt; again and again he'd raise it an inch from the holster and thumb the safety back and forth. Each time I'd feel my sphincter contract.

Now those flat eyes hit on Grady sipping a beer in a corner, and once more the General voiced his obsession. "I'd be delighted," Grady answered gravely.

The musicians played a ragged fanfare, something like the first few notes of a cavalry charge. Bin Zaki cried, "Follow me!" A pair of Qazwini's stalwarts, their faces still caked with chicken blood, stood aside and we entered the Throne Room. The vassals bowed and we followed their example.

"The Hall of Harmony!" Shakir yelled.

As in the Hall of Fragrance, the structure was ribbed with a proliferation of pillars which jostled each other and, in this case, took the form of serpents. But serpents out of a daunting nightmare, rampant, with miscellaneous permutations. The heads were horned, the mouths slit to the ears. The bodies had manes of stiff bristles, and backbones prickled with spines. They had powerful, scaly legs, feet with cloven hooves, and claws like a vulture's.

From a rafter hung the provincial flag, a great red-and-yellow bird against a field of white. The powerful wings were spread, the curved beak gaping, the red eyes turbulent. In one yellow talon was a clutch of spears, in the other a gnarly club. The creature simulated all the warlike characteristics of the shrieking, emblematic eagle, so often the metaphor of a nation's pride. But in this case, possibly unique in the annals of heraldry, the bird was a chicken.

The color scheme found further expression in the throne itself, a sworl of reds (for power, in the chromatic scale of Assama) and yellows (for royalty). On it sat a man with ropy old muscles. He bore a resemblance to Abdul that time could not totally erase, but the hair had thinned and the jowls had grown puffy. A smell came off him, a pungent, old-man smell like a worn-out tire or a decaying rump roast.

"King!" cried bin Zaki. "Supreme Organ of the Land! Greet the *ademi chandiperoki smarelaj champungar domkeladi.*"

"What's that mean?" I asked in an aside to Abdul.

"It means 'Those who wear tight pants.' Literally, 'Those who keep their farts in their pants.'" He moved to his father's side.

Bin Zaki gestured imperiously and bearers came forward with our gifts. The King seemed unimpressed. In a hoarse, muted voice he said something I could not make out. The ministers closest to him chuckled dutifully, nervously, I thought, and Abdul turned as pale as the pigment of his skin allowed.

There was an awkward silence. Grady, our resolute leader, said, "I beg Your Highness's pardon. Would you mind repeating...?"

The Supreme Organ of the Land did not mind. He smacked his lips and a hush fell over the assemblage. He pointed a finger at Valerie.

"I want her," he said clearly.

A shockwave of anxiety rocked the group. The ministers sensed discord, the visitors felt fear. Each camp affected a momentary deafness, yet, as though driven by some instinctive force, they moved protectively toward their own kind until the room was divided into two logjams. All except Daphne, too pissed to perceive impending doom, too unversed to comprehend that his words had the power of thumbscrews. I sprang to her side, snared her traveling bag. She said, "What're you doing, Juddie?"

I strode to the King, a parade of one, eyes unaverted, carrying the thick batch of eight-by-ten glossies. "See, O King, what a jewel I've found for you," I said, trying to sound like Derek in one of those Biblical nosebleeds, dialogue out of Cecil B. DeMille. He'll never buy it, I told myself. I'll be the first to die.

I thrust out a deck of maybe a hundred glossies. The King took them and stared at the first. I had the temerity to lean over his shoulder, and together we studied the oeuvre of Daphne Titsworth.

There were nudes, full frontal and profile; half nudes, bottomless and topless; close-ups of clit and scut, even of her face with the hot, hungry eyes, the gaping mouth, the lolling tongue. There were shots of her back, of her belly, of her *ear* for God's sake. She was a little old vehicle of prurience, yet the intensity of her dedication to posturing lust made it kind of funny.

But not to the King. A ruttish nerve began to throb at his temple.

"Look at her, there, across the room," I said in a pimpy voice, "a gift any king would envy. A movie star."

He looked, pulling his eyes reluctantly from the pictures, and I went to Daphne and led her to the throne. They smiled lewdly at each other. I breathed a croupy sigh of relief, having somehow steered Valerie through the crisis, and stemmed the tide of spoliation. That was, I hoped, the end of it, but it was far from a certainty. In this alien land, where passion and violence were capriciously and uncompromisingly entwined, who could predict what tomorrow would bring? The King was at the moment enthusiastically occupied with his movie star, but how long before he switched preferences or, such being his polygamous bent, wanted them both?

So the plaguey coda of a king's inconstancy stretched far into the night, long after the bash was over. We had been shown, Val and I, to our pied à deux. It smelled of a thousand rotty seepages. I rolled and tossed on the bed of septicemic rat skins, listening to the scurry of paw pads in the bush. A bird flew into our nest, squawking as if he owned it. Valerie stirred, turning to face me in the bright pallor of moonlight.

"What's that?" she asked.

"Nothing," I said. "It's a beautiful bird."

"Terrible voice."

"I think it's called a fark-fark."

"In the middle of the night you got to be scholarly."

The bird flew off, still squawking. Softly she said, "You could have been killed, you know that? You were pretty damned gutsy."

I shrugged. I hadn't thought much about my performance. I was too worried about having to do it again.

"You saved my ass. Literally."

"What I did, it had nothing to do with valor, or anything like that."

"I think it did," she said. "You're a valiant fool." She pulled me to her. "That's the best kind," she added. "Thanks."

She curled herself around me like a sweet-smelling cocoon, and we slept.

TWENTY-EIGHT

CUSTOMS OF THE COUNTRY

She was still asleep in the morning when I walked out of our hut into a solid mass of heat, weaving a little under the havelock I had improvised to ward off the sun.

The path was straight and narrow, and led through a stand of droopy trees to the town a quarter mile away. Yet the topography was such, with its successive twists and turns, that the human eye couldn't penetrate more than a fragment of the total distance.

So it was that I heard the keening before I saw the keener. She squatted where the street began, her long gray hair under the hejab. The brown teeth drooled betel juice on her schmatte as she chanted an incantation over a pubescent youth. He knelt before her, foaming at the mouth, trembling in an ecstasy of stress as she cut three slits like frown lines in his forehead, rounded them with a twist of the stone blade, and rubbed dirt into the wounds, making a paste with the oozing blood. Then she ate the surplus paste.

Before her was spread a lacework of interwoven palm fronds and on them was laid out a pharmacopoeia of magic potions and elixirs. She smiled up at me through the emulsion of blood and betel juice, making obscene gestures not as a sexual enticement but to make clear that she was pushing aphrodisiacs. And all the time we were attended by a skulk of yellow dogs, sniffing and scratching and pissing, with nothing better to do, just hanging loose. Then a big hand shot out from behind me and grabbed me firmly by the balls. I jumped a good three feet, straight up, twirling in the middle of the air to face my assailant.

Hashim Pachachi stood there with a warm smile, but by the time I returned to earth the smile had vanished; he looked shocked and aggrieved. His abusively attentive right hand I had in my flight managed to free from its assault. His injured eyes found mine, seeking a clue to my erratic behavior. I too groped for an explanation that could rationalize his.

"Don't grotz me. Back the hell off," I snarled, discarding caution and diplomacy in one fell swoop.

"Grotz?" He was puzzled. "I do not know the word."

"Keep your goddam mitts to yourself. Is that clear?"

"But I…" He was holding a roll of untidy, cream-colored paper in his left hand; he twisted it agonizingly in his discomfort. "If I am not to… grotz…"

"That's right."

"…then how am I to greet you properly?"

I shuddered to imagine what an improper greeting might entail, but I was beginning to understand.

We in the West approach friends with the requisite handshake, a gesture of goodwill whose original purpose, it is thought, was to demonstrate that we carried no weapons, not even a fist. Some of us are even friendlier: the French with their cheeky kisses; Hispanics with the sedate *abrazo,* an embrace accompanied by a few swift, fluttery slaps between the scapulas.

The Assamans went further. They greeted by clutching each other's genitals—what could be friendlier that that? And it did accomplish its aim, a weapons check to ascertain if a knife were hidden in a codpiece or, in the case of a woman, beneath her robe. Still, it was unnerving and required a bit of getting used to, and it happened so often in the days that followed that there seemed to be time for little else; the mind was inclined to dwell on it.

Both the Secretary of Commerce and I were eager to establish an amicable relationship after the salutatory rift.

"Here is the report." He thrust his rolled paper into my hand. "The investment code I promised you."

I riffled the pages. It was my turn to look bewildered. "You promised me?"

"Last night. The Disneyland projection. Read it at your earliest convenience," he offered graciously. "And now let's find a suitable spot for your theater."

Comprehension dawned. "I think," I said slowly, "you have me confused with Derek Bronson."

"Impossible," he said. He tilted his head sharply, as if the angle might improve his sight. "You are not the drama teacher?"

"Afraid not."

"Sorry. It's very confusing."

"What is?"

"Well, quite frankly, you all look alike to me."

"But Bronson is blond, and I'm dark..."

"Looks are superficial, wouldn't you agree? Thing is, I suppose, you all *act* alike. Anyway," he added, "read my report. Then we'll get together and kick it around." He smiled again, reached for my balls, thought better of it, and waddled off.

Those first few days I spent mostly with Val, studying our new habitat, intrigued by the statues in the square, drawn to (and repelled by) the ever-ominous People's Tower, a relic, we were assured, of the long dead and buried past, from which enemies had been launched for ganching. It was disturbingly reminiscent of the "baby drops" in prerevolutionary China from which unwanted little girls were thrown.

In the company of Grady I examined the architecture, searching for the key to its construction, which we couldn't find. The buildings were bulbous and baroque, in their own way magnificent, but nothing man-made in this trembling furnace of a country seemed to belong, nothing could compete against the desert, which was inhospitably in command.

About six miles north of Coproliabad we followed a narrow valley and climbed a hill to see what was on the other side—more valleys and more hills tumbling, it seemed, forever. The high ground was contoured with rocks like great gnarly muscles and pocked with caves occupied by creeping beetles and unblinking newts and bats that beat about, dipping and soaring as if borne on waves. The sharp rise and fall of the topography made it unfeasible for a nuke site, and so we pushed on, always without a guide because Grady found covert operations irresistible. We asked about likely terrain of the country people who tried his patience with their unspecificity, for Assamans generally exhibited an emphatic carelessness about the passage of time and the fixity of space. His inquiries followed a precise pattern, first describing what he sought. "You know of such a place?" he would ask a native.

"Yes," was the invariable reply.

"Where is it?"

"Around."

Pointing a finger: "There?"

"Yes."

"How far over there?"

"Not far."

"How long does it take to get there?"

"Not long."

Then Grady would thank the man with a peppermint candy, raise his glasses to their habitual resting place along the supraorbital ridge, shake his head, and say, "Jesus, these guys are fun to be with."

Sometimes we'd start out before dawn, and walk all day without seeing anyone, for humanity in this pocket of the world maintained at best a vague and shallow enclave, made vaguer still by the impacted heat that obscured and distorted the landscape as if it were coated with a film of petroleum jelly. We slogged through it each morning, a solid suffocation as it thinned, faltered, and beat down again, the hot wind thrashing the trees and wailing like a prophet of doom. At times, on the north side of the mountains, lightning ripped open great channels in the sky. Thunder slammed them shut. Then it was gone for another twenty-four hours, leaving in its wake dripping messes of vegetation and the vision of a gem-splashed world.

Not for long. Even as the mold sucked softly under our feet, the garnet sun broke through, consuming all creation in its painful, unremitting fever.

While it is true, as you may have noticed, that I've never adapted to any clime, nor have I ever looked back with longing to wherever I've been before, yet in this roachy kingdom my mind in a curious warp of time and space kept reverting to New Haven. Something in this stagnant cesspool reminded me of Yale.

The land above the rain shadow on the windward slope of the mountains, so fresh and green with the paint of rain, had assumed ten minutes after the storm subsided the look of faded stone, not unlike the pale, medieval gloom of Yale's dominant architecture—and of so many exhausted New England schools badly in need of a restorative—but that wasn't the connection. The towering trees with their intertwined limbs and their astounding motility creaked and groaned like the old wooden ships riding at anchor along the quays of the Connecticut tributaries; that wasn't it either. The floor of the forest gave off the ammoniacal smell of vegetable matter, a gagging effluvium that scorched the nostrils, salted the eyes, and lodged achingly in the temples—and then I knew what crystallized the association: the gassy stench, there in this corner of a foreign field, was Armbruster's office.

What dispelled the tedium in town were the surprising but inevitable clamors and crises and alarms that no day was without. Most of them—those which concerned us—involved the quasi-King who held a forthright and empirical attitude toward our gifts. He used the tennis racquet, it was whispered, to swat the blimplike bugs. The tennis net went to the royal bird catcher to snare the iridescent birds for the pot. The pit bull he ate in a puree of toothpaste, washing it down with the hair dye. One of his concubines tried to bathe a child in the washing machine, but no real harm came of it.

All this made for considerable excitement and gave us something to talk about. We Americans shook our heads with awe and wonder at the superb efficiency of Saeed al Sadr's digestive tract while our hosts wistfully and endlessly discussed the prerogatives of royalty. They made up songs about it, their black eyes staring for inspiration into the desert. They were a weather-resistant people, tempered and toughened by the heat, wearing their robes to insulate themselves against it. In the ghostly pale of dawn and dusk they took on a phantasmic, deathlike insubstantiality.

The Assamans spent much of the daylight hours foraging for provender. They netted birds and bats and frogs, they tended their few chickens and the modest sorghum crop. They hunted and trapped rats and gerbils and snakes and small scaly animals with tapering tails. They gathered nuts and berries beyond the scope of any known botanica. There were some recognizable trees, including a few gnarled and stunted cherries; the people refused to pluck the fruit, waiting to pick it off the ground once it had fallen. The same with firewood; dead limbs and rotten branches were collected, but only from the floor—their animistic way, perhaps, of honoring the vibrant earth. They went about their chores without rancor or resentment or resignation, and without being too strenuous about them. They were kind to their children. They were good to the verminous dogs. They seemed generally to enjoy life despite the limitations imposed by a community not known for a rich variety of diversions, where extravagant self-indulgence meant a laundered robe for each seventh day, not unlike workers in the West, all gussied up once the workweek was done. At twilight, they emerged from their digs in Coproliabad to stroll and strut around the square, like the population of a little Mexican town doing the *paseo.*

When, mercifully, the sun finally went down and streamers of mist drifted among the treetops, the people returned to their shanties and kindled fires outside the doors to ward off evil as the hour of the ghosts approached. The squall of chatter and the furry calliope laughter subsided. The women like heavy-haunched Picassos sat out the night, eyes glowing like the embers of the fires before them, while moths dove close to the flames, flirting with suicide, and the men sang in praise of themselves, their good fortune, the ancestors within them, revelries, triumphs. They bayed incantations to the moon, their shrill, unrounded notes scaring off vultures while thousands of invisible frogs joined in the chorus. They danced, communing with the forest, floating through the mist like low-flying ghosts in a graceless stomp. There was something unnerving about it; Val gripped my hand tightly as we watched. Grady quoted *Dracula.* "'The children of the night,'" he said, "'are making their music.'"

TWENTY-NINE

SEE AND TALK TO LIVE NUDE GIRL

The jingle of tiny bells draws closer, a moving carillon. Daphne Titsworth minces into my cage wearing a modified bikini—two small saucers of fluff on her chest and a gauzy triangle that doesn't quite contain the shrubbery on her pude.

A piece of yarn, attached to the lowest point of the triangle, ducked under her thighs, disappeared between the chubby cheeks of her ass, and, reemerging, looped around the girdle of bells at her waist. Her spike heels give her trouble; still she bounces toward me as if the uneven floor were a burlesque stage, an altogether strange and unsettling apparition lugging a canvas tote inscribed BLOOMINGDALE'S.

"How've you been?" she asks, taking from the sack a flagon of beer and a battery-driven vibrator. "My bag of tricks," she says, arranging her wares in the middle of the cell with a kind of fussy, impulsive zeal, as if they were invested with totemic significance.

"I'd get you out of here," she goes on, "if I had half the clout I used to. But I don't, so I'm here to do the next best thing." She leans toward me, blinking behind the sequined glasses. "You ever go around the world?"

"Actually, this is the first time I've been out of the U.S."

"No, I mean like when a girl starts at your toes and licks up and up until it becomes," she grins, "heavenly." She takes a swig of the beer. "What I thought," she says, "I thought I might give you one last, sweet, fancy face job. Or a straight-out, old-fashioned stevedore fuck if you prefer, something you won't forget if you live to be a hundred. So," she clicks her spike heels and salutes, "at your service, sir."

"That's very thoughtful of you."

"'S'nothing, Judd. Just a pit stop on our way to hell."

We stand there a long time, uncomfortably.

"What's the matter?" she says. "You think Valerie would mind or something?"

"Well, we do have this commitment. Not that I don't appreciate…"

"It's okay. I think it's wonderful, being faithful and all that." She takes another swill of the beer.

"Have you seen her?"

"No," she says, "I've been kind of busy. She hasn't been around?"

"Not lately."

Despite their brevity, those two words were at best a varnished truth. I haven't seen her since Abdul locked me up. Which starts me wondering—is the leash he holds her on so tight, so prohibitive that she can't cut loose from it? Never before has she yielded to restraints, so why now from this power-nut of a pseudomonarch? Unless… not seeing me is her decision.

Daphne sees the worry on my face. "There's no satisfaction, is there? Whatever you do. Here you got Valerie, she's your main meal and she's a no-show."

"She has her reasons," I say, "I'm sure."

But I'm not at all sure. My doubts, my confusions burst on me like a flurry of Chinese firecrackers, as vivid, searing, haunting as my obsession with the ganching tower.

"Sure," Daphne repeats. "Not that I mean to pry, but even when a person goes legit, gets really married, or zeroes in on a significant other, it still sucks. I know."

"Have you ever been married?"

"Once. Come to think of it, twice. Didn't work, so I went back to playing piggy games, but that didn't work either. Hell of a life, right?"

She flops down on my rat-skin bed.

"Maybe," she says, "there's something wrong with me—anything's possible. Like when I'm screwing I scream, I moan, sometimes I even bark like a goddamn dog, but I'll let you in on a secret." She looks up at me, her eyes clown-sad. "I've never come in my life," she says, "except maybe once in the seventh grade."

She kicks off her shoes. "No kidding aside, my troubles began even earlier. When I was a little baby I cried and cried. They finally found out my arm was broke. I was so fat they hadn't noticed."

I sit down beside her.

"I went through a stage," she says, "it went on for years. I was so nervous I pulled out my eyelashes. Don't you want any beer?"

I take the flagon and drink.

"I started screwing regularly in high school," she says. "I mean for money, to save up and buy a fur jacket which I wouldn't do it now what with all the stink about killing live animals and I agree. But I never did buy it, that is, because I was sure I'd die before I wore it out even a little. I always had this panicky feeling whenever I was screwing in the back of a car that somebody invisible was up front. You're a good listener," she says. "Shit, I wish I had brought more beer."

She takes off her glasses, holds them to the light, runs her tongue across each lens front and back, and squints around for something to clean them. She settles on the patch of gauze at her crotch.

"The best job I ever had," she says, "was working for this guy on Forty-second Street with a hair lip. He had a sign outside: SEE AND TALK TO LIVE NUDE GIRL—$1. All I had to do was sit there. Everything else in my whole life has been a hard hustle." She settles against my shoulder. "But it's kind of all worked out in the end. Maybe not for you, Juddie, but Abdul gave me a place to live and I don't have to do anything I don't want, not even talk to some pimply-faced kid."

I put my arm around her. She sighs contentedly. "Sometimes," she says, "I used to wonder if Elvis was really alive."

We sit there I don't know how long. Darkness falls. I rock her in my arms and she goes to sleep.

THIRTY

MUCH IN DEMAND

The site for the nuclear plant that Grady ultimately located lay about twelve miles east of Coproliabad, a broad sandy flat scarred by a few outcrops of schist. Within a few weeks, construction was well under way and proceeding with unexpected efficiency. A large rounded shell had sprung up in the desert, like some fatso in a sandbox, sheltered on one side by a few stunted trees. The core baskets and the fuel assemblies for the generators had been requisitioned, and were on their way across the ocean. Chatterton and Gorelik were tooting away in their wing. In the vast, comparatively cool basement, like the keep of a castle, Grady had installed *his* band of brothers—more accurately, stepbrothers, as he was too inaccessible, distrustful, and secretive to merit "fraternal" as a modifier in his relationship with his workforce. As a gesture of goodwill, he had invited the Assamans to build the facility with their very own indigenous ingredients, in hopes of giving himself the chance to examine the BRITs up close and unimpeded. And so he spent his days shadowing them, scrutinizing mixing pits and dung heaps, secreting samples back to his lab for analysis.

"We've got the recipe," he insisted one day, "we know the process, the approximate ratios..." But he never could get his shit together. Trembling with pique, in a tantrum of frustration, he whined about the ineptitude of his gurus in the lab, with their PhDs and their failed expertise. "They think they know more about BRITs than Einstein knew about relativity—charges and currents and procedures—more than this whole damned population of primitives rolled into one, but these stumblebums can put it together and we can't." His moaning fused imperfectly with the singsongs and clickity-clacks that the Assamans who did all the ball-breaking labor produced in unison, an atonal yowl whose constancy turned my stomach and ground my teeth.

Grady was a bundle of convulsive energy, full of weighty decisions, crackling with his own brand of voltage as he led Assama toward another colonization. He was always moving, obsessively demonic. Somehow he managed to maximize the reluctant grunts, wringing more sweat out of them than they had to give, as if they were dehydrated tea bags.

"These people are an impediment," he said to me, "and you're not much better."

True. I was no help to him, out there half-dissolved in sunlight.

"Whatever I do," he said angrily, "your heart's not in it."

He was right. Maybe my heart was in the highlands or somewhere east of Suez or over the rainbow, but it sure as hell wasn't in this tacky desert galvanizing Assaman grunts.

"You might at least mingle with the rank and file while I am otherwise occupied."

"I do mingle."

"No, you don't. You *affiliate.*"

It was true. Time and again I found myself drawn in to the position of mediator between Grady and the workers.

"I thought it might help if I kind of hung out with them. Allayed their confusions. They don't know what they're doing here."

"Let's not forget what *we're* doing here. If you knocked off this buddy-buddy crap and just nosed around a bit, maybe you could come up with a clue about their shit-bricks."

I took a shot at nosing around, three shots, in fact. With my first two targets I used the same approach—admiration for the statues in the square. "What are they made of?" I asked Shakir bin Zaki, Minister of Information and Culture. He had no idea, he answered, and then invited my reflection on the decline of English literature since the demise of William McGonagall.

Yussuf Chapouk, champion rat-catcher, also had no idea about the mysterious fixative that so enchanted Grady, but he launched into a lather of detail about one remarkable day eight years ago when he came upon the most arresting, freaky creature of his career—a rat with one pink eye and one blue.

Turning to Abdul, a source no more unlikely than my two previous flame-outs, I began, not with a prying query but with an expression of wonder and delight in the palace sculptures, those behemoth figures whose privates went wall to wall, holding the ceiling in place—I got no further. Abdul gaped at me, his eyes glittering unpleasantly, as if he were mad Ahab and I were intent on telling him what a really cool dude Moby Dick was. "I hate those fucking things," he told me, "those literally fucking things. Their... whadayoucallit—eroticism is a laughable embarrassment, an affront to civilized architecture. Soon as I'm... soon as I can I'm going to destroy the hell out of them—get some U.S. engineers and build a decent palace of glass and stainless steel and translucent plastics and toilets that flush." Contempt (that could only have been meant for me) snarled his handsome face, creased his brow, twisted his mouth. "I can't believe," he said, "you like that barbaric shit!" And he strode angrily out of the room.

The triple failure was auspicious enough, I thought, to impress Grady with my total inadequacy in the field of BRIT detection. Once I'd reported it all to him, he couldn't ignore the futility of assigning me to any crazy-assed quest again. And that for me constituted a thunderous triumph.

I hurried to share the good news with Grady, but he was off, I was told, at the airstrip. Waiting for me instead was an old Assaman. He bore a note from Chatterton, inviting me to drop in on him. "I think you'd be interested in seeing what we've been up to," he had written.

I heard what he'd been up to long before I saw it. In the cramped pile of BRITs that served as Chatterton's laboratory, Gorelik coaxed shrill glissandi from his flute, and a few of the local performers who had provided the fanfare on our first night fitfully emitted a few responding blasts. They greeted me with extravagant inattention, just as their predecessors had that morning when I first appeared among them in Maryland; some things never change. Chatterton, despite his invitation, hailed me like a man preoccupied, as if I had intruded on some gorgeous fantasy he was intent on pursuing.

"We are on the cusp of a breakthrough," he shouted, beguiled as always by the misty splendor of his dreams. He shouted because the tumult his musicians raised was thunderously reproduced by an entanglement of mikes hooked up to a clunky but effective generator. "How are you, my boy?" he hollered.

At the far end of the complex, Gorelik and his backup band stood surrounded by Copros, like the bulb of an onion within its concentric leaves. Gravely they crowded in, ignoring the din, paying homage not to the reedy voice of his flute but to the hump on his back. *K'tu Bomumbojum,* something like that, they called him, Lord Camel, for the hump, like madness, was of divine origin and proved he was favored by some animistic tutelary.

I had suspected that Chatterton's madness would have qualified him as a candidate for veneration, with an adoring claque all his own, but it didn't. I had expected to find him jubilant, as he had been on the plane, by the prospect of having landed a receptive home for his crew as they untangled the sweet mysteries of ur-science, but he wasn't. Rather, he was full of frowns and fidgets, scratching his bare arms and legs fiercely, as if to mortify the flesh, and with no relief from whatever it was that tormented him. He dug his nails into his scalp as if the source of the itch resided there. When finally he quit scratching, he looked well enough in his loose-fitting toga. The cloak was knee-length and knotted at one shoulder, of a kind that elders of the tribe threw on to ward off the evening chill whenever the temperature dropped below ninety. Despite the immoderate exposure of wrinkled and raddled skin, he carried it off with the lumbering grace of a Clydesdale; he looked better in his toga than, say, Caligula, and it was a large improvement on that travesty of a bathrobe he sported back home.

"Ah," he said, crooning a nostalgic song, "we had some grand old times in Maryland, didn't we, when we were all pulling the load together."

I wasn't aware of them, but let it go.

"I've been waiting for you to reappear," he said. "Correct me if I'm wrong, but you don't seem to be heavily occupied with Grady in whatever frivolous venture he's been up to since he walked out on me."

"Well, I'm not as involved as he'd like."

"Then let me offer an alternative. Come back and work with me."

"Thank you, but..."

"I'm willing to make concessions," he went on tolerantly. "I won't prohibit your reading, although," he added, "for the life of me I cannot comprehend why you insist on seeing everything secondhand."

"I was raised that way," I apologized. "I believe I learned to read before I learned to talk."

"Or to think. But you must remember, I raised you from a sprout and I'm a flicker from being your father-in-law. Come back with me and I won't even expect you to think—if you find cerebration that difficult."

I didn't want his job, not in a millennium of Mondays. But I was curious. What kind of job encouraged a total absence of thought?

"What kind of job?" I asked.

"I just told you," he said, "that we are on the verge of the most desperately needed watershed in the history of the human race." He gestured at a bowl of wild cherries sitting on a low table. "I've put the fipple flute and the cymbals and all the rest of it together—that was the key, you see, mixing the frequencies—and I've seen a whole batch of cherries, not two or three, cavort and prance to the music. Observe, and try to be objective."

I did both as he gestured at the bowl of cherries. In it a few drupes popped about, as if prompted by an invisible hand. "And now," he yelled, "the time has come to record our progress so that, soon as the breakthrough comes, we can submit it for publication. I want you to write down what I tell you and then kind of trick it up, you know, the way writers do? I'd do it myself if I had the time."

"It wouldn't require any thought on my part?"

"Goodness, no," he said, "why should it? I'll give you all the data, and supply the biographical background. All you have to do is rearrange it a little and you'll have a runaway best seller."

I could scarcely believe my ears. Here he was, a bludgeoner of books whose contempt for the written word bordered on hysteria, and suddenly hell-bent on sweet-talking me into doing a book about his obsession. I was the alembic that would transmute him, in a few hundred tricked-up pages, from kook to Mme. Curie.

And then I knew why he fussed and fidgeted and scratched: that sacred, anonymous drive to discover the engine that would bring peace and plenty to a world endowed with neither had been somehow diverted to an itch for fame. Old Man Chatterton, whose churlishness was a mask for the corruptibility he claimed to abhor, had become an eager victim of the world he sought to raze, a seeker for personal glory, for the flotsam of—poisonous hiss of a word—celebrity.

He was scratching again. "When can you start?" he asked. "Tomorrow?"

I was beginning to feel itchy myself. I rubbed my chin, to prove how pensively I considered his offer. Stalling for time, my eyes swept across the cluttered laboratory—dominoes strewn about, my dented old tuba gathering dust, the Gorelik clangor in a corner, by turns tremulous and deafening, circled by a group of Assamans in a demotic sing-along. The air was thick with their snufflings, and they shuffled with a kind of boneless grace—the whole room seemed to shuffle to the discord.

"I can't do it," I said, sealing my extreme regret with a suitable sigh. "If I did he'd turn you off like a spigot."

"Would he dare to deny survival to humankind in the only world we've got?"

"I wouldn't doubt it. He's capable of anything."

Chatterton stared into the far distance as if to seek sustenance from the world Grady would deprive him of, and I took the opportunity to be on my swinging-ass way before that itchy Chatterton fungus got a headlock on me. I never told him that I too had seen his cherries cavort and prance—without, however, the benefit of orchestration. Take a bite of an Asso cherry and you get a mouthful of worms.

Grady wasn't at the airstrip. I headed home in the thickening darkness, only to find him waiting for me with Abdul at the edge of town.

"Where's Valerie?" Abdul asked, trying to hide his apprehension. "Is she with you?" Certainly he could see that she was not. "She's gone," he said.

"Maybe she's with Daphne," I said.

"I checked," Abdul said. "She's nowhere about."

"Then where the hell could she be?" My voice croaked like a man dying. If fear could kill, all of a sudden I was a corpse.

"I've got an idea," Abdul said, "but I was waiting on the off chance she was with you. Let's get Qazwini and the Number One Rat-Catcher."

"What would they know about it?"

"We need them," Abdul said. "Qazwini for fire power, Chapouk for tracking. I think she's been stolen." He walked fast, back toward the town.

"Who would do a thing like that?" I asked, catching up with him.

"I don't know exactly," he said, "but the night we got here, at the reception, there were tribal chieftains from the North. Any one of them could have kidnapped her."

"Why?"

Abdul shrugged. "Any number of reasons," he said. "Tribal animosity. Vengeance for a real or imagined affront. A yen for a particular woman, or just some mess-maker with a bug up his ass. Although," he went on, "you might have sparked the idea when you told my father—and we all heard you—'Look at her,' you said, 'a gift a king would envy'—something like that."

"I was talking about Daphne."

"Daphne, Valerie, it makes no difference. My guess is, some chief figured if my father got one of them, he should have the other. A matter of power or prestige or Christ," Abdul said. "What difference does it make when the important thing is to get to her before he does."

"What happens if we don't?"

"Well," Abdul said carefully, "in the North they have certain practices before a chief takes a captive bride. Practices performed on her."

"What?"

"Nothing unheard of around here, but something of a shock to those who are unfamiliar or unprepared for them."

"What?"

"Take it easy, kid," Grady said.

"What, goddamit!"

"Well," Abdul said in a tight voice, "genital mutilation. What they do, they sew up the lips..." His handsome face reworked itself into a painful frown. He swallowed audibly. "...the lips of the vagina. Then a week later they snip the stitches and cut off the clitoris and take her into the forest, where she is, ah... covered by the warriors who captured her. And then she is presented to the chief. He shears her hair, braids it into a whip, and beats her..."

"That's enough!" Grady said.

"Well," Abdul said, "he wanted to know. And it can all be averted if we get there fast enough." Impelled by his own words he started to run.

It took no more than a couple of minutes, interminable as they seemed, to enlist Qazwini and the rat-catcher. The four of us headed north into the desert, still a pale red flare in the dying sun. Yussuf carried a scimitar and my powerful flashlight. The General toted a horse pistol on each hip. For ballast fore and aft were a brace of knives. I had suggested that he conscript his entire constabulary to the cause, but Abdul rejected the idea. "The fewer the men, the faster we move," he said, pumping shells into a rifle I didn't know he owned. I also didn't know that Grady carried a Navy .38 until the moment he slipped it from the waistband under his shirt and for some reason pressed it on me.

The desert floor was rough and insubstantial in the half-light. We filed along after the rat-catcher as though we were adrift in some refractive, underwater dimension. Not a word was said, but only Yussuf was silent. Abdul's shotgun slapped loudly against his sweaty shoulder whenever he lost his footing, which was often. Qazwini snorted like a beast of burden, weighed down by his arsenal, and bellowed, absolute in his conviction that if he bellowed loud enough the raiders would hear him, and in a frenzy of fear return Val to us, roll over, and beg his forgiveness. I tripped and sprawled with a great deal of noise, which was lost, along with the din created by Qazwini and Abdul, in the tidal winds wailing and flailing the wasteland. Outcrops had the unnerving habit of taking on the guise of crippled giants with claws clutching at me while I, their not so nimble prey, floundered to elude them.

Yussuf led us on, his long body under the Pooh blanket bent over the trail, his nose inches from the ground, scarcely breathing.

"Watch out for snakes," Abdul said. "This place is full of snakes."

Don't think about them, it can only impair your feeble efficiency, I told myself. My mind swung back to Valerie. I felt she was threatened not only by the men who had snatched her, a reinforced regiment, for all I knew, but by her dubious rescuers as well. Yussuf had only his sword and my flashlight; he was defenseless against firearms. With Grady's .38, I couldn't hit water if I fell out of a boat. What worried me most was the General and his bullets. Once he started firing, Val would be vulnerable even if she were thirty feet from his target. The same was true of Abdul's scattershot.

The moon came up, throwing a white radiance over the sandscape. Yussuf hesitated on the trail, fussing, sniffing, sweeping the beam of the torch in front of us like a windshield wiper, while we waited, as we would for a trusted bloodhound. Qazwini made the most of the delay, peeing where he stood, guiding the spray with one hand, the other cocking and uncocking his pistol. Abdul leaned against a tree and I collapsed where I was, beside a rock, among the snakes and God knows what else. I knew if I closed my eyes, the chances of opening them ever again were pretty slim; I resolved not to shut them at all. Then Abdul was shaking me roughly. "Wake up," he said, "you've been screaming in your sleep."

Yussuf straightened up; he had found tracks. He started off again, chewing on a strip of rat jerky. We fell in behind him. I glanced at the luminous hands of my watch: nine fifteen. "How long was I sleeping?" I asked Abdul.

"About five minutes."

Yussuf pulled up short and stood motionless.

"Lose the track again?" Abdul asked.

Yussuf shook his head and pointed. "Rat," he said. "Fat rat."

"Let's go on," Abdul said impatiently. "You can spear it on your way back."

"It was beautiful," Yussuf insisted. "I want to kill it."

"Yussuf," Abdul said, "we've only got about seven hours."

And of course it was true. In seven hours the rain would come, drowning every sign of the raiders.

The white moon waned. The sand went black. I couldn't see Qazwini's thick shoulders six feet in front of me. I couldn't see my hand brushing the sweat from my face. Yussuf flicked the flashlight on and off, moving with swift assurance down what to him was a trail. I thought I heard sounds, sounds of what could only have been a moving enemy presence, but Yussuf gave no sign of awareness and certainly his hearing was more acute than mine, and his imagination less febrile. One consolation: daylight would soon dispel the night's obscurity, but it would also herald an end to hope. Even if Val survived the experience she would probably prefer that she had not.

How far we lurched and stumbled I do not know before a faint sliver of light broke through from the east. We came to a slot of gingko trees, bobbing and weaving in caloric waves. Before us stretched a scabby plain, totally devoid of life except for an immense cloud of insects that hummed and tumbled and pulsated, beating their translucent wings like fans, as if to keep from frying in the heat. Yussuf squinted at a thin, solitary wisp of smoke curling up on the horizon. "There they are," he said.

"How many?" Abdul asked.

"Nine," the rat-catcher said. He glanced at the sky grown suddenly dark. A flock of hysterical birds, thousands of them and out of nowhere, circled like a screeching tornado and swooped down on the bugs for the morning kill.

"What are we waiting for?" I asked.

"The rain," Abdul said, "or they'll spot us."

We waited. Not long. The sky opened up and the deluge came. Lightning turned the earth an electric blue. Red columns of thunder slouched across the plain and hammered my skull and I thought of my father scorching the earth of Vietnam as an artillery lieutenant. For the first time in years I remembered his stories of loud destruction. Odd, I thought, those stories told with incongruous relish by a quiet man about his days of bedlam. The notion had often crossed my mind that those war years were the happiest of his life.

We advanced across a sea of mud. The rain stopped abruptly; just as abruptly, the sun beat down again. The air was lustrously clear; we should have been able to distinguish every contour of the Jungfrau, about twenty-four hundred miles away, but there was nothing to see. Not a bird, not a bug, not the smoke of the fire Val's captors had built. They had disappeared like jinn into the emptiness.

"Where are they?" I asked.

To our right appeared a hairline fracture in the earth, which shimmered even as I watched, detaching itself from the mud and climbing upward. It hung in space, seething uneasily, a restless island in the sky. It was toward that hanging island that the rat-catcher pointed.

"It's a mirage," I said. He shook his head. I squinted into the painful luminosity and made out a thick, hazy stand of trees. They could have been dwarfs or giants; the very purity of the air diminished reality, intensified illusion, skewered distances. This place, alternately drenched by sun and rain, was as unstable as the enchanted boglands beyond Camelot, and Yussuf's pointed finger, like Merlin's long ago, gave substance to a capricious terrain, and we hurried to the trees before they vanished. There were noises ahead, the frail snapping of twigs, human voices. The rat-catcher was running now, we were all running, and the General was bellowing again as he fired his howitzer and the slugs screamed and ricocheted.

And then I saw nine large men and Valerie. They fanned out and fled, eight of them swallowed up by the desert, but the ninth was impeded by Val, whose wrist was cuffed to his by a rope of vine. He jerked her across the forest floor, reaching for his knife to cut the bond between them. Her face was swollen and misshapen, frozen by a gag, a kind of primitive bridle. She dug in her heels and threw herself to the ground and in a vortex of flailing arms and legs he went down with her. I got to them but Qazwini stormed up, flinging me aside. He shot the hand that held the knife. Bone, flesh, and blood exploded all over us. He fired again at the other hand and it came off, extracting Val from the rest of the body.

Qazwini stood over the man, his gun holstered but still smoking. His knife jumped out and he sliced strips of flesh down the man's chest and peeled them off, clavicle to groin. The man tried to lie still but his body twitched uncontrollably as he sucked air. Not once during the surgery did he cry out, not even when the General cut off his penis; it was as if he expected it. Now only his eyes were alive, and the General began to work on them. He gouged out the first—all this happening faster than it can be told—and turned to the second. My trembling .38 was an inch from that dreadful socket when I fired, and the warrior finally stopped twitching.

THIRTY-ONE

THE STONE-AGE MONARCH

I closed my eyes, tired of waiting, and with nothing better to do, opened them again. I tried not to listen, although I couldn't seal my ears.

I was in the presence chamber of the sheik. The room was covered wall to wall with rat skins sewed into carpets and stacked haphazardly, reminiscent of a warehouse in which only a rug merchant might feel at home. There were other touches, not unlike a dental office in the West. Old magazines were scattered about, not copies of *Sports Illustrated* or *Newsweek* or *House & Garden,* but of stroke books, their photos faded and smudged from thumbs and scrutiny over the years.

The sheik had summoned me to express his undying gratitude, so I had been led to believe. With two of his top panjandrums and his only legitimate son, I had been instrumental in averting a full-scale war with the tribe that abducted Valerie. For my dual role as guardian of the peace and warrior in the field I was to be embellished with a weighty decoration, at least the Assaman equivalent of the Distinguished Service Cross; such was the consensus of my fellow Americans. I remained skeptical. If, indeed, some sort of recognition was forthcoming, I felt it might more closely approximate the kudos accorded to Paul Revere's horse. The local citizenry in their evening sing-alongs had already documented the valor of our little expeditionary force, and particularly Val's stellar role as the focus of it all.

Valerie. Upon our return, she had sunk into a spiral of silence from which it seemed she would never surface. She avoided people, including me, whether to relive those long hours of captivity or to sort them out or to bury them or to discourage others from digging them up, I didn't know. I never pressed her with questions, but she knew I was there if she wanted me. And then she started to talk, an act of catharsis that, once begun, I thought would never stop.

"Life," she said.

"What about it?" I asked tentatively.

"Jesus," she said, "it's an endless trail. You never know what's waiting to pounce."

She sounded a little loopy. "At first," she went on, "I thought they'd be after you know like gang rape, but they weren't in the least interested. They behaved like little gentlemen, never laying a hand on me—maybe they were afraid of repercussions if the boss wacko ever found out. Even when I got rough with them, kicking or scratching, they just grinned."

She flicked a bug off her blouse. "But on the other hand," she said, "they wore a hole in me. They were one bunch of mean mothers, charm sure gave them the slip, a wad of wrecking balls. They put a gag in my mouth, tied me to a tree, ran me over rocks, Jesus, I thought I'd never be able to whistle again. When I put on the brakes or just collapsed, they'd drag me along like a kid pulling a busted toy."

A tremorous sigh. She wrinkled her nose. "And they were a little rank," she said, "all the time hawking and spitting, God, it looked like rice at a wedding. And they stank, Jesus, worse than the curs in town, like a pack of hyenas farting upward."

She shuddered. "The worst thing about it was not what those guys did, but Qazwini blowing that poor bastard to bits, and using a knife on him." A wobbly shake of her head. "That Qazwini, he was like a... a fanged vampire released from a coop who hadn't been fed blood for a while."

Her face twisted into a hard grin, spreading her lips without parting them. "But that's the way it goes, right, Charley?"

She seemed to harbor no hatred, no grudge, no deep resentment against her oppressors. She even apologized for them. "I don't mean to put the knock on those guys," she said. "I guess they only did what they had to do. And what did it all amount to but a long walk in the sandbox? Maybe I'm making too much of it."

Thus she dislodged the horror of it all. No irreversible damage had been done. She did not intend to mope around anymore, pondering the cruelty of fate. She had found her way back into the daily flow of Assaman life. Or so I thought, and so did she.

From somewhere beyond the alcove came the unmistakable gasps and whines and kabooms of coitus—Saeed al Sadr and Daphne at it again. The sounds of their frolic diminished, gave way to five minutes of lost whispers, muffled laughter, occasional coughing, and then the sheik appeared, clad in a bathrobe of many colors, Chatterton's gift.

He had changed since the night of the reception. He seemed thinner, and that wheezy cough bounced intermittently around his chest with the flat resonance of a muffled drum. On a shoulder was perched a strong-smelling monkey with arrogant, evil eyes, wearing a necklace of blue glass beads I had last seen at Daphne's throat. The sheik brushed the ape aside—it seemed to take some effort. The beast bared its yellow teeth in a snarl and scrambled up a phallic pillar.

Saeed called, "Zun!"—that's what it sounded like, more of a snort than a directive—and a moldy old gnome of a man appeared. Draped over an arm was a rat-skin pouch containing an aba, the burnoose worn by desert nomads—this, then, was my reward for gallantry. It symbolized, I suppose, my validation as one of the boys, an honorary citizen of the wasteland. "Accept this garb," said the sheik, "as a token of our esteem."

I accepted it with soldierly restraint, and we lapsed into silence. I thought I'd be dismissed at any moment; not so. Time dragged by; finally the old man said, "You did well against the pig-fuckers of the eastern *kasham beit*."

I nodded modestly.

Then, gesturing toward the aba, "We don't expect you to wear it," he added with a smile, "except on public occasions."

"I'd be proud to," I said. Not exactly the truth, but the truth at times can be unfruitful.

"That's hardly the case with your friend Abdul," he said. "He feels it is the uniform of backwardness. He does not approve of our ways. Nor does he approve of me."

That too was true—another unproductive subject I had the prudence to ignore. Once, long ago, in our shared ostracism at Chatterton's place, Abdul had alluded to his father as "the last of the Stone Age holdouts." Saeed al Sadr didn't look like, nor did he sound, Paleolithic to me. His speech was a trifle stilted, like that of a highborn Indian who had maintained the language of the ruling Brits long after the raj had expired. Despite his leanness and his cough, he remained an imposing specimen. Although his muscles had gone lax with time, he conveyed the power, the dignity of those sages on the ceiling of the Sistine Chapel.

The gnome had settled down in a corner. Who was he, I wondered, to sit in the presence of the sheik?

"He's like that damned monkey," al Sadr said.

My eyes went to the gnome. Indeed, there was something simian about him, the way he hunkered, his hands, too large for his body, dripping over his knees.

"Not Zun," the King said. "Abdul. He and that monkey share a certain attitude toward me. I have great affection for him…" he gestured toward the sullen little ape. His finger had a jagged gash in it. "…and he bites me."

"Abdul wants to modernize Assama," I said. "He is a man of purpose."

"He is a boy of rash purpose, hell-bent on making us into a pygmy, mock America. If he succeeds, he will destroy us."

"Then why did you let him let us come in?"

"I am an old man," he said. "I wanted Abdul back, and this was the only way he'd come. I thought he might change." Again his deep black eyes sought mine. "Do you think it is possible?" he asked.

It was another question I preferred to leave unexplored. Fortunately I was saved, momentarily, by a bell, a little silver one pealing thinly on the hinge of Daphne's wrist. She had lately discovered the bells of Chatterton's lab, and was not above lifting a few.

She traipsed in on us, all tarted up in a kind of see-through sarong. Saeed gestured with an almost imperceptible tilt of his head in the direction from which she had come. Daphne got it and, bell tinkling, traipsed off again. He turned back to me. "What about Abdul?" he asked.

And then, of course, I realized what I was doing there: he wanted to put the find-out on me—whose side was I on, regarding Assama's future, his or his son's?

"About Abdul…" I shrugged because I didn't have an answer. The best I could mumble was, "You'll have to be patient with him."

"If only *he* had a little patience… But he's become an American, and patience is the least cultivated of American virtues. So," he added, as if he were trying hard to integrate whatever enlightenment I might provide, "so, what really can you and my son offer us? Our values are so different."

"Who is to say that one set of ethical standards is superior to another?"

"You do. Or you wouldn't try to impose yours on us. Matter of fact, some principles of conduct are certainly better than others."

"Ours for us, yours for you."

"Generally, yes, but there are exceptions. Some of our most disturbed people embrace your values—Hashim Pachachi is obsessed by commerce, General Qazwini is preoccupied with guns. And they're not alone."

I nodded. "We're all hooked on one damn thing or another. We are all full of discontents."

"How'd we get that way?" he asked. "Was the whole human race irreparably flawed from the beginning? Genetically?"

I shrugged, lacking answers to his quiz, and somewhat confused by his rather formal lucidity in my language.

"I don't know either," he said. "Perhaps it started with the division of labor, when one man worked for another, or many worked for a boss. Perhaps it started with our first backaches, the result of walking upright, instead of on all fours. Or perhaps it started with an irreversible error committed by our distant relatives about two hundred and fifty million years ago. Our forefathers, the foolish amphibians, took the wrong evolutionary turn and left the sea, our home, our mother. We've been going downhill ever since."

He was quite serious. I suppose his jeremiad was no more absurd than any hypothesis of Original Sin or the Fall of Man, yet I found it worrisome. I stood there, haunted by the grisly inheritance of doom that he had bequeathed to me as if its very dubiety held some hidden truth. Were we lost, all lost, routed by some ruinous predestination, foreordained to live and die in darkness, without hope of self-deliverance or free will?

Curious and confusing, this old man and his hypothesizing on the source of human unhappiness. How was he even aware of the perceptions he spouted, this inconsiderably minor eminence on a rat-skin throne? Had he arrived at them by swilling his all-purpose beer, going into a trance to receive signals from some omniscient ancestor? Or did he, brooding in the wilderness, gedanken them through in a way that Chatterton would have approved of? I approved, but reluctantly. He'd thrown me off balance.

To say the least. Here he sat, cross-legged in a stifling room, a withered, knobby stalk of a man, still as a boulder in his burnoose schmatte, or some highly irregular vegetable that had cropped up out of the earth, yet with a mind as sharp and swift as a spear. He examined any idea that popped up. He espoused notions that might have been construed as faulty (who was to say?) but certainly he understood more about his world and mine than anyone (that is, I) would have suspected. That, I think, was what jostled me. And there was more to come.

"Of course, what I'm talking about are conjectures. Nobody really knows how or when or where it started." He winced, he frowned. "But I do remember when I became aware that there were vividly spookish people in every society. I was at Cambridge rooming with a young man from the Lake District who'd relax from his studies by eating glass, preferably crystal..."

Now all his pronouncements and meanderings became clear, once I knew where he had picked them up, along with his curious vocabulary. It was beyond mannered or stuffy, beyond the broad, clipped fricatives of sprucey English. Had I misjudged this dog-eating pooh-bah?

The King registered my surprise. "Abdul never told you I went to Cambridge?"

"Not exactly. He said you went to an English school; I thought it was a missionary school. Elementary. Here."

"Not quite the case. When the British ripped off a large chunk of Mesopotamia and manufactured Iraq out of sand and shale, they tried to make friends by bribery, or to influence the noncompliant by sending their sons to university, just as the Yanks sent my son to Georgetown.

"Still, Abdul prefers to think of me as backward and uninformed. I'm his skeleton in a closet that has to be swept clean. He of course would like to do the sweeping, and I think he'd like you to help him."

"I'm not good at that sort of thing."

"And why not?"

"Because I don't want to be."

He nodded slowly. "Would you be interested in keeping the closet the way it is?"

I hesitated, stalling. Saeed al Sadr waited patiently, and so did the gnome. He leaned forward, head cocked to indicate his curiosity, aroused at long last.

"I'm not sure," I said. "I'd have to know more about what's in it."

And then a dog bounded into the room, barking gaily, and threw himself into Saeed's arms: a ghost of a dog, a second coming, back from the dead.

"Where the hell did he come from?" I asked in a bloodless voice.

Saeed grinned. "You thought I ate him?" His fingers kneaded the ears of the ecstatic little beast. "According to Saint Paul," he said, "the Corinthians suffered fools gladly. I refuse to suffer them at all. But they're always with us; they petition me consistently for one damned thing or another.

"I don't wish to appear inaccessible to my people, so I've found a way of having *them* avoid *me,* by the simple expedient of spreading rumors about myself—that I am mean and eccentric, that I do frightful things, like eating a puppy and defying the label on a poisonous bottle of hair dye. Which also enhances the legend of my indestructibility, and that is not bad at all." He paused, then added, "I think we've had enough for one day."

We shook hands, and I galloped off in my burnoose tent.

THIRTY-TWO
THE CAVE AND THE ETHNOGRAPHER

Val and I loved to wander across the yellow plains, combed by the hot wind. (What, you say, I thought you hated the place? Well, I say, the world is full of hellholes, inhospitable and cruel, from Oymyakon in Siberia, where the temperature falls to minus eighty-nine point nine, to the Kalahari Desert, but, I say, even a pilgrim in Gehenna might be moved, even purified, by the sights—"Hey! Look at that there fiery pit!"—and sounds—"Just listen to those sinners scream!"—if he were in the company of someone he loved and cherished, and with whom he could share the experience and shape the remembrance.)

So we walked to the north, across the rifts and wide savannahs, to a rise where stunted casuarinas grew out of fissures in rocks split by lightning. Where, it was said, a sacred river once ran uphill, carrying golden leaves of a perfect tree in a holy place that sounded suspiciously like Paradise, an unparalleled eminence assigned to Mesopotamia (and what would now be Iraq) by Johann Durchfall, the early Moravian explorer and missionary. In a biblical controversy written months before he died, Durchfall propounded the notion; it was no more than that because he offered no physical evidence to support the hypothesis, and his logic was fuzzier than his theology.

I digress; to get back to Val and me—our hill—Val's and mine—had a crest as might be expected, and along its slope was an aggregation of caves, in any of which we could have woven a secret life. One of them had a mouth that was no more than a slit in its rocky face, and this was our retreat, a refuge from Grady's impositions, a cozy nest we had surfaced with a couple of rat-skin rugs after her rescue. Bubbling up from a rock-ribbed pond was the most delicious water I'd ever tasted.

We went there often, but on this day it was occupied. The Reverend Dewey Lipgloss, in the hallowed tradition of his calling, reclined in the missionary position and was being bounced all over our rat skins by a fat native girl. It was an egregiously private moment, and politely we turned away. But Lipgloss, entwined as he was, called after us.

"Be finished in a jiff," he gasped. "Then it's all yours." And he turned back to the business at hand.

I wanted to get out of there, but Val whispered, no, it would be discourteous, he was being friendly, he might think we were critical. So we settled down on the far side of the hill in a little bower shaded by flames of bougainvillea and tufted with springy bracken. Good as his word, Lipgloss and his partner soon appeared. Upright they made a peach of a pair. He was half her size, a scrawny little man with shoulders the breadth of her thighs and arms scarcely thicker than her fingers.

"We have spent the night in vigil," he said in a booming liturgical voice that seemed to echo in his beard. The beard tilted upward; he might have been smiling behind it, up at the fat girl. "A night of devotion," he boomed. "I've been meaning to get in touch with you. Shall we take a meet? Tomorrow? My digs?"

"Well…"

"Splendid. See you then." And he loped off down the slope with the girl.

His hut stood on the outskirts of Coproliabad, windowless and conical according to custom but larger than its neighbors. He sat cross-legged on the dirt-packed floor, studying a spread of tarot cards on what I first perceived in the gloom as a thick, low table. He greeted me and then spoke a few words to the table, which promptly levitated and changed, as if it were the thrall of a prestidigitator, into a prodigiously fat woman. The cards went flying off her ample rump. It was another rump, not that of the lady on the hill. Dewey Lipgloss, it seemed, was simply awash in steatopygous women.

"I hear you have your doctorate," he said, gathering up the cards.

"No, you were misinformed."

The girl sat silently on her haunches in the deep shadows. Now she had become something like a miniature tank.

Lipgloss frowned. "But you did graduate work at Yale?"

"Unsuccessfully."

"What was your field?"

"English lit. But…"

"Rats!" With that lame expletive the Reverend achieved a facile blend of vexation and resentment. "I had hoped," he went on, "it was theater arts or cinema or… Let me show you."

He got up, lit the wick of a tarnished brass lamp, and replaced the cracked chimney. Squat acrobatic shadows danced on the walls. I was aware of the sweet-sour reek of yesterday's flowers wilting in a tin can, tinged with the sharp decomposition of mildewed paper.

He picked up the lamp and led me into the adjoining room. A congestion of notebooks, stenographers' pads, and legal tablets rose in packs and piles from floor to ceiling.

"For more than twenty years," he said, "I've been doing an ethnography on the Coprolian people. Assamans, from the time they quietly broke off and established, so to speak, an independent fiefdom from Iraq. It covers just about every area of their culture. It could make a sensational documentary, a series that could play on TV forever, with somebody like a young Bette Midler narrating. I was hoping you'd help turn it into a screenplay."

"The man you should see," I said helpfully, "is Derek. He knows all about theater and film and—"

"I don't like him," he said forthrightly. "I don't think he knows all about anything."

He reached for the topmost legal pad, flipped it open, and pushed it toward me. I looked at the constipated little ciphers crowding the yellow page. They were faded by time, foxed by nature, stained by beer.

"I can't read it."

"Suppose I dictate? You'll find it fascinating and instructive."

It was a fanciful and presumptuous statement. "I really don't have the time," I said.

"Hold on," he admonished, "let's not be hasty; do you know their story of Genesis? They have one, despite their absorption in animism. They believe somewhere out there a conglomeration of gods got together in a kind of celestial circle jerk and created the world and the Assamans by a few strokes of divine masturbation. They have an Eden myth, with a slight twist—*their* Adam and Eve were prisoners of the demon Snake, bowed down, quivering in a fiery pit, until they got the Snake shit-faced on beer, and escaped to the desert, where they and their offspring lived happily ever after. They believe that if you step on the shadow of the sheik, he dies. He's supposed to be the descendant of the rooster deity; Balakar, the mother of the gods, was a chicken. That's why, with all the chickens around here, the people won't eat them, except in the performance of some kind of rite or other."

He had an unsettling habit of punctuating his sentences with snorts, sudden little tic-like explosions, as though he were afflicted by a channel-blocking allergy. Even more repellant was his habit, following every snort, of wiping his nose on the crusty hair of a forearm before he launched yet another anthropological zinger.

"They believe," he said, "that fireflies are the restless souls of infants who died before the rite of purification was performed. I could go on." He snorted.

Please don't, I thought, but the Reverend Lipgloss wasn't one to short-stroke a sermon. "They've got a thing about snails," he said, "you know about that? They eat raw snails with relish and trepidation, then they place the empty shell on a dish and pour out beer as an offering. They crave pardon of the ghost of the snail, beseeching him not to tell his brothers and sisters how he died. If he did, the family would dispatch a sick but heroic snail to tempt the man who upon eating the martyr would himself take deathly ill. Their word for 'sick snail' is *razrustam,* which is also a word for foreigners. They believe foreigners are rotten inside, each of them born with a hundred and ninety-eight evils within him, but how to dislodge them nobody knows. Prayer doesn't do it."

He ran his hands through his hair, as if he were plastering it down with water. "They might be right," he said. "I tried."

He moved to a prie-dieu, a relic presumably of his former life that he had transported to Assama. His hairy hands gripped the high straight back as if it were a pulpit. He was just warming up, I realized, for a long, chewy, confidential homily, the kind that he believed was just as fascinating and instructive as his unborn screenplay. The kind that, as it turned out, would have probably enthralled the bejesus out of his stateside parishioners.

"When I was young I tried everything," he confessed, "to purge the evil within me. Prayer. Fasting. Mortification of the flesh. Would you believe I even tried abstinence? A wretched experiment, but from it I learned that chastity is the only perversion known to man."

His eyes burned in the light of the brass lamp. A flicker of keen satisfaction settled over his face—that part of it uncluttered by the beard—as he explored the depth of his depravity. His bronzy voice held a certain swagger, the secret pride of the truly unrepentant that was at discord with his testament.

"I stupefied myself," he went on, "with drink and drugs, seeking salvation and a Sign, finding no gladness, no Jesus-joy in them. I was like a grimy old wino, yearning to bathe in the Lamb's blood of the Lord, draining instead the bitter dregs of self-estrangement and a lost faith.

"Somewhere along that road to ruin I seem to have suffered a loss of memory. One Sunday morning I couldn't find my church. I realized I only liked it when it was empty.

"I had physical problems. My hair fell out. My face sprouted pimples. As a Protestant, I found myself oddly engaged—praying to Guido von Eichbuchl, patron saint of sinners with boils.

"I had to start afresh, to walk the lonely places of the earth, to find myself by losing myself. So I came here; I haven't had a sleepless night since I got off the boat. Would you believe my hair started growing again? That clerical collar, like a noose, was cutting off circulation to my brain. I discovered that there is indeed life before death, and that it is good and meaningful. Withdrawing from the world, I became part of it, became what I am today— a peaceful and a happy man."

"You simply showed up one morning and they accepted you, no questions asked?"

"At first they were a bit suspicious, even hostile you might say. But as soon as I understood something of their customs I was able to fit in, even contribute. So it wasn't entirely a one-way street. I paid my dues. I filled a gaping need."

"For what?"

"Well," he said, "the Assos, unlike the Muslims, take rather a dim view of virginity. They find defloration not only messy but a dangerous business to be avoided if at all possible. So I volunteered for the job—somebody had to do it—and I became the more or less official virgin eradicator. It worked out fine for everyone concerned."

"You've treated this aspect of the culture in your ethnography?"

"Couldn't honestly avoid it. You'll find it in the chapter headed 'Stomping Out Virginity.'"

"Are there other chapters where you appear?"

"Only in about half of them. About fifty-fifty," he said modestly. "You know—primitive man emerging in the modern world, and a modern man groping his humble way among the primitives. Quite a nice balance, don't you think?"

"Quite."

Lipgloss leaped on the word. "Then you will take it on?"

I thought about it. I hadn't escaped graduate school only to drown in a pool of Lipgloss's disintegrating notebooks. On the other hand, I needed to show Grady something more than my bedsheet of a burnoose, and these cryptic scribblings at least *resembled* research—maybe there'd be something about the BRITs in there. I scooped up some notebooks and Lipgloss beamed.

"Banshah!" he called to the soft fat girl in the other room. She slithered through the door, holding the deck of tarot cards. She lay down before him in sections, like an elephant entering a mud bath. He shuffled the cards on the bulge of her ass, and that's the way I left him.

The theater was a craterlike depression in the earth.

"Energy!" cried Derek. "Otto, give me some energy!"

The actor called Otto looked stunned.

"Leo!" Derek shouted. "Remember the subtext!"

Leo blinked and regarded him blankly.

"All right, Gilda," Derek said to Daphne. "Take it from the top. And this time let's shift into high."

Something sounded vaguely, disturbingly familiar, like a sudden onslaught of déjà vu.

Daphne said, "Okay, but, Jesus, where the hell's Ernest? How can I play the scene without Ernest?"

Nobody knew where Ernest was.

Derek said, "Okay, just do it. I'll feed you Ernest's lines."

Daphne bowed her head, then shook it wildly. She breathed deeply, in, out, and whirled to face Derek. In a fruity, relentlessly Oxonian accent, "I'm sick of this studio," she lilted. "It's squalid! I wish I were a nice-minded British matron, with a husband, a cook, and a baby."

"Oh, shit," I whispered in Valerie's ear.

"What's the matter?"

"He's doing Noel Coward. *Design for Living.*"

The previous evening Val and I had been sitting outside with a couple of beers and watching the world go by. Carefully she put her bowl on the stoop beside her. "I heard from Derek today," she said. "He dropped by when you were out."

I had seen little of him since the night of the welcoming bash—God, could it have been a month ago? Once we met on the street for an interminable ten minutes devoted to his complaints. His hut was too small, too dark, too uncomfortable, too accessible to the sounds and smells of pedestrian traffic. He objected to spellbound people in a noisy trance or coupling at all hours before his entryway; like most rakes he was excessively conventional.

His hair dryer didn't work. He was sure Chatterton or Grady or Daphne had extra batteries that they refused to share with him. He was denied the use of the sheik's washing machine, and his dashing white bush jacket with trousers to match (bought in lower Manhattan, probably from some theatrical costumer) were turning yellow as the leaves of a New England autumn.

I had been lazily tracing doodles in the dirt; now as Val mentioned him I calcified.

A man has feelings that range from mild dislike to sheer loathing for the former lover of a present love; whatever the ferment, it is invariably tinged with the glacial residue of fear. There's always the chance that some spark of affection has survived and might be rekindled into a conflagration, a terrible awareness that sexual history has the nasty habit of repeating itself. I was sure that Val remained unaffected by the proximity of that narcissistic clown, but yet... and here he was, calling on her. When I wasn't around.

"What did he want?" I asked in a throwaway voice, flattened to stress casual disinterest.

"He's preparing his first play," she said. "He wanted to know if I'd be in it."

"And you said...?"

"What the hell's the matter with you?"

"You said that to him?"

"I'm saying it to you, Breslau. You really believe I'd be interested? I hate plays anyway. I can't even read them, they're all such bullshit."

"Comes in handy, I bet, having an elegant yet earthy, all-purpose aesthetic..."

"Come off it, Breslau."

"...that dismisses in one word the entire corpus of drama."

"Why don't you go screw, all right?"

"Just don't exaggerate. Some plays are wonderful."

"You mean like *Hamlet*?"

"*Hamlet* and many more."

"Well, I read *Hamlet* in high school. Son of a bitch stands around scratching his ass, can't make up his mind to do a simple thing like off the louse who offed his daddy."

"So what did you tell him?"

"Derek? I told him thanks but forget it, I got other things to do, like trim my toenails. Still," she mused, "I'd like to know what he's up to, wouldn't you?"

So there we were, watching Derek squeeze a performance out of his actors as if they were so many tubes of dried-up toothpaste. When the ordeal was over, he joined us.

"What do you think?" he asked, fishing for plaudits.

Valerie stifled a tiny yawn. I nodded my head with slow approval, a solemn aficionado of the arts.

"I know we're just blocking it out," he said, "but did you catch the nuances?"

"It has your imprint," I said.

"Derek," Valerie said, "you've done it again."

"What about the architectonics?" Derek asked. "I mean, doing it in the round, in the open, the interdigitation of the actors with the site, defining space, merging it with content, you know?"

"Absolutely," I said.

"That's what I like about working here," Derek said. "Broadway's so stifling, so commercial. Here I can free my instrument."

"Yeah," I said. "You can't get any further off Broadway than this."

"Yeah," he said gravely. "The vehicle needs work, but there's something there. I'll just have to keep digging for it. Problems, problems." He dabbed at his brow with a neckerchief of a vile color, made more so by the stains of honest sweat. "As soon as I stomp out one brush fire, another one starts. Would you like to play Ernest?"

"I don't think I'd be up to it," I said.

"I'd work with you... But no, I guess not. *My* Ernest has a certain decency—integrity if you will—that's rare and beautiful. But it's hard to sustain, particularly when he doesn't show up. Still, I'd better stick with him."

"I understand."

"Well," he said, "back to business." And he strode off, the imperator of the boards, burdened with responsibility, burning with a luminous mission.

The noise was deafening, an erratic, high-decibel fury that blasted my ears long before my eyes were close enough to identify the source. Nerve-jangling, tooth-rattling, it seared the brain pan and drowned out the farts of the generators. It shook the earth and trembled the sky, and it came from the site of the nuke facility.

The impacted flat was swarming with Assamans in their bright orange hats, raptly attentive to the spasms of sound as they went about their chores. Grady sat in his jeep at the edge of the field, his sharp and scornful eyes on the working stiffs as they toted hunks of BRIT from one unlikely place to another. He watched them with a kind of imperious complacency, the way Cheops (as Chatterton had reminded me long ago) might have observed the Israelites building his pyramid. Without a word he motioned me into the seat beside him. We drove for five minutes before he cut the engine and removed his earplugs.

Silence did not reign, but the din to some degree was diminished by distance and a propitious sirocco that blew the tumult away from us. Although the irregular beat of the discord, even from far away, was hardly restful, it was no longer deafening.

Around my head a flawless purple-rumped butterfly fluttered. A long way off the orange hats of the Assos glistened and swarmed like the helmets of a Roman battalion.

"Well. The gang's all there," I said.

He snorted. "You know how many of 'em are working for me?"

"Looks like, I don't know—five hundred, a thousand?"

"A vast multitude," he said. "Maybe a hundred."

"What are the rest of them doing?"

"Whooping it up for Chatterton. He's got some kind of crazy-ass notion about acoustics—increase the volume, multiply it and its echo again and again and again, and it'll somehow agitate his dominoes into motion. The Assos are having a hell of a good time, crowding into his lab and beyond, blatting and bleating and... and..." the more he talked the madder he got, "...drumming and banging." With swift impetuosity he ripped off his pith helmet and slashed at the butterfly. He missed, which did nothing to defuse his anger. "Goddamn bugs," he said.

"Why don't you stop them—Chatterton's recruits?"

"And lose my hundred grunts? As it is, whenever Chatterton calls a two-minute time out to adjust a mike or a generator or something, they all stand around like statues until it starts up again."

"There's a big desert out there. Why not send 'em deep into it?"

"Because my hundred grunts would go with them. They love the noise." He gulped a Maalox. "It's a goddamn dilemma," he said. "Where are you with the BRITs?"

Nowhere, I should have told him. But stalling, I said, "I picked up Lipgloss's ethnography..."

"Quit stalling," he said. "What did you find out?"

"I found out he's got hundred of notebooks, and every one of them is totally illegible."

"So decipher 'em. Sooner you do, the sooner I'll put you and your doxy on a plane. With a creepy smile he added, "Just get started, and you'll be happily surprised at how fast it'll go."

THIRTY-THREE

PLOTS AND PLANS

In the early days of my imprisonment I had concocted energetic plots, devised feverish plans of escape. To overpower my jailers was inconceivable but to outfox them was certainly within the realm of possibility. People less self-reliant than I were always managing to do it. They drugged guards and expropriated their uniforms. They masqueraded as corpses or a bowl of sushi—the list was as long as the catalog of B movies. But with all the know-how books I had read and all the television I had seen, I still couldn't figure out how to evacuate a tenth-rate slammer.

I tried a number of maneuvers; example: bribing a jailer I took to be corruptible with a jar of salted peanuts Chatterton had left behind. The man accepted the lure with an air of entitlement. It never occurred to him that he was being greased, and my attempt to enlighten him was met with stony incomprehension.

Another tack: flattening myself against the wall beside the door and screaming until I was hoarse, steeling myself for the guard flying in to investigate and my flying out to freedom. It was a project that came to nothing, because my howls were totally ignored.

Failure generates resignation. Although I don't have a precise day and hour of execution, the more that time goes by, receding from the future and galloping pell-mell into the past, the more I am aware of its running out.

I haven't seen Valerie for ten days, maybe eleven. Does Abdul have a lock on her? Or—a far worse possibility shivers me—is her absence a personal decision that Abdul has nothing to do with?

I hear footsteps like the muffled beat of a drum coming down the dark corridor. Could it possibly be Val, checking in at long last? Or is this my appointed hour of doom, time to get shafted on the stakes? Who else could be calling? Anybody, but nobody I could put a name to.

I freeze in a stupor of anxiety. The thick crossbar that bolts me inside the jug disengages. Slowly the door creaks open, like the promise of doom in a horror flick, and I cannot believe I'm staring at Derek. He says, "Hi," as if we were neighbors meeting in the supermarket. Then he says, "How's tricks?" Before he can ask, "What's new in your line?" or some such fatuous question, I cut in.

"There's something," I predict, "you'd like me to do for you?"

Immediately, he gets to the point. "I need money," he says. "I figured you wouldn't be needing what you got, so...?"

"What for?"

"Well," he said, "I'm kind of hooked a little on drugs..."

"Hard stuff?"

"I don't know."

"How can you not know?"

He shrugs. "I get 'em from the witch lady who runs the head shop. We don't speak the same language."

"You got any idea where Val is?"

"No. I could get you some uplift from the old bag."

"I don't think so. I've got to keep alert in case—"

"You could feed it to the guard. And when you get past him you slip it to Abdul."

"How could I do that?"

Again he shrugs. "Maybe your friend, the blind old geezer in the palace, would help." He's getting carried away, like any gutter punk talking smack, and he isn't through yet. "Then," he goes on, "you might stir a little into Grady's ice cream."

"I doubt if I could."

"How do you know if you won't give it a whack? Jesus," his eyes sweep upward, appealing to an invisible authority. "He's about to get hit with an axe and he's squeamish. Don't you at least want to see what she's peddling?"

It's my turn to shrug, and suddenly I'm drained. His chumminess exhausts me.

"How much do you want?" I ask.

"As much as you can spare. The more the better." he looks at me, flushing with monstrous sincerity. "I really appreciate it," he says as, thank Christ, he leaves. The night closes in, black as hell.

THIRTY-FOUR

THE CARRIER OF LIGHT AND POWER

In the words of the old hymn, there's more than one way to fuck a duck. I battered my head on Lipgloss's clubfooted prose, mindful of Grady's gloomy threats. I spent an entire afternoon deciphering about a dozen pages, with the Reverend a witness to the struggle, dawdling breathlessly for some word of praise. I waited for a segue to my target, and, finally, after a few false starts, I found one.

"It's fascinating," I told him.

"Wait till you get to the oral histories," he said, preening with pleasure. "It's steamier than the Boccaccio of Decameron. What these guys try to do with their tools you wouldn't believe."

"That's what interests me," I said. "Tools. And building materials." I put down the legal pad and plucked at my lower lip, evidence of deep thinking. "I suppose you devote some space to them?"

He frowned. "It's in there somewhere," he said helpfully. "You'll just have to plow on till you come to it."

"It's hard to wait," I said. "I got this limited attention span."

No answer.

"So tell me," I persisted, "how did these people manage to construct the sheik's palace, for example, without lumber or steel or…"

"You know what they use."

"But how do they hold it together? What's the glue, the adhesive?"

"Beats me," he said. "I think it's in here somewhere."

"But you don't remember exactly."

"Can't say that I do."

Some sudden incongruous twist of mind tilted my probe to Chatterton. "Is it possible," I digressed, "that the… the edifice complex of the Assos could be in any way connected to the building of the pyramids? With acoustics, maybe?"

"Why? Would that encourage you to write my screenplay?"

He was searching for any convergence that might whet my appetite for his script. Hell with that. "Tell you what—I just remembered—I got to wash my socks."

"When will you be back?"

"Soon as I… soon as I get my glasses from the States. I'm practically blind, you know. That's why I have such trouble reading your material."

"When do you expect your glasses?"

"You never can tell. You know how the mail is these days. Gone to pot since the Pony Express." I got to my feet. He was watching me suspiciously. Small wonder.

"In the meantime…?" he asked.

"I'll make do with one of those white canes."

"I mean, what am I to do in the meantime?"

I froze. "You hear that?"

"Hear what?"

"I thought it was a plane. With my glasses on it."

"I thought it was that durned music."

"I got to check it out. The sooner I get my glasses, the sooner I'll be back." I moved toward the door and sprinted for safety.

When I walked into our scratch-house, Val said, "Grady's been looking for you."

"What now?"

"What's ethnography?"

"It's a branch of anthropology dealing with a group's culture. Why?"

"Grady's got some kind of a wild hair about Lipgloss's ethnology. Says he wants you to get with it."

"No way. I can't do it."

"Can't do what?"

"I can't even read his writing. It's illegible."

For a moment she was silent, chewing a lip, scratching a bruise on her arm.

"You don't get it," she said at last, "do you?"

"Get what?"

"Don't you realize we're stuck here till Grady gets his recipe for BRITs? That he won't leave unless—"

"So let him figure it out."

"You like it here? Enjoying every moment? Waiting till we cook to death one day or freeze to death some night or flake out from malaria or dengue or scurvy or just plain squat to death from diarrhea?"

"Val, what Lipgloss calls ethnography is just a hybrid of what he imagines he's heard and seen with an added scoop of porno fantasies."

"How do you know if you haven't read it?"

"He told me."

"In five minutes? Ten minutes?"

I didn't answer. After a moment, "Oh, for Christ's sake," she said, "I'll do it."

It took more than a moment before her sturdy decision registered. When finally it did, "What a good idea," I said.

Grady was desperate for workers—every day, another armada was sweeping out of the sky, C-130 Hercules transports and giant helicopters flailing the earth with the arrogant roar of their engines, depositing yet another consignment of strange twisted girders, coils of metal, vats of chemicals for the nuclear complex. It was Chatterton who guilelessly ensnared Grady's ragtags; nine-tenths of them, it seemed, were irresistibly drawn into his inharmonious orbit, which left a constantly diminishing few in the field to haul all the components of atomic alchemy into place: reactors, breeder cores, axial compressors, blocks of graphite, beads of resin, assorted acids, corrosion resistants, enricheners, processors, converters, reflectors, centrifuge assemblies, jet-nozzle separators, vortex units, explosives and implosives, sealants, coolants, claddings, concrete shields and diffusion barriers, extruded aluminum ladders and landings, consoles of instruments that measured ergs and rads, curies and dynes, switches, knobs, gauges and computers, protective clothing, air conditioners, fire extinguishers, iodine tablets, Band-Aids, a library of manuals and advisories, a rash of closed-circuit TV cameras and screens for under-the-plume monitoring, and an ice machine (for Grady's parfaits and martinis). Just off the airstrip, all was readied to receive the more volatile elements of nuclear fusion, the climactic excitants scheduled to arrive later, but there was near to nobody to do it. They all preferred turns on my old abandoned tuba.

Grady took up the workers' delinquency with Pachachi, his straw boss, who suggested the application of a thicker stick. He approached other ministers who, he thought, had some clout; thus he learned that they had their own grievances, with little time and less inclination to tackle his. And yet their rebuffs were tinctured with envy, and that odd commingling added to the stress. Racism was the fundament, a loose and loaded cannon rumbling across a slippery deck, threatening to crush and destroy everything in its path at any uncertain moment.

From the day our plane first put down on their unpropitious soil, the ministers had been divided in their attitude toward us, and particularly toward Abdul. Some of them, like Pachachi, welcomed him, anticipating in his enterprising presence an increase in their prestige, while others feared the erosion of ancient values. They saw that their fiefdom was soon to be torn between the robust inertia of the sheik, their champion of the past, and the diligence of his son, that paradigm of the future. They saw in Assama's predicament a singular opportunity to thrive or (unthinkable alternative) to languish, reduced to insignificance as political bastards on the doorstep of the palace.

Much was at stake and the time for decision was short. For there was something in the hot, combustible air, something beyond the flummery and the infighting of officialdom, an aura of disaster that presaged the approaching storm, an expectation of doom about which I was but minimally aware. It was remote yet immediate, unreal yet insistent, as if the ministers, like friars of some mysterious faith, held an inscrutable secret they would not share with the rest of us. But secrets have a way of spilling out convulsively, given a little time, and so it was with this one.

* * *

That night I woke with a start. The man standing over me continued to knead my shoulder. "The sheik wish to see you," he said.

"In the middle of the night?" My voice was raw with fatigue.

"Now," the man said. "Please, you come."

I slipped out of my rat-skin bed, interrupting the sweet quiet rhythm of Val's breath. She said, "Wha...?" and went back to sleep, and I staggered to my feet.

The town was silent, the street empty under the pallor of a high full moon as I floundered toward the palace. My mind was floundering too, in lockstep with my body. What the hell could he want of me? In his presence chamber two weeks ago he had mentioned, possibly out of politeness, that he'd like to renew our acquaintance, but, Jesus, at four o'clock in the morning?

The palace was brightly lit. Swiftly I was ushered down a long and narrow corridor I had never seen before to the royal bedroom, its walls and vaulted ceiling forming a tent of light, billowy wool.

He lay back on his pallet. His eyes smoldered. His breath came in shallow little bursts, as if it were pumped from a defective bellows. He looked smaller than life, meager. Standing over the bed was Abdul. Beside him was Zun, the big-handed gnome who had attended my award ceremony. He was visibly moved, stunned, as if he were witness to the irreparable collapse of his country.

"...natural-born casualties, all of them," the sheik was raging in his delirium. "They're carriers of greed, bred for trouble," he went on in a dull rasp, "parasites who prey on all living things." He paused, gasping, the eyes burnished by fever, the flesh desiccated, the color of timeworn cork, the parchmenty skin of a mummy.

He saw me. "I'm dying," he said. It was less a statement than an apology. With difficulty he refocused his eyes on Abdul. "I want you," he said, "to get the foreigners out of here. I think your friend Judd will help you. I want your promise..." He looked up pleadingly at his son. Not a line in Abdul's face responded; he wore a mask of numb inscrutability. The old man reached out. His fingers tugged feebly at the sleeve of Abdul's Brooks shirt. Abdul said, "I promise." The hand fell back on the bed.

After that, silence and the surdy whisper of the oil lamps as the epilogue of Saeed's life trickled out of him. With some effort he managed to maintain his great dignity despite the dark spittle that ran down his chin, despite the diarrheic plasma that fouled his lower body. Zun wiped the pollution from his mouth and his limbs. Then the rattle of death in the shriveled throat signaled the end to the people waiting, listening behind the curtained portal of the airless room.

The messenger appeared, and Daphne ran in sobbing.

"I killed him," she wailed.

"Be quiet," Abdul said.

"It's my fault," she insisted. "I overfucked him. And he was so good to me."

The ministers, when they filed in, were solemn, although their grief lacked the extravagance of Daphne's. They declared Saeed officially dead when a naked fourteen-year-old girl was placed on the bed beside him and he didn't raise a finger or anything else. The honor had been offered to Daphne, showing on the part of the funeral committee an exquisite sensibility for her feelings, but she balked.

"Jeez," she said to me, chewing on a lock of hair and twisting the frames of her glasses, "do I have to? I mean, I've climbed in the kip with a midget, Siamese twins, a Shetland pony, and once a duck. But a stiff...?" She shuddered. Zun led her away.

An ingenious nest of boughs was built in a tall tree, and Saeed was hoisted to his grave by eight strong and acrobatic pallbearers who passed him upward from hand to hand and branch to branch until he was high above the shadows, where the rays of the sun lacquered his flesh with a somber cobalt sheen. The sweating bodies of the pallbearers floated and swayed in the treetop like an arrangement of dewy flowers. I wore my aba.

"You're really going to do it?" Valerie had asked as I undressed for the funeral.

"It's a matter of respect. Don't you think I should?"

"Do you think you should?"

I nodded. "Although Grady'll think I'm some kind of nut."

"Screw what Grady thinks."

Daphne too was more than fugitively visible at the tail end of the cortege. Her head was bowed, her eyes downcast. She walked shakily, wearing corpse maquillage and a snug black dress that possibly inspired rescue fantasies in the two men who supported her, Reverend Lipgloss on one side and Qazwini on the other.

The acrobats tied the sheik safely in his swaying bier with a skein of vines. When they were done he seemed part of some intricate puzzle from which extrication was impossible.

For human beings, perhaps, but not for vultures. Directly they came and peeled off his flesh, until nothing remained but the tumbled hair and the unyielding milk-white bone. Hair and bone were collected and studied by the Number One Rat-Catcher, who served as the diviner of auguries. He also slit open a few sacrificial rats and examined their entrails for signs and omens. He scrutinized pebbles drawn from a heap, and globules of melted fat dropped into water. When he foresaw no immediate disaster—an eclipse of the sun, a thunderbolt, a freaky hailstorm like that which savaged the capital a century earlier—the funeral party became the coronation committee and Abdul was forthwith enthroned.

His acceptance speech was rich in political mantras. He promised peace and goodwill for the fief but warned that state stability would not countenance adventurism from the tribes of the north. He gave his sacred pledge to preserve the country's terrain and topography, but he pointed out that bringing unprecedented plenty to the people would require a bit of geographic surgery. He looked into the future and saw an age of unparalleled prosperity for his people, but warned that they might have to tighten their abas in order to achieve it. He said the old world of tradition and the new world of technology would coagulate to create a wondrous political and social order that would become a mirror for all mankind. He said he would not appropriate any power other than that traditionally accorded to the sheik but he would become director of the energy and strategic-resources program, just to speed things along. He thanked the spirits that the augurs had been propitiously interpreted and he thanked the people for their faith in him. He said he was humble, and proud of it. He said they would always have direct access to his presence, but they must remember that he was a busy sheik. He described himself as the Carrier of light and power, Devourer of time and space, Greatest Servant of man. Thou hast put all things under our feet, he concluded.

The people clapped elbows. The wheezy band played "Anchors Aweigh" again. The young women danced to the music, weaving and gliding among the young men, who darted and leaped on grasshopper legs. They all got shitfaced on beer and so did most of the foreign legation, myself included.

I fell to musing about that last, galvanic encomium Abdul had lavished on himself, "Carrier of light and power. Devourer of time and space"—strong stuff. It had a familiar ring, and, recollecting in drunken tranquillity, I remembered what it was: the inscription on an emblematic statue extolling Electricity in Union Station, Washington, D.C.

Abdul walked among the celebrants, who greeted him warmly, clutching his genitals nimbly to avoid stepping on his shadow. He made his way toward me. "Come back to the palace," he said. "We have to talk."

He eyed me in my aba, not as he would the Carrier of light and power, but as if I were a carrier of smallpox or a damn fool gussied up for Halloween. "But first," he said, "get out of that clown outfit and into something civilized."

"What's he want?" Val asked, back in our shack.

"Let you know when I find out."

"Five'll get you ten it's bad news." She was in her office, a corner of our hut where spread out around her were the stacked and scattered substance of Lipgloss's gleanings—twenty-some years of notes and observations of Assama's people. The notebooks Val had finished were stacked neatly in columns. She chose a beer-stained tablet from a haphazard pyramid and opened it. Five minutes later, as I was going out the door, "Holy moly," she said. "Here it is."

I stood there, hexed by her words. She said, "What Grady calls BRITs, it's a big secret handed down as a sacred trust from—get this—sheik to sheik, from Saeed to Abdul. Grady," she added, "is going to wet his drawers."

We sat in the throne room drinking the dry, light Rhine wine we picked up at the Leipzig duty-free shop on the way here. Abdul held his father's bowl, carrying to his lips the touch of flesh that had lately been feeding vultures.

We talked hardly at all, although something clearly was on his mind. So I sat and waited, providing an obbligato to his silence. I wanted to say, "I thought we came back here to talk," but the wine was pleasant and so was the silence, and there was about him a newfound air of regal inaccessibility I wasn't going to challenge. It didn't seem like the time to ask him to reveal his shit-brick birthright; all of a sudden, Grady was no longer the most imposing power-monger in my life.

Finally, "Isn't wine supposed to be a mood elevator?" he asked.

"Or a depressant."

He shrugged. "About Grady: he's trying to scam us. It's the wolf and the lamb, in spades. Well, the time has come for the lamb to kick a little ass."

"Not literally, I hope."

"Why," he asked scornfully, "do you always deplore violence? There is no quicker remedy, no better medicine for dealing with violent people." He paused, sipping his wine.

I said, "Don't."

"Don't what?"

"Do anything drastic."

"Drastic?" He scowled at my soppiness. "Christ," he went on, "what an insipid word for a... a long-overdue response to provocation."

"What kind of response are you talking about?"

"I haven't decided yet, although we can do whatever we please," he said. "Would you refill our bowl?"

I poured. The earth seemed to be quaking but, no, it was my hand.

"Don't be alarmed about Grady," he said. "We have no intention of stripping the skin off his back or cutting off his balls or..." he was warming to the subject, "or flattening him under his own bulldozer or firing him from the mouth of a cannon, as our ancestors once did to a British provincial governor, after chopping him up to fit in the barrel."

"That limits your options considerably."

He emptied the royal bowl. It resembled rusticated stone, which it wasn't, being of the same material that composed the palace and the rest of the public works. A speckled snake in hollow-relief sinuously encircled the vessel; the blunt head met the tapered tail and swallowed it to close the ring in a self-perpetuating, self-consuming paradox.

He plunged back into speech: "Many alternatives are available—when the time comes. Grady..." he spoke the name like a malediction, "he thinks he's so smart with his managerial know-how and his runaway skills—attributes which have propelled you Yanks into so many global messes. He talks about improving the lot of our people, but all he wants is a big piece of the action." Again the smile. "Sorry to bad-mouth your..." his voice dripped disdain, "mentor, but what's ironic—he's so greedy it affects his sight. You follow me?"

Me. So deep was his concentrated hatred for Grady he had relapsed to the plebeian *me.*

"No, I don't."

"What we mean, his brains seem to small up, confronted by any potential beyond his immediate goal. Once he supplies us with two four-forty-megawatt reactors for electrification, what are we going to do with them?"

"Attract industry."

"Suppose we develop our own? And tell Grady," he added with relish, "to go shit in his ice-cream machine. What do you think?"

"Think you can do it yourself?"

"We can with your help. Interested?"

Before I could demur, Qazwini barreled in. At his waist were two guns and a knife with a nasty blade. In each ear was lodged a U.S. silver quarter. On his face were dark aviator glasses and the turbulent scowl of a Mescalero. Abdul's attention was still riveted on my sweaty brow. "We've confided in you," he said, "knowing you won't betray our trust. Let us confide a bit more."

From the square came the sound of the muted voices and shuffling feet of the people as they strutted in their hard hats at the end of the day.

"General Qazwini," he said, "wants an army."

"I see."

"What do you see?" Qazwini asked belligerently.

"I see that an army would be something the General would enjoy."

"We are not put on this earth to enjoy ourselves," the General said in a voice that took me by the lapels. "We are here to be tested."

I turned to Abdul. "What do you think?" I asked him.

He said nothing.

"There are threats of subversion," the General said darkly. "We face tribal strife. Enemies are at our borders. Without an army we encourage them to commit acts of terror and aggression."

I turned back to Abdul. "You think the Goths are at the gates?" I asked.

"We must make our fatherland safe from those cannibals in the north," Qazwini insisted, "so nobody can come here and eat us. Have you forgotten what they tried to do?"

"You've managed to thrive for centuries without an army."

The General bared his teeth at me. They were blackened by betel nut. "Times have changed," he said. "Now our enemies are envious of our king, of the wealth he will bring us. They will attack to get it, and we will be powerless against them. Our defense system consists entirely of two second-hand .20 millimeter guns from World War II that the British left here, so you know how worthless they are."

He turned to Abdul and unleashed a torrent of words in his tribal argot. The sheik smiled. "He wants to know," Abdul translated, "why you're so oppositional to affairs that don't concern you. He wants to impress on you the fact that we stand at the threshold of world power, and no power in the world exists without an army. He also hopes that two hundred and fifty syphilitic salamanders grow in your belly." Abdul yawned. "All this talk is beginning to bore the bejesus out of us," he said.

"Would you welcome a candid opinion?"

Abdul said, "Not particularly."

Qazwini's fusion of strut and vinegar had touched a nerve of resistance in me. Now Abdul's curt incivility had inflamed it to flashpoint.

"In that case," I heard myself saying, "what the fuck am I doing here?"

Qazwini gasped. An inky driblet of betel juice bubbled from his mouth and leaked down his chin. Abdul favored me with a fierce, granitic stare. His fine face was coarsely altered, resembling itself as a bad photograph might, but for only a moment. Then the ferocity and the stoniness vanished, as if a soft hand had passed over them, and the features relaxed and he was handsome again, gazing calmly at me, restoring harmony.

"You must try to understand the General," he said.

That, I thought, would be like trying to understand the daydreams of a rhinoceros.

"It's an embarrassment to him that despite all the pips on his shoulders he doesn't have even a platoon to command, just a sorry, shredded scrap of a constabulary."

"With all due respect to the General," I nodded deferentially in his direction, "I don't believe he could train an army."

"We'll get advisors from the best land force on earth. We want you to draft a letter—that's why we asked you here—to the Israeli Defense Minister, requesting an instructor to organize our military."

"Who will pick up the tab?"

"We're sure Grady would respond, to protect his investment."

"But—"

Abdul cut me short. "We have reasoned together. We intend to proceed with our plans," he said, "with or without you. It'll take a while to get rolling, so you'll have a little time to decide. We can't make you do what we ask," he added soothingly, "we can only make you wish you had."

Knowledge is a dangerous thing, multiply dangerous because I was privy to a couple of particulars Grady with all his sagacity did not suspect, and I was hesitant to share them with him.

Should I have confided that Abdul planned to kick him out of the country and gain control? That it was Abdul alone who knew the formula, and he had no intention of sharing with Grady, who was hellbent on snagging it? What could such a confession have accomplished? It could only have intensified the discord between them, and precipitated a showdown that would be disastrous. It was not beyond Grady's influence and resentment to call in the Marines in the North, under the guise of safeguarding American lives and property. Assama had so far escaped the war on the other side of the mountains; now it would become another battlefield, with Coproliabad immersed in a bloodbath as were Baghdad, Kirkuk, Mosul.

A wall was being built between Grady and me, as strong and substantial as that which existed between him and the Assos. I was for the first time consciously aware that I was on their side of the barricade, and for reasons that I was not quite able to grasp. Was it guilt, aggravated by the act of bringing grief, however indirectly, to a disadvantaged race? Or shame, in being identified with the aggressor? Or was it an excess of pity for the afflicted masses?

All I knew, the affinity existed. I wanted their friendship (by which I possibly meant approval), knowing they would resist any attempt on my part to gain it, not only because of the skin I wore but because of the company I kept. I felt terribly alone, isolated from them and, by a curious inversion, from my own kind. In the slow, sleepless hours of the night thoughts of doom like panicked bats flopped crazily and uncontrollably around my head.

The arsenal of fear has many weapons. When a man knows that the baleful eye of the enemy is on him, particularly in the dark, he is prone to finding it as disturbing as the application of a knout. I'd lie on my shoddy pallet, scarcely breathing, bathed in flop-sweat and jolted by the race of my heart, alert to the crack of a twig or the quiet footfall of somebody out there, or was it just another rat restlessly scurrying? I'd get up and look around. There'd be nothing under the black sky, nothing that took the phantom shape of a spy in the surging silence, so I'd go back to bed and with a mind still unrelieved wait for that inevitable midnight knock on the door.

I wrote Abdul's letter, but not without a certain somatic recalcitrance. My back ached as I bent over the too-small desk. My head ached in the fumes of the oil lamp. My eyes, even when I closed them for a moment, stung in the feathery penumbra behind my lids. My face felt scarlet in the lamplight, as if I had a fever.

Certainly it was no concern of mine, as Qazwini had correctly observed, if Abdul's fief or province or whatever it was got an army. Yet I wanted no part in getting him one, or of placing such power in his dirty hands. I saw myself as Harry Truman, drafting the paper that ordained the devastation of Hiroshima, a vision that was palpably absurd, yet persistently approximate. Do not most countries (with the possible exception of Switzerland and the Vatican) sport an army only in order to use it? I pitied the poor Assos on the verge of conscription, the tools and toys of a bullheaded butcher, this student of mayhem who had flunked civilization, who was now in the process of inventing a perilous future for them.

And I still felt I was being watched in the night.

"Somebody's out there," I said, glancing up at Val from the letter I had written.

"It's your imagination," she said. "Don't let him gong you."

"Abdul's not gonging me," I said irritably, "and neither is Qazwini. It's just," I rubbed my eyes; they were as rough as stucco, "I haven't been sleeping lately."

"They've been destroying you, even when you sleep, starting with your teeth. You grind them all night long."

"Bad dreams."

"Sure," she said, "well, let me tell you something: it's getting to me. When you started grinding, a couple of weeks ago, I'd put a finger in your mouth, and you'd relax. Last night..." she held up a red and swollen finger as evidence, "you damned near bit it off."

"Sorry."

She shrugged. I lifted the sheet from the platen of the typewriter, reading:

Headquarters, General Staff
Israeli Defense Force
Jerusalem, Israel

Sirs:

Invoking the comity of nations, coupled with a deep regard for your country and a personal admiration for its leaders, we are prepared to seek the expertise of our Israeli friends in the task of establishing an infantry brigade for Assama, Iraq.

Pursuant to that goal, it is our wish to promote the earliest convocation of a conference between your representative(s) and ours, to take place on Assaman soil, with the purpose of exploring ways and means of effectuating a military arm including subsystems and ancillaries, technologies and instruction in all categories that comprise a highly efficient and tactically sound land force. We therefore respectfully request the attendance of an officer, of not less than field rank and of your choosing, under whose guidance our aspirations might become a reality.

Please accept the assurance of our high esteem, and with it the hope for a favorable response. We remain,

A twig snapped loudly. I strained to listen. It was all I could do to keep from raising a cupped hand to an apprehensive ear and whispering, "Hark!"

"You hear that?" I asked.

"Jesus!" Val said. "Here we go again. It's the wind in the trees."

"I'm going to have a look."

"Why? I mean, if nobody's there, it's a waste of effort. And if there is somebody, the sensible thing would be to avoid him."

"I want to know." I doused the lamp, waited a moment until my eyes grew accustomed to the dark mucilage of the hut. Then I slithered out the door.

There was nothing I could detect in a night so suffocatingly black it had no gradations. It was like being inside a mountain, and just as reassuring. Still I stumbled ahead, from one shrub to another, and then I saw a dense shadow weaving about, close to the ground, like a large warthog rooting for acorns. I squinted; now I was not more than twenty feet from him, but he didn't notice, so intent he was on... on what?

My foot caught a creeper. I did a kind of loopy half gainer, landing on all fours and eye to eye with the warthog. The warthog blinked first, aware of my shadow, and shied from it. He said, "You come out to help me look?"

"Look for what, Derek?"

"I dropped that goddamn bowl of beer," Derek said, cottonmouthed. He smelled sour. "Can't find it anywhere. R'diculous."

"Come on in," I said, wobbling him to his feet.

He sagged in a corner, curled in the fetal position. "I'm sick," he said, digging his fists uneasily into his crotch. His face was sullen and flaccid. "I want to go home." Unexpectedly, untheatrically, he started to cry.

Valerie and I exchanged a muddled glance. "Going home shouldn't be too hard to arrange," I said. "Haven't you seen Abdul about it?"

"He won't see me. We're not friends anymore. We just don't see neck to neck…"

"What about the play?" I asked. "It's not going well?"

"Nobody cares, not even the actors. They just laugh." A tear like a vagrant tributary veered toward his nose. He brushed it away. "I've been wanting to ask you," he went on, "would you talk to Abdul for me? I've been hanging out there for a week now, trying to build up the courage to ask."

From far off on the square came the jangle of a native band jiving in the night. The muffled beat of rat-skin drums, the rattle of wooden tambourines, the eldritch shrill of nose flutes supplied a fitting accompaniment to Derek's plaint.

"I hate that music," he said. "These people spook me. I feel faint all the time, like when I was back in my father's mortuary and the smell of formaldehyde made me sick." He began to retch at the memory.

"Derek," I said firmly, "everybody lives in some kind of sweatbox or another. You've got to pull yourself together."

"Sure, that's what my father'ud say. He knew I was scared of the stiffs, and it was a weakness he couldn't accept. So he'd lock me in the embalming room with a corpse. That supposed to pull me together?"

"Your father was a scary bastard," Val said, "and you're too sensitive."

"My mother scared me even more," Derek said, taking, I thought, a peculiar pride in her frightfulness. "Like one Saturday when my father was away on business. Soon as he left the shop I bolted for home. In the house the radio was playing loud and there she was, pissed as usual, dancing naked before a wad of neighborhood kids."

He blew his nose on his colored neckerchief. "I got to get back to New York," he rambled, "where I won't die, and get ate by vultures. Maybe I won't go to New York. Maybe I can find another place to glow—go."

"Don't worry," Val said, "you're going to be all right."

"Sure," I lied. "You'll be sadder but wiser for the experience."

"Screw that," Derek said. "I'd rather be happier and dumber." He straightened up, standing tall, although his eyes still had a hopeless look in them. "You'll talk to Abdul?" he asked.

"Of course."

He left. For a moment Val and I said nothing.

THIRTY-FIVE

THE GOOD AMBASSADRESS

Less than an hour ago the morning rain stopped with the suddenness of a plugged spigot. My cell is already charged with accelerating heat.

The lean old woman comes in, a pouch of rat skin draped over her wrinkled shoulder. Her eyes have trouble tracking, and above them on her brow, an inch below the peak of her beautiful white hair, is an embroidered band of green beetles. She sinks to the floor with the effortless grace of a dancer, sitting with crossed legs and a spine as straight as a sapling. From the pouch she takes little packets of powder wrapped neatly in palm leaves. She aligns them before her like a druggist dispensing restoratives.

"I have been told," she says in a parched whisper, "that you are interested in my magic. What is your wish? Birds' claws for courage? Rats' teeth for happy thoughts? Bones of a lizard to fight off demons? Wings of a scarab for toothache? Sorghum and swordgrass to lengthen the penis?"

That muddling fool Derek, zonked out on even he didn't know what. "No," I say, "I think he got it a bit twisted..." And then I think, maybe it was I who got it twisted. What could I lose, exploring the possibility of feeding a rack of goofballs to the sentry, Abdul, Grady? "Have you got some kind of knockout drops?"

"For a sleep? A long sleep or a short one? Or the sleep that does not end?"

"One that lasts a day or so."

We speak—I haltingly—in her dialect. My usage is both blunt and fragile, without subtlety, the pronunciation abominable, lacking the correct stressses and the requisite sound shifts. Still, she understands me, for she nods sympathetically. Her bedside manner is impeccable, although she's pretty close to nodding off—a healer who obviously dips into her own nostrums.

"How much do you weigh?" she asks. "In stones?"

I hesitated. How many pounds to a British stone? About fourteen? I wasn't sure.

"I have to know," she persists, gently, "if you do not want the sleep that never ends."

"It's for two smaller men," I say. "Maybe one hundred and sixty pounds. Almost twelve stones. And a larger one."

She stiffens. "Not for you?" she asks dubiously.

I've said something wrong. "What difference does it make who it's for?"

Her tranced eyes are on me, as if I were a dangerous child playing a deadly game whose rules I don't fathom. Slowly she gathers up her philters and replaces them in the pouch.

"A man cannot force a journey on someone else."

"Why not?"

"Our lord and leader does not allow. We have the new ways, now that we are modern." The tone of her ancient voice rather than the words of homage spoken make it clear that she equates modernity with derangement.

"When I was a girl," she says, "just starting to learn The Mysteries, then we served the people well, providing for their every need and comfort. If a patron wanted riddance of a foe, I'd take half a gourd of water a corpse had been washed in and mix it with swine snout. I made figurines of mud and pitch to induce boils. Chalk and fresh-fallen wood of a lightning-struck tree would with a few well-chosen words cause sickness and the witherings. Crushed river stones sprinkled with the finest rat oil and lit with a sacred flame would bring on the trembles and the madness." She smiles sadly, reliving the triumphs of a golden age. "Then everything was possible. But today..."

She gets to her feet. We're being watched by a fat squirrel at the window; he looks like a poorly animated Japanese teapot. How had a squirrel climbed seven stories to my cell? Why? I must be unhinged, I think, invoking the metaphysical *why* to shed light on the locomotion of a squirrel.

"I cannot help you," she says, "unless you wish to make the journey yourself."

She is the good ambassadress from the country of the dead, offering a passport and the means of getting there: a soothing anodyne that seamlessly transmutes sleep to rigor mortis, which is certainly preferable to impalement, the only other option I have.

Thoughts of my suicide freak me out. But even the self-slaughter of those with whom I had no more than a nonpersonal, perhaps idiosyncratic contact lather me in cold sweat. Like Val's mother, in the photograph in the cluttered attic staring blankly at the camera as if for her passport. Like Thomas Chatterton, boy fuckup, eulogized by Coleridge as well as by Wordsworth, doing himself in at seventeen.

Now the voice of the drug lady pulls me back to reality, such as it is.

"Without the journey of the good sleep," she says softly, "you are like the serpent bound forever to the earth. But with it, you will look inside yourself, you will fly like a great bird forever."

Just a few weeks ago I would have been tempted. But I'm still alive. Perhaps there's time (ten days? twenty?) before I'll be made to fly on my own power off the roof and down to meet the bamboo stakes. Perhaps I might still puzzle out how to avoid the trip altogether.

"Forever is too long."

"Ah." She reaches back into the pouch and waves a palm leaf folded like an envelope in front of me. It catches the light of a million dust motes.

"Is it," she asks, "that you wish the short time passage? To make the outward journey that is inward and come back to crawl the earth again? To break the cord that binds you to this world and become the dragon, master of the earth and the sky? Just for a while?"

"The dragon is the master?"

She nods. "The serpent with wings." Again she waves the palm leaf. "The seeds of the dragon. Very good price. Five of your dollars."

I give her five dollars for the house call and take the packet. I don't want to be shamanized, boxed on drugs, blissed out when Valerie comes. But in case she doesn't...

"Why is it," she asks compassionately, "that you Tallow Faces have so much, and yet your hearts go on bleeding? Why is it that you do nothing to stop the blood except to run after the things that made you bleed in the first place?"

I have no answer for her.

THIRTY-SIX
THE SOLDIER

The people lined the street. An air of carnival washed over them, a tide of excitement that erupted at times in laughter and in sudden spurts and flurries, like a school of fish responding to an indiscernible stimulus. Above their heads a banner hung limply. COLONEL MENACHEM BEN ISH-CHAYL, it read, WELCOME.

The unpredictable bus assigned to gather the Colonel up from the airstrip clanked through the outskirts of Coproliabad, audible but unseen. The people stood breathless, all the better to listen, and clapped in anticipation. And then the bus appeared, a floundering whale that staggered down the main drag and collapsed in a gear-stripping halt. The skiffle band churned up a sour rendition of "Ha'Tikva." With Daphne at my side I watched, about fifty yards away, as Ish-Chayl stepped down out of the bus.

He was a ramrod of a man in the starched and immaculate uniform of the Israeli Army. A manifestation of verdict girded his long, lean frame, the only body within a radius of a million square miles, I'd venture to say, that wasn't sweating. He had a certain serene swagger that I found mesmerizing, as if he enjoyed being the focus of the event and at the same time somehow being above it. Mine were not the only eyes that clung to him obediently, unable to resist the pull of his charisma. Struck dumb, I watched as he strode gravely to Abdul, and then a voice at my ear said softly, "Have you talked to him?"

I turned to face Derek. "Yes," I lied, "but I don't have an answer."

I looked back at Ish-Chayl as he and the young sheik exchanged greetings. They were joined by Val, who demurely placed a garland of flowers around the Colonel's neck.

Ish-Chayl stood in the square, the quintessential soldier-operator, tall as a cedar of the Psalms, surrounded by Abdul's ministers. His bearing was such that to each he seemed to give his undivided attention, and to all at the same time. Each shift of his body was economical, at once fluid and restrained, reflecting an assertive self-possession denied to most mortals.

Yet there was something familiar about him; where had I seen that man, that Lion of Judah, before? On the illustrated pages of a book, some saga perhaps of the Israeli wars? In a documentary? On TV?

And then in a slant of sharp sunlight the Colonel turned his face toward me, and I found myself racing toward him, stumbling and sobbing. "Pop!" I howled.

Even in the highly charged, somewhat aberrational tableau of our reunion, the Colonel had lost neither his bravura nor his colossal dignity. As for me, I was staggered by the wild intoxication of the advent, unaccustomed as I was to the sight of a father. Certainly when I swooped down on him he gave no outward sign of recognition, and for a valid reason: he hadn't the slightest idea who the hell I was. But of course there was a rich variety of reactions from the gallery.

Nonplussed, Abdul watched and listened, waiting for further proof that this random convergence was indeed all it presumed to be. Qazwini smoldered with resentment and disbelief, suspicious of all encounters not of his making, as if I were the upstart instrument of some pell-mell plot to undermine his eminence. Grady, the great manipulator, who but a moment ago had been thinking (Oh, I could read each dip and blister of that churning cerebrum—it took little imagination, considering our long alliance—so I knew, I knew) *I've picked up the tab for this paragon,* he'd been thinking, *this pitchman's dream. How can I use him?* In a wink of time he had modified the question, seeking further advantage. Now he asked himself, How can I benefit from a consanguinity not my own?

As for Chatterton and his minions, they observed the unfolding scenario with a slit-eyed, tight-mouthed skepticism, uninterested in a discovery from which no foreseeable harvest could be reaped. Or maybe they were just having trouble hearing my joyful yelps—they must have been half-deaf from all their cacophonous harmonics experiments by now.

Now Abdul and Qazwini eyed me with a kind of uncertain suspicion, as if I had conjured him up with some kind of sorcery and unleashed him on Assama.

Only Valerie responded to the radiance of the moment. Unpuzzled, she accepted the reunion for what it was—just another goose by the fickle finger of fate. She was happy for me; possibly she figured I might share the Colonel with her. Certainly she had need of a father, even a surrogate one, and I would have been glad to oblige.

But there was nothing to share. His very remoteness was chilling. Perhaps I'm being unfair, for he could have been as shocked as I was by the encounter and, moreover, he must have been carrying a heavy bucket of guilt for having abandoned wife and son (was I projecting?), which my presence did nothing to assuage. Maybe he saw in me a discomforting reminder of that segment of his life he'd have preferred to forget. He did seem slightly embarrassed by our kinship. After all, I was the only imperfection, the only inelegance that could be grafted to Ish-Chayl (more projection?).

"Why do you make excuses for him?" Valerie asked later.

Her opinion of fathers had reverted to a minimal expectancy.

"He has a lot of good in him," I insisted doggedly.

"Sure," she said, "he just never lets it out. I think he's kind of weird."

"Why? Because he's so superior to the general run of men?"

"No. I don't know. Because he's so stern and unbending."

"Well, what the hell, nobody's totally sane."

Whatever the reason, Ish-Chayl/Breslau chose to meet the challenge I presented with evasive action, avoiding engagement until he had a better handle on it. He did say, almost in an aside, "We'll talk later," as he strode off with Abdul and Qazwini, and more than a week went by before I saw him again, before he sought me out.

He had been closeted with the General. Rumor had it that the going was rough, that their styles simply did not jell. Certainly Qazwini's oppositional voice rose loud and late into the night, every night, except for the evening when my father materialized at our door.

His fine shoulders sagged, his face was sallow, not at all the calm adornment it had been a little more than a week ago. He settled himself in a director's chair I had managed to lift from the nuclear site. He closed his eyes exhaustedly and rubbed the furrows on his brow. His stomach rumbled; he grimaced. "How can you stand the food?" he asked. "How's your mother?"

I told him. He nodded. He couldn't have cared less; tranquilly he moved on to another subject. If indeed he'd sustained the wounds of earlier conflict, they had stopped bleeding. We talked for an hour, as impersonally as strangers on a plane, and then he left without even a hint that we might meet again.

Valerie said, "He'll be back."

"We'll see," I said, feigning an indifference to match my father's. But I was stung by his heartlessness, his insensibility, whatever the hell it was, although I wouldn't admit it, not even to Valerie. "Maybe when his stomach feels better he'll be more... paternal, you know?"

"Paternal or not, he'll be back," she repeated, "because he needs you."

"You think so?"

She crossed the room, bent over, and kissed the top of my head. "What I mean," she said softly, "is he wants something from you."

"What?"

"We'll find out."

And we did on his next visit, a few nights later. He reinstalled himself in the director's chair as if it had his name on it and took a brief stab at sociability ("Let's see—how old are you now?"), segued into nostalgia ("Remember when you were five or six we used to play chess without pieces or a board, just in our heads?"), and made a foray into sentimentality ("Your mother hung your first baby shoes from the rearview mirror of the Ford") which consumed me with doubt. Mother in a moment of abstraction might have hung me from the rearview mirror, but not my shoes.

Then he said, "I need a sounding board. Someone who knows these people better than I do, to take notes, lay plans, to diagnose, analyze. Will you work with me?"

And so I gave him the fidelity I had denied Grady and Chatterton, Lipgloss and Abdul. Each day, like a glittering knight, he ignored the thunder in his bowels and sallied forth to joust with the knavish Qazwini, whose ideas about the formation of a modern army were, to say the least, bizarre. And I trailed after him, his loyal and worshipful Panza.

Those daily disputations in the General's House of the Martial Spirit were a litmus test of Asso-Israeli amity, a confrontation in a minefield which my father tried to defuse, seeking solutions even as Qazwini yelled and blustered. The very air reeked with the clash of their arguments; the General's sweat mingled with Ish-Chayl's redolence of myrrh and sandalwood.

They fought over everything. Every discussion sooner or later went sour, as sour as the General's sweat. High on Qazwini's agenda was the question of uniforms. He favored scarlet tunics with gold-braided fourrageres, like the dress regimentals of British officers he had seen in books.

Ish-Chayl tried to point out the advantages of camouflage. "Red scares off enemies," the General replied. "We get red tunics or godammit I'll push you through a wall."

"We'll put the question of uniforms on hold. Let's move on."

"What about the question of weapons? We put that on hold yesterday."

Qazwini wanted Uzis for his troops. "Not until we can maintain some modicum of discipline," Ish-Chayl said. "An army must have fire power," the General said. "Give them Uzis and they'll damned well learn discipline." "They'll shoot each other dead and then you won't have an army." "Uzis," the General said, fingering his horse pistols, "or I'll shoot you so dead you'll stink before you hit the ground."

"We'll talk about it tomorrow," the Colonel said, resisting arrogance with arrogance, as if he were bulletproof. "What's next on the agenda?"

"Helicopter."

My father stared up and away at the sculptured trusses of the enormous room; such was his habit when talk with Qazwini reached an impasse. As in the Hall of Harmony, the beams and columns were carved like snakes with scaly legs. The Colonel seemed to find them fascinating.

"Helicopter," the General repeated. "Can't you hear me?"

"We've been through this before."

"I want a chopper to observe maneuvers. If I do not get a chopper I will drive a rock through you."

"I suggest you control your impetuosity."

"Why? I am a General. I outrank any Colonel in the whole world."

On and on, again and again, Qazwini threatening mayhem like a club.

And all the while, and equally incompatible, was Abdul's reaction to the war of words. He listened to both warriors, but he ratified nothing, serving not as a judge but as an aloof and lofty deity who refused to intervene in the affairs of men, letting them find their own solutions or, as in most cases, dig their own graves. Indeed he simply sat there, the visible, inaccessible incarnation of the tutelary deity Regat Punbela, whose name meant "God of Those Who Trip Over Their Own Pricks."

I'd come away from those meetings in something of a state of shock, stunned and shuddered by Qazwini's bloodcurdling rhetoric and intransigent, hell-for-leather diplomacy.

"He's a hundred and ten percenter," I'd say to my father as we rehashed the day's entanglements or shaped the morrow's strategies. "He wants his own way in everything."

"Even the angels want their own way," the Colonel said imperturbably.

"He wears me out. I don't like people who think they're right when they're merely unruly."

My father shrugged. "In the military business, even in Israel, you sometimes have to deal with dinosaurs. The important thing," he went on, "is to keep the channels open."

"I may be clogging them."

"You?"

"He dislikes me. Intensely."

"Can you think of anyone he doesn't dislike?"

"No."

"If you were to disengage, wouldn't he consider it at least a partial victory, a strengthening of his position, one less adversary to contend with? Stick around," he said. "Don't let your hatred be self-defeating."

"I loathe the son of a bitch and the things he says. Like yesterday when he said he'd sit on your face till it turned blue."

My father smiled. *"Ma'asim, lo diburim.* That's what's important."

"What's it mean?"

"'Deeds, not dialogue.' Anyway, it's the Divine Will."

"How could that be?"

"God allotted loud mouths to those who have them. Perhaps to test the righteous."

God figured prominently in both my father's deeds and his dialogue. Gradually, as we conferred, his attitude of disinterest and remoteness toward me changed. Imperceptibly at first, but it was I suppose inevitable, in spending so much time together, that something of himself would infiltrate our discussions. Slowly a personal history emerged.

Morton Breslau had become Menachem ben Ish-Chayl, warrior of God, forsaking secular scholarship to embrace a born-again faith. His was the commitment of a mystic who had overcome apostasy to find something fresh and fulfilling, an old untrodden path of hope and promise. Israel gave him the opportunity of exercising a potential he never suspected he possessed. What he gave in return was a deep and unqualified devotion so boundless it could more accurately be called love. Thus he learned that God works indeed in mysterious ways, and that there is good in everything.

"What happened to us—our separation, our reunion—was mandated," he told me with that air of moral certitude. "Man finds his own preordained pathway. The infidel finds a path to God," he went on, laying on me another of his rabbinic pensées, "the misanthropist to his fellow man, the estranged father to his son. Sometimes it is no more than a trail in the wilderness, the half-hidden beast-track through the jungle. According to both the *Targum* and the *Midrashim,* there are thirty-two pathways back to Eden. And one of them," he said, "leads through Assama."

"Eden? The Eden of Adam and Eve?"

He nodded solemnly. "The Cradle of God," he said. "Eden on earth. It's somewhere out there," he went on, "toward the uncharted northeast. Somewhere beside the ghost of a stream that once fed the Nile or the Tigris or the Euphrates. Waiting to be rediscovered..."

He was watching me closely, looking for some sign of challenge. I nodded, rearranging my face to show how seriously I took his teaching. Apparently it wasn't seriously enough.

"You think I'm some kind of zealot?" he asked with a twisted smile. "A fanatic? Let me tell you, it's the fanatic who keeps the faith alive. Everybody else backslides into deracination." His flinty eyes burned into mine until I was thoroughly cowed.

Satisfied, he went on: "This place, Assama, this land of desolation, is holy land."

It didn't seem so to me. There was a too-muchness of everything about it.

The sun that baked the brain. The rain that turned it spongy. The exhausted earth, the insipid shrubs standing like a stunted army of blind sentinels, the sapless stalks, and always the smell of rot, clogging the nostrils with its putrescence, clouding the eyes. This was holy land?

"It's a most unpromising country," I ventured, "as far as you can see."

"We Jews," my father said, "have always been interested in what lies beyond the horizon."

"How can you ignore what's all around us?"

"What's all around us?"

"Dishevelment. Untidiness. Chaos."

"I don't ignore it. I like it, I welcome it."

"What's to like?"

He thought for a moment. "In Genesis," he said, "God, the architect of the world, introduced order and harmony. But if God is the Prime Mover of the universe, did He not introduce what came before? Was He not the agent, first, of chaos? And is not then chaos the initial stage of harmony, the weed of God that became the flowering of Eden?"

He paused, giving me a little time to grasp his words. I wanted to take seriously everything he said, even the conceptions I couldn't accept. I didn't want another rift between us. We had known enough stress and strife back in the States to last my lifetime. But all I could think of was Valerie's words. Indeed he was kind of peculiar.

"And here," he went on, "the cycle has started again. Assama wallows in chaos. The rest of the world with its wars and unruliness won't be far behind."

"It seems a long way," I said, "from here to Paradise. It'll take an eternity."

"Perhaps not. Just one rousing catastrophe could do it—some cataclysm of nature or of man and it's Genesis revisited. And this time, maybe we'll get it right."

I had had enough of my father's lurid eschatology. "I think a compromise might be in order," I said.

"God doesn't compromise."

"Not God. I was referring to the stalemate between you and the General."

"What do you suggest?"

"Something that would make both of you happy. Relatively happy."

He thought for a moment. "I have a box of hand grenades. We could divide them up and toss 'em at each other."

"You could teach the troops to toss them. At inanimate targets, I mean, taking proper safety cautions."

"Hmmm..." Brows knit, he began to pace with the long stride of an infantryman, spurred, presumably, by my suggestion. Peculiar or not, he's always center stage, I thought as I followed him with my eyes, whether he's alone with me in a hovel compounded of mud and shit, or in the midst of a crowd in a marbled hall. I wondered if that radiating glory was infectious, whether those high-intensity chromosomes would one day assert themselves in me.

THIRTY-SEVEN

QUESTIONABLE BEHAVIOR

In the piercing afternoon light the sky hung like an angry bruise over the nuclear facility. The shell was completed, and sealed with a flat roof. Its geometrics were so free of ornamental frills that it looked less designed than engineered, an exercise in hypertrophic packaging, so long and so wide that, despite its twelve stories, it most resembled a clay-colored sardine can on a concrete slab. The land like a reluctant partner in miscegenation refused to embrace the monster that lay on it.

Although Abdul, since his ascension, had ordered Chatterton's prodigious symphony reduced to a few otherwise unemployable tooters and all able hands over to the plant, Grady still raged against the slow pace. Whenever his baleful eye turned elsewhere, the workers dawdled on the side of the building away from the sun, like ravens crowding under the wings of a condor for precious shade.

I worked my way through them and pushed open the smoky glass doors that led to the lab, unchallenged by a pair of Asso guards wearing hard hats stenciled SECURITY. I was privileged personnel, as was everyone with a white face. I sauntered past the turbines to the containment area, the concrete shield and steel shell housing the steam generator, and the reactor rigged to percolate the first kettle of atomic fuel as soon as the awesome ingredients arrived from the States. I moved across the control room banked with dials and switches to enter the executive lounge with its coffee machine, pool table, steel bookcases holding technical journals. I had a mission I was determined to discharge. I was going to liberate another director's chair as a gift for my father.

When my old man first asked me to enlist in his slugfest with Qazwini, I complied with no excessive display of enthusiasm. But inwardly I beamed with pride and pleasure; it was as if I had swallowed a new toy, and it was hopping around inside me. In the evenings that followed, when we talked and planned and explored not only the military agenda but, ranging far and wide, the riddles of God and man, I wasn't much taken by his rather peculiar theology, his ruminations of some lost Elysium, but as we raised our bowls and drank our beer, I was happy just being there with him; I was wrapped in delight. Somehow it brought back a wonderful memory of his lifting me high in the air when I was a little boy.

So I wanted to do something for him. Nothing spectacular, if indeed that sort of extravagance had been within my power to disburse, just a little something to let him know that...

"Well..." The voice behind me dripped irony. "So kind of you to spare us a visit."

Of course it was Grady, seething in a controlled tantrum of affront. Fortunately all the chairs were in place; I hadn't yet decided between the one with the blue or the green canvas. He wore the remotest of smiles, and he chose to bypass even the most customary of obligatories like How are you?

"I've been waiting for you to show up," he said testily. "I almost sent for you. What's taking so long with Lipgloss?"

Suddenly, uncomfortably, I realized I had to quit deluding myself—I couldn't keep it from him forever. If nothing more, I had to tell Grady that the elusive formula for BRITs, according to Lipgloss's records and Val's research, resided with Abdul. Of course, as Val had predicted, he like to wet his drawers. I stared at my shoes for fifteen minutes, until his rage diffused into a rant.

"He's your friend," he said, "so get it out of him."

"How?"

"Stroke him with honeyed words. Rub him the right way. Fawn. Grovel. You know."

"No, I don't."

"God damn it!" he exploded. "Would it hurt you to kiss his ass a little? What the hell kind of business partner are you?"

"If I suddenly changed character on him, he'd know something was up. And that would be the end of it. He hasn't exactly become any more solicitous since his coronation. If you try to gouge or wheedle it out of Abdul, you'll only succeed in antagonizing him."

"Why should he be antagonized when it's to his advantage in the long run? Particularly if our strategy is laced with subtlety...?"

"I'm familiar with your stratagems," I said. "They have all the subtlety of a cyclone."

"You're letting me down," Grady said. His glinty eyes pierced mine, never blinking. "I swear, since you stepped off the plane you've given less than a diminished performance."

"Yeah," I agreed, "and it'll probably get worse." Why don't we, I was about to add, just forget our partnership, tear up the contract? But no. I'd had enough of confrontational fireworks.

"Tell you what," I promised, "I'll try to do better."

He stared at me, trying to determine the depth of my sincerity. Finally, "Okay," he said stiffly. "But you'd better start pulling your weight. And you can begin your reformation by returning my director's chair. You think I don't know who stole it?"

Somewhere, about halfway along the road that stretched from Coproliabad to the nuclear compound, was an ill-defined, unfrequented track, overgrown with exhausted foliage. It led off at a right angle into an especially desolate footpath, one of many that had been used, then abandoned, then forgotten by the people somewhere in their misty past.

Colonel Ish-Chayl, at the head of a straggly column, held up his hand and halted. Immediately he was challenged by the General.

"Why here?" Qazwini asked petulantly. The Colonel didn't answer. He squinted through the latticework of rotted trees, anchored not by their roots but by the iron grip of vines that snaked from trunk to trunk to keep them from falling.

Qazwini was annoyed. This was not the first time that Ish-Chayl had halted the apathetic constabulary, examined the terrain briefly, and then continued on down the road. Nor was it the first time that Qazwini had questioned him without getting an answer. And so the General did what he had done on each previous occasion. He called the troops to attention and strutted down the ranks, reviewing them as if he were Patton and they his crack regiment. Whenever he paused in his inspection, jutting his heavy jaw and gluing a gimlet eye on one of his men, "Why," he would roar, "you such a fuckup? Why you such a shitbird?" He had picked up the nomenclature from his favorite movie, which was about the U.S. Marine Corps. He had seen it eight or ten times.

Ish-Chayl stood there, drenched in sunlight. Head to one side, he seemed to be listening rather than looking. He reached a decision; whatever prompted it he did not share with Qazwini. He raised a hand above his head and then shot the arm forward, as if he were throwing a baseball. The General recognized the sign. "Move out!" he bellowed. "Follow me!" and trailed by the troops he trailed after the Colonel, off the road and into the boondocks.

The path was less than a hairline fracture into, of all unexpected places, a reach of woodland. Somehow, it seemed to me, we were drifting backward in time. There was no sound except for the muffled tread of the barefoot soldiers, and now and then the crack of a snapping twig. There was the smell of another world, lost, dead-aired, and ancient, the smell of a subterranean cave sealed off from sunlight, the pungency of wild apples.

We came to a clearing of sharp and oily grass, bordered on the far side by a slight depression that snaked out of one stand of dead trees and disappeared into another—probably what, in the morning of the world, had been the bed of a river. A faint insectal drone quavered in the strange, soft, airy light, but there were no insects to be seen. The drone gave way to a teasing whisper, like an echo without a source, the relic of an epoch when humanoids with flat faces and moist snouts pranced and capered among the lions and the lambs.

"We'll set up here," the Colonel said.

A dozen men broke out picks and shovels. When the trench was dug and the earth piled before it, Ish-Chayl moved front and center. He took one of a half dozen fragmentation grenades from his web belt. He showed them the cast-iron serrated body; carefully he pointed out the detonating fuse. He stressed the destructive potential of the bursting charge, two ounces of flaked TNT. He emphasized safety precautions. He repeated the entire procedure, this time pulling the pin, releasing the lever, throwing the bomb, and ducking behind the parapet with the rest of us.

We heard it explode forty yards away. The earth trembled; we staggered against the agitated air. Dirt and pebbles rose like a fountain from the dry riverbed where the grenade landed, and smoke curled up from the battered branches of the dead trees, a second killing.

"My turn," the General said. His belt like Ish-Chayl's was studded with bombs. He grabbed one, pulled the pin with his teeth—that too he had learned from the Marine movie—and threw it. I sighed with relief as it exploded not far from the Colonel's.

Qazwini snared the arm of a recruit. "You," he ordered, handing him an olive-drab pineapple.

The man, whose name was Salim Nafi, took the grenade. Salim was well known to all of us: he stood out in any crowd. People thrown in with him for the first time would whisper, behind their hands, "Who is that man?" What made him unforgettable was his incessant belching. He sounded off like a broken-down calliope, and with the regularity of a metronome. The fumes of his emissions were like those little dark green clouds that hover above the decomposing body of a beached whale. His proximity withered leaves, stunned small birds, and moved strong men to tears.

Something was also wrong inside Salim's head. The valves that opened to transmit messages to the brain in microseconds were in his case jammed for relatively long periods.

Now he blinked at the grenade in his hand as if he had never seen anything remotely like it before, and I knew then, as the adrenaline kicked in, that we were all in serious trouble. Calmly the Colonel said, "Hold it a minute," and moved in on him, but it was too late. Salim pulled the pin. He reared back and threw it a mile, holding on to the grenade.

The troops let out a wild collective yell and led by Qazwini took off, mostly in my direction. I fought against the human tide to my father—terror brings out the best in some of us—as he struggled to separate the grenade from the grenadier. The seconds were ticking off. I saw blue flames and smelled sulfur; I was that close to the abyss. I saw Ish-Chayl pull a grenade from his belt. In a blur almost too fast for the eye to follow he slammed it against the side of Salim's skull. The man crumbled; before he hit the ground the Colonel had the bomb. Too late to help, I stood there transfixed as he whipped it into the wadi. Following through he swarmed over me, pulling me down and under him as the grenade exploded somewhere out there.

"You all right?" he asked.

"Yeah. You?"

He nodded, shifting his attention to Salim, who lay there, rigid as any proper corpse. A pair of hands like catchers' mitts pushed me aside. The General stared down at the motionless dogface with a look of keen satisfaction.

"He will be buried with full military honors," he said sonorously.

"He's not dead," Ish-Chayl told him.

"Not dead?" Qazwini repeated unbelievingly. "We do not have a body count?" He kicked at Salim. "How," he asked, "can we have a great army without a body count?"

"We're not at war yet," the Colonel said.

"Is he not badly wounded?" His jaw shot out in the direction of the Colonel. "You trying to fuck me out of a body count?" He glowered, fingering the howitzer at his belt. "Do not bad wounds deserve consideration?"

"Of course they do," I said quickly. "The man's at death's door and that's close enough."

Qazwini stared hard at Salim, who was beginning to stir. A lump the size of an orange appeared at his temple. The General knew damned well that I knew nothing about body counts or the determinants governing them, but all of us, with a little encouragement, find truth in what we want to believe.

"The man deserves a Purple Heart," I said, "with an oak leaf cluster. For action above and beyond—"

"We're all above and beyond," Qazwini said, fancying the phrase. "All of us should get one."

"Certainly *you* should. As the commanding officer." I reached out a congratulatory hand. He took it and, son of a bitch, I should have known, guided it to his scrotum while he in turn gripped mine.

Salim groaned. Ish-Chayl helped him to his feet. "I think we've had enough for one day," he said.

"Awright, you fuckheads!" the General yelled, like John Wayne on Iwo Jima. "Let's saddle up and shove off!"

He led them out of the clearing. The Colonel and I remained there for a moment. He ran a hand over his eyes. "Good God," he murmured. "What a mess."

"Actually, we've accomplished a lot."

"How do you figure that?"

"Now we've got Qazwini by the balls—figuratively speaking. Now we know how to deal with him."

"We do?"

"Sure. In any emergency, give him a medal."

My father tilted his head and studied me with undisguised appreciation. "For one so young," he said, "you are a master of damage control." And then he added his finest compliment. "You'd do well," he said, "in Israel."

I found the Colonel the next evening at his desk, pursuing his paperwork, preparing a T.O. for his war machine.

"Where've you been all day?" I asked casually.

"Oh, here and there. Floating around the backcountry. Moving around helps me think." He smiled ruefully, and with a kind of gracious regret, added, "but now I've got work to do."

Thus I was dismissed, puzzled by his clueless secrecy.

And worried about him. True, he had changed considerably since his days at Corn Pone U. No longer was he given to ranting and raging, no longer did he scourge his colleagues (and his son) in the snide, measured accents of an Oxford don. No longer did he blame anti-Semitic assailants for his failures; indeed, he was no longer a failure. He had even changed physically. His stooped shoulders, once so pronounced, and his air of tortured weariness had given way to a vigor and a drive that would have been esteemed in a ten-wheeled locomotive.

Still, he was a bit strange. He didn't seem to need people. He shied from affection, tenderness, warmth. And certainly his approach to the earliest chapters of Genesis displayed an eccentricity of mind, a view that was wildly, recklessly deviant from that of most scholars. He had become, I thought, an exceptional man, invested with an odd and unpleasant prominence. But what was he concealing from me?

And why? I asked myself as I walked out of the sunset scorch into our dusky hut and stopped short, blinking at Val disbelievingly. She stood in the middle of the room, clothed in nothing but a wreathed smile, a flimsy sheath in folds at her ankles, and her astonishing beauty. Zun, the silent gnome who had sat in the presence of Abdul's father—it seemed ages ago—was palpating her breasts with his enormous hands. Immersed in his probe, he was totally inattentive to my arrival. A look not of bliss but of blindness clouded his eyes as he squeezed her ripe melons. So deep was his fixation that his mouth hung open as his slow fingers swept downward, over the flatness of her belly, the inspired rise of her buttocks, tracing the subtle curvature of her thighs, knees, calves, and up again between those lovely long legs to the lustrous electric floss and on, up still higher to the perfect brown cheekbones. It was as if the apperception of all his senses was wired to his fingertips.

"Hi!" she said, totally ignoring those two marauding paws.

"What the hell's he doing?"

"Getting the feel of things." She giggled.

"I can see that. Goddammit…"

"He's the resident sculptor."

At the mention of his title, the wizened little man smiled around an oval of intermittent teeth.

"He's the sculptor?"

"Yep," she said. "He's going to put me up in the square. Abdul's orders."

"Why?"

"Because Abdul said I'm the Minister Pleni… Pleniposanctuary—something like that—of Tourism and Hospitality. He said I served with honor and distinction in welcoming your Daddikins."

I was about to combust like a spectator in the first row of a burlesque show. I turned toward the door.

"Where're you going? You just got here."

"I can't watch this. I'll explode."

"Stick around. He's about done."

And he was, in another few minutes that seemed an eternity. As soon as he'd gone I said, "Don't you see why Abdul's making such a big-assed deal out of this?"

"What big-assed deal? So he sends around a nice old geezer to sculpt me."

"Once back in Maryland he said he wanted to make you his queen."

"That's the dumbest thing I ever heard," she said. Her voice had an edge to it. "Problem is, you're jealous."

"Of course I am. But there's another problem. I think you're pissed off at me for not taking better care of you."

"I can take care of myself."

"Maybe if I'd been more—I don't know—alert to the vibes around here, showed more devotion, been more attentive…"

For a moment she was silent. Then softly she said, "You spent too damn much time with Grady."

"That's my job."

"And now it's your father."

"You think I could've prevented your kidnapping?"

Suddenly she realized that she was adorned only by her nakedness. She reached down for the sheath at her ankles. "Look," she said tonelessly, "this is getting us nowhere."

"Don't," I said.

"Don't what?"

"The sheath."

She hesitated.

"I don't want to fight with you. I don't even want to spar or bicker or... ever again."

Her face softened. She opened her arms to me. My hands followed the route of the nice old geezer's.

THIRTY-EIGHT

PATH TO GLORY

He ploughed along that backcountry footpath as if he were blinkered, looking neither right nor left. The khaki shirt was plastered to his back, the
stain spreading across the scapulas and down his spine. He carried a pick
and a long-handled shovel. Over his shoulder was slung a canvas musette
bag, Israeli Army issue. A large paintbrush and a small one made bulges in
his pockets, along with a spading fork. On his cartridge belt were lashed an
entrenching tool, a canteen, and a knife with a six-inch blade. Small wonder
he was sweating.

I had spent a sleepless night asking myself the same question: What the hell
was he up to? His solitary expeditions had more of an aim than he'd claimed
they did—I was sure he was keeping something from me. It wasn't until the
cusp of dawn that I realized the way to find out was to follow him, a simple
expedient that, for reasons I cannot imagine, had previously eluded me.

Early that morning I hid in the woods behind his hut. When he emerged,
I waited two or three minutes before I shadowed him down Main Street, into
the trees, over the road that led to the nuke station, always keeping between
us as great a distance as I could without losing sight or sound of him.

He moved fast, despite the oppressive heat and the cumbersome weight of his gear, yet the overall effect was that of a man in a shambling trance. I suddenly realized that we were following the same route we had taken last week on our training mission with Qazwini. A moment later he turned abruptly into the wilderness, down the wisp of path that led to the clearing. On the bank of the dry riverbed where the grayish stones had been overturned by the grenades he unloaded his tools. The shovel and the pick clanged in the silence as he dropped them. He ran a wet sleeve over his wet forehead and raised the canteen to his lips. Then he started to work.

The clearing was bathed in a brilliant whiteness. Perhaps that blaze could have been dismissed as some phenomenon of nature—the amber eye of the sun slanting off the lacquered vines, thousands of leafy mirrors gleaming like the facets of an emerald. Or perhaps my vision was intensified by the light that filtered through the prism of sweat beading my eyelashes. I brushed the sweat away. The glow persisted.

And there was something else, an aberration perhaps, a fraudulent offshoot of the light-headed exhaustion I felt from lack of sleep: an air of tremulous expectancy seemed to hang over the white clearing, as if it were under a spell and lay waiting for some long-delayed magician to unlock it.

Ish-Chayl's pick rang out in the riverbed, glancing off a rock. He exchanged it, first for the entrenching tool, then for the fork. Finally, with the utmost caution, he flicked the paintbrush over a bulge in the riverbed. So intent was he on the bulge, so close was his nose to it, that I was only a few feet from him before he noticed me.

"What the hell," he said nastily, "are you doing here?"

"I wanted to ask you a question."

"Couldn't it wait?"

I shrugged.

"Well? What is it?"

"What are you doing here?"

He glowered at me, then shifted his wary eyes to the bed of the dry river as if he possessed some colossal secret he was reluctant to share. Finally he crossed to the far bank and rummaged through the musette. He scooped up a few lusterless pellets, a gummy globule that smelled faintly of myrrh, and a half dozen shards of black and whitish-blue agate.

"Know what these are?" he asked.

I didn't.

"The nuggets are gold. The ball of resin—it's still fragrant—that's bdellium. The marbleized stone is onyx, right?"

"If you say so. How'd you happen to find them?"

"I came back here the day after the grenade debacle to check out the damage." His skin was flushed—it could have been the heat—even his foxy eyes were inflamed. "No," he went on, "I don't know why I came back, unless it was..." The sentence hung in the white silence.

"Unless it was what?"

"Well... preordained."

"What's preordained about your finding the gold and the rest of it?"

"Perhaps God pointed the way. I was His instrument."

The presumption of divine intervention in human affairs violates my sense of an orderly and comprehensible universe. I gazed at him in bewilderment—the kind of confusion that borders on panic.

He went to his knees and with meticulous little strokes flicked his paintbrush over a bulge in the wadi.

"Why," I asked, "would God be so concerned with your find?"

"Because," he paused, looking up at me. Again those eyes burned feverishly. "Because it holds a vast and unique significance for His people." He stared off into the dead, gigantic, twisted vines. He seemed to be poised, listening. I heard it too, a deep and persistent resonance, not of insects nor the hot wind but of the throbbing, unbounded energy of the cosmos.

"Of course," he said dismissively, "what we have here could be just another yield of the earth's inexhaustible riches. Or," his voice rang with the steely timbre of total assurance, "it could be something special, the most overwhelmingly extraordinary find in history." He held up a nugget, turning it slowly between thumb and forefinger.

"Gold has been found before," I told him. "So has onyx and bdellium."

"But only once in the same place. So you must realize the significance."

"I can't say that I do. I see nothing unique or extraordinary about it."

His eyes went back to the dust of the wadi. "'And a river,'" he said, "'went out of Eden to water the garden...' Genesis Two: Eight. Remember? Then, in verse thirteen: 'The gold of that land is good,'" he quoted, "'and there is bdellium and the onyx stone.'"

He smiled at me, the smile of a man of many wiles—action and scholarship, soldiering and exploration—beamed on his son, who lacked all of them.

"You're saying that this is… was the Garden of Eden?" I glanced around at the decomposing cluster of vines. "And your source is the Bible?"

"An excellent source."

"But not exactly a scientific text, if you're going to examine the origins of the earth and of man. The Garden of Eden was a Hebraic trope, symbolic, not to be taken literally."

He exchanged the nugget in his hand for the lump of bdellium. "Would you…" he sniffed it pleasurably, "go so far as to say that my find warrants investigation?"

"I suppose so," I said, allowing myself to be drawn in to his delirium, the better to restrain it. Again I glanced around at the purple vines, dense, murky, unfruitful. "But wouldn't you agree," I said guardedly, "that the chances of this place ever having been any kind of garden, much less Paradise, are pretty slim?"

"What about outer space?"

"What about it?"

"The odds against intelligent life existing in outer space are well over five hundred million to one; still we reach out, probing the heavens in the hope of coming up with an answer. Are the odds against finding Eden any greater? Whatever the odds, the search cannot be dismissed as nonsense.

"There are those who call Genesis a cosmogony of folklore. Eden was not a geographical fact but a dawn myth. Just about all the world's peoples have something like it.

"And every people has a flood myth, but we know now that sometime between five thousand and four thousand BC there occurred a universal phenomenon—the Flandrian Transgression—which caused a sudden rise in sea levels. Through the study of Babylonian texts and the recent application of satellite photography, three ribs of an ark have been found on the south slope of Mount Ararat, just where Noah was said to have beached it. So what was for centuries considered a legend has been supplanted by historicity.

"Water?" He offered me the canteen. I shook my head. "And let's not forget," he went on, "that Troy was a Homeric myth until Heinrich Schliemann found it in Turkey, and the palace city of Knossos was a myth until Arthur Evans found it in Crete. And now…" He paused, conjuring up, no doubt, an image of himself as the inheritor of the great tradition, taking up the torch ignited by Schliemann, held high by Evans.

"Before you make any claims, don't you need a bit more confirmation...?"

"I intend to get it, in Israel. I'm sure the wizards at the Weizmann Institute will come up with something."

"I hope so," I said, "and I hope I haven't offended you with my skepticism."

"That's okay," he said, "I can understand your doubts. I'm proud of you, son."

Son, he called me, something he had never done before. A shiver of exultation ran through me. "Why proud?" I asked like a ham actor milking a scene, no amount of applause ever enough.

"Not once," he said, "during my rather lengthy recital did you respond with outrage or hysteria. It's good to know that you can disagree without being disagreeable. I'm sorry to leave before we really got to know each other." And to his regrets he added the tribute of a melancholy sigh.

"Must you leave so soon? What about your commitment here?"

"I'm getting nowhere with Qazwini. I don't think I ever will. But what about you?" he asked. "I don't know what you're doing in Coproliabad, but..."

"You never asked."

"...but whatever it is, you don't seem to find it all that gratifying. Come to Israel with me."

He had spoken impulsively; the invitation surprised both of us, but he made no attempt to retract it. "We'll test our doubts," he went on serenely. "We might even find convictions."

It was a tempting offer, a way to bow the hell out of Iraq, to fly over the hills and far away from Abdul and Grady. All I'd have to tell them was of the deep, affectionate bond that existed between my father and me, and there was more than a grain of truth in it, certainly on my part. I'd lost him once. I didn't want to lose him again. Not after he called me *son.*

"You'd like the country," he said in a voice that held excitement and a challenge. "And so would Hilary."

"Valerie."

"Yes, of course. Valerie."

"I suppose I could find something to do in Israel?"

"Do? You'd be my assistant."

"In the Army?"

"Army!" he scoffed. "The least I should be getting out of this is a full professorship at Hebrew University."

He looked glazedly into the middle distance, dreaming of a future way beyond anything he had known in the past. "It's an opportunity—" he lowered his eyelids, the better to savor the impossible dream that was about to come true. "The kind that doesn't come often—to achieve greatness. World-class renown."

The passage of the years had done nothing to diminish his ambition. He said, "I'll teach you all you have to know."

The offer came too late. As of that moment I knew I no longer wanted to walk in his footsteps, to shadow his substance, to replicate his life.

"You too?" I asked.

"Me too, what?"

"The big fish bone."

"What are you talking about?"

I didn't amplify. How could I tell him that even, at long last, as he accepted me, I couldn't accept him? Here he was on the tenure track all over again, digging for fame, yearning for stardom. This immaculate warrior, this servant of God and master of Byron, was a blood brother of Chatterton throbbing to save the human race from self-destruction whether they liked it or not; of Grady driven to shelter the homeless with houses of shit whether they liked it or not; of Abdul caught in a snare of meanness as he carved a niche for himself in the Asso pantheon by flogging his people into the twenty-first century whether they liked it or not; even of Derek with his genius for ineptitude, seeking a peacock throne, bringing art to the masses whether they liked it or not. All of them puppets of their own passion, whose goal was to look out on the lesser world from the cover of *People* magazine. All of them motivated not by the love or the virtue of what they did but by a craving for celebrity, and so entrapped that they'd rather have been notorious than unknown.

"I'm still waiting for your answer," my father said.

"Thing is," I said, "I'm not very ambitious."

"What's wrong with ambition? Particularly when it's in the service of mankind?"

In the service of mankind. A ringing dedication, shrill, clear, and dangerously self-deceptive. Perhaps my experience was limited, but I'd never known a honcho who didn't feel that his all-consuming mission wasn't in the service of mankind. All of them saw themselves as God's partners, whether in the pursuit of peace or plenty, beauty or truth.

"I guess nothing's wrong with ambition," I said. "It's just that I don't have any, and greatness requires an awful lot of energy. I don't really care about making a big bang in the world. I'm kind of lazy."

He thought for a moment. "I hate to say good-bye, just when I'm getting to know you."

I crossed the riverbed to the bank where he stood. I put my arms around him. I kissed his cheek. His body was rigid; he didn't return the embrace. I had only succeeded in startling him.

THIRTY-NINE

TO THE DARK TOWER

It was a week of pomp and commotion. First, the nuclear soups and mashes arrived on the thunderous wings of helicopters. Grady supervised the off-loading of the yellow steel receptacles stamped DANGER and the red super tough polymer drums stamped HANDLE WITH EXTREME CARE in four languages.

Everybody stood around, poised in a sprinter's crouch, ready to take off at the first sign of a signature mushroom cloud. Even the Assos were charily energized in their assigned duty to keep the dogs from peeing on the containers. There was a general feeling that anything, even dog piss, could set off a chain reaction. Nobody trusted the buses either, so the more unstable emulsions and miscibles were transferred to the facility in Grady's fleet of two jeeps. And slowly. It took a couple of days.

Twenty-four hours later, an airplane swept out of the sky, bearing the Star of David insignia. My father and I stood on the tarmac bidding our last good-bye, he eager to be gone, I hovering for the last time in his encumbering shadow.

The Colonel's steely reserve, which had not abandoned him since my outburst of affection in the clearing, made us both self-conscious, he out of fear, I suppose, of bending a little, I out of fear of bending too much.

Fortunately we were saved from further abashment by the appearance of General Kalid Qazwini. He grabbed my father's gonads with a warmth I'd never thought him capable of expressing.

"It is difficult," he said, "to stifle the gratitude that fills my bowels. Thank you for the hand grenades."

"Use them well, and respectfully," the Colonel said.

"Trust me," said the General. His eyes, always so angry, were bright with anticipation as visions of a record body count danced in his head.

"May God look down on you—"

"'Look down on me...?'" the General said peevishly, the old anger flaring momentarily.

"It's an expression," the Colonel said, "a blessing. May God look down on you and give you peace." Quickly he amended the invocation: peace, he realized, was the last thing Qazwini wanted. "...And give you heartsease."

I thought my father was doing rather well. It's not easy to bless a man while he's gripping your balls.

"Until you return, " Kalid said, "all our voices will be silent in their grief."

With a final tug of the genitals, he turned and clanked off in a military manner. The Colonel and I were alone again.

"Well, time to go," he announced redundantly, tapping the musette bag that held his treasure. "All our explorations are before us, freighted with promise, and perhaps a surprise or two."

"You might even surprise God."

"Nothing surprises God," he said. "To suppose that such was the case would be to impugn God's omniscience. No, the world begins again, not for Him but for us. I'll miss you, my boy."

I supposed he would, in his fashion, if I ever happened to cross his mind. And I would miss him; rather I would miss what he might have been, what I wanted him to be. But the reality of what we were, each to the other—that I wouldn't miss. As fathers and sons went, we shared at best a fragile and unharmonious alliance; we were not made for each other.

He mounted the aluminum ladder, paused at the top rung, waved, and disappeared into the cabin. The plane quaked and fled down the runway. It rose, became a dot on the horizon, and was gone.

I stood there in a sudden grip of loneliness, wondering, Would I ever see him again? Probably not.

Valerie was immortalized a couple of days later. Her statue in the square stood next to Abdul's, just as she, during the unveiling ceremony, stood at his side in a kind of makeshift winner's circle.

The statue of course was forged from the ingredients Grady had come so far to identify. He stood to one side watching the fanfare, bitter with the realization that he still had no clue as to what they were and steaming with fury as Abdul thanked Valerie for serving the province so well. He called her a walking welcome wagon for Assama's distinguished visitor from Israel. He was sure that Ish-Chayl was only the first of a grand confluence of VIPs in the near future. In appreciation of her service he presented her with a necklace of semiprecious beads pried from the saddle of a horse, and a bamboo cage of butterflies. The band struck up "You Are My Sunshine" and the crowd dispersed.

"I thought it was a generous gesture, the jeweled necklace," Val said later that evening in our rat-infested snuggery.

"If he's generous," I said, "I'm Mother Teresa. Or," I added, "if you're making a joke, it's nothing to laugh at."

"Who's making a joke?"

For a long moment she leveled an unblinking gaze on me. Finally I said, "You don't dig it, do you?"

"Dig what?"

"The gifts. And that pukey music."

"I thought it was all kind of touching."

"Touching, my ass. He's zeroed in on you." I felt a sudden surge of fear, as though my words forged a threat beyond what existed before I said them.

She was silent, biting her lower lip. "I guess it's true," she said in a small voice. "He's been trying for years to climb on me. How much time you think we've got before he pounces?"

"Not much."

"How do we get out of here?"

"We can't."

"What *can* we do?"

I had no answer, just an uncertain notion I didn't know how to express.

"These people," I began, "will screw anything that moves—"

"What's that got to do with—"

"But they're all monogamous. They might not like it if he busts up a marriage—tramples on the... the sanctity of wedlock."

"On the other hand they might not give a damn. Abdul might not give a damn. Still…"

And then we both said, as in a timeless stage duet, "Let's get married."

Next afternoon I stood with Lipgloss, the vicar of Assama, solemn in the sunlight. Aware of the reverend's prodigial eccentricities, I had arrived early to sound him out, to preview how he intended to conduct the ceremony, how to restrain his ecclesiastical excesses to a dignified minimum, and to make sure that he wore pants over his usual raiment, which was a little less than a jock strap. I wanted to have Lipgloss in order operationally and sartorially before Val arrived. She was due any minute now.

Odd, it seemed to me, that the first wedding I ever attended was my own. I felt a serenity of mind and at the same time a keen subcutaneous excitement that quickened the pulse and sharpened the eye.

I saw our guests unindividualized, as in a crowded frieze, yet I was aware of isolated shapes, sounds, responses… Daphne, maid of honor, misty-eyed and sniveling; somehow she understood that a proper attendant of the bride was expected to fight back tears. Shakir bin Zaki, poet laureate, floated about with a pad and a stub of a pencil, composing an epithalamium. Old Man Chatterton—holy moley, it dawned on me, my father-in-law in a dish-dash as filthy as any bathrobe he ever owned, trying with difficulty to sustain a little interest in the proceedings.

At the back, General Qazwini stood at spit-polish attention, the quarters in his ears newly shined. With him was a scattering of Assos, many of them feigning polite attention. The rest were under the trees, abstractedly scratching the screw-tailed dogs that moseyed about.

Abdul was elsewhere. I could not have concealed my impending marriage from him, but, to pour as little oil as possible on the flames of his unrequited love, I made sure he was the first to know. I asked him to be my best man. He declined, even offering an excuse; if he were to accept, he said quietly, he would be expected to perform that function at every nuptial in Assama, a task he found too daunting. He offered felicitations, but in his eyes was a look that I would long remember.

Grady was not in attendance either, having refused to yield to a custom that promised a profitless hour of boredom. The rear of the crowd was starting to rumble impatiently among the vermian cherry trees, so I wasn't aware of the jumble of uniforms until they surrounded me. General Qazwini pointed a large pistol at my head. He snarled, "Freeze." To make his point he fired a slug an inch from my ear. My hair singed. Lipgloss yiped in a fluttery falsetto and went fetal at my feet. Everybody else, including the dogs, ran.

At dusk I stood before Abdul in the throne room of the palace. He sighed sternly and shook his head in sorrow, disappointed and puzzled by all the trouble I had caused. Kalid and his bravos stood by, staunchly at the service of their sheik.

"You haven't behaved well," Abdul said.

"That's a crime?"

"You want charges?" He was thoroughly enjoying himself, titillated as if by some unspeakable perversion. "You're guilty of anti-Asso activities. Malicious and provocative hooliganism. Prejudicial cosmopolitanism. You murdered an honorable and defenseless warrior."

"Who?" I was baffled.

"A tribesman from the north."

"You mean"—I couldn't believe it—"Val's kidnapper? He was an enemy!"

"We do not kill enemies when they are tribesmen."

"No. You just cut off their cocks."

He shrugged. "We have our traditions. It is not for you to change them. And then," he added, "there's espionage. You've jeopardized our security with false, deceptive, and misleading practices. You stole state secrets to accommodate a foreign power, that pissant Grady. You violated our trust."

How could he have reached that conclusion? Because he wanted to. We could have done without all this blather, these allegations, but my pain and my fear pleasured him.

A faraway glaze darkened Abdul's eyes. He cleared his throat. "Valerie came to me earlier this evening, after you'd left her. She revealed that you'd been taking our confidences to Grady, so that he could exclude us and profit from them. You might as well know that while—"

I stopped listening. It couldn't be. It couldn't be.

"Where is she," I croaked.

"—conspiring to deprive the province of its most valuable—"

"Where is my wife, Abdul?"

I didn't feel much like a husband. I felt like a corpse—a premonition immediately reinforced when Abdul said, "She's not yet your wife, is she? In any case, she's safe with me now. Her forthrightness will be rewarded." He rose from his throne and approached me, as if a closer proximity would intensify the verdict. "And you," he said, "will be going to the ganching tower."

The sentence was evil; the way he pronounced it was villainous. He engorged the words, wrapped his mouth around them as if they were candy or dope, as if they gave him some deep and obscene satisfaction. I sprang at him, driven by multiple motives: in panic there is an exultant need for physicality; in desperation there is always the question *what have I got to lose*; and in extremis, death loves company. The least I could do was rip off an ear or tear out an eye before I died, before he took Val from me forever. I'd be damned if I'd go to dust unpartnered.

Blind rage was not fuel enough. I never reached him, although he was only a few feet away. Qazwini and his apes closed in, gang-tackling. I went down with the butt of a rifle hard against the side of my head. The torchlight wavered, dimmed, and went out altogether.

FORTY

CONSPIRACY

I get through the days on a kind of muscular memory, eating little, writing less, assailed by wild, careening thoughts. In the night they continue to sweep over me like a stormy sea and I sink into a spiral of frightful confusion. I dream dreams of terror, mostly about an eagle, both wings broken, crying in a cage. I'm obsessed by mountain climbing.

The nightmares return, although I try to fight them off at their source by refusing to sleep. I trudge in the dark, feeling my way as the blind do, with fingers for eyes, and by memory and the peculiar aura that emanates from solid objects otherwise undetected by the senses.

Some days pass swiftly. For hours on end I totter on the verge of coma, totally inattentive to the passage of time. Or I waver between resignation to the inevitable and the soothing conviction that this couldn't possibly be happening to me. Somehow, just before the end, the cavalry will swoop down with flashing sabers of deliverance, and I'll ride off into the sunset with Val. I can see her smiling face wavering before me. Slowly the face ages, slackens, and solidifies. A small dark man with phosphorescent eyeballs stands over me like a shade, like some Gothic rendition of Death. In a hand he carries not a scythe but a rat-skin sac in the shape of a bota. Expressionlessly he stares at me.

"I have brought you goat's milk," he says. "It will help your diarrhea."

I mumble my appreciation.

"Perhaps you don't remember me. I am Zun Alawi. Zun the Sculptor. Advisor to the late sheik."

How could I forget him? The blind gnome who had ravished Val with his thick, inquisitive hands. "I've admired your statues in the square," I tell him.

He nods slowly. The skin of his face is like the bark of a tree.

"We met when you gave me an aba. And again when the old sheik died. I suppose you were doing his death mask, or something."

And then a disturbing thought disrupts the exchange of pleasantries. "Is that why you're here?" I ask. "To do mine?"

"No," he assures me, "that's not why I'm here. Or why I was with the old sheik when he died. He was my older brother. I was there to smooth his bed of death."

"And now you've come to smooth mine?"

"No," he repeats, "let's just say this is a social visit. But I don't want to exhaust either your limited strength or your patience. Is there anything else you'd like?"

"Well," I shrug, "I'd like to live, and..." I wave the rat skin, "this should help me do it."

"To what end?" he asks. "To what end do you want to live?"

An insensibly pointless question. The goals of life are hardly worth pondering when your feet are in the fire and the flames are creeping up.

"I suppose I could list a number of reasons," I say. "Let's just say I prefer it to death. It's a personal thing, not the least cosmic. My dying won't affect the fate of nations or anything like that."

"But your living might." He steps toward me, a most persistent catechist. Those glistening blind eyes hold mine, and there is nothing consoling about them. "You are a gifted and rebellious youth," he goes on. "Just how rebellious are you?"

"Not very."

"Come now, young man. I heard you talking with my brother. I got the impression that you might have agreed with him."

"About what?"

"About the encroachment of Western ideas, and keeping them out of

Assama. However, I am not a man of power or persuasion. All I can do is offer you a proposition."

"Whatever it is and however I feel, don't you think it comes a bit late? I'll be dead in a week or two."

"Perhaps you won't. You've remained alive so far, despite Abdul's wish to have you killed an hour after your trial."

"I thought Abdul's word was law. He *is* your nephew?"

He nods. "There are some of us who oppose my nephew. We do not like his ways, and we have so far succeeded in putting off your execution."

"But how...?"

"You have a good friend in Yussuf Chapouk."

"The rat-catcher?"

He nods. "And your comrade in arms and a traditionalist."

"He has more clout than the sheik?"

"He is adept at augurs and portents. The entrails of a special rat, a ring-tailed rat, foretold him of disaster if you were to die so soon."

"And Abdul believed it?"

"No, but the people did. Abdul does not wish to oppose the will of the people. Not yet."

So the rat-catcher kept me alive. To what purpose? "What do you want me to do?" I ask.

He's silent for a moment, peering out of the rib-vaulted window as if he can see the shaggy vines beyond the square. "This land," he says, "is the best place on earth because it's possibly the last place to succumb to the ravages of civilization." He turns back to me. "That doesn't make it a utopia, and it won't remain an unexploited frontier forever. But for a few precious years..." Those penetrating eyes gleam; could it be a trace of tears? "Would you help us keep it this way?" he asks. "We'll need advisers, counselors—people more familiar with Western tactics and procedures than we are. We'll need an envoy to the World Health Organization and perhaps other organs of the U.N., and to represent Assama if need be before the Security Council, and when the war's ended, to deal with Iraq as our parent state."

A stillness comes over him, as if he were suspended in that dark space of a cell, as if he were one of his own statues in the square.

"Would you consider?" he asks. "Or are you shocked by the prospect?"

I could embrace him—of course I'll consider. Particularly (and this

I don't mention) when the alternative is doom, without ever regaining the feel of Valerie in my arms or the heat of the Asso earth under my feet. Our pledge is sealed as, with a firm hand, he grips my scrotum.

"We'll try to keep you alive," he says, raising the remaining pouch looped over his shoulder. "Here's to our future together," he adds diffidently. He drinks.

"What about the present?" I ask.

He smiles slightly, for the first time. "Don't know how to dispatch a dozen armed guards?"

"Afraid I don't."

He shakes his head. "Sometimes," he sighs, "I don't know what we ever went to university for. I know your being in here is an acute... inconvenience."

We share a long silence. It should have swelled into a tremulous vibrato, like in a gut-wrenching movie. Instead he says, "We'll do what we can." And with a final, robust squeeze of my plums he's gone. But...

Instead of dwelling with high hopes and good cheer on my future as Zun sees it, for reasons I cannot explain I zero in on my past, a history so brief that I wonder how there had ever been time for it all. Which leads to an uncanny quietude, a resignation not unlike old people are said to experience with the approach of ineluctable death. How can I possibly escape? Zun, the nice old geezer, was trying to set me at my ease, if I had one. I don't. There is no way out. Period.

FORTY-ONE

THUNDER AND FLAME

When Caesar died, they say, many dire prodigies and apparitions augured the event. The black sky was suddenly pierced by ghastly light. Wild winds fanned storms of fire. The earth trembled and a lion stalked the temples of the Forum.

To compare myself with Caesar would be, even in my state of precarious balance, an act of indulgence beyond hyperbole. But strange things happen when a hero dies, and I am no less the hero of my life than great Caesar was of his. There is no grieving lion to presage my death, but there are lion-colored dogs howling in the street below my cell window, and dust devils that swirl in the high wind.

It begins with a *crack!*, unimaginably loud, of a rifle inconceivably large. The blast staggers me as if I've been struck by something big and altogether invisible, as if I were trapped in a wind tunnel struggling against a current so strong it seems solid, so loud it pops an ear. A runnel of blood sluices down the lobe.

My jailhouse rattles until I am sure not one brick will be left upon another. Darkness engulfs the sun and the earth shakes, thunder rumbles across the sky. Strange, for the morning storm subsided hours ago. Yet the thunder and the lightning slouch back hand in hand, and a thick gray spear of smoke rises up in the south, in the vicinity of Grady's compound. Never before has a lightning bolt ignited anything, not with the deluge that accompanies and extinguishes every stroke.

If there's an explanation for the display, it escapes me. True, my powers of observation are weakening. I see things as distortions, floating and weightless, as a straight twig underwater appears to be bent; still I know that something in nature has blundered and gone out of hand. I blink, shake my head, focus my gaze once more on Valerie's statue in the square. But now I see it as a wavering, ghostly image across which sparkling silverfish swim, while tiny black nuns dart about like waterbugs. And then, between peals of thunder and the high wind, I hear the approaching splat of shoeless feet, and I know that at last they're coming for me, that my time to be fed to those hungry stakes has come. Somewhere over the rainbow I see my bleak future—a perforated mote in infinity.

I pull my eyes from Valerie as the door of my cell rocks wide on its hinges. Standing there, in a mephitic cloud of heartburn, is Salim Nafi, the sponge-brained, fire-belching veteran of the grenade maneuvers. Expressionlessly, he stares at me.

"What's going on?" I manage to ask.

His answer in stress combines the poetry of his ancestors with the vocabulary of his trade. "The gods shriek in the sky," he says, "but something is all fucked up." He turns and disappears, cloud and all. In his place is the narrow, empty corridor promising freedom.

I stagger through the door, down the pestilential hallway, light-headed, overwhelmed, bursting into the open, boundlessly unconfined. For a moment my retina is ruddled and scorched by the brilliance of the earth, the pungency of life.

The blindness recedes. The world is splendidly, astonishingly beautiful, grassy-green, sunlit.

But only for a moment; now the wind thrashes, settles down, thrashes again, carrying a whiff of sulfur. Suddenly it gusts, snarls, and an uncertain darkness shadows the sun.

It is a tenuous freedom at best, not to be achieved within the confines of the fief. To be seen by just about anybody is to be apprehended and returned to the brig. I wobble down the steep, vertiginous ramp of the prison. Salim has evaporated, as if in his own acidic juices. The streets are empty, abandoned to the dogs baying fearfully at the shrouded sun. Not a bird peeps or screeches or caws. They too have disappeared, taking their voices with them.

I have to find Valerie, and with her make tracks for the nuclear compound, to commandeer a copter and a pilot, at gunpoint if necessary, and wing out of Assama. But the compound lies miles away, through enemy country. I need a weapon. There's only one place where I might possibly find one. But first things first: I have to conquer the shakes and the reelings. With great effort I manage to subdue the nuns, the silverfish...

There are none of the usual guards at the entrance of General Qazwini's House of the Martial Spirit. No one is within, not even a flunky, not the General himself. I breathe a little easier as I drift from room to room, rummaging for a gun, or even a knife. I find nothing—presumably he's armed with every weapon he owns. But there in a corner of his trophy room is a squat green chest with a Hebrew stencil. Grenades. I scoop up a half dozen.

I limp over to my old hut. Empty. I know the most likely place I'll find Val is the one I least want to find her in.

I enter the royal grounds. A clutch of people sit silently under a palaver tree. Among them and the dogs and the dust devils is the old woman with her aphrodisiacs. To the east, near the power plant, the sky is lustrous, bloodshot, black-bruised, coining a color that has no name.

As soon as I slip into the palace I hear the tense voices. I creep down the hall to the presence chamber and peek into the throne room. Qazwini stands, posturing, hands on his guns. Zun stands in the shadow of a mad, vast tectonic penis, head bowed. Abdul is pacing back and forth stiffly, like a troubled old man with too much on his mind. A .38 is holstered on his belt.

Valerie slumps in a corner, as if she's been thrown there like a sack of grain. Her hands and feet are bound. For a moment, I get a rush of perverse exultation, realizing finally that her absence from my cell was not her choice. The gag in her mouth somehow makes her eyes seem extravagantly wide. Sniffing around her is the puppy. He prances and cocks his head, confused by her inattention.

I duck back and scuttle into a reception room, pondering how I might neutralize Abdul and Qazwini without murdering Valerie. All I can feel is fear. I take a grenade from the cluster of six at my belt. I pull the pin and throw it against the far wall. It bounces off with the flat, leaden resonance of a cracked bell. I wait, crouching behind a phallic column. A thousand and one, my head is saying, above my bursting heart. I have ten seconds before the explosion, when Abdul and the General will come tearing in to investigate. A thousand and two. I'll drop them with another pineapple, cut her bonds, and escape with her. A thousand and three.

Into the room bounds the puppy. He sees me, wags his tail, but what commands all his cocked-headed merriment is the oddly shaped toy that ticks provocatively in the corner. He pounces on it, sniffing. He growls and slaps it with a paw. He worries it between his jaws.

I sprint across the room, smack the grenade from his mouth, grab him by the scruff, carry him to the entry, and throw him like a bowling ball as far down the corridor as I can. He lands, rolls, and takes off like a scalded-assed ape. I dive back to the protection of the pillar. The grenade frags in a fountain of debris. Running footsteps stumble into the room, blinded by the dust. I expected both of them but, Jesus, the General is alone. He trips on a chunk of penis dislodged from the ceiling in the bombardment.

There is nothing protracted about our negotiations: I grab the shard and bring it down with such force that it shatters against his skull. For an unending moment he wavers, a disabled tank, then he sinks to the ground and is out. I unbuckle his belt with the two guns and the two knives and drape it over my shoulder like a Mexican bandolier. I draw a gun, moving into the throne room, weighed down by the hardware at my waist. I fire point-blank at Abdul, hitting the wall behind him, arresting his hand as it reaches for the .38.

"Don't move!" I tell him, and, astonishingly, he doesn't. I feel a surge of power and with it a ridiculous sense of embarrassment, talking like that, acting out this ancient and improbable ritual borrowed from so many fictions. "Drop your gun!" I say, and again I'm shocked when he does. I kick it across the room, toward Zun. Abdul stands there, benumbed, as I cut Valerie free. As I pull the gag from her mouth she screams and points behind me. Brandishing the hard hat like a cestus, Qazwini bears down on us. His skull is a scrambled omelet. Blood covers his face, drips from his thuggish jaw. I fire and miss but the next three shots take him in the belly and the chest. Still he keeps coming, a wrecking crew, a war party, harder to kill than Rasputin. The fifth slug catches him (did some god of rectitude guide my trembling hand?) in the genitals. He falls, finally at the end of his extraordinary capacities. Two pools of blood, one above, one below, mingle, spread.

Abdul dives for his gun. His fingers close over the grip as I shoot him. I don't know where the rounds hit.

His spittled mouth hangs open. His eyes hold a sad, flat puzzlement. Tonelessly, fumblingly, he murmurs, "Why you do that?" He falls. I stand over him, doubly tainted by this second murder, astonished by what I have done, exalted by the violence I so thoroughly disapproved of. Suddenly I feel sick, faint. Think about it later, I try to tell myself. Abdul looks up at me. He says, "You. My best friend…"

"Let's go," I say to Valerie, grabbing her hand.

"Go where?"

"The compound. Get a chopper from Grady and take the hell off."

"You can't go out there," she says sharply. "Don't you know the whole damned place is radioactive?"

My scalp tingles, my heart loops. Of course, I think. What other explanation could there possibly be for the thunders and the flames, the clouds of smoke that swirled in the sky to the south. The howling dogs, the silent birds. We're up to our ears in another nuke apocalypse, our very own Three Mile Island.

"How do you know?"

"All I know is, Qazwini came bopping in here with one of his guys on guard duty out there, a couple of hours before you showed up. Then Abdul told me the reactor had gone haywire, that he was leaving the country and he was taking me with him. I said I wasn't leaving, no way, not without you. Jesus," Val says, "what'll we do?"

"We'd better start walking," I say. "Into the wind, before it changes."

In the courtyard a fiery wind blows in from the northeast. We cross the square. I glance for the last time at the icons of the illustrious. Can they withstand the cankers and corrosions that will buffet them with the changing of the wind? Probably better than the heroes they immortalized.

Then I hear the helicopter. It swoops out of the sky like a sudden storm, flashing its rotors, quaking and clattering, a monster of a bird pounding its chest. It hovers over the square and settles down in the clearing, churning up a cyclone. The overhead prop continues to swing, but slowly, and the dust subsides. The door slides back and Grady stands in the frame, armed with his

.45. He displays no surprise in seeing me, but he does seem impressed.

"Glad you're out," he says without enthusiasm. "Abdul grant a reprieve?"

"Abdul's dead."

"Dead?" he repeats. At once he notes my arsenal and the acrid reek of the weapon I've just used on Abdul. His eyes take fire. "You killed him," he says, "and the BRITs died with him, thanks to your... your apostasy."

He's shouting now, his rage churns his bellow into a shrill falsetto. ""You stupid punk bastard," he yells, "I came back here, risk life and limb for one last shot of talking some sense into fucking Abdul about fucking BRITs and you killed him before I had a fucking chance!"

Christ knows how much longer he would have seethed, but his focus drifts to something of greater immediacy than the tale of Abdul's death. I follow his cautious, walleyed gaze.

Out of nowhere, people are converging on us. They stand around, too damned close, like haunters of the landscape, their dull, dusty eyes watching us expressionlessly. They hone in on the copter, surrounding it. I feel menaced in the blowtorched air, although they menace no one. Valerie feels it too. Swiftly she climbs into the aircraft, and I follow her. I turn to look back on Coproliabad for the last time. Above the heads of the people I see the palace dome, the prison tower, and for reasons I cannot attempt to explain I feel the unmistakable pangs of melancholy and regret.

Then I see Zun. He stands away from the crowd, far back, his gaze piercing me, exclusively, shutting out everyone else. Despite the distance between us, he seems to lean into me, so close that his long hair falls about my shoulders. His face is like a thin flame, a part of my conscience, and his eyes are a deep well of light even as the day grows darker.

I climb out of the copter and run to his side, to that still, sad look of his.

"Come on," I say, in a voice that is hushed and commanding. "You come with us. We have to get out of here."

He doesn't budge. My fingers bite into his arm, prodding him. He doesn't respond, not with so much as a blink of a blind eye or the brace of a muscle. He simply stands there, unalterable as a rock.

I walk back and board the copter. The pilot is blond, boyish. I vaguely recognize his small neat features, the rakish cap, the high polished jodhpurs. He revs the engine with a look of devil-may-care languor meant to tell us that any activity not requiring an absolutely gruesome courage is in his lexicon a bore. As further proof he whistles nonchalantly between his teeth. The chopper trembles. The rotors are a shrieking blur somewhere above us.

Then Val stiffens. "Oh, Christ!" she says. She springs out of a bucket seat and twists the safety latch on the door.

"What the hell are you doing?" I yell.

"My father," she cries. "I got to find him."

"Your father's dead," Grady tells her.

She looks at him, stunned.

The copter lifts slowly, screaming as if in pain. It's a few feet off the ground when one of the spectators, so passive until this moment, sprints to the side of the ship and grabs the radio antenna. Then the rest surge forward, clinging to the skids, dangling from the stabilizers.

The aircraft shudders and tips. The main rotor slices into the earth, smashing people into a bloody gruel. The tail boom guard skews, throwing us hard against a bulkhead. The aircraft flips over. The three of us in the cabin slam against what had been the overhead and is now the deck. The shaft of the rotor snarls, breaks jaggedly from its mooring. It twists and spins through the fuselage and like the giant bore of a rotary drill plunges into the pilot, eviscerating him, brains and bowels, as suffocating smoke engulfs the cabin. A little white finger of fire points to a break in the fuel line. We throw ourselves out of the copter as it becomes an orange and scarlet fireball.

We run until we are numb with exhaustion. Then we walk and stumble until we fall to the desert floor. I don't know how far we've come, but when the helicopter explodes it sounds a long way off, even as it fuses with the untempered catastrophe that surrounds it.

We lie back in the ocean of sand, walled in by a thick and pondrous outcrop of rocks that make it impossible to tell if the wind has changed.

"How did my father die?" Valerie asks.

"Do me a favor," Grady says breathlessly, "save your questions for later." He drags himself to his feet. So do Val and I. Grady uses abbreviated gestures to point out the dictates of his compass.

We cross the mountains not a hundred yards from the cave, *our* cave, Val's and mine. We go on. The shadows amplify. Darkness falls as suddenly as a meteor.

Wherever I look I see Zun's face. It won't go away, while all around him the intense heat and the eccentric wind spews radiation into the atmosphere.

"I've got to stop a minute," Grady says. He collapses among the ferns and the mosses, his back to us, inaccessible.

"What about my father?" Valerie says.

He lies there wrapped in sweat and silence. Finally, "The whole place," he says, "it was like a moonscape, like the end of the world..." Slowly he turns to face us. "At first I couldn't understand—we had taken every precaution against accidents. I figured it must have been some flaw, some internal failure of a reactor." He brushes a lump of earth from his forehead with a shaky hand. "But it wasn't a failure," he says, "and it wasn't an accident." Suddenly he flaps his hands on his thighs, on his buttocks, on the patch pocket of his shirt. He pats his forehead. "Shit!" he blurts savagely, "I must've lost my glasses."

How long will it be before somebody's satellite catches a whiff of the poison? A matter of hours. In a few days the helicopters of a dozen energetic nations will charge in to drop wet sand, lead, and boron over the site. In less than a week physicians and scientists from the West will arrive at a catchment center far from Assama to which the victims will be flown. They are tireless men, these missionaries alleviating pain, but they themselves cannot agree on the life span of thermonuclear particles or the extent to which they are absorbed in human tissue.

Whatever my life span, I owe it to Zun, to Yussuf Chapouk, the rat-catcher, the interpreter of entrails, to those people back there, his supporters, whoever they are, who kept me alive. Are they dead? Dying? Has the nausea, the vomiting, the hemorrhaging already begun? Are they lying somewhere, unaccounted for? Will they soon be etherized on an overtaxed operating table, tapped for bone-marrow transplants? Or are they still on their feet, moving among the people to help those less fortunate than they?

"If it wasn't an accident..." Val says, "what was it?"

For a moment, in silence, Grady squints at her. The wrinkles around his eyes etch a scowl. "Your father," Grady says, "started the whole mess. Trying to move a goddamn domino by blasting it with his horns and clappers and Meistersingers. What he blasted was my instrumentation. It went berserk."

"How," I ask, "could an increase in volume, no matter how intense, cause that kind of backlash?"

"If could if it was loud enough. An airplane breaking the sound barrier has been known to shatter plate-glass windows five miles below."

Again, methodically, he goes through all his pockets, and again comes up empty. "I told him to knock it off," he says. "But he was delighted that his nuttiness worked—he and his fucking gooks. They enjoyed the mess as much as he did—the guards couldn't keep them out. He started prancing around for more evidence—maybe a couple of dice doing the Charleston—who knows what? And somehow when he came upon the reactor he got the idea that I was concocting some kind of nuclear bomb. Your father pulled a fire axe off a wall and started waving it like a madman." He pauses, frowns. "There's one thing, though... Maybe his rage wasn't so sudden."

"He planned it?" Val says.

"All I know, your father wasn't as bumblingly eccentric as a lot of people thought. There was something... devious and creepy about his playing the clown. Plus he always suspected I was up to something he didn't know what."

"He sure got that right," I say.

Grady ignores me. "So maybe," he goes on, "he was looking for a way to foul me up, and here, at last, he damned well succeeded. He started hacking away at the reactor coils. The coolant spilled out—that's what triggered the first explosion. Soon the whole damned complex was burning at temperatures of five thousand degrees which, if you don't know, is twice that of molten steel. A goddamned inferno."

He unscrews the cap of the canteen at his belt and, bringing it to his lips, hesitates. "I wonder if I ought to drink this," he says. "It may be contaminated." He screws the cap back on.

"Fucking gooks," he repeats, "They liked your father, you know, and they seemed to... well, approve of what he was doing. By the time I stopped him the damage was done."

"How'd you stop him?" Valerie asks.

"Me? I pulled him away... It wasn't easy. He had an axe."

"But you had a gun," she says.

He stiffens. "You don't think for a moment that I...?"

"I don't want to, Grady, but..."

"Then don't. Christ, I couldn't save everybody."

In a week, possibly less, a wave of technicians with their tools will swerve out of the polluted sky. I can see them in lead protective gear, more suitable for a lunar expedition than the solar blaze of Assama. They'll wave their Geiger counters slowly, like wands, and hold them close to their eyes behind the filtered masks. They will stagger with the heat and the exertions of altruism.

I could wear a lead suit, like those technicians, like the engineers who soon will tunnel beneath the reactor, coating the underside with concrete in their attempt to protect the subsoil and the water table. Or will they entomb the entire complex (what's left of it) in a steel and concrete sarcophagus, to seal it for centuries?

"Who did you save?" Val asks.

"Most of them. I got most everybody in the cargo plane..."

"So what are you doing here?"

"I came back for you and Judd and Abdul."

"You came back for Abdul, period," I say. "Because you figured if you saved his ass you could return with him, maybe in a year's time, partners in the shit business."

In a year's time, two years, if the damage isn't as fearful as my imagination foretells, then the radioactive emissions will, possibly, normalize. Nuclear carpenters will build an eight-foot chain-link fence around the colony, banishing four hundred square miles, twenty by twenty, from the face of the earth, as if it were an enclave of Hell. When the fogs and fires subside, will the rest of the country be safe for men and other living things?

"You're badgering me," Grady says. "Why?"

"Oh, I don't know," Val answers for me, "maybe because I find no pleasure in your company."

"You'll have to accept it. We have a strategic dependency on each other." He sniffs the wind. There is a faint smell of iodine and cesium in it. "Let's move out," he says. "We can discuss personalities and accomodations and other dazzling issues when we're on safer ground."

He walks off, assuming that we will follow.

"Where are we going?" Val asks.

"Northeast, I think. Uncharted country. Clean air." And in that instant my mind veers off, embracing a reluctant notion. Painful and hazardous, it has been hibernating on the threshold of consciousness; now it pounces. I try to evade it, to think of something else. I think of my father.

"Once," I tell Val, "my father thought Eden was somewhere out there."

"Your father was mad. Although maybe he was right. We got the cast for it—you, me, and the snake."

I'm not paying much attention to her. By next fall, I'm thinking, all the experts will be done with Assama, returning to where they came from. The doctors and the scientists, back at their computers, will establish new, improved, and redundant safety systems that somewhere, sometime will fail again. And Asso's floodgates will be open to another wave of specialists, the banner-bearers of enterprise, the go-getters, the carpetbaggers, the leeches, the loan sharks, the hucksters, of everything from shit to Shinola. Here is a market to assault and a virgin race to ravish. But maybe not, that monitor in my head persists.

We stumble on. For about ten paces. I pull up short. Grady is already out of sight.

"What's the matter?" she asks, and again I heed not her plaint but the disquieting voice in my head.

"The prospects," that voice is saying, "are bleak. The pain may be unendurable, and that's just for starters."

"It's not yet time," I tell the voice, "to reach for the morphine."

Not if Zun and the rat-catcher and others like them rally round that silly, chicken-limned flag. They could in time rebuild the wreckage, maybe even bring back the animals from the wilderness and the veldt. Do a little of this and a little of that—but most important, embrace again the holy cause of lethargy and let the country go back to sleep for another hundred years. The rest of the world, in the immortal words of Gorelik, can take a flying fug to the moon.

I feel my face twitching slightly, just enough to be out of control. "I'm going back," I say to Val.

"Back where?"

"Assama."

"Now?"

"Soon."

"You're crazy," she says, "your father's son. And where do you intend to hang out, between now and soon?"

"In our cave. There's fresh water, and bats and lizards..."

"Gracious living."

"No worse than the rat stew we've been eating for months."

"You're not serious."

"Assama's the last, best, ugliest hope on earth. I want to help Zun save it, if it's at all savable, from people like Grady."

My words are highfalutin and suspect. They sound so turgid with false heroics and a craving (my father's son, she called me) for the scalds of glory.

"I can't explain it," I tell her. "I don't want to argue. I don't expect you to understand."

"Maybe I do," she says. "Maybe you have to do what has to be done, and there's nobody else to do it."

"Maybe."

"Well," she says, "I'm not going on with Grady, that's for goddam sure." She puts her hand in mine. "What the hell," she says.

We turn and walk back through the night.